Catharsis

Dr. Leslie

Thank you for contributing to
the formation of future
pastors and scholars!

In friendship,

3-17-17

Catharsis

Maldonado's Journey through Grief

a novel

Luis R. Perez

RESOURCE *Publications* · Eugene, Oregon

CATHARSIS
Maldonado's Journey through Grief

Resource Publications
An Imprint of Wipf and Stock Publishers
199 W. 8th Ave., Suite 3
Eugene, OR 97401

www.wipfandstock.com

PAPERBACK ISBN: 978-1-5326-0565-9
HARDCOVER ISBN: 978-1-5326-0567-3
EBOOK ISBN: 978-1-5326-0566-6

Manufactured in the U.S.A.   DECEMBER 19, 2016

Dedicated to Jeremiah A. Perez-Peña,
the source of my happiness and creative energy

In memory of Mercedes Rosario-Silva, Jose Ines Rosario,
Luis Rosario, and Marianna Torres for nurturing my ambitions
and supporting my work

Contents

Acknowledgments

I WOULD LIKE TO thank:

My editors, Arthur Gowran, Esq., and Lawrence Aaron, for their fine editing and faithful companionship

Diana Peña-Perez for always recognizing my interest in story-telling and deepening my affection of Dominican culture and teaching me to live life with joy

My parents, Lydia and Benedicto Perez, for sustaining me with your faith and instilling in me a deep love for reading and sharing stories

My siblings, Jose, Benny, Loyda and Noemi, for loving me unconditionally

The Rev. Edwin Tirado, M.D., and the Rev. Martha Tirado for giving me light to see my way clear in life and for teaching me how to give the best of myself to humanity when I didn't know how

The wonderful people of the Wipf and Stock Publishers for acknowledging my gifts and giving me my first opportunity in publishing

The Rhinebeck Reformed Church, my beloved friends and congregants, all of whom allow me to exercise my vocation with the utmost joy

Dr. Kathy Armistead for your wise counsel and resourcefulness

Dr. Carlos Eire for your guidance, mentoring, and friendship

Dr. Bruce Chilton for your unwavering support and meaningful insights

Dr. David Asomaning for your inspiration and guidance

The Rev. Dr. Bob Gram for your unwavering support and positive feedback

Anna Laufer for your editorial feedback and technical support

All who have contributed to my human development in the past, and to all in the future who will join me on Catharsis' literary journey, I thank you for your friendship and support.

Chapter One

The Nostalgic Search

THE STOUTLY BUILT MAN sported a Fedora and sour mood. He felt impinged upon by his mother's request to drive her sister, the man's aunt, to the airport on a Wednesday morning in 1980. The car, a Chevy Nova SS Coupe, was his prized possession. He didn't like to take it on the road during the winter months. But his mother convinced him that family honor compelled him to act charitably toward a relative, especially one who routinely returned from vacation trips to the tropics with ethnic delicacies for the family. So, his conscience and the pull of his ethnic cravings obliged him to make the trip to the airport. He donned his polyester jump suit and fake gold necklaces and bracelets. He removed his car's winter cover and placed his aunt's two suitcases in the rear of his car. One of the two bags was packed with her clothes and the other one was filled with hand-me-downs, counterfeit perfumes and colognes from Chinatown, and bargain clothes from Delancey Street in New York. He then asked his aunt to sit next to him. She did, and soon became alarmed at the speed he was driving. About 15-minutes into the ride, he slowly looped toward the drop off area, while pressuring his aunt to quickly tell him the name of the airline she was ticketed on. She had already given him that information, but he had forgotten it. She repeated the name of the airline, but he didn't recognize it, because it was new. He quickly became frustrated and started to complain about the congested drop-off lanes and the gas he was wasting, even though his tank was nearly full. He was abrupt and treated his aunt poorly.

"I am going to drop you off right here. I can't help you with your stuff. You have to get out quickly," he said.

His aunt was flustered by the brusque behavior. She whispered *malcriao* (ill-mannered in Spanish), grabbed her purse and scurried out of the car. She motioned to a skycap to retrieve her suitcases from the backseat. Momentarily, distracted by the flurry of other voices asking for help, the skycap left one of the two suitcases in the backseat. The traveling aunt didn't notice. She was digging through her purse for money to tip the man, and when she looked at the luggage cart, there was a suitcase that looked like the one that was left behind. Her nephew wasn't paying attention to what was going on. He was busy entertaining carnal fantasies. A young woman, who was graced with long legs and the face of a porcelain figurine, was struggling to carry her luggage after getting out of a taxi. He saw this as his opportunity to make a gentlemanly impression.

He uttered a flirtatious remark, which was common in his circles.

"Ay, *mami* (*mami* in Spanish can mean sexy baby), if you cook like you walk, I will eat everything, even the scraps."

He then adjusted his hat at a rakish angle, put his car in neutral, and emerged from the car, leaving the keys in the ignition. Using his suave charm and macho strength, he hoisted the woman's suitcase on his shoulder and marched inside the terminal with the sexy damsel at his side. When a person is objectified, and when an unregulated libido is not reined in, even in a moment of faux gentility, a mistake is bound to happen.

A fugitive man, William Maldonado, who was standing nearby and waiting for a bus, took advantage of the fact that the car was unoccupied and running. Maldonado jumped into the car and sped away. Within 15 minutes, he became awestruck by how quickly the clear winter skies underwent a gloomy transformation.

On the horizon, gray clouds unfurled like a canopy across the sky. To Maldonado, the darkness brought on the scene of a barreling storm. In a flash, the car was struck by rain mixed with hail. The torrential drubbing on the car's retractable roof sounded like bursting popcorn. Crystal drops of ice bounced off the car's hood resembling marbles. Little by little, what had been a peaceful atmosphere, a pristine snowfall in an urban landscape, soon turned into murky lagoons awash in froth and sewage spewing debris. A nauseating stench rose from the foul waters suggestive of an apocalyptic pestilence.

A minute or so late Maldonado thought that he could take a detour from the unfolding chaos. He veered left onto a side street. Almost immediately, the car was soiled by a mass of dirty snow and jolted by a series of gaping potholes. The hard-hitting bounces gave Maldonado a frisson of dread; those feelings of fear increased as the car slid and nearly collided into a doubled-parked station wagon, where a young man, Javier Martínez, wearing a vintage sheepskin coat, was unloading grocery bags from the wagon's tailgate. Javier gasped and jumped out of the way when he heard the car's horn sounding like a wheezing pipe organ. In his haste to remove himself from the path of the swerving car, Javier recoiled and upended a bag full of glass jars of peanut butter, baby food and pasta sauce. The snow layered on the sidewalk served as a thin cushion for some of the jars. A few of them cracked and bled sauce onto the pavement. The spattered sauce resembled a pastel mosaic on the concrete canvass, causing the pedestrian to confront the grim reality: when one is poor, it is almost impossible to overcome life's miseries and reassemble the shards of broken dreams.

Javier was an unemployed recovering alcoholic with three young children, ages two to six, all born out of wedlock. He had just completed his monthly visit to a local church food pantry using a borrowed station wagon belonging to the C & C Bodega where he ran errands for tips and self-respect. Full of anger at the near collision and spilled food, he launched a barrage of curses at the driver.

Javier concluded his string of obscenities by blaming the driver for his mishap.

"Watch where the hell you're going! You messed me up, man!," he said to the car as it proceeded ahead with no sign that the driver ever heard a word.

Javier shuddered at the thought of telling his family what had occurred on what was supposed to be one of his routine, though clandestine, shopping errands. He thought about returning to the pantry to explain his circumstances and plead for a second handout. He vacillated about returning to the pantry. Ultimately, however, he dismissed the idea as unrealistic and too late. He concluded that the volunteer staffers at the pantry would interpret the freak accident as a stunt designed to get more free food.

Javier said to himself: "No! No! No! They *ain't* never *gonna* think that I dropped it. They *gonna* think that I sold the stuff to get me some booze."

When Maldonado regained control of the car, he took a quick glance through his rear view mirror and guessed that Javier's flailing hands and contorted facial expressions were signs of his seething rage. Upset by what he saw, Maldonado mouthed words of consolation unheard by the furious young man he had left behind in the street from the relatively safety of his vehicle. "Take it easy, friend. Take it easy. Nothing happened. Why the exaggeration?"

The shock of the near miss accident forced Maldonado to maneuver the slippery streets. He realized that an accident would require him to furnish identification that he didn't have. Furthermore, it would compromise his anonymity as a fugitive from justice. What mattered most to him was finding a place to ditch the hatchback sedan he had stolen from the passenger drop-off curb at a Newark airport terminal.

Maldonado was prodding himself to come up with options: "Where can I abandon this car? How can I get rid of this problem?"

Concerned that he was not going to be able to repair his broken life, he mused, "I've got to get this right. I may not have many more chances to achieve what I am going after."

Not too far ahead, a dangling traffic light rapidly turned from a yellow to a red signal. Maldonado hated the delay, but he didn't try to beat the light. He plucked out a handkerchief bearing his WM monogram from his grey trench-coat. After using it to wipe the foggy windshield, he could peer through a clear patch and continue his search for an open parking lane. Once the light turned green, he steered with one hand, while searching for a classical radio station with the other. He wasn't sure if he was going to get a clear signal. There was a twisted metal clothes hanger, shaped like a deformed treble clef, inserted where the car's original antenna had been. He turned on the radio and moved the dial counterclockwise. But just as he surmised, the reception faded in some spots on the dial, and projected a buzzing static on other frequencies.

Annoyed by the radio's poor reception, Maldonado parked in front of a glass sheltered bus stop that was without a single commuter. He manually lowered the driver's side window, and stretched out his bulky left-arm to adjust the makeshift antenna until he managed to get a clear transmission. Making the radio work was more than an indication of Maldonado's unrelenting spirit; it was a foretaste of an innate personality trait. He got the radio to work. J.S. Bach's *Air on the G String* was playing, and the elegant pitch of the violin stirred memories of his mother, Dolores Loubriel-Maldonado, coming to his room to check on him at night. His mother knew that he suffered from a gnawing fear of pitch-black darkness. She knew that his fear of the dark intensified when rain drops ricocheted off the accordion-style exterior shutters of their home.

For a few seconds, he reflected on another vignette of his childhood. He closed his eyes and let the baroque music infiltrate his thoughts. Instantly, he zoned out and experienced a series of affectionate moments. Aglow in his mind was a barely lit, yellow novena candle of Saint Lazarus—the patron saint of the poor and sick—that stood erect on the center of a mahogany table in his bedroom. That candle flickered and barely illuminated a 5 x 7 framed picture of his father in his winter blue U.S. Navy uniform. Next to the framed picture was a three-point, folded American flag inside a memorial case with two ribbon medals. Then he looked up from his bed when he heard a squeak. There was no doubt in his mind that it was his mother making her way to his room. Her soft and rhythmic stroll on the scrap-wood floor sounded like the time signature of three beats, for graciousness was the essence of her nature. His mother, a classically trained violinist at Mannes, would sit on a plywood chair and softly play Bach's Air G on a rustic, but phenomenal, violin. The violin had been purchased for her by his dad, Navy Sgt. Ernesto "Ernie" Maldonado, as a ten-year wedding anniversary gift when he was stationed in Asia.

"Mamma would always say that dad was on an extended trip overseas," he said in a faint, wistful voice. He paused.

"One day I was old enough to understand that his soul was permanently docked at the harbor of a celestial city beyond time and space."

Maldonado temporarily forgot that he was parked illegally, and he continued to revel in the enduring memories of his mother's nightly visits. His thoughts drifted to the forever memorable occasion when her hovering shadow descended upon him. She lifted a mosquito net that veiled him and immediately was greeted by a scent of jasmine on her long, wavy hair. She sat on the edge of the bed next to his crumpled body, placed his head on her bosom, caressed his nape, and hummed an interpretation of *De Colores,* a Spanish folkloric song, in the form of a lullaby. Vexed by the flashback, he lapsed deeper into the corners of his memory and recalled how his mother's sweet hum persisted even as a tropical storm rattled their wood-boarded home and threatened to yank the leaking sheet metal roof from its beams.

Maldonado sorely missed the comfort of his mother's attention. Though she passed away when he was a young adult, he was still grieving her death and lamented not having her around for moments like the one he was experiencing in this shaky period of his life.

"If mamma were only here. She always made everything bad go away," he despaired, sighing as he reverted to the needy child he was 30 years before.

As the music spun inside his head and in the car, Maldonado's eyes blinked with gusto. He was hallucinating and imagining the sensations he experienced when his grandmother's crème brûlée clung to his tongue. Somewhere between melancholy and nostalgia, the power of the lyrics and the music unleashed a cascade of emotions. To calm himself, he practiced a yoga breathing technique he had learned from a Christian prison chaplain steeped in Buddhism. Just like a chaplain trained at Union Theological Seminary in New York taught him during their weekly yoga and spirituality sessions, Maldonado breathed deeply in and out from his diaphragm. He did this repeatedly to temper his revved up emotions.

"Stay calm," Maldonado chanted repeatedly in what sounded like a Benedictine incantation.

It seemed to work. The tightly braided muscles in his back loosened, and his mind was momentarily purged of unsettling thoughts. He felt a serenity like he only experienced when he navigated his maternal grandfather's

16-foot bark-built dory on the sapphire waters of his native town Cabo Rojo in coastal Puerto Rico.

As the memory unfolded, Tomaso Vitali's *Chaconne* played on the radio, inspiring him to envision a tropical sailing adventure, where he saw himself steering the boat through the soft waves of a cove known as *La Playuela.* The experience seemed so real that he felt a light and dry salty breeze feather his face. He saw on the horizon, the *Faro Los Morillos,* a lighthouse built in the 1880s, arching from the top of golden limestone cliffs. The imagined cadence of the waves and the stunning beauty of the panorama created an outlet for him to escape his roiling world.

He sighed deeply. "Aahh! This is so divine, so relaxing."

But in Maldonado's personal universe, moments of tranquility were lived in brief spurts. Just when his mind and spirit were settling into a nautical groove, an alarming cacophony grew closer and closer, disrupting his meditation. Rather then experiencing abiding peace, he felt terrified, once again.

Chapter Two

Feeling Bushwacked

Maldonado groaned, "Ay, and now, what?"

A yelping sound coming from the background prompted him to sneak a peek at what was going on behind him. He spotted an emergency vehicle with flashing dazzling lights drawing closer to him.

In peeved disbelief, he struck the steering wheel with the palm of his left hand. After absorbing the sting of the whack, he turned off the radio and took a quick look into his rear-view mirror.

Maldonado asked, "Hell, how is this possible?"

The threat of being caught before he could fulfill his aching desire to avenge an oozing emotional wound triggered additional anxiety and nervousness.

He pulled the car over to the curb, tilted his seat backward and crouched to hide his presence. No sooner had he readjusted his seat than the emergency car whizzed by with a repetitive screeching sound—Woop! Woop! With each of the siren's electrifying screeches, his nerves altered and his body compressed, resting in a fetal position. He recalled the day more than 10 years ago when he laid down on a sofa in a similar posture listening to an organ piece in D Minor in his apartment. The macabre-styled music made him feel that his mother's presence was with him during a time in which he felt lonely and worried about his fate. He had been waiting 48 hours, hoping to hear back from his business partner, Angel Santana, about the insurance fraud case Maldonado was accused of perpetrating. On that day, someone entered the building and ran up the stairs. The visitor knocked repeatedly on Maldonado's door with a fierce thump, causing his heart to palpitate with anxiety.

Maldonado lowered the volume of his record player. He approached the door cautiously and asked in an anxious tone who was at the door.

The visitor responded in a familiar voice, "*Guillo*, it is me."

Maldonado swung the door wide open, thinking that it was Santana. The person on the other side of the door sounded like Santana. Santana was the only one whom Maldonado allowed to call him *Guillo,* an affectionate form of William. But the visitor was Santana's oldest son, Gregorio. Both Gregorio's casual greeting and Santana's inexplicable absence troubled Maldonado.

"You sound more and more just like your father," Maldonado said. "Where is he?"

Gregorio did not respond. He barreled into the apartment, gasping for air and trying to conceal his nicked up forearms. Gregorio's forearms were not the only thing Maldonado noticed was out of the ordinary. Gregorio's hazel eyes were watery and his wavy mane, which hung over his ears, was disheveled. After a futile attempt to compose himself, Gregorio tried to justify his father's absence.

"My father would have loved to come, but he couldn't. He would have been followed here. He would have led an angry mob to your door step," Gregorio said.

Those words gave Maldonado a chilling feeling. He could not believe he had earned the animus of the general public.

"An angry mob?" Maldonado asked.

"Yessiree, it's bad," said Gregorio.

Gregorio took a seat on the sofa. He said he was nervous and spoke in an inarticulate manner about how Maldonado's decision to switch to a new insurance company had backfired.

When Maldonado asked for specific examples, Gregorio became defensive and accusatory.

Gregorio said, "I have nothing to do with the mess that is going on. The bottom line is that the new insurance company does not exist. People thought they had insurance coverage and they didn't. You are being labeled a charlatan. It looks like you were carrying out a shell game."

Maldonado felt bushwhacked. Gesticulating with his hands, he asked, "How is this possible? How can I be accused of fraud?"

Gregorio said softly, "I don't know."

Maldonado thought about what to say next. He was a partner with Gregorio's dad at a multi-service, small business geared to working class people. He had become an entrepreneur after his unsuccessful doctoral candidacy at New York University. Out of a 20 x 50 space in a four-story building, Maldonado and Santana sold car and home insurance, and airplane tickets. Also, they offered translation and notary services and prepared income taxes. The storefront business was a staple in the community. It employed three full-time people, including Gregorio, who served as Maldonado's clerk and as the bookkeeper. Gregorio handled the cash and money order payments that customers either mailed or dropped off at the business.

After briefly assessing the the problem, Maldonado became increasingly more strident with Gregorio.

"You were the one who talked me into finding a new company to help the customers save money. You had me talk with headquarters over the phone. You mailed out the declaration letters to each customer. Those letters provided clear and specific information on how much coverage each client would get," Maldonado said.

Gregorio rose from the sofa, scratched his gashed forearms, and walked slowly toward the darkest area of the room. With his back turned to Maldonado, he spoke in a somber voice.

"We messed up. The declaration letters should have not come from our office, but directly from the insurance company. We are simply the middle people. To make matters worse, my father is not insured as an agent to cover the exposure. His coverage lapsed," Gregorio said.

Maldonado was perplexed. He sensed there was insincerity in what he was being told, but decided not to quarrel with Gregorio. Instead, he asked Gregorio to arrange a meeting with his father, Santana. Gregorio nixed that idea, arguing that an imminent danger was looming. He threw out the names of notorious gang members to intimidate Maldonado. He went as far as to suggest that the gang members were on the prowl for Maldonado. He entreated him to flee.

"You have to leave the area. They are coming for you. You must leave immediately. Some of the victims have told their story to family members with gang ties. The word on the street is that those dudes are riled up and are threatening to put a serious hurt on you," Gregorio said.

Maldonado dug in. He didn't think that running away was the solution to the problem.

"I am willing to face my accusers. I can overcome this problem if your father stands by my side. You know that I am innocent. I can argue my way out of anything. By the way, your father is not returning my calls. What is going on?"

Gregorio gave a laconic answer.

"He is depressed," Gregorio said, pulling a folded airline ticket from his pocket and handing it to his bewildered business associate.

"Dad bought you a one-way ticket under a different alias. He asked me to tell you that he will send for you when things get cleared up," Gregorio said.

Maldonado was confused, but he grabbed the plane ticket. He did not want to run the risk of an attack by a vigilante. He gathered a few belongings, asked Gregorio for a ride to the airport, and left to Puerto Rico. There, within six months, Maldonado found work as a policy analyst for an elected official. His tenacity and intelligence contributed to a quick career ascension in politics. He became the chief of staff. But after five years on the job, he ended up in prison for obstructing a bribery investigation case involving the politician who hired him. In a prison cell, he tried to discern who or what was responsible for his predicament. He considered the possibilities and wrote them down in a journal along with the questions on his mind.

He asked himself, "Why am I not recognized as an intellectual genius, the academic artiste that I am?"

"Why am I always hitching myself to the wrong people?"

"How come I end up getting my wings clipped?"

Maldonado vowed to find out the answers to his questions once his release was granted by the Bureau of Prisons. About a month after making that personal vow, the prison chaplain asked Maldonado to meet with him. At his office, the chaplain gave Maldonado the news that his release was granted earlier than expected, but that he had to attend a substance abuse facility as a condition for getting parole. Maldonado did not use drugs or alcohol, but he managed to convince his caseworker and the parole board that he was committed to overcoming his addictive behaviors.

Maldonado had no intention of attending a half-way house in Puerto Rico. He had planned for months to purchase an airplane ticket and flee to a half-way house named *Healing Hearts* in Jersey City. It was a facility he discovered through a relationship he cultivated with a lay chaplaincy couple, Anthony and Maria Romero, both of whom ran a bi-annual, faith-based, educational weekend program at the prison. Even if Maldonado wanted to remain in Puerto Rico, he felt that his career options winnowed in the aftermath of the *Cerro Maravilla* case, which involved high-ranking politicians accused of employing the police to ambush a couple of young activists. Maldonado ascertained from the newspaper coverage of the *Cerro Maravilla* case that cynicism toward politicians was rampant, and that he was going to be looked upon with suspicion for his association with an incarcerated politician. The prospect of having to uproot himself and start all over again enraged him.

More than once the Romeros stressed the importance of forgiving those who had aggrieved him; they encouraged him to explore new and honest ways to make a living in Puerto Rico. But Maldonado was in a mental state that wouldn't let him move on. He was angry at the world and wanted someone to pay for his lot in life. He channeled his anger toward Santana. He wanted to know why Santana never sent for him or returned his phone calls from Puerto Rico. He harbored feelings of abandonment and betrayal toward Santana. He jumped on a plane to Jersey City and then stole a car.

The moment he got behind the stolen car's wheel, Maldonado reasoned to himself, "You have to steal because life will take from you."

This was Maldonado's sense of social retribution. It was a way of thinking that complicated his life. His life was going to get a tad more complicated with a new problem that was waiting for him just around the corner.

Chapter Three

An Air of Feeling Stuck

THE PASSING EMERGENCY VEHICLE's siren had long faded. Maldonado rationalized that he had the freedom to forge ahead.

He readjusted his body and pulled out onto the road. Out of desperation to get off the main streets and possibly find some place to abandon the car, he took a right turn onto a back alley in the downtown section of the city. There he encountered a team of workers standing idly on the loading docks of one of the retail stores that dotted a stretch of Jersey City's Santini Street. Work had temporarily halted due to the weather. He slowed down and took a quick glance at his digital wristwatch. It was 9 o'clock in the morning. He was gratified to know that he had a full day ahead of him. But unbeknownst to Maldonado, Wednesday was the day of the week when stores in the city's retail district prepared for the anticipated blitz of customers who sought short-lived happiness in the newest and trendiest products on sale—clothes, shoes, perfumes, electronics.

When the mix of bad weather conditions tapered off, the workers scurried to make up for lost time. They replaced non-selling clothing and electronic merchandise with the newest fashion attire and electronic gadgets that were delivered to the store. It was difficult to know for sure, but Maldonado sensed from a combination of things—the workers' anxious vibe, the "neon" layaway signs, and the familiar holiday symbols decorating the area—that there was extra pressure to keep the shelves stocked.

Maldonado had a knack for analyzing behaviors, an aptitude he developed as a teenager by observing how his baptismal godmother, Petra Nales, a Santería priestess, would help her clients overcome personal problems by intermingling supernatural phenomena with straightforward street advice. Nales would "bless for pay," as she would lightheartedly say, any person who sought her spiritual intervention and cosmic influence. Nales called on her power of divination to forecast the future or unravel clients' enigmatic dreams. Her skills also included producing homemade healing ointments to cure physical maladies and emotional afflictions, and sprinkling magical powders on her clients to ward off the spells cast by a rival shaman. Maldonado's exposure to underground spirituality helped him refine his understanding of human nature. It made him appreciate the value of interconnecting language with human motive, regardless of coded idiom, explicit bodily movement, and camouflaged or transparent intentions. He remembered Nales once saying to him, "Language is more than words. If you stay attuned to what is being said and to what is not being said, you will be able to gather information and unravel what people are up to."

Fortunately for Maldonado, he also was equipped with sharp analytical skills, an ability he harnessed by reading the works of social psychologist Kurt Lewin and anthropologist Ruth Benedict, first as an adolescent, when he spent idle time at his grandfather's study, and then as a doctoral candidate in social psychology at New York University. Not only was he adept at making sense of arcane scholarly works, but he was also skilled as a debater. He displayed his best form when he engaged in Socratic-styled debates with fellow graduate students at the university's commons area. On infrequent occasions, he also jousted verbally at a Greenwich Village pub with a community-affairs newspaper columnist who published her work under the byline Maribel Gibbons.

With his windows tightly closed, Maldonado continued to drive through the heart of Jersey City's downtown shopping and business district, scoping out people and always conscious of the hot car he needed to get rid of. A pudgy man, whose legal name was Freddy Jimenez, but who was known among them as "Fredito-Franco" for his short-size and hyper-tyrannical management style, was directing a crew of laborers unloading inventory and moving it into *Pepe's Clothing Store*. Maldonado took note of Jimenez's flamboyant attire, a blue dress shirt with cufflinks and a blazing red tie. He was religiously tracking inventory on a clipboard and using a quirky intercom to holler directions and garbled outbursts, which sounded like a scratched vinyl record. He knew that in the confusion and frenetic pace of the business district a person desperately trying to cling to anonymity might find it there.

"This *revolú* (pandemonium or mess in English) is really good. It is conceivable that I can get lost in this place," he said. "People are so immersed in their own worries that a stranger is reduced to a moving shadow, an insignificant passerby."

The flurry of activity did not distract Maldonado from picking up on a cue. He arched his bushy eyebrows, signifying his interest in the meaning of the Police Community Outreach Fund, PCOF, badge-shaped decals and placards that were attached to the stores' metal gates:

"Cops and merchants undoubtedly support each other."

"Everything and everyone around here is interconnected like a tree."

"Who is the trunk? Who are the branches? Who are the limbs? Who are the leaves?"

Maldonado recalled being asked by his ward councilman, Derek Jones, to serve on a task-force, prior to his imposed exile from the city over a decade ago. In many respects Maldonado's appointment to a task-force made sense. Jones needed to quell a controversy during an election year, and Maldonado wanted to assure himself of being able to succeed on his own, without his business partner or male authority figure taking credit for one accomplishment in his life.

At one time before the insurance scandal Maldonado had been on an upward mobile path that might have eventually led to a prestigious city position. Who knows? His thoughts reverted to the press conference where the task force initiative was rolled out and the members of the committee, including Father Roberto Sebastiano, a Jesuit priest, were introduced to the general public by Councilman Jones. In his usual colorful flare and amusing theatrics, Councilman Jones thanked the members of the committee in advance for their service to the city. But when he came to Maldonado, the task force's committee chair, Councilman Jones lavishly praised Maldonado's business acumen and academic achievements, even making a passing reference to Maldonado's doctoral work. Not mentioned by Councilman Jones during his presentation, but picked up by a clever reporter when she filed her story, was the fact that Maldonado stood to gain from the controversy. She described him as the self-appointed mouthpiece for a community in one of the city's more pivotal voting districts and financially up and coming sections. In her community affairs column, Gibbons wrote, "The recent explosive confrontations between some members of the police and some ethnic minorities threaten to drown Jones's message in a highly contested election. The media is abuzz over the conflict and the variety of proposed plans to bring a resolution. Appointing Maldonado, a Hispanic-American with cross-cultural appeal to work on the police and community relations, will allow Councilman Jones to temporarily stem the problem by creating the myth that the conflict is just a matter of people blending in."

Maldonado did not like the slant of her column. It made him look like a political lackey and the committee members were portrayed as pawns. He had the inclination to write the editor-in-chief and the publisher a letter to protest the reporter's angle and to request a personal meeting with the editorial team to ask for a retraction. He withheld that consideration. He knew how to get a hold of Gibbons and didn't want to destroy her credibility with her bosses.

Even though the leading newspaper expressed wariness about the task force's purpose, Maldonado ignored the paper's skepticism and the slant on future stories. He focused primarily on taking his chairmanship seriously. He started his job by recruiting a select group of ordinary citizens and retired officers to reexamine reams of arrest records. He then assigned committee members to conduct follow-up interviews with primary sources, which included meeting with the arrestees. The committee drafted a report. It concluded that the clashes between the ethnic minorities and the police officers were primarily generated by questionable traffic violations, such as whether a driver made a complete stop at a stop sign, and by a handful of uncooperative and oversensitive drivers, some of whom goaded police officers into an argument at a checkpoint. As a member of the city's non-paid task-force, Maldonado helped create an outreach program that focused on a number of issues: driver safety and responsibility; racial sensitivity training; recruiting and adding qualified minorities to the police force; and launching after-school police-operated programs for underprivileged children across the city.

He was largely happy with the quality of the project. He reasonably expected that the neutral recommendations put forth by his committee were going to work. He did not hide what appealed to him personally, and he laid out some of those views in the closing recommendations of the report. He remembered arguing: "Essentially, these problems are going to carry over if we don't promote synergy between law enforcement and the general public. We need to start by recognizing that we are not constituted the same and thus we react in a variety of ways, and this is not an oversimplification, since differences are not an easy thing to resolve. Outreach experiences, however, that foster trust can help us neutralize fear. It can help us override the impulse to hurt each other out of mistrust, particularly when a response to a conflict is not in proportion to justice."

The old days made him speculate that the donations from the businessmen to the PCOF enhanced the police department's public image. The police in turn rewarded the interested loyalty of the merchants with police decals for windows. The props were used both as a symbol of community pride and involvement. A blustering wind jolted him back to the present with a sheet of ice blown from a roof top and onto his windshield. The sound of the ice splintering made Maldonado realize that he had to curtail his scholarly rumination and not get further sidetracked, so he asked, "Where can I leave this car?"

He resumed driving slowly around side streets of the retail district. Some of the usually available parking spaces along the stretch of the retail hub were not available. There was a disabled car barricaded by obstinate frozen mounds of slightly melted hardened snow that encircled the car in a puddle. The car had a makeshift sign on the inside of the windshield that read, "Doesn't Start, Please Don't Tow." There was another car immobilized with a boot placed on the driver's side front tire by one of the city's parking enforcement officers. The boots were saddled on cars that had outstanding parking tickets or on cars that did not have a city pre-approved permit to park in a residential area. Then there was a dry cargo delivery truck parked in an awkward position, occupying two parking spots on purpose.

Maldonado shifted from spying to hiding to analyzing. His mind started to tinkle like *Zimbelstern* bells, so he empirically collected data and surmised, "if everyone described in the parking scenario comes across as egocentric, they are being misunderstood. The driver who pleads not to be towed, the traffic agent who enforces parking rules, and the truck driver who hordes two parking spaces, are responding to a primordial 'self-sustenance trait' genetically coded into every human being by Nature.

Maldonado had put forward the 'self-sustenance trait' theory in a paper for a doctoral seminar, and, in an excerpt of his argument, he said:

> *"Human acts of aggression, regardless of whether they are latent or overt, are motivated and propagated by an innate desire to establish proprietary dominion over lesser things. An aggressor may seek to justify aggression as a righteous response to an ominous or self-created threat that promises to compromise an individual or a community's safety and security. An aggressor may even persuade him or herself and, in some cases, the masses, that an aggressive act was spawned by heroism, patriotism, goodwill or stewardship. There are times when the behavior of an aggressor finds shelter in societal institutions and mechanisms that succeed in rationalizing and promoting the act. But aggression is nothing more than an irrational response to the fear of becoming violable. Aggression is always a selfish act because the aggressor seeks to take away through hostility that which Nature freely and abundantly provides to all without reservation and impunity, namely the freedom to claim autonomy and self-preservation."*

The concept of the "self-sustenance trait" sought to explain the root cause of aggression. It was a concept imparted to Maldonado by his grandfather, Dr. Ivan Loubriel, a well sought-out clinical psychologist who originated the theory based on Abraham Maslow's hierarchy of needs. Dr. Loubriel illustrated the premise of his theory by discussing tangentially some of his more fascinating cases, without breaching confidentialities with Maldonado, whenever he took him out to sea on his sailboat. Maldonado knew whom his grandfather was talking about. And he knew quiet often.

He was able to connect his grandfather's clients and their individual stories, always given in the third person, to newspaper accounts, local rumors and gossip, and the pantheon of celebrity-framed photos that decorated his grandfather's palatial office at a colonial-styled home in Old San Juan.

A part of Maldonado took comfort in the "self-sustenance trait." He got absorbed in that theory to reduce the impact of problems, help him make sense of human motive, and plot his life. He continued to slowly track social trends and look for a place to park, and he continued to find himself drawn to retracing how he ended up maligned, disgraced, and exiled. The messy weather conditions and feelings of persecution were keeping him subdued.

Even though Maldonado was not devoted to institutional religion, and even though he became less of a believer on supernatural phenomena as an adult, moments of desperation lured him back to tinker with spirituality and the religious practices he had grown up with. He ran his hand through the layers of his clothes feeling around for a black cocoa-beaded rosary that was given to him by his mother as a Confirmation gift when he was twelve. He carried it as an amulet, and every time that he was in a quandary, he would rediscover a conduit to God in a side pocket. When he felt the crucifix on the string of beads, he clutched it and asked for God's intervention. Maldonado was possessed by the self-contrived idea that God could be bargained with under the pretense of prayer. He subconsciously thought that he could trick The Almighty into accepting his feigned piety.

"My God, help me!" he muttered in a hushed voice. "I just want to settle down. Forgive me. I know that I have not been faithful."

After a brief pause, he concluded his supplication with a paraphrase of a biblical verse that he remembered from one of his Confirmation classes.

" . . . [But] the sun comes out for the just and unjust alike . . . "

Chapter Four

A Rotating Problem

MALDONADO'S FRAME OF MIND led him to think that he could cajole God into resolving his deep-seated problems, since beneficial events marked his life every time that he prayed. He could not fathom the mystery of prayer, and he could not understand why his life was marked by acts of divine favor, given that his prayers were not said in liturgical formality or mediated through a priest. All he knew was that his entreaties harkened the deity, the Spirit, to help him out. Whenever that help came, more often than not, it took place in unexpected ways.

After Maldonado concluded his prayerful petition, he watched and hoped. Ten minutes had slowly trickled away on his digital wristwatch, but it seemed much longer. Cooped-up in a stolen car, he felt imprisoned in a chamber of interminable uncertainty. Understandably, Maldonado felt a sense of relief when he noticed that a parked car was flashing its left signal light in preparation to pull out of the space and enter the driving lane; the best thing about the situation was that the parking space that he was about to claim became available near the busy center of the city's retail section.

Maldonado said, "Finally, something goes my way."

Maldonado flickered his high beams twice to get the attention of his fellow motorist.

About five minutes went by and the car did not pull out.

"All right, just move out and move on!" Maldonado implored, talking to himself inside the car. "C'mon, what is taking you so long?"

The driver went through a ten-minute futile routine of realigning the wheels, pausing briefly, and revving the car's sputtering engine. She was stuck. The ice was preventing any traction.

Maldonado became preoccupied with fatalistic thoughts. "Should I get out of the car or not? What if the person inside the car recognizes me and calls the cops at the corner pay phone?"

He continued to wonder.

"Now, stay positive . . . think positive . . . ," he kept repeating in a soft voice. He wanted optimism to overcome his pessimism.

Once Maldonado surveyed the area, he slowly emerged from his car and walked through a slushy surface to help the driver stranded inside a classy looking red Lincoln Continental, Mark VI. When Maldonado stood beside the driver's side, he gingerly tapped on the window with his key ring. The driver lowered her window half-way.

Still feeling paranoid about being recognized, Maldonado started his conversation in a masterfully deceptive hoarse voice, attempting to somehow disguise his identity.

"I will help you, ma'am," Maldonado said in a husky voice.

He forced a cough.

"I will be right back. Just keep the engine running."

Before he had a chance to turn around and walk away, the woman inside the car pursed her lips, and with composure, determined to extricate her car through force of will.

"You don't have to," she exclaimed. "If I honk my horn long enough, one of my husband's workers will dig me out."

The woman was Brigid Santini, the wife of Francisco Santini, affectionately known by the locals as Don Frankie, a retail store magnate who also owned a vast number of apartment buildings occupied by rent control tenants. Brigid's marriage to Don Frankie and her genuine partnering with him gave her enormous social standing which influenced how she related to other people. She was suspicious of those who offered to do unusual favors for her. Such acts of altruism were often accompanied by an invitation prodding her husband to join a board, make a donation in a suggested amount on a pledge-card, or an invitation for her to attend a fundraiser dinner, a request for a job or a rent-controlled apartment.

Hunching over the roof of the car to create a sense of security, Maldonado said, "um, don't aggravate yourself, ma'am. We don't need to interrupt your husband's work schedule."

Leaning sideways to the passenger side, she responded with cold and condescending body language that said, "Do you know who I am?"—implying that he should have known who she was, and should have respected spatial boundaries.

Brigid thought, "I wonder what he is up to?"

She continued to speculate. "I have never seen this man spending time around this neighborhood."

Maldonado looked into her mahogany brown eyes and picked up on her obvious apprehension.

"Be careful, be careful, I can't come across as overbearing," he cautioned himself as he stroked his French beard with slow and deliberate movements.

Meanwhile, he did not want to make Brigid suspicious of him. He spoke in the humble tones using language employed by those who want to create a charming personality that soothes the fears and calms the heart of the listener who is leery of deception.

"I am going to help you get your car out, if that's is alright with you?" Maldonado said.

Brigid's expression assured Maldonado that she was willing to let him help her out. He thought about her silent approval and breathtaking beauty. Quite unexpectedly, she stirred his heart with nostalgic feelings. Her glistening braided hair, succulent full pink lips, and genial manner reminded him both of his mother and the girl of his dreams. Maldonado had no reason to know that Brigid looked considerably younger than her actual middle-aged years. She ate healthy and took great care of her complexion. For instance, she scrubbed and lubricated her face daily with natural products imported from the Dead Sea. She had two other peculiar characteristics. She did not moisturize her hands with lotion. Some surmised that she purposely allowed her hands to feel like the surface of a crater as a way of remaining grounded in her working-class Irish roots and as way of staying in touch with her subordinates; they loved her.

Her other idiosyncrasy was not covering up her hands, with either working gloves or weather gloves, to protect her two prized pieces of jewelry from losing their polish; one was her wedding ring and the other her graduation ring from an Ivy-league business school. There were times that she did not wear her wedding ring. Some of her gossipy employees speculated that this was her way of retaliating against her husband whenever she felt under-appreciated. The same intrusive employees also noticed that she almost never removed her graduation ring, a symbol of academic achievement which she wore on her fourth finger. It was a 14-karat, gold solitaire ring with a crimson ruby in the middle. Embossed on one side of the ring was the insignia of her school, on the other side, her initials, B.A.M, for Brigid Anya McCann, and her graduation year.

With her waving hand, the one with her graduation ring, Brigid directed Maldonado to look at a commercial sign on the crumbling red brick façade of her husband's flagship store. She was listed in small letters on the sign as vice president of operations and marketing. Maldonado could not possibly have read her name and title on the sign from where he was standing, but she was hoping that her allusion to Don Frankie would accentuate her clout, just in case the seemingly good Samaritan was intentionally using the rescue mission for a malevolent purpose. Even though Santini Street, named after her husband's family, was relatively safe, she knew that one can never be completely protected from malice. She would quite often say half-jokingly, that "a squirrel creates a den in an unattended cavity."

Unsure of Maldonado's intentions, she continued to question his motive.

"Is he doing all of this gratis?" she asked herself.

She shrugged, and then a strange look appeared on her face.

Maldonado pretended not to notice her already worried eyes. He looked away and thought about what to say next. He looked at the crumpled bill board sign with flaking paint and fading letters. The sign spelled, V I C O R, so he surmised that the place was called VICTOR'S. What Maldonado and many others did not know was that Brigid purposely allowed the sign to decay. That way she could have the upper hand in negotiating deals with her customers. If she didn't use this ploy, her customers would speculate that business was teeming with profits, and they would complain about their finances and haggle for additional discounts above and beyond the coupons she and Don Frankie provided customers. When her customers asked for lower prices, she did not budge. But Don Frankie quite often succumbed to his customers' appeal to their common Puerto Rican heritage. He had a soft spot for teary-eyed stories that invariably began with the self-pitying phrases *la piña esta agria* (the pineapple is sour) and *la cosas están del color de hormiga* (the outlook is as bleak as the color of an ant), underscoring how people felt overwhelmed by raising costs and a slumping economy.

Maldonado mistook her kindness for someone who was demure and flattered by compliments and namedropping.

"I just had breakfast with the president of the Fashion Institute, and he was sitting as close to me as we are."

"Oh, the things that were said about this store would make Victor feel so proud."

"Victoria!" Brigid quickly corrected Maldonado. "The store is named after my late mother-in-law, who recently passed away."

The blunder mortified Maldonado, but he did not spend time dwelling on his mistake. He quickly downplayed his gaffe.

"Yes, I know. I affectionately call your husband Victor, even though I don't know him too well, out of honor and respect for your late mother-in-law."

Honoring Victoria gained currency with Brigid.

Victoria was Brigid's retail mentor. She was the legendary seamstress who tastefully glorified sexuality by designing and tailoring outfits specifi-cally for her clients' anatomy and voluptuous curves. Any favorable mention of Victoria and the store made Brigid feel that her mother-in-law's legacy was being upheld and her own work honored. Brigid nursed the secret re-sentment that she was not properly credited with taking a small store and expanding it regionally. Her husband, on the other hand, grandstanded and received adulation from the local service club, the business chamber of commerce, and the newspapers. They elevated him to an iconic business-man status. Brigid felt that Frankie received all of the attention in the print-media because his full-page ads greased the engines of the printing press. He gained unmerited attention and lofty praise, Brigid privately murmured, because he gave generously of his time, talent and treasure at the expense of their marriage.

Brigid put her feelings of disappointment about her husband aside for the moment. Maldonado had just brightened her day with his pro-feminist bias and his praise of her mother-in-law.

"Bless your soul," she said as she marked herself with the sign of the cross.

It was important for Brigid to get on her merry way to the indoor ten-nis games that she attended on Wednesdays.

"Oh, that is so nice of you. Well, dig me out, then."

"Well, let me get going with it," Maldonado said with a roguish grin, knowing that he had just slithered out of a potentially embarrassing situa-tion. Maldonado crossed the street to scavenge a dumpster, and he found a piece of cardboard that he used as a mat to kneel on one knee. He started to use his bare hands to gouge the soggy snow and clods of dirt from around the tires, residue from a plow truck that hemmed in the tires of Brigid's car. Quickly his hands swelled up. His frozen nose became flush-red and numb, discharging a watery fluid that moisturized his prickly mustache. In the midst of this, strange and disabling thoughts invaded his mind.

"She is losing confidence in you."

"Things are getting worse."

"She is going to blame you for keeping her stuck and wasting her time."

Afraid that Brigid would become exasperated and go inside the retail store to ask for help, he drifted to her window and mumbled a semi-confi-dent remark.

"It shouldn't be long."

"Are you sure?" asked Brigid through her barely open car window.

She added: "I am qualified to take care of this problem."

Maldonado insisted he could be counted on. After digging a bit more, he exhorted her to "step on it!"

She did. For a moment the car seemed to have enough impetus to pull out, but it couldn't get any traction.

Not only did the car refuse to budge, Maldonado was beginning to feel trapped by the negativity of his own thoughts. To liberate himself, he offered one last pragmatic idea.

"I am going to rock you from behind as you step on the accelerator, ok?"

A befuddled Brigid asked: "Why this way?"

"Aren't you overdoing it?"

Maldonado responded: "This will help you gain momentum. I hope to time it perfectly and spring you out."

Brigid was as disciplined about following her itinerary as she was scrupulous about appraising a person's skills. She did the hiring, promoting, and firing at her business. With a specialized business degree in human resources, she knew how to evaluate talent and performance. She made an exception on this occasion because she was taken in by Maldonado's gallantry and refined looks. She became deferential to him, even in the face of his clumsiness.

Maldonado knew that he had to make a good impression quickly. He covered his nose with his monogramed handkerchief to avoid inhaling the car's sooty and noxious fumes. He used the side of his foot to kick the snow away from the tires. He lasted a few minutes doing this, but the heaps of snow were difficult to remove. Quickly, he said, "Pull out! This time it will work."

The car's back tires rotated and the car's engine roared but there was no forward movement out of the space. It was pointless. Wasted energy. Maldonado stopped rocking the car back and forth. He tapped on the window to present her with another idea that might work. As he spoke, he was forced to react to an odd remark he heard over his shoulder that came from a man who seemed to appear out of nowhere.

Chapter Five

Parking Spot Becomes Available

THE FIGURE, LIKE AN apparition, was a gimpy vagrant. He dragged his right foot as he filled the brisk air with a charming jingle, "If you have some spare change, my generosity has boundless range."

Scrappin' Steve, as he was known locally, was a college-student and vagabond who pounded the streets for cash-yielding opportunities. One of Steve's economic niches was scrapping recyclable materials. He rattled them around in a grocery cart that he borrowed from *Felix's Fine Foods*, a family-owned supermarket in the heart of the Spanish-speaking downtown. Aluminum wheel caps, car batteries, empty glass bottles, squashed beer and soda cans, and sawed-off pieces of copper pipes, the latter extracted from either condemned or burned-out properties, were part of the cobbled junk that he wheeled in his cart. He paid Javier a nominal fee to have him haul his junk in a station wagon to the *Pete's Scrap Yard*.

On this particular Wednesday, Steve had parked his pushcart under a timber bridge, fastening it to a steel staircase rail with a thick chain and impregnable bolt. The bad weather made it difficult to wheel objects around. His foot and leg injuries made it challenging for him to shoulder a garbage bag full of crushed cans and empty bottles. A cart full of scrap metal could be even worse. Steve had recently turned his ankle by stepping on a badly placed paving block. Some of his ligaments were damaged. The injury occurred soon after lacerating his leg on a steel gate on a unfastened fire escape. The accident happened when he acrobatically straddled the gate so he could enter and exit a nearly abandoned building full of squatters, vagrants, vagabonds, runaways, addicts and assorted homeless folks.

Living there was a way for him to assert his independence from his troubled family situation. In between the junk collecting and substandard living, he attended college classes to earn his degree.

Steve's college academic advisor, Dean Mike Smith, insisted that he work with his college counselor, Esther Walker, to resolve his housing issues.

Smith told him that if he didn't establish a safe and legal address, scholarship, grants and other university-related funding for his studies would be stopped. This admonition motivated Steve to raise money to rent a studio apartment, paying for it with his supplemental income from hauling and selling junk.

Now and then on Wednesdays, Steve worked as a "lumper" doing manual labor and odd jobs for Junior Morales, who was one of two volunteer bus drivers ferrying congregants back and forth at his childhood church. One of the things he liked the most about the lumper job was that he was paid on the spot in cash. But with the weather messing up the roads, it meant that he was going have to find another way to make money. Brigid's stuck car was possibly his only option to make some petty cash.

As he sauntered toward Maldonado and Brigid with a jaunty gait, Maldonado tensed up.

"I don't have a good feeling about this bum," said Maldonado to himself. "Is this guy going to try to hurt us?"

Maldonado's visceral fear was increased by *Scrappin'* Steve's thuggish demeanor. Steve swiveled his head with a funky *mojo* as if disco jams were playing inside his head. He twirled a push-broom stick like the blades of a windmill. He followed each dazzling circle motion by hacking the polar ends of the stick forcefully on the surface; the synchronized thump was intended to sound like those of his favorite percussionists. Maldonado, however, saw the maneuver as a prelude to a possible physical attack. Steve used the broomstick to steady his uncomfortable walk, but Maldonado, who was becoming increasingly nervous, thought that the vagrant was brandishing the stick as a tool of intimidation and perhaps violence. Steve's shabby, dirty clothes and physical appearance exacerbated Maldonado's stereotypical fears of who the vagrant was and his motives. Steve was unkempt and disheveled. An untrimmed beard bristled around his face, and he sported a wild Afro that spread around his entire head like an open umbrella. Sticking out from the side of his Afro was an ornate, upraised-fist-handle, Afro-pick.

Maldonado had a predetermined view of human appearances. He said to himself, "The outer shell is a manifestation of an internal condition—of what is in the mind."

Maldonado forced a weak smile and waved Steve away. He gazed intently at him and even spoke words of calm and competency. He did this to deter any motive Steve might have to act with aggression.

Maldonado softly said, "Everything is under control."

Steve pretended to ignore Maldonado, while at the same time drawing closer and closer to him. When he was about ten paces away from

Maldonado, he started moving his top teeth over his lower lip, a twitch he displayed whenever he was overly excited.

"Yo, homey. I was checkin' you out from over there," Steve said. "And what you are doing is dangerous."

In a nervous frenzy, Steve shared the rationale for his concern.

"If the car skates backward, it is going to bowl you over and pin you against the fender of the car sitting behind you."

When Steve said that he was "checkin' you out from over there," he was making reference to the loading dock that connected to the *Victoria's* bulk storage room. During the summer, he used the loading dock's overhead roof as an awning to shade himself from the blistering sun. During the winter he used it as a *porte-cochère* to shelter and protect himself, as best as he could, from the frigid weather. For Steve, the warehouse's higher-ups even made an exception. They allowed him to roam inside the warehouse to warm-up and use the bathroom to freshen-up, as long as he didn't distract workers with his notorious wild tales and silly jokes. Steve watched and laughed as Maldonado tried to no avail to dislodge Brigid's car.

Maldonado listened to Steve's response in silence and studied the young vagrant. He was modestly impressed by Steve's ability to insert himself into a situation.

Maldonado, not wanting to be dismissed as a fool, started to justify his car intervention strategy: "I was trying to—"

Scrappin' Steve cut him off and said: "Nah, man. You are more lost than a cross-eyed service dog."

After sharing an underhand remark, *Scrappin'* Steve proposed a practical way of resolving the problem.

"You have to dig deep trenches around the outside part of the front wheels so that she can properly position them at 30 degrees, and then you have to create a small path and layer the surface with dirt or something solid, like a plank, so that the wheels can get a firm traction to run on."

Though Maldonado was not amused by *Scrappin'* Steve's canine analogy—comparing him to an inept service dog—he was struck by the junkman's ability to seamlessly shift between the common language of a street person and his well articulated solution to the stranded car dilemma.

"This guy is not a fool," Maldonado said to himself.

With the push of a button, Brigid lowered her car window all the way down, popped her head half-way out and greeted Steve in a sweet tone.

"Hi sweetie," said Brigid.

Maldonado started to wonder, "Not only is this guy sharp, he is well connected. Who is this guy?"

Scrappin' Steve strutted toward Brigid to make conversation and ex-change pleasantries. As this occurred, Maldonado felt a tingling sensation on the upper portion of his neck, then imagined hearing the reedy voice of Petra, his dead godmother, whispering a warning to him.

Petra said, "Remember, you are never alone. There is always a presence watching over you. The realm of spirits takes notice of your actions and employs creatures, angelic or temporal, good or evil, depending on your conduct, who gravitate to you and influence your world order."

Petra's words created a tremor in him, but he did a good job at hiding his fear and awe. If he didn't, he realized, he would telegraph to Steve that he was awkward and afraid, and in an uncertain and vulnerable situation. He knew that any sign of weakness would be an invitation for evil to be visited upon him.

"I am not going to give this guy permission to hurt me. I have to look at him straight in the eyes and not display any signs of intimidation," Maldonado said. Like so many of Maldonado's troubles—in the past and the ones to come—he was in a situation of males fighting for the dominant position.

Brigid, who minored in Spanish at her undergraduate college, kept her fluency in the language by attending a weekly Spanish-table at her alma mater's club in midtown Manhattan. She also selectively practiced her Span-ish with employees, clients, and family friends. She progressed to a point that she spoke better than many—like Steve—who claimed it as a birthright, their first language or language spoken at home.

Scrappin' Steve visited with Brigid on Wednesdays when he picked up leftover recyclables which she set aside for him in a waste basket. Though he enjoyed her company, he did not appreciate her speaking to him in Spanish. *Scrappin'* Steve was raised in a household where Spanish was the first and dominant language, but his Spanish-speaking skills were limited. He had a tendency to mangle pronunciations and use Spanish out of context. Under-standably, he avoided speaking it in public to avoid derision and stigmatiza-tion. There were some educators who floated the idea that students learning two languages simultaneously ended up confused.

This unsubstantiated claim had devastating implications. A number of Steve's contemporaries from Spanish-speaking homes were mistakenly diagnosed with learning disabilities when they failed to learn English within the school district's established timeline. Students who lagged behind were tracked and shuffled to a special education program where they were cru-elly taunted during recess by fellow students. This was ironic because the students doing the bullying were themselves only doing minimally better academically than those they tormented.

Brigid, along with other educational advocates, suspected that the bullying of the misdiagnosed students was a major cause for their high truancy rates. Her bicultural marriage to a man of Puerto Rican ancestry gave her an understanding of the complexities and pressures of cultural adaptation. After she was elected to the city's Board of Education, she got a clearer picture of the often unreported causes of student dropouts, including failed programs for non-native English speakers. Brigid sensed that Steve was dabbling in cultural repression. She thought that a clever way of drawing him out of his sense of isolation was by subtly blending the familiar identity with the repressed identity. One way she tiptoed around this challenge was by starting a sentence in one language and completing it in another.

Brigid asked: "*Hola*, Steve. How are you doing?

¿Cómo van los estudios? (How are your studies?)"

Scrappin' Steve timidly said in a broken Spanish:

"*Estoy bien* (I am doing well).

I just finished my second year."

Steve was studying electrical engineering at a four-year institute of technology known for its selective admissions and prominent alumni in his field of study.

Brigid validated Steve's academic accomplishments:

"*Muy bien* (Very good)," and she proceeded to ask, "and your *familia* (family)?"

The question engendered melancholic thoughts in Steve.

"*No se* (I don't know). Dad still does not allow me *to pasar por casa* (to stop by the house). Not even for special holidays."

"Well, you know that can always count on me as family," said Brigid

Scrappin' Steve flinched, lowered his head and moved away. Brigid's benign questions induced in Steve feelings of shame over his unhealthy and hurtful family dynamics. Her question laid bare the antagonistic relationship he had with his autocratic father. Steve pretended that he did not hear Brigid's pledge to be his family. He was jaded and did not believe in another human being's sincere interest in him as a person. He muttered something inaudible and turned to the traffic problem. He looked so natural at what he was doing that it did not occur to Brigid that she made Steve uncomfortable. Maldonado, for his part, listening silently for clues as to how this unlikely pair came together, sensed there was discord in the young vagrant's life, and he concluded that a family conflict was the basis for the sense of chaos surrounding him.

It didn't take *Scrappin'* Steve long to recover from his sad mood. Within five minutes or less he returned gripping a plank dislodge from a wooden pallet. Steve said to Maldonado, within an earshot of Brigid, "this piece of stick can be used as a shovel to clear out the snow and slush." Steve bent over and with a fixed determination dug ditches around the wheels until he ran out of energy. He pushed himself a little more, before he took a break and asked for a little help.

Gasping for air, Steve asked Maldonado, "want to try?"

Maldonado obliged. He started to dig through the problem his own way. He used his left bare hand to push through the remaining snow. He dug and dug and the black street surface was not visible. "Surreal?! This is just like an endless problem," Maldonado said.

Steve had second thoughts about having Maldonado take a turn as a digger.

Steve said, "You are working twice as hard, unnecessarily."

"You can get sick . . . get frostbite if you use your bare hands."

Steve retook control and had the audacity to say to Maldonado, "Just follow my lead."

"My digging technique allows you to get closer to the surface of the wheel."

Even though Steve's body was taking a break, his mind was not. It was churning, and as customary within him, every time a spontaneous idea surfaced, he would pursue it, particularly if the idea had the potential to augment his income.

"I'll be right back," said Steve.

He hurled the piece of wood aside, crossed the street and—even with his bad leg—gamely scampered up a platform connected to an electronic warehouse dock that was adjacent to *Victoria's*. Once Steve was on the platform of the electronics store, he jangled an iron gate and ripped a trilling whistle. Steve was talented at making noises and whistles that were animal-like. His mimicry covered parrots and other animals native to Puerto Rico like a little bird called *spindalis,* and the tiny tree frog *Coqui.* Behind the same gate was a tinted glass door, and from behind that door a man named Johnny Cruz could be heard expressing his anger at all the commotion. He vowed to reprimand the riff-raff responsible for the unrestrained wildness. That was until he realized that it was Steve.

Cruz greeted Steve. "Heeey, *negrito,* what brings you by?"

Steve turned away from Cruz. He felt insulted by Cruz's use of *negrito.* He had repeatedly asked him not to use that word when addressing him. He knew that Cruz used the word casually when saluting any male, regardless of his skin color. He used the word as a form of cultural endearment that was common among Puerto Ricans.

Steve understood the argot of his ethnic kin, but thought it was awful to be referred to by the color of his skin. He felt that allowing others to address him by the shade of his skin would make him standout for the wrong reason.

"Now that is flat-out disrespectful," Steve said.

A puzzled Cruz asked, "Disrespectful?"

Steve said, "I am fine with Steve or my street name *Scrappin'*. I gave myself that name. But I don't go around slapping people with a label as if they were an object. I don't think that by adding the suffix *ito* to the word somehow softens its stigma and makes the word acceptable. I don't say to this one or that one *hola, calbito* (hi, baldy), or *hola, goldito* (hi, chubby), or *hola, bajito* (hi, shorty), or *hola, feito* (hi, ugly)."

Cruz, brushing a curly mane of hair from one side of his head to the other to cover a receding hairline, waved his hands and said Steve's reaction was out of touch with the culture of his ancestors, and was an example of political correctness.

"That's an American thing."

Steve countered, "No, that is a respect thing."

Before Steve could get away, Cruz expressed his affections for Steve as both his son's, Eddie, and Steve's father's best friend. Johnny then tried to explain his use of *negrito* in reference to Steve.

"There is nothing shameful about being black. I am *trigueño*, a little lighter than you. I think you are smart and handsome, and I am always promoting you. I admire black people, um, Sammy Davis Jr., Celia Cruz, Jackie Robinson, Roberto Clemente." He went on and on and on, trying to take the sting out of the insults.

Steve sighed and did not reply. He listened out of habit and thought for a moment that perhaps there are attitudes endemic to a culture which are hard to overcome.

"Okay, I get it. You don't reject black people," Steve said. He gave Cruz a handshake and wandered about looking for scrapped items, discarded little things that may prove useful to someone. When he found what he needed, he returned outside and found Maldonado and Brigid gabbing. He pulled out a folding-knife from one of the pockets of his cargo pants to cut and divide some mesh wire into four, layer pieces. He then ordered Maldonado to place a piece of mesh in front of each wheel. Maldonado went along with his directions.

Steve asked Brigid to drive in reverse.

"Ok, Mrs. Santini, back up gently."

Steve knocked on the hood to get Brigid's undivided attention. It worked. Brigid suddenly stopped driving and fixed her eyes on him. Like a traffic controller at an airport runway, Steve started to use hand signals to guide her out of her entrapment.

"Slowly, slowly, angle your wheels in this direction. Okay, okay, that is fine," said the vagrant to the high class lady. Steve was amused by the power inversion.

Then he motioned Brigid to gradually step on the gas pedal. He started his open hand gesture at around his chest and slowly descended to a complete stop at his bellybutton. In an animated tempo, he coached, "Stay focused . . . slowly, slowly, slowly . . . "

For some unexplainable reason, Steve spoke sharply to Maldonado in commanding language.

"Take your hands out of your pocket and scoop out more snow!" Steve ordered him in very forceful tones.

Maldonado was revolted by the sharp tone in Steve's directive, but he did not allow it to get the best of him. He perceived Steve's order as a way of elevating his stature in Brigid's eyes.

"How can I help?" asked Maldonado. He did not want Brigid to see him as uninvolved, and he did not want to get into a conflict with Steve.

After some additional jostling and maneuvering, Brigid's car was dislodged from the snow and ice. She pulled away but not before gently tapping her horn twice and waving goodbye with the hand that proudly wore her graduation ring.

Steve stared at Brigid's tail lights. His eyes were tired after their ordeal. He extended his empty hand, hoping to be rewarded with a generous tip. Brigid was already going through the next traffic light, happy to be underway and feeling no sense of owing anything to the street person who'd just liberated her. That was the natural order of things. Steve felt ignored, left behind and not properly acknowledged for his hard work. Maldonado, for his part, did not think that he owed Steve anything. He jumped into his car without saying a word and set off to park.

Chapter Six

Playing with Loose Change

BRIGID'S OLD SPOT WAS still a mess and would require too much work for him and help from Steve for Maldonado to fulfill his original goal, to park his car. Steve, notwithstanding, was on a mission to claim an accessible parking spot by standing in it. He was preoccupied with the thought that another motorist would appear out of nowhere and jump into the newly-available parking spot.

"This is you," Steve said, as he simultaneously pointed downward to the vacant space and walked backward onto the curb.

"Come in slowly, this is you. A little closer, this is you," Steve said.

Maldonado wanted to get as close to the curb as possible without risking an accident.

Maldonado lunged from the car. He cautiously walked by Steve to fetch his American Belting Leather briefcase from the backseat of the car.

"God forbid that this guy thinks he is now my friend. He can't know anything else about me," Maldonado said to himself, trying to ease himself painlessly out of the thin bond that had formed by the shared success of freeing Mrs. Brigid Santini.

Steve was taken aback by Maldonado's indifference. He would have been even more furious if he'd known that Maldonado was getting him involved with a stolen vehicle. He could not grasp what prompted the sudden change in Maldonado's disposition. Steve, however, did not allow Maldonado's standoffishness to deter his plans.

In the past, Steve would crawl into an emotional shell. He would walk away from an opportunity to make a friend or he'd refuse to claim what was rightly his when he sensed that his presence was not wanted or that he was not welcomed in one social setting or the other. The self imposed social isolation from his peers was one of the main reasons that he abruptly left his free college dormitory room to live as a transient on the streets. His roommate shared a common ethnic heritage and was the son of a prominent business owner. He habitually made snide remarks about Steve's working-class family. Steve thought, as a first-generation college student, that a world-class college would provide him with access to world class people. He thought that an ethnic kin would offer him an unbreakable bond of brotherhood and an entry to success. But much to his dismay and disillusionment, he discovered early on in his college career that not everyone who shared a common background with him was interested in his upward mobility. He learned that not everyone who roamed the halls of higher learning was concerned about the dignified treatment of others.

His college counselor, Esther Walker, a gifted psychotherapist, was teaching him to overcome his negative self-image, and his homelessness. His homeless peers coarsened him and instilled in him the necessary edginess for survival, enabling him to deal with insults no matter what environment he found himself in.

"I have to slow this guy down," muttered Steve. His strategy was to contain Maldonado through engagement. Just talk to the guy about anything that interests guys. Cars, Business, Sex, Sports. There must be something that will make Maldonado talk.

Steve started to ask casual, but incisive questions.

"You are traveling, right? You are not from around here?"

There were conspicuous signs that Maldonado was from the tropics. He was wearing a pair of top-sider boat shoes on a wintry day, his complexion radiated a shiny bronze color. He spoke English with a sing-song accent.

Maldonado was evasive with his response.

"What makes you think that I am not?"

Steve responded to the question with a sarcastic compliment.

"Nice tan, bro."

Steve then looked inside the car, and then at Maldonado. He looked inside the car again and noticed a 26-inch, hard-case suitcase lodged between the front and back seat of the car. Steve, who saw a funny side to almost everything, called attention to the luggage with a wisecrack.

"Homey, the only time I see a guy around here carrying a suitcase in his wheels is when his girl gives him layoff for doing something stupid."

Steve broke into a silly laugh.

He then began a cat and mouse chase for information from the humorless stranger.

"What did you get busted for? Were you fooling around?" Steve said.

"Did you get fired from your job, and she *ain't* going to take care of you anymore?"

Steve's remark underscored another oversight by Maldonado. Steve was trying to laugh at the occurrences of everyday life, but Maldonado took Steve's remarks as personal insult.

Maldonado acted like Steve committed a capital offense.

With icy eyes and a curt tone, he said, "oh, you are so imaginative."

Maldonado's attitude did not deter Steve from wanting to know more about him. The stranger had given few clues to shed light on his identity, his past, or where he was headed. But then, hadn't they only just met by chance? Getting more required finesse.

There was something about Maldonado's enigmatic backstory that sparked a fascination in Steve's mind.

"Let me treat you to a cup of coffee," said Steve.

His aim was to make the stranger relax, get comfortable and reveal more of himself.

Maldonado rebuffed the offer. He did not want to entertain any expectation of conviviality.

"I can't. I have research to do."

Steve straddled the line between being tenacious and overbearing.

"I know the perfect place. It is clean and quiet. And on the way there, we can pick up a cup of coffee."

Just to prove Steve wrong, Maldonado asked, "Where?"

Steve responded: "The library."

Things fell into place for Maldonado. The library was an ideal location for him to quietly evaluate his next moves.

"Good idea," Maldonado said insincerely, as he was planning to park the car and finally abandon it.

"You are so prescient. How could I have failed to think of that?" he said.

Ah, but not too much time went by from the time when Maldonado offered Steve a compliment before Steve demonstrated his real motive.

"Can I have your spare change?"

Maldonado patted himself spryly from his chest to his lower hip area. The self-frisk did not produce the characteristic clink of coins from someone in possession of spare change, but it did elicit a satisfactory smile on Maldonado's face, as if to prove a point.

"I don't have any on me."

Steve smiled back and, with a devilish twinkle in his eye, pointed inside the car.

"How about the change sitting in the ashtray in your car?"

First the suitcase. Now the loose change. It seemed like the younger man was inspecting him to sniff out bits of factual information, or collecting clues to build a profile of him. The probing sent Maldonado into a bad mood. Part of Maldonado wanted to give Steve the change to avoid a conflict over what appeared to be a small amount of money, and he also wanted to hold back from giving a gift. Besides, in no way did he owe Steve for the job they'd done freeing Brigid from her parking space. Maldonado felt that a tip for Steve could be interpreted either as the overture of a friendship or the admission of guilt. Not surprisingly, Maldonado leaned on his grandfather's "self-sustenance trait" theory to help him sort out his feelings and guide his decision.

"Help yourself!" Maldonado said, gesturing with his head toward the the dashboard.

Steve opened the passenger side door, scooped up the loose change, and scattered the coins on the wet, snowy surface to wash off the powdery residue.

"I hate the smell of cigarettes," Steve said.

Steve added: "You know, come to think of it, I think that I am allergic to the smell of cigarettes, and I definitely hate to hustle for money."

Maldonado snorted. "Not according to your bighearted slogan of change and range."

" . . . you are not allergic to money, right?"

Steve repositioned his Afro pick as if to stimulate his brain for a deeper level of discussion than they'd been engaged in up to that point. He put forth his economic philosophy.

"Money in itself is not toxic to the soul. We all need some type of currency to meet our basic material needs. You just cannot get anything without something. The problem is greed. Greed is the toxin that metastasizes into a ravaging illness that destroys a person, institutions, and the fabric of a nation. As long as one is honest in making money then one is justified in amassing as fortune allows," Steve said.

Maldonado was not impressed by the vagrant's sense of philosophy.

"So, does it boil down to honesty? Is honesty the antidote to greed?"

To make his point crystal clear, Steve responded definitively, "yes, and honesty can never be dismissed!"

Maldonado thrust his elitist nose heavenward and snobbishly remarked, "iiiiin-teresting."

The scholar then posed a question that forced Steve to explain.

"So, honesty is the most important of all the virtues in your ethical schema?"

Steve wasn't sure if Maldonado was praising or making fun of his theory.

Steve said: "I don't know what you mean by 'ethical schema.' What I am clear on is that greed makes people do unethical things, and to take unnecessary risks. Selfishness is the primary cause of failed and strained relationships."

Maldonado's heart was tugged by Steve's remarks. He offered a straight-forward response.

"Your insight is very powerful!"

Steve nodded and deposited the sparkling coins in his pocket.

Chapter Seven

Bad Food Service and Kitchen Politics

THE TIME FOR FORMAL acquaintances arrived.

Steve, the junkman, removed one of his working gloves and offered the stranger, Maldonado, a cordial right-hand shake.

"I'm Steve, Steve Rosario. But I am known in the streets as *Scrappin'* Steve."

Maldonado returned the salutation also with a formal business-style handshake.

"I'm William Maldonado," he said.

After their introductions, Steve and Maldonado made their way through uneven narrow lanes to the college library, located four blocks east of the spot where they'd met. Steve took an alternate, slightly longer route. He was cold and hungry, and he fancied a *latte* and hot breakfast burrito from a truck cart operated by Dominican Joe, an Irish-American married to a Dominican from *El Cibao*, a rural area of the Dominican Republic.

Joe was popular for his specialty Dominican style-burrito, which was a melange of diced *chorizo*, green and red peppers, plantain bits, shredded white Dominican cheese called *queso de hoja*, all rolled up into a scrambled egg. He topped off the serving by adding either a homemade syrup of guava or mango served over a slice of open *casabe* bread. Steve imagined the scent of sizzling *chorizo* on the grill. He imagined savoring the crispy and crunchy palate of plantain bits in his mouth. The Dominican burrito was one of the very few delights that Steve's meager income allowed him.

Steve was able to get his *chorizo* Dominican-burrito fix on Wednesdays, after he earned money working on the docks. Steve always managed to place his order just before Joe's was swarmed by retail and factory workers on their scheduled 10:15 a.m. coffee break. Customers picked up coffee, burritos, cigarettes, and pastries from Joe's.

"Yummy! I can smell it all the way over here," said Steve.

Maldonado paid Steve no mind. He flipped the collar of his raincoat upward and tucked in his head to seek respite from the stinging cold wind.

As he walked, he silently reviewed the events that led to the implosion of his career and reputation. Maldonado wondered if he and Santana had ever been reported the fraud bureau, and wondered why the families who had paid their monthly insurance premium were not covered for property losses and loss of life.

Steve snapped Maldonado out of his deep reverie with a simple question.

"Hey man, what time do you have?"

Maldonado looked at his digital wristwatch.

"It is about 9:43 a.m."

Steve replied, "Good! We've got time before this place gets busy."

Maldonado was perplexed.

"Busy from what?

Steve said, "lots of people come here for a bite on their break."

Maldonado wanted to avoid the crowd of workers.

He said: "I thought we were just getting coffee."

"I've got to get me some protein," said Steve.

"Take it easy, man. Everybody is behind schedule today. The weather has messed us all up."

Before they knew it, they were in front of Joe's truck. The white exterior of the truck had been decorated by a graffiti artist, known in the streets as *Jay-Skee*, aka Javier Martinez, who had designed the tricolored Irish and Dominican flags on opposite sides. The truck also had a hallmark leprechaun business logo. The leprechaun was donning a Dominican peasant straw hat, wiggling his hips, and hopping on one foot. Clearly, the sign was designed to portray the leprechaun dancing an Irish jig to the rhythm of *Merengue.*

Joe, a freckled faced middle-aged man with a swatch of cinnamon dyed hair and emerald eyes, appeared behind the sliding window.

Joe knew what brought Steve by his food truck. In his characteristic tenor voice, he asked, "amigo, the usual burrito?"

Steve nodded and said, "Yep, the Wednesday special (burrito)."

"Add pepper, salt and ketchup on the side," Steve said.

Joe turned slightly and repeated the order to his younger brother, Evan, the grill chef. Joe used a microphone to pass along the customer's orders.

"A Dominican burrito on cassava."

Evan was grilling his specialty diced-up homemade fries, made up of green and red peppers, mushrooms and onions. He slammed his tong and lashed out at Joe.

"Stop bossing me around! I am not deaf! I can hear what the customers want!" Evan fumed. "I hate that stupid microphone!"

Joe insisted the microphone was necessary to drown out the noise. The food truck was noisy because of its ventilator and the funky music that blared from Evan's portable radio. Joe had been looking for a way to help Evan compensate for his attention deficit disorder. Bungled orders were costing his business money in wasted food and dissatisfied customers.

Joe was embarrassed by Evan's tirade.

"Ok, calm down. We've got customers," Joe said.

"We will discuss the problem later. We pride ourselves in being professional, at all times."

No matter how much he tried, Joe could not succeed in calming his little brother's easily irritated personality. It did not matter that Joe was mild-mannered when he spoke to his brother.

Evan kept grumbling, cursing, and slamming kitchen objects.

He slammed the pots, the tong, and the egg ring against the counter.

Joe's patience had reached a plateau, and he responded with a tantrum of his own. His voice screeched in agitation, and he yelled out his brother's full Baptismal name—with his Confirmation name thrown in for good measure—in advance of an insult.

"Evan Patrick Michael Kyle Thomas Kelly! You are so damn oversensitive and worthless!"

A fracas broke out. During the verbal sparring, Joe and Evan took turns flinging the most hurtful, indecent, anatomically-laced, scatological words imaginable. The pent-up emotions over kitchen politics and family dynamics reached a boiling point. They engaged in personal attacks covering personal setbacks and flaws. Evan diminished Joe about a struggling culinary career, even though Joe had earned an associate's degree from a renowned culinary school. Joe didn't hold back. He expressed his disappointment over what he perceived to be Evan's under-utilized military career opportunities. He also alluded to his little brother's bizarre relationships.

Evan was the first to launch a barrage of insults.

"I don't see why you have to wear that expensive chef's coat when you are just running a four-wheeled grease pit," Evan said.

"Huh! Who are you trying to impress?" Evan asked. "Man, you are such a phony!"

Joe, who took pride in wearing his immaculate, white chef coat, sulked for a few seconds before responding.

"It's about keeping a professional image. . . . this coat makes me feel good about myself, my business," Joe said.

Then Joe criticized Evan's ill-fitting military trousers, which the veteran wore daily to work, and his recent shamrock tattoos, sketched on each side of his little brother's neck.

"How about you?" Joe asked.

"Your appearance is a disgrace to the family, and it is hurting the image of my business."

"What's wrong with the way I look?" a bewildered Evan asked.

Taking a deeper dig at Evan's appearance, Joe said, "you are out of shape and out of place to be in those pants. It looks like you are wearing spandex. You are not eighteen anymore. There is more to life than the ongoing celebration of your military career."

Joe continued his verbal barrage with comments as jagged as the steak knife in the oak wood block inside his truck.

"And those awful tattoos . . . "

But before Joe could finish off another blistering remark, Evan interrupted and fought back.

"This is Irish pride," said Evan, as he pointed to the tattoos. "What's a matter? Don't you have respect for tradition anymore? "

"Oh, I get it." Evan added.

Evan even accused Joe of exploiting patriotism by sporting a flag pin on his coat to score points with the veterans who patronized his business.

"Why are you always making yourself to be more patriotic than George Washington?"

"You're always mouthing off about protecting the country, but you have never shot even a water pistol in defense of this country."

"Huh! How crazy is that?"

Joe, though agitated, did not want to debate the issue any longer. He wielded his paternalistic-level, big-brother authority to bring the conflict to a resolution.

"Again, get off your military soap box. There are other ways of proving loyalty to our country, but you're not taking advantage of opportunities available to you now that you're stateside."

"Just remember, in this truck, you are a private! You take orders from me, whether you like it or not!"

Joe could not conceal how the quarrel with his brother was affecting him. His face flushed red and his cracked lips quivered. With a flourish, he stepped out of the truck, reached into his custom-made executive chef coat for a cigarette and popped it into his mouth. Once it was lit, Joe had the idiosyncratic habit of rolling a cigarette from one side of his mouth to the other.

After a few puffs, Joe grunted repeatedly. "I can't take this aggravation anymore."

"This is kinda the problem with hiring family. They want special treatment."

Steve nodded. Maldonado remained quiet.

When the breakfast order was ready, Evan repeatedly pounded a hotel service bell that Joe recently had purchased at an estate sale. Evan's anger was designed to incite Joe into a cussing rematch.

"Take it easy, Evan, the customer can hear you," said Joe.

Evan reminded Joe how inconsistent he was.

"Aha, Mr. Double Standard, now you know why I don't like it when you use the mike. It is unnecessary. I can hear you."

Joe wanted to teach his brother a lesson that would have a lingering impact.

"Steve, can I borrow your stick?" asked Joe.

"I feel like whacking him across the head!"

"Cut it out, man" said Steve. "Cut it out."

To break up the bickering, Steve walked toward the breakfast truck to get his food and check.

"Cash me out."

"Make it $11," snapped Evan.

Steve extracted crumbled bills from his pocket, and a fistful of the cadged coins that he had mooched from Maldonado's car.

"Also, give me a butter roll, and two coffees with milk. No sugar," Steve ordered.

Steve then turned to Maldonado and asked, "How do you take your coffee?"

"Just black, regular," Maldonado responded.

"Evan, make it two coffees with steamed milk, and one regular."

"Do you want a pastry? The sugar doughnuts here are great," said Steve.

"I am fine," said Maldonado.

"Let's bounce," said Steve.

The breakfast order was placed into a foam container and deposited into a recycled plastic bag bearing the name and logo of *Felix's Fine Foods*.

Chapter Eight

News Flash

STEVE WALKED WITH A choppy gait, steadying himself by holding on firmly to the handle of his broom stick. Maldonado trudged along, clutching his briefcase. Together, the oddest of companions, they plodded on snow paths forged by previous pedestrians. Not for long. Steve abruptly trotted across the street and headed in the direction of an open newsstand, leaving Maldonado perplexed by the sudden change of travel plans.

Maldonado lifted his head and asked briskly, "Why are we making another stop?"

Steve turned around and mumbled the words, "Just chill!"

The street-slang made things confusing for Maldonado.

He shook his head and asked, "Just chill?"

Steve grinned and tried to explain the meaning of his hipster jargon.

"Just take it easy. Just relax."

Steve then said: "Wait for me right there. I've got to buy something very important."

Maldonado did not see anything good coming out of another detour. He was exhausted, worried and cold.

"We've got to keep moving. It's really cold out here."

Steve scoffed at Maldonado's take on the temperature.

"The weather situation is all mental!" Steve said, vaguely alluding to his companion's tropical mindset.

Maldonado sighed and grumbled, "This guy doesn't take anything seriously."

Steve advanced toward the newsstand, wanting to buy a Spanish-language paper known for its ample coverage of the Caribbean baseball winter leagues. In customary fashion, he dropped loose change on the counter, tucked the paper under his armpit, and curled up in a namaste posture. Steve tried to curry goodwill with the newsstand's owner, Krishna Patel, and the Lord Krishna shrine tucked in a corner.

Steve said, "Mr. Patel, *Asirratham*! (which can mean blessing in Hindi)."

Patel hardly looked at Steve. When he did, he said very little. Patel blew air from his mouth into the hand not covered up by a wood carving glove. He had become cynical of Steve, feeling that the vagrant tried to soften him up with polite gestures and inquisitive questions about India's culture as a presage to a ruse.

Patel said to himself, "It is all a fake, a distraction tactic."

Over time, Patel had become convinced that Steve was the customer who purchased newspapers, candy and chips and paid for those items by leaving a mixture of American and foreign currency if he was distracted when his store was crowded with customers. Adding to Patel's growing *sub rosa* dislike of Steve was the rumor that a bum with a physical description very similar to Steve's stole a bundle of newspapers. They had been dropped off by a delivery truck at his store before it opened for business. Patel was informed by the same source that the vagrant wore a nylon vest bearing the newspaper's logo and a fake company identification card, all in an effort to fool commuters into thinking that he was legitimately associated with the paper.

The stolen papers were sold by the vagrant thief at a lower price on a Path Train subway platform, not too far from Patel's store. The vagrant allegedly told rush-hour commuters that the paper was being sold at a discount to get new subscribers. Since Steve fit the description of the culprit according to Chico, the source of the rumor, Patel thought that Steve was the person hurting his business. Chico was Steve's father, and he was upset with Steve's decision to go to college. He wanted Steve to work as a second generation cabinet maker at a local factory and succeed him one day as the company's foreman. Patel had been unwittingly drawn into a family feud initiated by Steve's father.

Patel's discomfort with Steve showed in his shifting eyes, soft, tremulous voice, and his back and forth body movement. Patel, a peaceful man, looked twice at a cane with a carved, elephant-shaped handle leaning against a glass self-display refrigerator. He wanted to hurl it in a preemptive act of self-defense. Steve wondered what was going on with Patel. The usually happy man had a contorted scowl, and his oak-brown face turned into a moribund grey. Patel scrutinized Steve's money longer than usual. He seemed to distrust Steve, which aggravated Steve to the point that he wanted to heave the spare change in the direction of the shrine and hurl invectives at the merchant. Just when he was about to create a scene, Steve remembered the words of his college counselor, Esther Walker.

During a recent counseling session, Walker said to Steve, "Anger is a self-preservation emotion given to us by Nature. Remember always to use indignation as a catalyst for resiliency and courage. Learn how to overcome your victimization by mobilizing your anger in a constructive way to correct a perceived wrong."

Steve forced himself to smile. He wished Patel a good day and limped away. He rejoined Maldonado, who noticed that Steve returned looking despondent. Maldonado, nonetheless, could not believe that Steve had the gall to leave him standing out on the cold. He asked in earnest, "Was that paper so important that we needed to make a stop?" Steve did not respond. After walking a couple of long, city blocks, Steve dipped into one of the take-out containers and fetched his sandwich. He took a couple of desperate bites and blurted out his displeasure.

"Ah, man! This is not what I ordered! Joe is right. Evan is unreliable," he said. "What a crappy sandwich!"

Evan prepared Steve a "barn sandwich," made up of two scrambled eggs mixed with cheese and sliced pieces of bacon, hamburger, beef sausage, and Canadian ham. With a prolonged slurp, Steve licked his greasy fingers and, in a basketball shooting motion with arched wrists, hurled the barely eaten sandwiched into a topless waste basket. His street manners and childlike playfulness irritated Maldonado. He mumbled something in Spanish about the vagrant's behavior getting progressively worse as the day unfolded. Steve thought that Maldonado was being fussy about the weather not easing up. Steve shook his head. He did not understand why Maldonado wasn't better prepared for the winter, and just wearing spring-weather shoes and carrying a briefcase without gloves.

"You've got to be crazy to be wearing boat shoes on a day like today," Steve said.

Maldonado did not respond. That's not all that Steve was curious about. He noticed that Maldonado was carrying his briefcase barehanded. Steve could not resist asking what seemed like an obvious question.

"What do you do for a living, may I ask?"

Maldonado took a gulp of coffee, in order to stall and give him time to provide an evasive answer.

He said, "I am conducting a comparative historical analysis of the Puerto Rican diaspora in Jersey City."

Steve reacted to Maldonado's research project with a wrinkled forehead. The focus of Maldonado's research project did not make sense to him.

"Why this side of the river? Why not a study of Puerto Ricans in Spanish Harlem? Or The Bronx? Or Brooklyn?"

Maldonado was taken aback by Steve's question. In a placid voice, he responded, "The foundation that awarded me my fellowship required me to undertake this specific research in this specific place as a condition of my award."

Steve appealed to Maldonado's ego.

"Wow! That's impressive! A fellowship! You must be a top dog in your field. What are you hoping to get out of this?"

Maldonado sighed softly. He was annoyed with Steve's use of the dog metaphor to refer to him under the guise of a compliment.

"What do you mean?"

Steve gave Maldonado a bemused look.

"Um, tenure? A landmark book? A posh position with a think-tank? A consulting job with a high-end firm?"

Maldonado downplayed the importance of his fellowship and the potential future professional opportunities that could result from his research.

"Just a job well done," said Maldonado.

Steve wasn't done probing. He snuck in another question.

"Where did you go to school?"

Maldonado answered proudly, "the Harvard of the Caribbean," which was a reference to his beloved undergraduate alma mater, the University of Puerto Rico in Rio Piedras.

Steve did not appreciate that remark, perhaps envious that he didn't get into the school of his choice, or perhaps thinking that Maldonado was making himself out to be smarter than he was. He launched into a series of pointed questions and remarks.

"What in the world is that supposed to mean? That you received an elite education? That you are smart? You either went to the real McCoy in Cambridge or you didn't. When you are smart, you demonstrate it in your work. You don't need to hide behind a school to make that claim."

Maldonado frowned. He didn't understand why Steve gave him a reproving speech. He was simply trying to underscore that he got into a selective school, and that he was not a schlemiel. The other reason he mentioned Harvard was because he had a soft spot in his heart for the school. As a boy, he had attended alumni gatherings at Harvard with his grandfather, Loubriel.

Maldonado said, "Yes, very well. It's not important where I went to school."

"How far are we from the library?"

"It is too cold to be having this kind of conversation outdoors."

Maldonado, in effect, wanted to avoid arguing over mundane things and broadcasting personal information.

Steve picked up on the cue. He stopped asking questions, but not before deploying a barb.

"You are right about the weather making things too uncomfortable to talk. But I was right about you not being from the area," Steve said.

Maldonado curled his lip. Though he was tempted to respond in a harsh manner, he decided not to challenge Steve's comments. The suitcase, the loose change, the tan, the island accent, the boat shoes, and the revelation of a research fellowship proved the validity of Steve's assumptions. For about twenty minutes, they walked in the deep, reverential silence like that often displayed by mourners walking in a cemetery to attend a committal service.

Chapter Nine

Hidden Reality

FINALLY, THEY ARRIVED. THEY walked past two ornate lamp posts and faced doors of modern glass with a hazy surface. The glass was an apropos metaphor since life was foggy for Maldonado. He did not know what opportunities life had for him on the other side, once the hinges to the doors swung open. His fate was in the hands of a vagrant he'd just met. Getting acquainted with Steve came with the dread of the vagrant's displays of immaturity and unpredictable behavior. Maldonado, however, did not dwell on the vagrant's flaws. The vagrant provided perfect company for an imperfect moment.

Steve opened the doors and deferred to Maldonado.

"After you, illustrious," Steve said.

Maldonado entered walking with stiffly upright posture past the first and second set of doors, two wood pocket doors each with a brass handle. He walked under a brass chandelier and stepped onto the foyer's marble steps. His feet were squishy and wet with discomfort. It occurred to him to dry his wet socks on a cast-iron radiator, if he could find one that was away from the public view. He spotted a restroom and was heading in that direction when something surprised him. There was an average height, rail thin man, named Eduardo Cruz, sitting on a wheeled office chair behind a cubicle. Eduardo, who liked to be called by his Americanized name, Eddie Cross, was sporting a shiny badge on a cheap, blue two-toned poly-cotton shirt with a patch of the American flag embroidered on one sleeve.

Eddie said in an authoritative voice, "Hey! Where are you going? You have to sign in."

Maldonado tensed up; an eery feeling of doom engulfed him. Eddie was wearing the traditional colors of a police officer from the island he escaped, and he had a nightstick and a walkie-talkie resting on his single-pedestal steel desk. Maldonado thought that Steve was either an undercover cop or an informant. He feared Steve led him to Eddie, who would arrest him.

That was until Steve placed a butter roll, a lukewarm cup of coffee, and a copy of the recently purchased Spanish-language paper on Eddie's desk. Eddie, flashing a broad smile, jumped from his chair and greeted Steve with an unorthodox handshake—swinging hands followed by two back-hand slaps. The greeting culminated with a light chest bump.

"What have you been up to, homey?" Eddie asked.

"Just *scrappin'*, man. Just *scrappin'* to make it one day at a time," Steve said.

Maldonado softened up. He figured that Eddie was going to engage him in the same soul handshake that he greeted Steve with. So, preempting the handshake routine, Maldonado gently grabbed Eddie's hand in a conventional business handshake.

A miffed Eddie asked, "Why are you dissing me like that? I am not a hoodlum."

It was an awkward moment. Eddie then asked, "Does this guy think he is a *blanquito* (implying a preppy Caucasian)?"

Steve bent over and laughed in a wheezing voice.

"He's cool. He's cool, man. He is an intellectual from the island. He *ain't* into jiving and fooling around," Steve said. He went on to mention Maldonado's university funded research project as their purpose for visiting the library.

Eddie, who was impressed by a fancy title or terminal degree, especially a degree from a well-known school, fawned in admiration and apologized profusely. "My bad. My bad."

Then the side of Eddie that Steve hated the most came out. Eddie broke into talking about sports with an irrational devotion and pompous attitude.

"I told you so!" Eddie said. Eddie quite often spoke in fragmented thoughts or in incomplete sentences. His inadequate communication skills left people guessing or attempting to translate what he was trying to say.

Steve asked, "You told me, what?"

Eddie pointed to a statistical chart in a glossy sports' magazine. He felt that he had the upper-hand. He had had an ongoing tiff with Steve over who was the greatest second baseman of all time.

Eddie said, "My main man is the best second baseman of all time. No question about it."

"Here is the proof."

Steve quickly took the opportunity to agitate his easily flustered friend.

"C'mon man! Your pumping out propaganda!"

"Just drop it. Your guy will never be better than Joe Morgan. Ever. The statistics you are citing are skewed. Your main man plays in a softball park. Any pop-up he hits is a home run."

Eddie's voice inflected, "Huh, hmm." He shook his head and started his defiance ritual. He rubbed his hands together in a rapid motion, clapped them once, and rubbed them together again vigorously. He ended his routine by crossing his arms across his bony chest. The posture made him feel self-confident. Eddie religiously went through the defiance ritual before debating anyone on any topic, even on complex issues that were beyond his level of comprehension. Eddie was argumentative by nature. His contentious spirit was stirred by provocative talk-radio personalities and opinion writers that he either listened to or read during his eight-hour shift as a security guard. Eddie was a hoarder of information. When he learned something new, he would bait others into a conversation on the newly learned subject to impress upon them that he was not an ordinary security guard. He was well-informed, well-rounded, well-connected, and well on his way to a future of imponderable success. Eddie argued passionately that, "Rivas (José) has a better career average and more gold gloves at this point in his career than Morgan did at the time of his retirement."

Steve countered with a slogan that his friend detested to the point of causing him to grind his teeth.

"You are more tangled up than a plate of spaghetti."

Steve did not care about baseball players. Not one bit. Steve raised the topic of sports, through conversations and newspapers, to provoke and amuse himself with Eddie's irrational devotion to a ballplayer and sports' teams. Steve was a master in creating friction. He knew how to spot people who showed a "symptom of neurotic fanaticism," as he called it, in sports, politics and religion. He provoked them with inflammatory comments. He loved to agitate a fanatic and have him talk about how he was going to resolve an invincible problem.

There were times that Eddie suspected that Steve riled him up for the sake of a good laugh. Eddie went along with it, knowing that in friendship sometimes pretending is an antidote to an unnecessary conflict. But when it came to Rivas, there was nothing funny about the seriousness of his conviction. Eddie was bedazzled by Rivas's wizardry on the field, and he was unabashedly proud of the player's connection to his parents' native town in Puerto Rico. It did not matter what statistical evidence a Rivas critic would cite. Eddie would insist that no other rival second baseman would trump his baseball idol as the greatest player at that position. Not Roger Hornsby. Not Rod Carew. Not Ryan Sandberg. No other canonized baseball immortal, active player, or upcoming and promising prospect was going to replace Rivas's iconic standing.

Maldonado glanced at his wristwatch. He tarried for ten minutes, listening to Steve and Eddie go back and forth with their contentious conversation. Maldonado said, "what a drag," before becoming prissy and letting out a sigh of exasperation. The implication of his remark did not work. Eddie and Steve carried on with their vapid prattle. Maldonado thought that the only way to make Steve and Eddie aware of their apparent lack of courtesy was to simply walk away. Before he did, it occurred to him that maybe if he dispensed one of his stories that he could create a favorable impression, making himself more interesting, more noticeable.

"Excuse me," said Maldonado, with eyes dancing all over the place.

Steve and Eddie stopped talking.

Maldonado cleared his throat and took on the subject of baseball.

"I played Double A ball in Puerto Rico for about four years. From my perspective, Morgan is slightly better. He was the catalyst of one of the more dynamic hitting lineups ever. This is why he earned two MVP awards."

Maldonado turned toward Eddie and asked a provocative question.

"How many MVPs has your hero won?"

"None, yet," Eddie answered, feeling disarmed and conceding, for the time being, that perhaps his guy was not the best second baseman of all time but rather of a generation.

Maldonado tossed out other ideas on the subject of baseball, encouraging Eddie to compare players by eras and not across the wide history of the sport. Maldonado spoke rapidly about statistical information and anecdotal stories that made him sound like a sports savant. Some of the information was common knowledge that Steve had shared with Eddie in the past. Maldonado's doctoral degree work and ability to package and present the same information made him sound like a luminary to Eddie. Baseball had been Maldonado's escape from the reality of his mother's jaundiced face as she lay dying of cancer.

Eddie was brimming with excitement. He complemented Maldonado. "You have a gift for explaining things clearly and precisely."

Steve looked at Eddie and saw his friend's eyes twinkle with wonder.

Eddie, indeed, beamed with admiration.

He drew closer to Maldonado and asked, "What position did you play?"

With pride, Maldonado said, "I was an all-star catcher."

"Whoa!" exclaimed Eddie, who almost immediately asked, "for what team?"

Maldonado shifted emotional gears. With a sappy look, he said, "the team was formerly affiliated with a major league team, but it folded due to a lack of fan interest. Kids became more interested in other sports and outdoor activities—basketball, volleyball, surfing."

"Why did you give it up? Did you get hurt or what?" asked Steve, noticing that Maldonado became evasive in answering the question about what team he played for.

To no avail. Maldonado continued to sidestep the questions at hand.

"In life you have to dedicate yourself to one thing, and do that thing well. If not, you become scattered and mediocre at many things," said Maldonado.

"So, you believe more in being a specialist rather than a generalist?" Steve asked.

"Oh, yes!" Maldonado exclaimed.

"Now, back to your question, Steve. Thoughtful reflection and scholarly work invigorate me more than hearing the boisterous eruption of thousands chanting my name after a home run. Mass frenzy and public adulation are transient, but knowledge is eternal. And when it came down to it, my academic interests superseded my ambitions on the diamond. This is why I gave up baseball."

"Wow! You are deep," said Eddie, as he removed his security guard cap and gave Maldonado a formal handshake.

Eddie continued to shower Maldonado with praise. "You are the man!"

After flashing a fake smile, Maldonado walked away from a phony story he crafted on the spot. He headed to the bathroom to hang his wet socks. On his way there, he wondered whether his fanciful story garnered him acceptance into Steve's and Eddie's clique. When Maldonado was in prison and then at an in-patient substance abuse program, he discovered that bragging about exaggerated criminal acts among fellow inmates and fellow substance abusers earned him admiration and acceptance into the group. Not being part of a clan in prison or in rehab was considered foolhardy, since it exposed an inmate or a client at a rehab program to disapprobation and unimaginable dangers. Until now Maldonado's way of earning respect was by inflating his sense of importance through fictional triumphant stories—including false tales of drug life that he embellished with incidents he invented from other people's experiences.

He opened the bathroom door and walked slowly toward a dingy vanity mirror. With his waist pressed against the basin, he stooped over the sink, removed his wiry glasses, and contemplated his reflection. He was troubled by his reflection, which, in spite of the tan Steve commented on, was nonetheless drained and ghostly.

In a disillusioned whisper, he spoke to himself.

"I cannot believe what you have become."

His epiphany, however, did not create an iota of remorse.

"My life cannot end this way. It simply cannot."

Chapter Ten

Work-Related Problems

WITH MALDONADO OUT OF plain sight, Eddie broached the sticky subject of business. Steve and Eddie were partners in an interior painting and roofing business. They were not happy with each other and found themselves in a tug of war over the future of their relationship and business. Steve was hoping that time would resolve the problem on its own. He would skirt conversations about business. It bothered him that Eddie called past and potentially new customers without talking to him and made commitments to undertake jobs that required an uneven sharing of the workload and yielded a marginal profit. Eddie was into doing every job that came along without confirming Steve's availability. If Steve was not able to take on the job, Eddie would cobble together a motley crew and take on the job, at times leaving a job unfinished, thereby sullying the company name. When Steve pressed Eddie to stop putting the company name and insurance policy at risk, Eddie would say that money and work were happiness. Steve doubted that Eddie's ambition had anything to do with securing happiness. He was convinced that Eddie was all about keeping people preying on him for money favors happy, and he was about subsidizing a showy lifestyle to keep up a pretense of success and prosperity in the community.

Not too far from Eddie's assigned security post, an enclosed phone booth was staked out by Eddie as an office phone. Eddie plopped himself inside that booth to discuss job estimates and negotiate renovation material prices with hardware store managers. To make sure that no one ever tied up the phone line between his 9 a.m. to 5 p.m assigned security shift, Eddie hung the handle of the phone backwards to prevent incoming calls. He even created a hand-written sign that cautioned:

"DANGER!

Under Repair.

Do Not Enter –Police."

During the winter, Steve and Eddie performed interior painting jobs. During the summer, they focused on laying down flat and slightly-pitched tar roofs. Steve used his push cart to haul materials to worksites, since neither he nor Eddie could raise enough money to buy a company car. Eddie boasted about the company's mid-sized crew and construction equipment. Whenever a customer asked about the whereabouts of the crew or the work van or the cutting-edge equipment, Steve offered lame excuses to cover up Eddie's fibs. He would either say that his crew was hunkered down at another site, the company van was being repaired or the equipment was in storage.

With Maldonado well out of sight, Eddie reached into his trousers, pulled out a piece of rice paper with a scribbled estimate for a new job lead and handed it over to Steve.

"She has called us twice," Eddie said in an exasperated voice.

Steve bristled.

He was offended both by Eddie's insistence and that Eddie was probably still dabbling in marijuana, as suggested by the rice paper in his pants' pocket.

"Pssss!"

"My studies come first!"

"I have been prepping for my finals and doing lots of research for my term papers," Steve added.

Eddie cocked his head backwards, crinkled his lips, and sighed in disbelief.

"Alright. Alright. I understand . . . But we can't let this job go. Just go by, take her a couple of paint charts from the hardware store, and give her a start date," Eddie suggested.

"We can do the job in no time."

Steve remained unconvinced.

He said facetiously, "We is too many people."

Then Steve painted an uncomplimentary picture. He pantomimed Eddie's unusual and unconventional painting style. Eddie then spun a drenched paint roller nap on a wall from bottom up, rather than the conventional form of painting from top down. There was also the problem of unfocused productivity, unkept timelines, and the sloppy painting skills displayed during the trimming part of a paint job. The latter resembled candle-wax drippings.

Steve's lampoon created a surprising result.

Eddie was speechless, at first. He then giggled at Steve's frankness.

Eddie said, "You are crazy, man!"

"I get it. I get it."

Steve was trying to dramatize how Eddie's lack of productivity hampered him. Instead of addressing the problem directly, Steve went off track and talked about the client's personality, and her default payment on a past invoice.

"She is a difficult person to deal with. She had me moving like a yo-yo, putting up and removing wall paper patterns until she settled on the one she liked. She still hasn't paid me in full for last year's bathroom wallpapering job," Steve said.

Eddie knew why the client did not make the full payment, but held back that information from Steve. All he was interested in was the opportunity to make a quick profit. He humanized Andrea, hoping to soothe the irritated Steve.

"Andrea is a selfless and lonely widow. She has been through a lot with her family. Her husband of 51 years died. She lost her son, Hector, to the streets. All she wants is for her place to get touched up before her first annual Christmas open house. She said something about having family visiting from Florida for the first time in a decade. It is a straight-forward job," Eddie insisted.

Steve shrugged his shoulders. Steve was worn out by Eddie's business tactics. Steve, however, struggled to end his relationship with Eddie. He was hoping that the passing of time would resolve the problem on its own.

More problematic for Steve is that he viewed Eddie as a surrogate brother by virtue of their upbringing at the same Spanish-speaking Pentecostal church. The bond of brotherhood appeared too hard to break. He felt conflicted and thought about Dominican Joe's prophetic words on the folly of getting into a business relationship with a relative.

Steve originally hired Eddie as an assistant to haul gallons of paint up a flight of stairs of an apartment building, or have him sweep debris off a roof top, prior to laying down a new tar roof. Eddie, however, complained about how unfulfilling and poorly paid those "menial jobs" were to him. Steve had trained Eddie in carrying out prep work. Steve, for his part, was on the road purchasing materials, pricing out jobs, or preparing specs. This effort proved to be a huge waste of time, since Steve ended up redoing most of the jobs. Eddie always seemed rushed in doing his work and distracted. There were occasions when Eddie skipped work because he claimed that one of his kids was sick; he had to bail from work on several occasions to take his mother-in-law to a medical appointment; pick up his mother from a bingo gathering; take his cat to the veterinarian, or tuck himself in one of the library's quietest spots to complete a college project. There was always something unusual affecting Eddie's work schedule.

More than anything else, Steve wanted to end his business relationship with Eddie, but he could not bring himself to do it. He could not overcome the guilt and the rules instilled by his religious and cultural upbringing. He referred to the latter as those "damn Hispanic rules." Steve felt that he would be reneging on the religious vows he made as a godfather during the baptismal ceremony of Eddie's youngest child. He recited promises led by the priest to help promote the welfare of the child. It was explained to him that the vows meant that he was partly responsible for the child's spiritual formation and material needs. Steve reasoned that firing Eddie would make a mockery of his public vows (faith), unfairly penalize his godchild, and cause him to abdicate the Hispanic cultural expectations of godfathering.

"I can't back away from my baptismal vows," Steve said, amidst a mixture of remorse and guilt.

"I should have listened to my gut. I should not have accepted Eddie's 'honorary invitation' to be the child's godfather. He's got me on the hook now with the *compadre* here and *compadre* there nonsense."

Steve was chiefly concerned that the culturally-imposed expectations of being a godfather were archaic and inhibiting. Yet nothing bothered him more than Eddie's lack of gratitude. Eddie was always complaining about something that Steve could have done better with the business. He suggested that Steve was preventing him from overcoming his financial and relationship problems. When Eddie yakked about money and business, Steve nodded his head to give the impression that he was listening. He tuned Eddie out.

Chapter Eleven

In Need of Counseling

EDDIE CONTINUED TO GRIPE about money problems. Steve nodded to gently appear empathetic. He was grasping for an excuse to wrench himself from one of Eddie's characteristically long-winded, monotone conversations. But he couldn't come up with a single place to excuse himself where Eddie would not follow him, not even the restroom. Wherever he went, Eddie was sure to continue his prattle. Eddie yakked and yakked, almost without taking a break for a breath; he was seemingly unaware of Steve's strained body language. Steve backpedaled a few steps and allowed his thoughts to drift, engrossing himself in his most recent 45-minute counseling session with Walker. At that meeting, Steve explored the nature of friendship. In a sorrowful plea, Steve asked Walker, "Why do I keep putting all of my energy into the business, when I know that I am going to fall short all of the time?"

Walker knew that the question stemmed from a long-standing conflict Steve had with Eddie. She remained impassive, jotting down notes and reminding him that he had been stuck in a behavioral pattern for a while.

"What you are saying to me today reminds me of what you said a year ago. You were upset with your business partner (Eddie) for slacking off and showing up stoned at roof jobs. I remember you telling me that he endangered himself and placed your business at risk, correct?"

Steve nodded. The problem had gone on too long, and he didn't know how to address it. He gazed down, fidgeted with his beard and asked a couple of soul-searching questions.

"Am I setting myself up for unrealistic expectations?" Steve asked. "Does Eddie really care about me as much as I care about him?"

Walker did not offer an immediate response. She wanted Steve to stew with his own questions and uncertainties, figuring out on his own what to do when the moment was right. She finally spoke.

"Sometimes things go as far as they should go. You have to learn not to allow losses to stifle your happiness and deprive you of your right to cultivate your own world," Walker said.

Walker was a strikingly attractive, medium-sized woman with a chocolate soufflé complexion, fleshy lips and black hair pulled back with twirling curls perched in the back of her head. She was easy on the eyes. She was easier to listen to and open up to. She was a gifted clinician. Her natural compassion allowed her to listen without judgment. Her breadth of intellect allowed her to draw from diverse sources, philosophers John Dewey and Plato, psychologists Carl Jung and Sigmund Freud, to share meaningful insights. But her wisdom and precious doses of practical insights came from her rich Southern upbringing. She wove anecdotal stories about her early life with her personal artwork to illustrate a broader point of view in her counseling sessions.

Walker knew what made Steve tick. She motioned to him and asked, "Do you have your Bible?"

Steve pulled out a pocket-size Bible tucked away in one of his cargo pant's pockets.

"I've got my sword right here," Steve said, referring to the Bible in the metaphoric language used in the sacred canon to describe its piercing-like words (Hebrews 4:12 and Ephesians 6:17).

"Okay, then," said Walker.

She gave him two scriptural references and asked him to grapple with a question as he read the stories.

"As you read the assigned stories, ask yourself, 'is it beneficial for anyone to tolerate someone else's self-serving motives that are obstructive to your own self-interest?'"

Steve was staggered by the profundity of the question.

"Aha," Steve said, "That is some deep stuff you just threw at me."

The stories Steve was assigned to read were largely concerned with friendship. One of the stories centered on the resolution of an ongoing squabble between two family members, Abraham and his nephew, Lot, and the second story focused on Jesus's expansive definition of what constitutes family.

Steve, still stirred by the weightiness of Walker's question, picked a red pencil out of a stack of yellow pencils in a coffee mug. He then wrote down the question on the margin of one of the Bible's pages. After he did, he leaned back and paused to think about Eddie. He knew that Eddie needed money to supplement his low-wage salary as a security guard. He also knew that a lack of residual income was going to provoke ongoing clashes between Eddie and his second wife, also named Evelyn.

Steve heard a knock on the door and turned around to see who it was. From the angle where he was sitting, he couldn't see for sure who it was. It was one of Walker's scheduled clients, and she asked him to return in ten minutes. He disappeared from sight and Steve returned to his conversation with Walker.

Steve started to feel the tug of guilt and Hispanic rules. He asked an open-ended question.

"Am I being sensible?"

Walker wanted Steve to clarify his thoughts and feelings. She asked, "sensible about what?"

Steve placed his hands over his face and let his mind wander off to retrieve fragments of a recent conversation he had with Eddie about his marital strife. Walker figured out that Steve was conflicted. She asked a question that caused him to swing his hands and open up about something else. He resolved to tell Walker that there was something else making him feel torn.

"I am trying to comfort Eddie and his wife," Steve said.

Walker said, "tell me more."

Steve explained that Eddie was struggling to keep his former and current wives happy, and that he was caught in the middle by serving as a sounding board and de facto counselor to Eddie and, on infrequent occasions, to Eddie's current and former wives.

Steve spoke solemnly: "Not only am I this guy's kid's godfather. I was also the best man at both of his weddings."

Walker, upon learning the new information, was surprised by how involved Steve was in Eddie's personal affairs. She was worried by the subtle glimpses of depression in Steve's voice that he was not creating clear boundaries and was co-dependent in a dysfunctional relationship with Eddie. She had a strong affinity for Steve and some thought that she cared for him like a son. She was tempted to say something more direct to Steve about his conflict with Eddie, but decided against it. She wanted the counseling process to do its work without her interference.

Steve became self-conscious about what he had just revealed. He was ashamed and imagined that Walker was going to have a less favorable opinion of him. Trying to justify his involvement, Steve trotted out a gossipy story from the past to show how badly Eddie was being treated by his former wife, Evelyn. Steve told Walker that Evelyn wanted Eddie to focus on securing a more financially rewarding job. Eddie disagreed with her. He felt that the job he had as a guard provided steady income and was part of a broader plan. Steve then chuckled and told Walker that Eddie's personal goal was to use his security job to gain valuable criminal justice experience so that one day he could work as a motorcycle officer like Erik Estrada of

Chips and then go on to law school and become a criminal justice lawyer like Perry Mason.

Steve said, "His former wife is always breaking him down. She once told him vigorously in front of me, " 'Be realistic! With your shoddy grades, I don't see how you are ever going to get into law school, and with two young kids who need your attention, I don't see how you are going to make it, even if you got in'"

Steve shook his head and said, "That just *ain't* right."

Evelyn previously worked as a paralegal for a Fortune 100 company, prior to becoming a stay-at-home mom. She had a tendency to tell everyone who would listen that she possessed a peripheral knowledge of the legal profession from her paralegal work writing briefs for attorneys and mentoring first-year law school interns. She would habitually unload sharp rebukes at Eddie for what she perceived to be his misplaced ambitions. She would say to him, "spend less time dreaming and more time with [y]our kids."

Steve heard a second knock. This knock had a nervous ring to it. Standing outside the half open door was Walker's previous client who had stopped by earlier. He had an anxious expression on his face. Steve's counseling session came to an immediate end.

Walker whispered to Steve, "our time is up. If there is one goal that you can accomplish between now and our next meeting, what would that be?"

Steve sat motionless. Steve was daydreaming. Suddenly, a hand squeezed his shoulder. Steve panicked, until it occurred to him that it was Eddie firmly pressing on his shoulder. Eddie fixed his eyes on him. Eddie was curious about Steve's decision on the bathroom renovation job. He was hoping that Steve would agree to take it after hearing his sobering money tales. In earnest, Eddie asked, "Are you going for it? What is going on?"

Steve thought for a moment and responded, "Just thinking about so many things. I still don't think that I should commit to the job."

Chapter Twelve

Making an Impression on the Spot

DISSATISFIED WITH THE RESPONSE, Eddie started in earnest to pester Steve in a manner that was marked by trash-talking and shadow-boxing. In the meantime, Maldonado had come out of the bathroom and was on his way to the library's lobby. Maldonado looked straight ahead and got a hint of what was going on when he drew closer and heard Eddie say under his breath, "Taking that job and collecting the money is as easy as throwing this combination and scoring a knockout." After that statement, Eddie shuffled his feet and uncorked a string of simulated haymakers.

Steve appeared aggravated by Eddie's flamboyant theatrics, but he remained cool and simply waved him off. Feeling concerned, Maldonado picked up his pace and decided to walk past them. He had every reason to believe that they were arguing over something inconsequential, and he did not want to get sucked into another one of their foolish quarrels; his head still ached from the lively conversation he had with them as to who was the best second baseman of all time. Maldonado, however, quickly brushed aside the idea of separating himself completely from Eddie and Steve. He did not want to be looked upon as ungracious. Maldonado approached them, adjusted his glasses, and motioned for their attention. Once he got their attention, he asked for directions to the library's reference room.

It was a strange question, Steve thought. Within his sight, a multi-lingual sign facing Maldonado provided the information he wanted. The question succeeded in calming the tiff between Eddie and Steve. The question also moved Eddie. He was elated that Maldonado, whom he viewed as an intellectual, had asked him for directions on something as insignificant as a room in the library.

Flashing a broad smile, Eddie said, "Professor, just take the stairs to the second floor and hang a left."

Maldonado displayed a smile and gestured a goodbye in a military sa-lute. The scholar's manners impressed Eddie, who grinned and reciprocated the greeting with a military salute of his own. Eddie removed his cap, raised his right hand to his temple and swiftly whipped his hand downward in a chopping motion.

Eddie said, "*Maestro, que la pase bien*! (Teacher, I hope you have a good one.")

Maldonado winked and responded, "You are kind and gracious. I must now excuse myself."

Eddie leaned over to Steve and spoke in glowing admiration of Maldonado.

"He's definitely the man. He's got brains and character."

Eddie's behavior caused a shade of anger in Steve. He did not fancy Eddie showcasing his Spanish-speaking skills, and it made him sick to his stomach that Eddie would accept things as fact from people with fancy degrees, and yet would challenge Steve on virtually everything. Steve, nonetheless, forced himself to give Maldonado a lukewarm smile and timid wave.

Steve was not easily impressed by theatrical platitudes, and he was not in agreement with Eddie's predictable lofty praise of someone with unverifiable degrees and unprovable stellar accomplishments, but he decided not to say a word, for he did not want to come across as repugnant.

Maldonado waved at Steve with some apprehension of his own. He noticed a hint of curiosity in the vagrant college boy's glance. With briefcase in hand, Maldonado left. He ascended the stairs, and with each step he took, he recalled Petra's observation in that self-discovery always requires an assent of some sort. Once as a nine-year-old, he was invited to sit on a spiritual consultation led by Petra. She was trying to enlighten a well-heeled, middled-aged client, who was concerned about his legacy and the fate of his barely productive sugarcane farm. After rotating some tarot cards on an oval table, Petra took the palm of the man's hand and delivered a message in the language of a medieval mystic.

"The closer you orient your mind heavenward, the easier it will be for you to abandon your temporal worries. The lesser you become worried about the affairs of the world, the clearer your mind will be to receive the purpose of your existence."

Petra's words gave Maldonado a sense of assurance. After arriving at the top of the stairs, he read with great interest the arrowed-shaped signs that pointed to the library's rooms and resources. The signs read: Copy machine. Newspapers. Tutoring Sessions. Conference Room. Documentary Section.

He entered the microfilm room and walked toward the file cabinets resting against the wall. He pulled rolls from the indexed 1970's section, loaded the microfilm machine and positioned himself in front of the screen.

When the machine warmed up, it projected a grainy newspaper story. Slowly and methodically, Maldonado turned the microfilm's handle, and with each turn, the motion showed past stories and unwelcome memories of the insurance fraud scandal.

He stopped maneuvering the handle, but the churning of bitter thoughts persisted. He placed his hands over his head and said a minute or so later, "I don't know if I can continue doing this."

He let out an agonizing sigh and asked in a whisper, "What good would it do to retrieve memories and stir up the past?"

An internal struggle ensued, tearing him up inside with questions about the purpose of his investigation. The inner battle gave him doubts about continuing the research. But, in the end, his curiosity overpowered him, causing him to explore how an insurance fraud case, destroyed everything he esteemed: his professional integrity, his ability to make a living, his social life and friendships, his love for a city, his faith in organized religion.

He rotated the handle and unearthed stories that covered the insurance fraud scandal. He read and discovered that the source of the fire was sparked by bad electrical wiring. The coverage of the story went on to report that the victims did not level a complaint with the city's consumer fraud bureau, in part because most of the victims mistook Father Roberto's sermon on forgiveness and the priest's advocacy of Santana as an absolution of guilt. Maldonado scrolled through the stories and seethed in anger when he realized how he had been labeled an agent of deceit, while his former partner was presented as a victim.

He was upset with his former partner in that insurance business and asked himself, "How could I have been the only one to inherit the wrath of the community?"

Instead he was the only one accused of carrying out an insurance scam that victimized working class people. It dawned on him that he had been framed, and thought that Santana had set him up to take the fall.

Outside the microfilm room, the rumbling doors of the elevator slid open. Steve limped out onto the second floor. He looked for Maldonado in the reference room, and after not finding him there, he walked toward the water cooler in the hallway. Holding a cone-shaped cup, Steve stood outside a French door and peeked inside. Out of mere coincidence, he discovered that Maldonado mined through articles and scrawled notes at a furious pace. Certainly Steve wanted to know what Maldonado was doing. He wanted to be inside the microfilm room and the scholar's head, if nothing else but to get a sense of what he was working on.

In the meantime, a rustling voice came through Eddie's walkie talkie.

Eddie responded in earnest, "Security, this is Eddie. How can I help you?"

On the other end of the walkie talkie was Makayla, an assistant librarian, working out of the second floor.

"Honey," she said. After a pause, she added, "There is a suspicious character roaming the hallway. I have a chilling feeling that he is up to no good."

Makayla's comments jump-started Eddie's law enforcement sixth-sense.

"Can you tell me the location of the suspicious guy without letting him know that he is being observed?"

"The second floor," whispered the librarian.

Eddie continued to probe and assess the situation.

"What does he look like?" Eddie asked, gauging whether or not to call the police for backup support.

Makayla spoke nervously and in long pauses.

"He's a man who is lurching . . . can't seem to stay still . . . He's got a gang symbol popping out from his hair. He's got a distinctive smell . . . he smells like, um, a combination of a musty book and burned rubber . . . He's a person of color, thereby a person of interest."

The flawed stereotypical description left Eddie aghast. But he did nothing to challenge her misplaced assumptions since she had power over him by covering for him, providing his supervisor, the security company's dispatcher, faint excuses whenever he showed up late to work or whenever he had to leave early to attend one of his college classes.

Eddie said in a sweet-talking voice, "Baby, you are way off. I know the dude. I'll take care of the situation."

Eddie marched upstairs and caught up with Steve. He put his arm around Steve, and couched his concerns raised by Makayla in anonymous terms.

"Dude, you know that I love you like a brother, but you've got to stop dressing and acting the way you do. You throw people off."

Steve gulped. The condescending remark led him to ask, "Who told that I am creating trouble?"

Eddie became defensive. He tried to convince Steve not to worry about who fed him the information. Eddie said, "Just let it go, man."

Steve insisted that he needed to know who was attacking him.

"Nah, man. If I am being accused of something, I've got the right to know what's up and defend myself." Eddie remained tight lipped.

Steve, however, knew how he was going to get Eddie to talk. He said to Eddie, "Alright man, I get it. If we can't trust each other, we can't work and walk together."

Steve's veiled threat to break up their personal and work relationship got Eddie's attention. The prospect of losing money shifted Eddie's sense of loyalty. He subtly directed Steve with his eyes to the source of the complaint.

Steve almost lost it when he realized who was badmouthing him.

"You mean the *friggin'* librarian who has a crush on you?!"

Eddie tried to calm Steve with his soothing voice.

"Calm down, man," Eddie said, who feigned a few sobs, a tear or two, and made a sad face.

"We are brothers. We can handle anything together."

Steve picked up on the cues and did not hold back his displeasure.

He said, "Are you losing perspective?"

"Who are you trying to impress?"

"You better get your act together with the Mrs."

Eddie was embarrassed and speechless.

"Man, it is hard to overcome who you are," Steve said.

"I've always told you that we are not all perceived the same way."

Eddie did not respond. But in reality, there was nothing to be said. Eddie and Steve temporarily parted ways. Eddie, for his part, trotted over to the assistant librarian and boasted about how he cleared up the misunderstanding. Steve limped straight to an area near the research room's entrance and took a seat. He found that sitting in that area would give him a good vantage point of Maldonado and his next moves. He succeeded. Not long after settling down, Maldonado emerged from the microfilm room with a haunted expression on his pale face.

Steve wondered what could have gone wrong. He whispered to Maldonado, "Is everything alright?"

"I am fine," said Maldonado.

"C'mon man," said Steve. "Something is messing with you."

Maldonado placed his left hand over Steve's shoulder and squeezed it firmly.

"Trust me. Everything is fine."

"This place stirs many memories."

Steve was taken aback. He asked, "Have you been here before?"

Maldonado started to fumble through his words, but stopped talking when he realized that there was a man in a far corner looking with an imploring glare for him to be quiet. Maldonado raced his forefinger over his lips. The gesture caused Steve to be quiet. The unknown man in the far corner tilted his head then buried his face in a newspaper and resumed his reading. Steve started to chit chat with Maldonado. The unknown man clenched the paper and gave them both an annoyed look, objecting to their talking and rude behavior.

Maldonado waved his hands and apologized in a whisper. Steve let out a sardonic giggle. Maldonado grumbled and implored Steve to stop his silliness. Steve, with a devilish smirk, slowly walked on tip toes, despite his ailing foot, toward the water cooler. He said, "I think I should excuse myself. You guys are too tight, too serious," Steve said.

The unknown man didn't tolerate the buffoonery much longer. He left the reference room. Maldonado could not believe Steve's behavior, but didn't think that it was grave enough for him to worry about the undue attention. He went to a section of the reference room to look at the classified section of the local paper. He read. It didn't take long for some of his original assumptions about the business district to be confirmed. There was a half-page advertisement by the PBA to encourage kids from low income families to register for winter basketball clinics, and there was a promo line that offered future scholarships for summer camp programs.

"I knew it," said Maldonado. "I rarely make mistakes."

Maldonado quickly became acquainted with Don Frankie. There were full-blown ads and photo-stories highlighting Don Frankie's retail monopoly and generous acts. The photo stories feted Don Frankie with effusively written captions. For whatever reason, Maldonado did not like the verbal bouquets tossed at Don Frankie and the excessive times he appeared in the photos. He shook his head dismissively and said, "Oof, it looks like this guy owns the paper."

"*Ave María purísima* . . . Look at the panderers and enablers standing next to him."

Maldonado continued to review the photos. He recognized some of the people in the picture from his days as a member of the town's Police Community Relations Steering Committee.

He ran his index finger through the caption, and his finger quickly became soiled.

He muttered, "Councilman Derek Jones is still here. This guy doesn't age."

"It says here that he is the President of the City Council. Good for him! He is a good man!"

Then Maldonado became critical.

"Sammy Mendoza, a member of Planning and Zoning? This guy couldn't even successfully plan the annual Little League parade one year."

"How did he get elected to this position?!"

"What a disaster!"

But he was not through identifying characters in the photo. There was another person in the photo who he felt lacked the political acumen to be an effective elected official.

"What? How? Who in the world would have ever thought that David Robles was electable."

Robles was listed in the photo caption as a second-term councilman. He represented the coveted Ward B on the Town Council. That section of city was considered to be the seat of the city's political and economic power. Ward B is where the prominent members of the city made their home. Maldonado shook his head in disbelief. He made the assumption that Robles slipped into the role when a more qualified candidate had to drop out of the race at the last minute as a result of some intractable scandal. Even though the photo caption said something favorable about Robles's role in government, Maldonado refused to give him any credit for his present accomplishments and professional growth. He dubbed Robles's ascent to power a fluke and indicative of a weak candidate pool.

"Couldn't the party bosses find someone else more qualified and dignified for the position?"

Maldonado stopped fussing. He understood that it was not going to do him any good to worry about someone else's success. He could not help wonder, however, what would have happened if he had remained in the city. Perhaps he would have been Ward B's Town Councilman, or perhaps he would have been one of the high-ranking members of Jones' staff. He might have even landed a city grant to prepare free tax forms for seniors, an idea he and Jones once discussed over a game of dominoes and shots of expressos. It was possible that he would have had these things and everything else that his heart desired had he faced his troubles instead of running away.

In a silent moment, he remembered a question he asked himself earlier. He concluded based on first impressions of the city's political landscape, that, "Frankie is the trunk. Jones is one of the branches. And the hacks are the limbs and leaves."

Maldonado continued to look through the photos and read the captions. He was struck by Brigid's absence at the social event where her company was getting an award, and by her place in a group photo whenever she attended an event. It did not escape him that Don Frankie always smiled ear-to-ear and stood erect in the center of a group photo. In contrast, Brigid appeared solemn and stood to the extreme left of Don Frankie. Maldonado assumed that she was treated like "a zero to the left," a Spanish saying meant to underscore how a person gets treated as if he is of no significance. The photos caused him to believe that Brigid was lonely and unhappy.

"She is withdrawn from the world. There is something missing in this marriage," he thought.

"Can this gulf of sadness be bridged?"

Chapter Thirteen

Surveying the Land

THE SOCIAL SECTION OF the paper yielded juicy information, but it was not biography or gospel. Maldonado knew that ultimately he could not bother with the gossip. He believed that the editor's selection of the photos was driven by an agenda. He turned his attention to the front page stories to get a sense of the city's broader societal trends. At a table, he arrayed *The Liberty Beacon*, the leading local paper, into seven piles according to the day of the week. Afterwards, he shuffled the papers and paid the closest attention to the captions and the lead paragraph of each story. He considered his first impressions. He wrote his thoughts in coded, short summaries. His intention was to review his notes later at a private location. For the time being, he accounted for everyone in the room by keeping a close eye on where each person was sitting and what they were doing.

After taking an inventory of the room, he jotted down as many things as possible. His notes were succinct. After an hour, he shifted his efforts to other matters of practical importance. He needed to find a job and a semi-permanent place to call home. He had arrangements to stay at a halfway house, but he was not really satisfied with that prospect; the prospect of getting stuck with an unsuitable roommate bothered him. He wanted a quiet, private place to adjust himself and assess his plans. He hastened to examine the classified section of the paper to get an idea of the market for rental properties. The median asking price for studio apartments and railroad apartments stunned him. It was evident to him that the real estate market had undergone profound changes in the ten years he was away. He lingered for a moment and wondered, aside from inflation, what caused modest-sized apartments, that he could once afford, to be so exorbitantly expensive.

He looked at his wristwatch and reminded himself that there was nothing to be gained from dawdling. He could not reverse economic trends, but had the power to recalibrate and move ahead with his overarching plan. So, instead of worrying about snatching an apartment first, he focused on securing a job. But he did not want just any job. He wanted a job that would allow him to remain anonymous; one that would not signal his background. He kept an eye on a job opening which would meet that criterion. He noticed an advertisement for a housekeeping supervisor at a motel. He circled that one. He discovered an accounting job at a local trucking company. He placed a question mark on that one. And then appeared a job lead that tugged at him because he felt that the universe customized it for his needs. It was an opening for a church sexton at a Spanish-speaking Pentecostal church that offered the "possibility of free housing" on the church grounds. He placed an asterisk on that one.

"This is it!" he said.

And as he read on, there was a potentially significant discovery in the advertisement that made his heart leap for joy: the name of the church's minister.

"I can't believe this."

"Is this a coincidence or what?" asked Maldonado.

He plunged his left-hand into his pocket in search of his Rosary. He held the sacred object in his fist; it helped him subdue his excitement. He closed his eyes and started to breathe in and out. He looked down on the help wanted ad for the sexton one more time.

In a soft voice addressing his inner self he said, "I cannot afford to make a mistake. I have to contain myself."

The Rosary and a breathing exercise calmed his roiling emotions, but he did not mistake his tranquil state as an invitation to idleness. He unclasped the rosary in his pocket. He was motivated to find out if there was any merit to his discovery. It dawned on him that perhaps the safest route was to talk to Steve, who was an apparently well-connected street person. Perhaps he knew something about the minister and the church listed in the advertisement. Maldonado looked around for Steve and spotted him hunkered down on a chair with his head slumped facedown and his bad leg stretched over another chair positioned directly in front of him.

Maldonado moved toward Steve. Steve did not fidget. Maldonado tapped Steve on the shoulder and said, "Stop dreaming, wake up."

Aroused from his drowsy half-sleep, Steve was immediately irritable.

"What the hell is wrong with you? Sneaking up on people like that."

"I am just taking a break."

There was an opportunity for Maldonado to confirm an important piece of information, and he was not going to pass it up, even if it meant interrupting Steve's repose.

Maldonado asked, "Do you know anything about the *House of Mercy Pentecostal Church*?"

"Yes," Steve said, but with a slight hesitation. He asked, "You woke me up for that?"

Maldonado responded in an irritated tone.

"I wouldn't have bothered you if it were not important."

Steve stood up, stretched his body and let out a yawn across the room.

Not wanting to experience another uncomfortable experience with another person at the library, Maldonado asked, "Can you please be quiet?"

"Now, what can you tell be about the church?"

A sudden look of bewilderment came upon Steve. He wondered what Maldonado was after, but he nonetheless answered the question.

"That is my home church."

"But I don't go there anymore."

Maldonado wanted to know the reason. He asked, "why, may I ask?"

Steve admitted the reason.

"That is where my dad, *Chico*, goes. We don't get along."

The comments shed light into Steve's earlier conversation with Brigid.

"I see. So sorry to hear that," Maldonado said.

"It's alright. It's best for everybody," Steve said.

"How about the pastor? What can you tell me about him?"

Maldonado was eager for the rumors of the clergyman's past or just a physical description that would confirm his hunch.

Instead, the vagrant provided a window into the pastor's soul.

"He's a good man, always helping people out who don't deserve to be helped. But he's got his hands full with the people in that place," Steve said.

"What is going on?" Maldonado asked.

"They are trying to get rid of him," Steve said.

"Why?" Maldonado asked.

"Politics, man. There are too many pastors in that place," Steve responded.

"So, they must have a large congregation to have more than one minister on staff," Maldonado said.

"That is not what I am saying. There are too many people with a pulpit complex in that church; too many people act like they are the pastor, spouting off their opinions and wanting to be the big shot in that little sandbox," Steve said.

"Got it!" said Maldonado, as he rubbed his goatee.

"Is the church far from here?" asked Maldonado.

"Not really. Why?" Steve responded.

"I want to make an appointment with the pastor," Maldonado said.

"Are you saved? Are you you looking for a place to worship?" Steve asked.

"What do you mean?" Maldonado asked.

"If you don't know what I mean by those questions then you are not a believer. You definitely are not saved," Steve said.

"What does being saved or being a church member have to do with wanting to meet with a pastor?" Maldonado asked.

Steve offered a simple forewarning:

"I am just telling you. There is a lingo to a religious community just like there is a jargon to any other clique or tribe. If you don't speak the insider's language, or if you don't know the ins and outs of the culture, you are going to start with a disadvantage in the culture and expose yourself to all kinds of criticism," Steve said.

Maldonado, who considered himself a self-trained sociologist, did not seriously consider Steve's argument. He challenged it, instead.

"Aren't churches in the business of embracing the outsider, the stranger?" Maldonado asked.

"It's not that they are not going to welcome you. Churches love visitors, and they love a visitor's money and volunteer time. But they are going to ask you all kinds of intrusive and freaky questions," Steve said.

To illustrate, Steve said, "Have you given your life to Jesus? Or are you ready for the rapture?"

Maldonado dismissed those questions as religious nonsense.

"My interest in the church is not religious."

Steve argued with a sense of desperation.

"That is an oxymoron. That just doesn't make any sense. That is like trying to ride a bike with a flat tire. You can sit on a bike seat and hit the pedal all you want, but you *ain't* going anywhere without air in your wheel. You can sit on a church pew all day long, but without knowing Jesus in a personal way, you are not going to move into the light and gain discernment," Steve said.

Maldonado sighed. He did not share Steve's understanding.

"Not everyone who manifests an interest in religion is willing to subject himself to indoctrination."

Steve felt that Maldonado was thinking too hard.

"So scholar, you want something, a favor from Jesus, right?"

"You must be one of those bread and fish Christians."

Maldonado wasn't sure what Steve was getting at and asked, "Now, what do you mean this time?"

Steve, a passionate reader of the Bible, incorporated one of the Gospel's feeding the multitudes stories to express his position.

"I am referring to the miracle where Jesus turned a few pieces of bread and a few fish into enough bread and fish to feed 5,000 people."

"Do you know the story?"

Maldonado remained silent. Steve figured that Maldonado had limited biblical exposure. He crafted his argument. Thus Steve said, "I am not going to give you a blow-by-blow account of the story, but let me sum it up this way. That story was about people who approached Jesus with insincere, ulterior motives. They admired Jesus as a moral teacher or as someone who could help them with hunger, but not as their personal savior. They were just interested in getting something material from Jesus."

Maldonado thought that Steve's argument amounted to a radical interpretation. He asked a couple of questions he felt would expose the flaws in Steve's argument.

"What is wrong with using one of Jesus' miracles to inspire moral goodness and promote almsgiving?"

"And if it is the case that the people were self-interested, shouldn't Jesus share in the burden of caving to their selfishness by literally feeding them, and feeding them abundantly?"

"Interesting?" Steve said, feeling a tad disarmed by the provocative questions. He readjusted his Afro-pick and made a slight concession, but he did not entirely accept Maldonado's biblical understanding.

"Scholar, you are partly correct," Steve said.

"Jesus knew that the crowd was hungry and perhaps restless, so he fed them. But after the miracle, he bemoaned the fact that they were probably after him for something else."

Thinking about his grandfather's touchstone self-sustenance trait theory, Maldonado shrugged his shoulder and said, "that is just human nature. If you can meet people's core needs, you can subdue their aggression and manipulate the masses."

Steve wanted the argument to go on.

"Well, that is not good enough!"

"You have to go to church expecting more than just getting a personal favor from Jesus."

"There are people who go to church because they want Jesus to hook them up with a date, get them a better paying job, get them a dream retirement home, get them a better credit score. Going to church should be about deepening a personal relationship with Jesus with no expectation of receiving material blessings as a precondition to the relationship."

"Scholar, you are a sociologist and you don't know this?"

Maldonado thought that the debate was counterproductive.

"You like to sermonize when you get on a point. I think that you should consider a career in the ministry."

"Hell no! You *ain't* never going to catch me on a pulpit."

Maldonado made the argument go away, hitting on a practical idea.

"It seems natural that the pastor of a church can be a reliable and good source for my research project in sociology. Churches possess archives and have long-standing members, some of whom can provide anecdotal histories of the community, and most of whom won't talk to a stranger unless their pastor says it is safe to cooperate with an outsider. I am a sociologist, and I do know this," Maldonado said.

"I am persuadable. That is a fair point," Steve said.

"Let me show you where the church is," Steve added.

Steve walked Maldonado over to the east side of the library. He leaned on a window and pointed to the church's location.

"It's just a stone's throw away," Steve said.

"I will be right back," Maldonado said.

"Where are you going?" Steve asked.

"I have to wash my hands and check on my wet socks," Maldonado said.

"Your what?" asked Steve.

"Wait for me right here. I will be right back," Maldonado insisted. Before he departed, though, Maldonado approached the reference desk and asked Makayla for two dollars worth of change. He claimed that he needed the coins to make photo copies of a reference book.

Chapter Fourteen

Running Past a Problem

EXCITED AND HOLDING A fist full of coins, Maldonado dashed down the stairs and zoomed past an unattended security station. Eddie saw Maldonado fly by and wondered what he was so excited about. He could not find out. He was in the throes of a conflict with his former wife. Eddie was pointing his finger to the floor, grinding his teeth, and sporting an angry scowl. It was not an uncommon scene. This is how he got whenever he was corralled inside the lobby's phone booth, embroiled in an argument with Evelyn, wife number one. His second wife, also named Evelyn, was known as Evelyn number two. She bore a striking resemblance to Evelyn number one.

Eddie and Evelyn number one were arguing about what had become a recurrent topic of delayed child-support payments. This time the argument reached a boiling point when she charged that Eddie was not only slacking off with his payments, but he was also not seriously involved in their son's extracurricular activities.

Evelyn number one admonished him to pay timely child support and show interest in their son's activities. She had developed legal insights from routinely watching two television judges, an English-speaking one and a Spanish-speaking one, dismantle specious arguments in their courts. On her own she had been able to achieve a victory at the local family court without the aid of an attorney.

"You are spending too much time with your new kid and not enough time with our son," said Evelyn number one. "You need to shift your priorities, or I am going to haul your behind into court and let that judge put another tongue whipping on you. Don't make me call that judge. Don't make me do it."

"This time on what grounds?" asked Eddie.

"Child neglect and abandonment!" she said confidently.

Eddie was bewildered by her threat. He did not think that she had a legal leg to stand on, but he exerted restraint and vowed to make amends with his son. He said that things were going to pick up financially for him. He claimed that he had an "exclusive connection" to a handful of business leads with promising substantial earnings.

Evelyn number one remained skeptical about Eddie's big-time statement. She had been disappointed in the past by his sweeping claims, which always hinged on the promise of an "exclusive connection" that never amounted to anything.

She answered in a mocking tone.

"Promises . . . promises . . . promises. It sounds like the time during our courtship you promised me that you'd arrange for a horse and carriage to pick me up and take me to the city's Gothic cathedral for our wedding because you had an 'exclusive connection' with the priest. I ended up driving myself, in my wedding dress and all, to our ceremony at the Municipal Court. Or it sounds like the time that you had an 'exclusive connection' to build me a house on an orange orchard to work on our juice business, and we ended up living in a ghetto shack, all cramped up, with a whole bunch of orange pickers."

Eddie got twisted by each of Evelyn's examples, since there were elements of truthfulness to each claim, but he remained remarkably calm.

"Calm down, dear. It is useless to live in the past," Eddie said.

Evelyn number one sensed that Eddie's gentleness was an attempt to pacify her. She drew delight from the power she had over his conscience and emotions. She drew on that strength to poke him one more time before slamming the phone.

"Just remember, I've got me an 'exclusive connection' too."

"The juuuudge!"

Click!

Chapter Fifteen

The Church Sign

ALONG THE WAY TO the *House of Mercy* Pentecostal Church, thick snow-flakes fluttered and settled on Maldonado's uncovered head. The trickling flakes, accompanied by a howling wind, managed to dishevel Maldonado's neatly combed hair and revive a sad memory. Nearly a decade ago, he took the chance of driving on the same street during the early stages of a snow-storm. The decision proved fatal. He was involved in a traffic accident that killed his passenger, Maribel. He was courting her, and he was hoping to marry her in the spring of that year at an open-tent ceremony at Liberty State Park. The powdery flakes blunted his vision and reminded him of Maribel: the oriental, aromatic smell of her body, the spark of passion in her voice, the glow of virtuous living on her face, the red blush on her cheeks. He also recalled the classical song they listened to on the radio as he held the steering wheel with one hand and clutched her hand with the other. He relived the scene leading up to the accident and agonized over not heeding her advice to leave work early that day to travel together on public transpor-tation to her apartment.

"Leave the car where it is," Maribel said.

"It will be waiting there for you tomorrow."

"Not a chance," Maldonado said.

He stroked the car's dashboard and playfully said, "I cannot abandon my darling." Treating the car with romantic affection annoyed Maldonado's beloved Maribel. He knew it, but did it anyway. He found the facial expres-sion she made, a sort of benign jealousy, too adorable.

Maldonado had never owned a car. He was worried that a freak ac-cident would damage his car. He thought about the possible dents and scratches created by the rumbling, sharp blades of a plow or the hacks of a snow shoveler. He paused and wondered why he was so overly protective of his car, allowing a material possession to outweigh Maribel's advice.

"Why, why was I so materialistic . . . so damn stubborn?

"Why didn't I meet her at the terminal?"

"We could have taken a train, a bus, and still be together."

Over the years, he replayed the scenario. He blamed himself for allowing his former business partner, Santana, whom he viewed as a fatherly figure, to talk him into disregarding the public safety radio announcement.

He remembered his business partner saying to him, "you know politicians. They like to exaggerate and make it look that they are always doing something heroic to protect us."

To offset any doubts, his partner would always say, "you are like my son. I want what is best for you and your career."

The partner succeeded in convincing Maldonado to downplay the severity of the storm. But that storm, Maldonado remembered, progressively blanketed the city and created blinding driving conditions.

"That greedy bastard never really cared about my needs and happiness! All he cared about was looking good in front of others and making money."

The walk from the library to the church was not long enough to seriously process his past grievances. The church, as the vagrant pointed out, was nearby. Before he knew it, Maldonado arrived at his destination. The name of the minister, the Rev. Angel Santana, was imprinted on a sign hanging above the main entrance. The name of the minister prominently featured at a house of worship infuriated him. He called the number listed on the church advertisement at a pay phone.

The rotary phone inside the church rang five times. Daisy, the church secretary, picked it up, but she managed to fumble it. She was heard saying in a mousy, sweet church voice, "Wait a minute . . . wait a minute."

She continued to struggle to pick the phone off the floor and disentangle its coiled cord.

Finally, she gathered herself and greeted the caller.

"God bless you, *House of Mercy*."

Maldonado blurted out what came to his mind.

"God bless you, as well."

Right after that, he showed himself to be graceful.

"Thank you for wishing me Godspeed. What a warm greeting!"

Maldonado did not know that saying "God bless you" was part of the standard lingo in that Spanish Pentecostal church; it was the ordinary greeting shared by the church members as a way of wishing God's protection and guidance, showing mutual respect, and offering hospitality towards individuals.

Maldonado reverted to his cunning ways. He gabbed about her office decorum to put her at ease and hopefully, get her comfortable enough to volunteer the information he was looking for.

Maldonado said, "The congregation is so fortunate to have such a kind soul as the gatekeeper."

The fawning comments fed the secretary's meager professional ego. It created in her the sense, even for a brief moment, of the vocational validation that seemed to have eluded her throughout her time working at the church.

"Oh thank you, I try," she said.

With much encouragement, she shared in great detail how she made the church run smoothly. Maldonado did not care an iota about her accomplishments at the church. He made all kinds of contorted faces as she spoke on the other end of the line. When he'd had enough of her, he asked a question which consisted of reverse psychology and story-telling techniques.

"Since you are so knowledgable, perhaps you can help me clarify a lingering doubt. The other day I met a short, medium-built man, who I believe was the pastor. He was with his wife, um, Minerva, right?"

The secretary was surprised by the caller's question. The pastor's wife had not been at worship in over a month because of health problems. But the caller got the name of the pastor's wife right, and she had no reason to believe that the pastor was with another woman in public who was not his wife.

"Yes, Sister Minerva is the minister's wife."

Maldonado, sensing that she was easy-going and forthcoming, took the opportunity to concoct a fictitious story right on the spot.

"I was walking my dog, and they stopped me to give me a religious tract. I have been touched by his outreach, and I would like to thank him for the message on the tract. His message was just what I needed to hear; it picked my spirit up from the depths of despair."

"When is he in the office so that I can stop by to thank him?"

The secretary was touched too, so she digressed. She was the one who ordered the tracts from a publishing company and stamped them upon delivery with the church's address. She then stacked them in a convenient spot in the church so that the members with a proselytizing spirit could pass them out to the general public.

She felt that something she did had the potential to attract new members to the church.

She, therefore, requested the finance chair to permit the order of additional religious tracts. Her enthusiasm about a potential convert was palpable.

"Ooohh! God is calling you. I can feel the touch of his Spirit at work."

"Why don't you come by and share your word of testimony with the pastor?"

"I feel the Presence. I feel a special anointing. This phone call is of God. It means that God is calling you," she said as she let out a cry, pinned the phone against her shoulder and rubbed the goosebumps on her forearm.

"Sinner, what is your name?"

"Would you pray with me over the phone as you give your life to Jesus as your personal Lord and savior?"

"Um . . . um. My bus is quickly approaching. I have got to flag it down. See you in church sometime." Maldonado said.

He hung up the phone, and thought about so many things. How the military graduation photo of his former business partner resembled his father's. How his former business partner vowed to be a surrogate father to him. How unfit his former business partner was for the holy vocation he had entered.

For Maldonado, this Angel lacked the divine qualities befitting someone in a sacred vocation. In Maldonado's mind, Angel was nothing more than a fraud wearing clerical attire.

"You can hide behind your religious garb and pious appearance, but you are not fooling me. You are a fallen angel," he said rehearsing the lines he might use when he confronted Angel the pastor, his former business partner and onetime friend.

Maldonado already knew from Steve's comments in the library that the pastor was involved in a conflicted relationship with his congregation. He relished the prospect of unleashing more chaos and anguish in the pastor's life.

"I know who you are. I know your history. And soon your congregation will know who you really are as well."

Chapter Sixteen

Wet Socks

BACK AT THE LIBRARY, Steve made a discovery. He learned that relationships are like a river during a season's cycles. Sometimes they are frozen and stagnant, and sometimes they are flowing and teeming with life. His emerging philosophy on friendship allowed him to live more readily in a world of constant flux. With an expanding philosophy on friendship, he was exploring whether it was possible to keep a personal relationship with Eddie and discontinue his professional one. That is why it was not an issue for him to banter with Eddie about the shenanigans they pulled off as youngsters at worship services and other church-sponsored functions. The stories were outrageous and touched upon the time they were caught by Deacon Jimenez playing paper football during a long-winded sermon; the time the church's run-down, old van broke down on a hot summer night as they traveled to a youth summer camp in upstate New York; and the time they doctored church membership rolls to include gifted basketball players from the public housing playgrounds on the roster of a Christian recreational basketball league.

Steve said, "You remember the look on our parents' faces when we were rebuked from the pulpit and exhorted to return the championship trophy for trying to pass off reprobates as members."

Now it was Eddie's turn. He said, "How about when you raised your hands in the shape of a football goal post, and the preacher thought you were praising the Lord, until the deacon caught us playing finger football and horsing around."

Steve said, "I told you to stop ripping pages from the hymnals to make paper footballs. We got busted and chastised by the women's guild that raised the money to buy the hymnals."

They carried on with their memories of youthful escapades. They rehashed classic stories amidst boisterous laughs, but acted with joyous surprise, as if they heard the climax of a humorous story for the very first time.

The memory of those blissful moments and their unadulterated motives made them wish those days had never ended. And the affection created by a shared memory was the only thing that still kept them together, since they were no longer united in purpose, mind and spirit.

They were in the middle of recycling another outlandish church story when Maldonado returned to the library. Maldonado walked in slowly. He was soaked and miserable. Steve was baffled by the dramatic shift in Maldonado's demeanor. He knew that there was something unusual, perhaps unsettling, about the change in the scholar's countenance. Eddie noticed too, but withheld commenting on it.

Very casually, Maldonado asked, "how have you guys been?"

Steve said, "A little surprised. You asked to me wait right here and left me hanging."

Maldonado erected a wall of defensiveness.

"I needed to look into something."

Steve, while Maldonado was away, used the men's room and discovered that Maldonado's wet socks were drying on the radiator. He zinged, "Yeah, I noticed. I was worried that you left without your socks."

Steve's barbed remark pricked Maldonado's sensibilities. He loathed having his actions called into question, especially in public, and particularly not by a person whom he considered below his intellectual and social standing. He was going to utter a sharp rebuke, but decided there was nothing to be gained by doing so.

Maldonado said, "I am made for war!"

Eddie nodded in approval.

"Yeah, I like that!" said Eddie.

Steve was annoyed by Maldonado's slick response and Eddie's validation of what he considered an empty slogan. Steve, very of matter-of-fact, said, "I think that you should try that line ("I am made for war") the next time you get into a battle with your wife."

"Tell me how that works out for you."

"That's stupid, man," Eddie said with a hardy laugh.

Maldonado, sensing friction and bad energy, asked for directions to a new place.

"I am expected at a place near Kennedy Boulevard. Is it hard to get to the road from here?", he asked.

Maldonado vaguely remembered Kennedy Boulevard as one of Jersey City's main drags, but it had been a while since he traveled on the road. He wanted the quickest, easiest way to get there, while not disclosing his familiarity with the area. His question, nonetheless, bothered Steve, who was quick to develop a bias. His antennae were up and the signals were strong.

"There is something illegitimate about this guy," Steve said to himself.

Eddie thought that question was sincere and gave him the perfect opportunity to create a favorable impression with a scholar, who could tutor him so he could earn better grades and write him a stellar letter of recommendation for law school.

"Kennedy Boulevard cuts across five cities in our county. That covers a lot of territory."

"It might not be so hard to figure out if you tell us what exactly you are looking for."

Maldonado smiled and made things less complicated. He plopped his briefcase on Eddie's desk and leafed through catalogued files.

"Here it is," said Maldonado. He pulled out a copy of a letter and disclosed the name of a well-known, in-take substance abuse facility named, *Healing Hearts*.

"I know where that place is," Eddie said.

The name of the facility created deeper doubts for Steve. He could not make the correlation between a place for the destitute, guys with drug problems, and the scholar's original desire to examine demographic patterns of Puerto Ricans in the city.

"You must be on a missionary trip to be mixing with the outcasts," Steve said. "That kind of project just doesn't make any sense."

Maldonado came up with another remarkably lucky answer.

"I am not being trite with what I am about to say. I am also working on something that is big time," he said.

"I am researching many topics including the links between depression and homesickness among immigrants," Maldonado said.

"Many immigrants resort to drinking to dull the pain they feel from living in a strange land with no family. I want to use the data to get people who fall into cycles of addiction help."

Maldonado repeated once more, "This is big!"

Eddie found Maldonado's research remarkably promising. Steve didn't see anything pure or novel about the research, but he abstained from passing judgment.

"How long will you be investigating?" Eddie asked.

"Roughly speaking, it may be a year-long project," Maldonado said.

Eddie then gave himself the highest possible words of self-promotion.

"If you need an assistant, I can show you around. I have got some serious investigation skills. I have been told that I am a criminal justice guru."

There was little question in Maldonado's mind that he had created an impression on Eddie. Maldonado tilted his head endorsing Eddie's self-assessed skills. He knew that he could keep Eddie under his control.

Maldonado had the type of personality that attracted people from all walks of life. He knew how to use his charisma to mobilize people and resources to serve his self-interests.

With no hint of urgency, Maldonado asked Eddie for directions to the *Healing Hearts* substance abuse facility which was founded by the Romeros, an urban missionary husband and wife team, who were retired and worked as lay chaplains in Puerto Rico. Maldonado started to sketch a diagram and take notes on the blank side of a subscription card to one of Eddie's sports magazines.

He thanked them, shook their hands, and asked when he could see them again.

"You can find me at *Victoria's* on Wednesdays, around the same time we met today," Steve said.

Eddie wrote down the phone number to the assistant librarian's reference desk on a piece of rice paper and gave it to Maldonado.

Chapter Seventeen

The Power of a Good Name

TWENTY MINUTES AFTER LEAVING the library, Maldonado found the substance abuse facility where he was to enroll as a temporary resident. It was a mid-sized, brick building fraught with tell-tale signs of neglect. One of the building's sidewalls had a mural of Gospel scenes covered in graffiti. The steps leading to the main entrance were crumbled and poorly lighted, and a section of the building's annex windows were cracked or boarded up.

"My goodness, this is not the place that I was told that it was," Maldonado mused.

Maldonado, nonetheless, drove his car to the main gate. He got out of the car, left the engine running, and read a sign attached to the chain-link, razor-ribbon fence that enclosed the building. The sign said that incoming residents must have a referral letter from the city's Human Services Department, and they must arrive no later than 3 p.m. It was already 5:30 p.m. It was nearly dark and cold. Suddenly he imagined hearing Petra's transcendent voice cut through the chilly air.

Maldonado heard her say, "Rules can have different standards of application, and rules don't mean anything if they are not kept."

Petra's words struck Maldonado's mind. Her message forced him to press firmly on the intercom's panel button. As fate would have it, the panel button often got stuck; when it did, it made a perpetual ringing sound that would send the senior counselor, Eric Cabrera, into an explosive rage.

To prevent the senior counselor from unraveling over the shoddy intercom, the junior counselor, George Ortiz, would lower the volume to near silence. There were times, however, that he would forget to restore the volume to a more audible level. George's oversight left people outside the facility yelling and rattling the gate, hoping to get the attention of someone inside the facility to buzz them in. Perhaps the most annoying aspect of the intercom was the galactic sound it made, making it difficult for people to have a conversation.

Maldonado was not aware of the manifold problems created by the defective intercom. He had just pressed the button and allowed a reasonable amount of time to elapse before wondering if his ring had fallen on deaf ears. He decided to press the button a second time. This time he pressed the button repeatedly and held his finger on the button a little longer after each ring.

The timing of Maldonado's arrival was inconvenient. The only two staffers inside the building, the senior counselor and junior counselor, were trying to get 30 residents ready for supper. Maldonado, of course, did not know the program was understaffed. He started to shiver. He cursed the weather and jerked the gate.

Maldonado questioned, "What kind of operation is this?"

He was about to find out.

George's squawking voice came through the intercom.

He asked Maldonado a question in a staccato voice, "What part of the sign don't you understand?"

Maldonado lurched forward and spoke confidently into the intercom.

"I come highly recommended," Maldonado said.

George couldn't control his temper. He responded in a stern voice.

"Sir, it doesn't matter who sent you. It's past 3 p.m. You will have to return tomorrow. The rules are the rules. No exceptions," George said.

Maldonado calmly responded, "The Romeros sent me."

There was a deafening silence, followed by the sound of a slight jam. Then, a few seconds later, an eerie creak cut through the silence of the nearly empty parking lot. The fence's sliding gate rolled open. Maldonado got into his car and backed it into a parking place. He pinned the car's tailgate against the facade of the building. The license plate could only be seen if somebody moved the car forward. After getting out of his hot car, he unscrewed and removed the car's front license plate with one of the coins he had received at the library. He deposited the plate into his briefcase to conceal his secret. He temporarily resolved one problem, but a new one was waiting for him inside the facility.

George was fuming over Maldonado's late arrival. He left the residents unattended at the dining room to field his intercom call, and that was a decision that earned him a scolding from his boss.

At last, Maldonado strode into the building with briefcase in hand. George did not hold back from welcoming him with a sarcastic comment.

"I thought you couldn't figure out what the doors to the building looked like."

"What took you so long?"

Maldonado said in a calm voice, "I had to take care of a small car problem."

George was puzzled by Maldonado's revelation.

"You have a car?"

Maldonado, for a moment, remained silent.

"Yes."

George shook his head and said, "You are not allowed to be in possession of a car while you are a resident in our program."

"You are here to work on your issues. You can't have anything around you that can be a distraction and cut into your treatment plan. We don't want you driving to places that you shouldn't visit," George said.

Maldonado said in a low voice, "The Romeros said that I can."

George sighed. He was skeptical, but decided he'd have plenty of time to check the stranger's stories out in the morning. He said, "Whatever. If they said you can, I guess you can. Just don't tell the other residents."

Maldonado then popped open his briefcase and handed George a sealed, signed letter. George used his pocket knife to open it. As he read the letter, George smiled. He was delighted that he was not lied to by an incoming resident. Everything that Maldonado claimed to be true was substantiated in the letter with the exception of the car story; that claim was a tad fuzzy. The Romeros said in their letter, "Please grant (William) Maldonado immediate admission to the program and give him a furlough to look for work and attend worship services as part of his treatment plan. . . . support him with his transportation needs . . . he has undergone detox and is ready to engage his treatment."

George continued to read the letter. In the meantime, Maldonado placed his hands behind his back, whistled softly, and drifted to an area of the room that was decorated with plaques, awards, and Congressional citations in honor of the Romeros. It didn't take long for Maldonado to recognize the special place that the Romeros held in the facility and in the hearts of the community. He then walked toward a pair of limestone busts dedicated to the urban missionary couple. Each bust was done by an artist who was a former resident at the program, and each bust had a dated inscription that read: "This sculpture is dedicated to the honor and glory of God and to Anthony and Maria Romero. Their vision and empathy gave birth to a healing center for those afflicted by the disease of addiction."

Maldonado read the inscription in a whispery voice. He was in awe of the Romeros' mystique. He planted a kiss on his hand and rubbed that hand on each bust. But he soon discovered that he did something that was considered inappropriate.

"Ah, ah, ah, no touching the art work," said Cabrera.

He added a Spanish-saying, " 'Touch with your eyes and see with your hands.'"

Maldonado stood in silence. Cabrera was upset that he had to come out of his office to break up an argument between two residents over food portions. He gave way to his frustration with George. He reprimanded him for leaving the residents unattended and for allowing a visitor to enter the building past visiting hours.

Cabrera asked, "Who is this?"

George, shrugged his shoulder, and said, "A new client."

Cabrera asked, "Another one?"

"Did you consult me before letting him through the gate?"

George couldn't believe that Cabrera was embarrassing him in front of a new resident. He had asked Cabrera in the recent past, during a heart-to-heart meeting, to stop correcting him in public.

He said to Cabrera, "He was sent here by the Romeros themselves!"

"He's got a personal letter written by them."

Cabrera remained skeptical.

"How do you know that the client's claim is legit?"

"Ay, Georgie, you have so much to learn, little one."

Cabrera's behavior offended Maldonado, but he remained silent. George, for his part, gasped for air as if he were choking. He held the letter to Cabrera's eye-level and said, "Come on, no one can imitate the Romeros' looping signature."

Cabrera snatched the letter from George's hand. He started to read it and immediately recognized the Romeros' language style and distinctive signature.

"I can hear them speaking in this letter. They always sign in blue," Cabrera said.

Begrudgingly, Cabrera gave way, but not without a little grandstanding.

Cabrera said to Maldonado, "We generally don't allow new clients past 3 p.m., but I am going to make an exception."

Cabrera was disappointed with upper management. He felt that they circumvented his leadership when they overturned his disciplinary decisions and sided with residents during an appeal. He felt disappointed with the Romeros for their ongoing meddling with the facility post their retirement, even though they had emeritus status. He felt burned out by the fluid nature of his job and the high turnover rate of junior counselors. His frustration was affecting his love-life, and he blamed that in part to late arrivals.

"What gets me in all of this is that some people just don't know how to let go and let others lead," Cabrera said. "I have a right to a social life too, you know."

The time for Maldonado to enter the program arrived. Cabrera asked him to follow him. He led Maldonado to his office to fill out the facility's mandatory admission forms. The process consisted of the following: a resident's psycho-social history; an overview of his confidentiality rights; a payment request form; a discussion of the house rules and rules of conduct for the residents; the facility's policies and procedures; a guidebook of the resident's privileges; and a screening and pat down in case he was trying to sneak in drug paraphernalia or a weapon. After going through Maldonado's briefcase and pockets, Cabrera discovered a car's license plate in the briefcase and a rosary in Maldonado's pocket. Cabrera held the rosary and glanced at it. He told Maldonado that he had one in white wrapped around his car's rear-view mirror for protection. He rambled on about his parochial school education and why he didn't attend Mass. But when he discovered the car plate in the briefcase things got nasty.

"What's this?" asked Cabrera, as he held the license plate in his hand.

Maldonado said, "I have a bad screw, and the plate was dangling, sliding. I didn't want to lose the plate. I removed it and put it away."

Cabrera grimaced. He found Maldonado's answer unbelievable. He said, "Well, it's against the law for you to drive your car with one plate. Take care of that problem or I am going to take away your driving privileges, which you shouldn't have anyway. For now, I am going to let it slide. I will give you 48 hours to fix that problem."

Cabrera shifted to the topic of religion. He said, "We have a list of churches that I have approved for the residents to attend. George can give you that list. It contains the names of the denominations, the times of worship, and the time the bus picks you up to take you to your church of preference."

He added, "I generally allow people to visit church after successfully completing the first 30 days of the program. I am going to make an exception. I am going to authorize you to go to church this weekend."

Maldonado did not make a comment. He knew that his letter of recommendation allowed him to attend worship services immediately.

Then Cabrera asked Maldonado to sit down and look him in the eyes. He was going to share the facility's most important rule.

"My name is Dr. Eric Cabrera. You can call me Dr. Cee or Mr. Cee, but you do not have permission to call me by my first name."

"I am in charge of this place, and you need to understand that. I am the counselor, and you are the resident. By definition, we are adversaries. I am not here to be your friend, but to help you work on your issues so that you can remain drug free, sober, and clean," Cabrera said.

Cabrera had a captive listener. He continued his self-aggrandizing monologue.

"There is a long waiting list of people trying to get into this place. I get phone calls every day from people begging me to let them in my program," Cabrera said. "You try one dumb ass stunt and you are out of here, okay?"

"I will give your bed to someone else in a heartbeat if you provide one dirty urine sample or if you don't follow my rules." To make sure his message was clear, Cabrera asked a rhetorical question. "What is my name?"

Cabrera's veiled threat and arrogant attitude offended Maldonado.

Maldonado deliberately looked at the floor to create the impression of submission before an authority figure. A few seconds went by without a response from Maldonado. Cabrera fidgeted, adjusted his bifocals, arched his bushy brow, and placed his sweaty hands over his knees. Cabrera did not know what to make of Maldonado's expressionless stare at the floor. He asked himself, "Is the new guy daydreaming? Is he stoned? Is he looking down out of respect, as generally understood in the Hispanic culture, or out of defiance?" All of these questions occupied Cabrera's mind.

The prolonged silence unnerved Cabrera. Had it been one of the other residents, Cabrera would have snapped and unleashed his wrath. Since Maldonado was recommended by the Romeros, he restrained himself. He removed his hands from his knees, uncovering the sweat stains left by his palms. He then twirled his tie over and over again, until there was no more thread to twist.

Cabrera prodded Maldonado. He said, "Uhm . . . well . . . "

Maldonado figured that he had kept Cabrera in suspense just long enough. He provided the answer that Cabrera wanted to hear.

Maldonado said, "Mr. Cabrera."

Cabrera said, "Good! We are understanding each other."

"Here are your fresh and clean bed sheets, pillow case, and blanket."

Not long after getting his bed linens, Maldonado heard the voice of a man singing and jingling a set of keys in the hallway. The man sang in an upbeat tone the verse: "I've got a joy like a river in my soul." The words of the melody were sweet and glorious, but the man's voice and his rhythm were offbeat. The man sang and rattled the keys repeatedly.

Suddenly, the singing and jingling came to an end. The man making the sounds showed his face. It was George. He just sounded different when he sang.

George asked, "Is he ready?"

Cabrera flicked his wrists dismissively. He had had enough for the day. He did not want to deal with Maldonado any longer. They had spent two hours together.

Cabrera, prior to slamming the door to his office, said to George, "You can take over from here."

Chapter Eighteen

When Religion (Really) Works

GEORGE TOOK OVER.

He gathered Maldonado's bed set into his hands and said, "Let me give you a hand. We've got other pressing matters to take care of."

Maldonado was glad that his time with Cabrera was over.

He responded to George, "Certainly!"

George asked Maldonado to follow him to his work station. They strolled past a bedroom unit in one of the facility's wings. Maldonado looked ahead toward the hallway and noticed young men with tattooed faces stared at him. The one with a tribal warrior tattoo gave him an unfriendly look from head to toe, while the other one with a tear-drop tattoo on his left cheek puckered his lips and tauntingly blew soft, nearly silent kisses at him. Maldonado stared back and saluted them with a micro-movement of the head while not saying a word. He felt sad that they were so young and wore masks made of ink to hide their raw potential and raw pain. He figured that the tattoos were going to make life tougher for them once they graduated from the program and reentered mainstream society. George knew that the young men were playing mind-games, perhaps trying to intimidate the new guy.

George said to the young men, "Okay guys. You know the rules. No hanging out in the hallway." George, however, was a little harder on one of the two young men. "You have been here before. Give an example to the new guy."

The idling residents complied and returned to their bedrooms.

At one point, George felt comfortable enough to ask Maldonado a question.

With a sneer on his face, he asked, "Did the doctor give you the low-down or the beat-down?"

"Or a little of both?"

Maldonado knew that George was referring to Cabrera. He faced George and gave an expedient answer.

"He is doing his job. I am here to do mine," Maldonado said.

Maldonado remembered what Steve told him at the library about church people. He figured that the song George belted out in the hallway and the Christian fish emblem pin on his shirt's collar were evidence that he was a person of a deep personal faith.

Maldonado added: "One has to be grateful to God for everything."

George clapped his hands in approval.

"That attitude is going to help you make it here and thrive in life. I love it."

Within a few seconds or so, George and Maldonado reached the work station. George started to review a bedroom chart. Maldonado put his briefcase down. He thought that it was strange that his name was on a blackboard. It was a blackboard that listed the chores assigned to the residents. Some residents were assigned to pick up and clear the plates. Others were assigned to manually rinse and wash the dishes, and dry the silverware. Others were assigned to store away the dried dishes and silverware. Others had to sweep, mop and throw away the garbage. Maldonado got garbage crew duties. His first job was almost immediate. He had to haul the garbage, with the help of three other guys, to a dumpster in the yard that very evening.

George said to Maldonado, "I update the board twice a day, in the morning before breakfast and in the evening before supper. It's your responsibility to know what you have to do. Assignments are non-negotiable, and they must be completed in a timely manner."

Maldonado nodded. He did not like things hanging over his head He asked if he could leave his briefcase under George's care and when he could throw away the garbage. George took him to the dining room and introduced him to the other members of the garbage crew. After George left, Maldonado, as the new guy at the facility, was told by the bald-shaved leader of the garbage crew, that he had to haul the garbage to the dumpster by himself, while he and the other guys dragged a cigarette and played dice. The bald-shaved man explained with a punching gesture to an open hand, that every new guy completes that task as a rite of passage, and does it without tattling.

Maldonado did what he was told without thinking twice about it.

It took a while, but Maldonado completed the garbage chore. His feet were sore and his back ached when he crossed the worker's station. He was on his way to freshen up and go to bed on an empty stomach. George, who was sitting at the station reading an enormous Bible, stopped him. He provided Maldonado with his room number, a covered meal on a disposable plate, and a set of clothes that were left behind by a former resident who graduated from the program about a month before. Maldonado took his dish and set of clothes and sat by himself in the dining room. He didn't care for the food after one bite; the heavy seasoning made it taste salty. He didn't care for the style of clothes; they were corny and smelled like a gym locker.

After a short while, Maldonado heard George rounding up the residents and noticed the flickering lights. George was enforcing the bedtime curfew. Maldonado picked up his briefcase from George and headed to his bedroom. Everything was quiet, except for a Christian-based radio station that George listened to and the roaring sound of the old furnace. At one in the morning, Maldonado leaned against his bedroom's door frame and tried to get George's attention, calling for him in a whispery voice.

The rules forbade Maldonado from walking in the hallway without the approval of a counselor once the bedtime curfew was enforced. George heard his name being called and walked in the direction of Maldonado, who was acting reticent.

George asked, "What's the matter? What's going on?"

Maldonado made a victim's face and pretty much told him that he had an upset stomach and couldn't fall sleep.

"I am having a hard time falling asleep. I don't think I should have eaten a heavy meal past 9 p.m. I think I read in the resident's rulebook that we are not allowed to have dinner after 7 p.m., unless we were returning to the facility from a medical appointment."

It was Maldonado's plan to stay up and read his journal, and he went about that plan with a hidden agenda.

"I am a new believer. Can I read the Bible for a while? Is there one that I can borrow?"

It was clear to George that he had few other choices but to let Maldonado stay up past rule-book bed time. Reading the Bible would be a flimsy but acceptable excuse if any residents or staff should happen to take notice that the new guy was getting a ton of special treatment.

"Sure," he said. "There is one in the visitor's waiting room. The cover is loose. Be careful how you handle it."

Maldonado asked, "I am a new believer. Where should I start?"

George gave a rapid-fire answer. "The Gospel of Matthew," he said as he walked away.

Maldonado entered the guest room, plucked the Bible from a book shelf, sat down on a sofa, and looked for the Gospel of Matthew in the index section. When he found Matthew, he flipped through the pages and focused on the headings of the chapters. There were two headings that intrigued him, and he read those passages. He specifically focused on two verses.

He read, " . . . Put your sword back into its place; for all who take the sword will perish by the sword (Matthew 26:52)."

Then he read, "In everything do unto others as you would have them do to you; . . . (Matthew 7: 12)."

Both verses troubled him, and made him remember two defining moments in his life. He put the Bible down and turned to his journal.

He read a journal entry regarding a sailboat trip he went on with his grandfather when he was a twelve-year-old lad. He remembered that his grandfather, Loubriel, used that trip to talk about the merits of his touchstone self-sustenance theory.

Loubriel said from the sailboat's rugged cockpit, "If you understand the proclivities of human nature, you will avoid many lamentations throughout your life."

Loubriel then looked away from Maldonado, tilted his head backward, and spat a slimy filter of a *Montecristo* cigar overboard. He rapidly shifted the boat's rudder and continued to lecture in a didactic manner.

"Remember, my little one, human beings possess a primitive fear of the future. The only way to relieve the angst created by the unknown is by making sure that one's basic, human needs are met."

"Are there exceptions?" asked a curious and intellectually gifted Maldonado.

"Oh, no!" Loubriel said in a tone of urgency.

"Our primordial ancestors left the cave to hunt for the saber-toothed tiger because there can be no laxity when it comes to survival. Modern human beings continue to emerge from the shadow of the cave to hunt aggressively for riches and conquer fiefdoms to ensure survival for themselves and the members of their tribe. Either you govern or you are governed, and when you govern, you must do so by aggressively securing core needs."

With a tone of sadness, Maldonado asked, "So papá (Maldonado's affectionate name for his grandfather, Loubriel), is there violence and aggression in everyone's past?"

"Undoubtedly! This is the only way we have made it to this point as a species, and it is the only way we continue to maintain our existence. We cannot reverse evolution; nature will not allow us to bypass the self-sustenance trait."

Maldonado let out a sigh of sadness before turning to the next page. The next page dealt with the meeting he had many years later with his doctoral faculty advisor to discuss his proposed dissertation topic. He closed his eyes and went back to that meeting. He sat in his advisor's office, stroked his goatee and rocked his knees sideways as his advisor read intently. The advisor cleared his throat and, in his pedantic Castilian, gave him the damning news in a faculty room at New York University in New York.

"You are potentially a good analyst, but your rationale in this proposal is discursive. I cannot approve your topic. Sadly, you will not be given an extension to proceed with your research. I truly had high hopes for you. I am sure that you will succeed at something else."

After making those comments, the academic advisor stood up from his chair, which Maldonado took as a cue that he should do the same. Maldonado expressed his gratitude for his advisor's time, totally contradicting his real feeling of total revulsion about the outcome of that meeting. He was actually feeling diminished and demoralized. He immediately headed to a bathroom on the same floor of his advisor's office. The bathroom was solely for faculty members, but Maldonado did not care about protocol at that moment. He went in and was startled by a mouse that crawled under a radiator. Maldonado, who believed in the concept of personification he learned from Petra, perceived the mouse to be the spirit of his dead grandfather in the form of that animal.

Choking back sobs, Maldonado started to talk to the mouse. He said, "Papá, I am sorry that I let you down."

"I promise that I am going to make this all work one way or another."

Lying there in the halfway house Maldonado became teary-eyed, but continued to read his journal in the imposed monastic silence of his temporary home. He shook his head when he resumed reading about the day he was notified that he had to move off campus. He received a university letter confirming that his fellowship funds were being discontinued.

Many years later he would reduce it to ashes at a noon-time, Ash Wednesday para-liturgical service organized by his friend from a previous life, Father Roberto, on the church grounds. Maldonado was a faithful member of the Holy Rosary Catholic Church, and he attended an annal event where Father Roberto invited participants to identify, on a scrap of paper, a painful episode that reduced a personal dream to ashes. Father Roberto instructed the participants to release the paper inside a metal barrel of burning fronds. For some people gathered around the bonfire amidst prayers, Psalm readings and weeping, the scrap of paper addressed a divorce, a loss of a small business or employment, a passing of a pet or family member, or even the loss of a body function due to age or poor health. Maldonado remembered casting away the rejection letter, which represented the devastating defeat of his scholarly ambitions. The Ash Wednesday ceremony soothed the pain in Maldonado's soul, but it apparently did not make everything bad pertaining to the incident go away.

Maldonado discovered years later, through a random encounter with his former university roommate, that a topic similar to Maldonado's original doctoral dissertation proposal was supervised by his former doctoral advisor. The topic helped the person who wrote it earn a doctoral degree, a book deal based on the dissertation, and a tenure-track teaching position at a big-time university. If only he could have reworked the logic and structure of his thesis, he might have been able to convince his advisor to give him another chance. The topic was OK. It was only arguing it that had derailed his project, and left it for another grad student to retrieve.

"This cannot end this way."

"I am not a slouch."

Maldonado closed his journal and laid his head on the sofa's armrest. He dozed off and fell hard asleep. George, who was doing his rounds, woke him up and asked him to return to his bedroom. He laid on his bed, slid his briefcase under his pillow, and mumbled, "I cannot be defeated."

Chapter Nineteen

A Pentecostal Handshake

THE NEXT DAY, A cooing pigeon perched on the windowsill of his bedroom heralded the break of dawn. The glare of light filtering through the dusty venetian blinds symbolized a new beginning for Maldonado. He awoke and pondered how small his life was in terms of the cosmos, as he observed the orbit of specs floating aimlessly in the spectrum of gleaming rays. He clenched his fists and stretched his body. He let out a soft yawn when he saw that his roommate's bed was empty. He smiled when he remembered his mother was in the habit of taking him a piece of toasted bread with butter and a cup of coffee in bed, as she said her version of a colloquialism, "*Levantate dormilón. Lo mejor que hizo Dios fue un día detrás del otro.* (Get up sleepyhead. The best thing that God did was a day after the next.)" But this was not his mama's house where he felt safe, loved, protected. This was a halfway house and he was equally a man on the run with a felony waiting to happen and a man trying to get back the stature lost ten years before he went to jail. The real world was much harsher than the one his mama and grandpa Loubriel created for him.

The pigeon ceased its serenade and flew away. It had been startled by George's rapping on the residents' bedroom doors with his key chain and characteristic loud wake-up call. It was a Biblical rallying cry from Ephesians 5:14, "Awake, O sleeper, rise from the dead, and Christ will give you light."

George's religious mantra irritated Maldonado.

When Maldonado's roommate came out of the bathroom, Maldonado could not help but ask him, "Is the jail keeper always this insensitive?"

The roommate asked, "Insensitive?"

Maldonado started to explain the meaning of the word.

"Yeah, it means . . . "

Maldonado's roommate waved him off.

"Let me stop you right there. I may not be schooled, but I think I know what it means. People around here just don't drop million dollar words," he said. "You must be an educated man or a good bullshitter."

Maldonado smiled and said, "A little of both."

A short burst of warm humor was breaking the ice between the two men.

The roommate said, "The jail-keeper, as you just baptized him, is just herding us to breakfast."

Maldonado sat on the edge of his bed, greeted his roommate and offered a handshake.

He said, "Good morning. I am *"Guillo"* William Maldonado."

Maldonado's roommate extended his hand and said, "I am Tito, and I am the point-man for anything you need. Cigarettes, magazines, calling cards, you name it. I will get it to you for a modest fee."

Maldonado nodded and said, "That's good to know."

Tito wasn't ready to let this untested stranger know that his contraband was stored inside the bedroom's air-conditioning box. Tito used the air conditioner's metal sliding sleeve box with loose screws to have objects come in and out of the building. He kept his cash in a brown bag hidden in an overhead drop ceiling in their bedroom's half-bath.

Maldonado freshened up and ventured to the dining room to have breakfast. He barely ate his bowl of oatmeal and fruit cup. He cleaned up his bowl and performed the errands assigned to him. He went back to his room to fetch his briefcase. Afterward, he went over to George to get a work furlough. George authorized his exit, but breaking the program's rules for the stranger again, he slipped Maldonado a cash gift through an exchange known as a Pentecostal "handshake." It's an informal friendly gesture practice in communities of faith when an almsgiver discreetly passes folding money to another person he's shaking hands with. Pentecostals at George's church believed that calling public attention to gift-giving is the type of pride and grandstanding that ultimately forfeits the giver's eternal reward.

"I always take care of my people," George said, thinking that Maldonado was truly a new convert to his branch of Christianity, although his grand hope grew out of only a little bit of Bible reading in the night.

Maldonado smiled and tucked the money in his pocket. He headed out the door, reattached the license plate, and drove the car to the downtown section of the city. He somehow got lost. The makeshift map he sketched the day before was useless. Some of the streets that he traveled were sealed off as a result of construction or an accident. No road traveled on is ever the same.

He meandered on his travels until a sandwich board outside the C & C bodega caught his attention. The board advertised the sale of toasted bread and coffee for 50 cents. The deal was too good to pass up. He decided to stop and have the special. He grabbed an employment verification log, where he had to jot down the places he visited looking for a job.

Maldonado had hardly walked into the store when he heard the bodega's owner, Carlos Roman, reprimanding his nephew, Javier Martínez, regarding the newly arrived gas statement and the mechanic's invoice for unauthorized repairs done on the station wagon Javier used for making the bodega's deliveries. Carlos was scolding Javier for wasting time and gas by taking longer routes to make deliveries to the store's customers, most of whom were elderly and homebound. Carlos also hammered Javier for taking the store's vehicle for his own personal use. He was filling the station wagon with food and household products Carlos did not authorize him to buy at the wholesale distribution center. Carlos bought cheap merchandise at the distribution center and then sold the items for a marginal profit at his bodega.

"I have asked you nicely to stop putting so much stuff in the car. It is not a truck. And I have asked you nicely to stop taking side streets to get stuff to people," Carlos said with his anger building. "Why can't you follow these simple directions?"

Javier pleaded his case.

"Uncle, I am avoiding bad traffic and streets dotted with potholes," Javier said. "What's the big deal, uncle?"

Carlos answered Javier and then sprang to the counter to tend to Maldonado.

"The big deal is that the customers are calling me upset over the milk arriving leaking out of crushed containers, and bloody juices leaking out of the package of meat. One customer said the bottom of the bag was so wet that all the cans had to be wiped clean so she could put the food away."

Javier shook his head. He sauntered to the back of the store to take a seat on an empty, upside down milk crate next to Carmelo, a 35-year-old man known in the community as a street philosopher and clever cash-making entrepreneur. For a modest commission, Carmelo operated a *Brisca,* a Spanish card game, and a Dominoes gambling table in the back room of the bodega. Carlos, who was a well-regarded member at the *House of Mercy* Pentecostal Church, felt horrible for allowing shady activities in the back-room of his business. The back-room was a former *siesta* room furnished with a cot and a black-and-white television that he used to watch boxing matches and baseball games. But his slumping business was shaking his faith and eroding his moral outlook. His faith was being tested by terrestrial realities—a cash flow crisis. He turned the back-room into a den of perdition or "a playground of adult devilish vices," as his wife would say.

Carlos tried to attract customers by offering a lay-away plan after years of denying people a store credit with a facetious sign that read, " '*El Que Fía No Está.Salio a Cobrar*'/ 'The lender is not in. He is out collecting debt.'"

The gambling sessions and the lay-away plan brought in a few more customers. Carlos eventually was not able to compete with the lower prices offered by the new supermarket, *Felix's Fine Foods*, the demographic shifts bringing more Asians and South Asians into the neighborhood, and the changing attitudes of some second-generation Hispanic-Americans. The younger folks were trending toward American fast food and choosing mainstream dishes over the traditional Latin cuisine dishes on which they were raised, and for which the bodega had formerly supplied exotic ingredients like yucca, cilantro, and homemade seasoning known as *sazón*.

When Carlos originally launched his business in the early 1960s, he was responding to the needs of the newly arrived Latinos from the Caribbean. Twenty years later, the apartment buildings that housed his working class Latino clients were being refurbished and re-offered at rental prices beyond the means of his working class customers. Many of Carlos' customers lived within walking distance to his store, so it was convenient for them to load their folding grocery push carts with purchased items and haul them home. Now many of these same regulars had to relocate to more cheaply priced rentals in other sections of the city, and they did not have access to a car or need to do business with Carlos. They naturally took their food shopping business to the bodegas in their new neighborhoods.

Carlos' wife, Carmen, had encouraged him for years to buy the building that housed his storefront business, to fire his nephew Javier, and replace him with an Asian store clerk, and to dedicate an aisle of his store to selling Asian products. Carlos ignored his wife's suggestions. It was a machismo thing. He would say to himself, "What would my friends think if they knew my housewife was running my business?" It was also the allure of easy money that interfered with common sense business decisions. But Carlos' way of doing things was not working. He got deeper and deeper into debt. He started publicly to blame the Asians for his problems, and to risk his store to Carmelo's gambling and the off-the-books underground economy.

At the back of the store, Carmelo was reading the paper and having a sip of wine. He encouraged Javier to take a nip and calm down. Carmelo purposely and playfully combined the words wine and down to evoke stillness in Javier.

"You need to 'wine-down,'" said Carmelo.

Javier chuckled at the play on words. He declined the drink.

He had marked a cross on the wall calendar to record his stretch of sobriety which was so far 20 days.

"I can't be having none of that," Javier said.

"If he catches me drinking, he will put on another show and take the car keys away from me.

Carmelo asked, "What's the matter now?"

Javier said, "I am having bad luck, man."

Javier ranted about how a restaurant deliveryman, who was riding a moped, tore off the station wagon's side mirror by recklessly cutting through traffic.

"The dude didn't stop. I had to pay for that out of my paycheck."

After that story, he talked with Carmelo about feeling mistreated by the volunteers at the church's food pantry when he goes there for food to take to his kids.

One of Javier's tormentors was a church lady he thought Carmelo might be familiar with. "That lady who comes here all the time and is a friend of your mom's—her name's Lourdes, right?"

Carmelo responded to a question with a question, not sure what Javier was getting at.

"What about her?"

Javier tried to discredit her by describing and mocking a congenital eye deformity. The disfigurement made her stand out as different and marginalized.

"She's got a scary set of eyes," Javier said.

Carmelo lifted his head and said that she had been good to his mother, Andrea, when his father passed away, bringing his mother care packages and taking her out shopping.

"Man, she is alright. She's probably upset with you," Carmelo said. "I would be mad at you too if you tagged the side wall of my building with graffiti."

Javier's total silence proved Carmelo's point.

"She had to pay *Scrappin'* Steve to have that side of the building wall power washed and repainted. That's extra time, extra money. You just can't act like nothing happened," Carmelo said.

"How does she know that it was me?" Javier asked.

Carmelo couldn't believe that Javier was denying his role in defacing the building.

"People around here know your work. You have a trademark design and signature," Carmelo said.

Javier avoided personal responsibility and made it about something else.

He said, "Everybody just resents me. I am ahead of the curve and people are threatened by what a visionary I am."

Carmelo said, "Okay. You may be a visionary, but you can't put your artistic freedom before property rights."

Javier was not responsive.

Carmelo then wove another point into his opinion of why the volunteers were giving him such a hard time. It had to do with his and their disapproval of Javier's sheepskin coat, $100 leather sneakers, and gold-plated, name medallion hanging on a fat gold chain around his neck.

He said, "You can't expect the volunteers at the pantry to like you or feel compassion for you when you are asking for a handout dressed like a "bad boy wanna be," and when you live on a pauper's budget but dress like a Hollywood celebrity, sinking money into brand name shoes and clothes but can't put food on your own table. The volunteers keep the pantry going by donating their personal time and food."

Carmelo's words hit a nerve. Javier lost it.

"Those church people don't like me, man," Javier complained.

"They always give me such a hassle over what I can take and what I can't take. I end up giving a lot of it away because they pack my bag with stuff that I don't eat and the kids don't eat."

Javier couldn't find words to express his frustration. He used a word not used in good company. It was the first in a litany of curse words that began to flow from his mouth in Spanish.

Carlos overheard Javier's loud profanity coming from the back of his store. He berated his nephew for the loud angry words that were making the bodega sound more like a barroom.

"*Mira* (look it), stop cursing in here. This is a Christian store," Carlos said.

The hypocrisy of the moment did not escape Javier. He looked at Carmelo, rolled his eyes, and continued to murmur about his negative experiences with the church pantry.

"There is this one woman who questioned the validity of my id card. I knew she was mumbling something about me in Spanish to the other volunteers," Javier said.

Carmelo tilted his head back, jutted out his chin and said, "Now wait a minute! You don't know Spanish!"

Javier said that he understood bits and pieces from listening to the Spanish radio and watching Mexican soap operas. And he knew enough to spew out some mean curse words.

Carmelo exhorted Javier, "You should become bilingual. You should take an interest in your family's culture."

Javier stood up from his seat, clasped his hands, and said, "The other language that I speak is music."

To prove his point, he stood up and broke into a song he wrote entitled, "Let Yourself Go."

"Don't be so uptight

It's gonna be alright

If you don't try new things

you will always live in blight

Let's experiment

let's go nice and slow

let's experiment,

just let yourself go

let's experiment

go with the flow,

let's experiment

it's the way to go"

When he concluded his song, Javier danced in a robotic style and then mimicked the sound of a turntable scratching. After that, Javier had a wide grin across his face and asked Carmelo for his opinion.

"How about that, yeah?"

Carmelo was appalled. He took a sip of wine and said, "The only thing you need to experiment with is college and job applications."

He added: "You've got talent, but your street poetry *ain't* gonna get you anywhere. You can't imagine me buying one of your records, or your uncle listening to that stuff. You've got to go with what is safe and sells. Tradition is safe. Salsa sells. Merengue sells. That stuff you just lipped off doesn't do it for me."

Carmelo was not done pontificating.

"You've got serious art talent, but you don't have serious, mature goals. You should be thinking about becoming an art teacher. You've got kids now. You should be spending your time battling financially for their future instead of battling another street artist."

Maldonado who had stuck around overheard bits and pieces of the conversation. He was intrigued by what he heard. All he could think about was how the older guy was afraid of the death of tradition, and how the younger guy wanted put his creative energy into something new, and how that newness, which was dismissed as a fad by the older guys, threatened the core of their traditional Latin ethnic identity. Maldonado thought that the conversation could be a great case study for his self-sustenance theory project. He pretended that he needed steamed milk for his *café con leche*. He went over to the coffee station to tune in better on the conversation between Carmelo and Javier and judge how it was going. When Maldonado accidentally dropped the coffee strainer on the floor, Carlos told him not to worry about it. He spoke in a rough tone, critical of his nephew, Javier, for wearing a baseball hat sideways inside the store and for not paying attention to the customer.

"*Mira.* Don't wear your cap inside the store and wear it like a gentleman. You represent the store and your culture," Carlos said.

"Pay attention to the customers."

"Chill, uncle. I've got this," Javier said.

Javier removed his cap, and when he did, Maldonado realized that he bore a striking resemblance to the young man that he nearly bowled over the previous day. Just in case it was the same person, Maldonado walked over to Carlos and paid in haste. He emptied out his pockets, placed a handful of coins on the counter, and scurried out of the bodega. He didn't bother asking the owner, who he wanted to put down as a prospective employer, to sign his job search form required by the halfway house.

He took quick steps toward his car, but stopped and turned around to see what created a sudden, clanking sound. It was a merchant raising the shutter to a Botánica. The merchant reminded him of Petra, and the Botánica's boutique displayed a collection of exquisite, sacred relics. For the first time in his adult life, he realized how motionless inanimate sacred objects made something within him come alive, and how inert sacred icons spoke to him across the continuum of time and space, connecting his narrative to his ancestors'. The religious objects were being sold at a discount price, since the store was going out of business. With the dollar bill that George had given him, which turned out to be $20, he decided to buy something and entered the Botánica. In an hour or so, he exited with a sweet fragrance of candles, and he carried a bag of objects that awoke dormant memories and passions. Something changed when he left the Botánica. The cultural and religious symbols made him feel at home again, even though he was far from the place of his upbringing, Cabo Rojo. He got into his car and drove away feeling confident, knowing that he carried with him a tangible, concrete representation of what made him human. And that discovery was a sacred moment.

Chapter Twenty

A Flailing Faith

A VILE PRESENCE LURKED. A foe prowled. An old debt had to be resolved.

Little did Pastor Santana know that as he sought to draw closer to his God, a new problem was heading his way. He was currently engrossed in a prayer and fasting retreat at his congregation for the third straight day. He was hoping that prayer and fasting would renew his spiritual strength and consecrate himself more intently to his ecclesiastical vows. He was wavering on his commitment to his call. He felt anxious because of the harassing tactics of a vocal faction inside his church that wanted him defrocked. He was in despair at the thought that he had been cut off from the loving presence of his God.

Pastor Santana wasn't sure what was fueling the antagonism against him. He viewed the hardheartedness of his foes through a cosmology of good and evil. He asked himself in prayer, "Was it complex personality disorders that melded into one rival camp?" "Was it satanic forces that were shaping his foes into vessels of aggression?" "Was it both?" He didn't know. All he knew was that his opponents did not see him as the legitimate successor to the founding minister, the Rev. Miguel Montes, of the first Spanish-speaking Pentecostal church in the city.

Two years ago, the founding minister, the Rev. Montes, announced that he was retiring and appointed Santana as the new pastor. The opposing faction, nearly 40% of the church members, were all biologically related and were upset that the founding pastor did not name his own son, Pablo Montes, as the new pastor. Even though sixty-percent of the congregation voted Santana in, and even though the installation service consisted of a special anointing with frankincense, ordination vows, the laying on of hands by other Pentecostal pastors, and a special reception luncheon after worship, the opposition continued to quarrel about Santana's legitimacy. Some said that he had not been at the church long enough, while others said that an opportunity for a thoughtful search, and discernment process had not taken place.

Santana's opponents pressured him to name Pablo, his predecessor's son, as the new co-pastor. Santana stiff-armed the idea every time it came up during the annual congregational meeting. He thought that it was nothing more than a scheme to supplant him. Pablo, for his part, shrunk under his father's towering success as founder of the church, and he had shared publicly that he was not sure whether he had what it took to lead a congregation.

Santana had reached a point where he could no longer subdue his desire to retaliate. The Sunday prior to the start of his current fast and prayer retreat, Santana tossed the idea of preaching a bristling sermon titled, "Reeling in Rebellious Sheep." His aim was to address rebellion as a spiritual attitude problem. If the sermon failed to influence positively his troublemaking members to repent publicly during an altar call, he was going to wield his pastoral authority and saddle them with disciplinary charges.

Disciplinary charges required Santana to publicly announce the individual names and charges brought against each person. The nature of the charges, and the length of the sanction, a process known as "discipline," would prohibit the offenders from public participation in services and from exercising a leadership role, from anywhere between six-months to a year.

Santana, however, feared that chastising his insubordinate members for their actions would create a backlash. His peaceful members, who avoided conflict at the church to the point of becoming shamefully passive and compliant, could view him as not sufficiently pastoral and leave the church. There was also the risk, he thought, that his opponents might become emboldened and create new problems. He was conflicted. He knew that his indecisiveness could be interpreted as weakness, and the perceived weakness could incentivize his opponents to push him harder. But he dismissed the idea of being vindictive.

He pursued piety and introspection as a way of dealing with his suffering.

He raised his voice in melancholic prayer.

Santana said, "You didn't quit on me when You were suspended on the cross. You took on the scorn, the pain, and the suffering until You completed your mission."

"How can I turn my back on You?" he prayed out loud in a mournful voice that was equally doleful in his head when his prayers were soundless.

He was trying to convince himself that there was something noble about suffering for a personal cause.

Chapter Twenty-One

A Pastoral Family's Cross

AT ANY RATE, THE pastor's personal suffering affected the efficacy of his pastoral leadership. Every word he delivered from the pulpit was scrutinized more than usual. Every church policy he proposed at a board meeting was arbitrarily challenged. Everything he did, and anything that he neglected to do was subject to criticism. He could tell when the criticism against him was increasing by the amount of written complaints deposited in a suggestion box located on his secretary's desk. That box was bloated with what he considered to be petty nonsensical complaints, and unrealistic expectations.

Even if he wanted to, he did not have time to go through the litany of complaints. His main preoccupation was with a graver problem: his marriage to his high-school sweetheart, Minerva, was strained, and his three children, one daughter and two sons, were growing resentful over the deteriorating family life. His children were old enough to pick up on the chatter and were growing resentful of the unrelenting criticism directed at his ministry. Unbeknownst to the children, they were being criticized too. The trendy, but modest, *Victoria* brand outfits worn by the pastor's daughter, clothing items which she was able to buy with an employee discount at her job, were interpreted as a brazen endorsement of worldly popular culture. The posters of sports figures, some of whom made the news for things other than athletic accomplishments, that were spread on the walls of his two boys' shared bedroom, were viewed as a violation of the first commandment's prohibition against idolatry, which in that faith community included the veneration of popular, cultural symbols.

At a church, particularly at a small church, it is hard to keep secrets. Word got back to Minerva about the all finger wagging going on about her children. She was troubled by the impact that the negative chatter could have on her children's psyche and faith, if they discovered that they were being criticized by church members. Minerva already had two kids driven away by church gossip, "snatched away by the clutches of Satan," she would say in her prayers. She did not want the three children living with them to adopt a prodigal path and abandon the faith.

Minerva was annoyed by all the fuss. She decided to tell Santana that everything was not fine in case he had not noticed. She was no longer going to allow him to calm her. His Bible-quoting and spiritual-warrior mindset, she felt, was nothing more than a ploy to mask the reality of their family problems. A few days ago, Santana was seated in his recliner eating a late dinner and watching a documentary show about Napoleon. She stood in the TV room and asked whether the ongoing skirmishes with church members and his children's hostility undermined his divine calling.

She asked, "At what point are you going to look at how your schedule is affecting our family?"

"You are never around, and when you are, you are either absentminded or stressed about something. You know, our children need you too. The more you make yourself available at church, the more people are going to expect from you," Minerva said.

Santana continued to eat and gaze at the TV. He ignored her. He thought she had the right to say what was on her mind, though he felt she was allowing their tribulations to get the best of her.

Minerva was not done. She peppered him with more comments. "Angel, they are saying that you are not fit to be their pastor," Minerva said. "Why don't you consider starting a new church, or doing something else with your life?"

"It's not that simple. You can't get out once you are in," he said.

"What is that supposed to mean?" she challenged.

He quoted a passage from Luke that made him believe that he had no way out.

" . . . No one who puts a hand to the plow and looks back is fit for service in the kingdom of God (Luke 9:62)."

"I can't be what you want," he simply said.

Minerva responded.

"You said the same thing when you went into the military and had us bouncing around from state-to-state," Minerva said, reaching back into their past as a family with tenuous roots. "You said, 'I am responding to a higher call.' You are always trying to be heroic and save something or someone. Look at how our older two kids turned out. You may have saved the country but our kids are lost."

Santana said nothing.

Minerva said, "All I want is for you to be a person to me. Hello, remember me?"

She then quoted verbatim a Pauline passage that was used against her husband as proof of his disqualifications to serve as pastor.

"Here is a trustworthy saying: Whoever aspires to be an overseer desires a noble task. He must manage his own family well and see that his children obey him, and he must do so in a manner worthy of full respect. If anyone does not know how to manage his own family, how can he take care of God's church?"

Santana felt he no longer could be cordial and indifferent. He chastised his wife.

He said in a harsh tone, "May the Lord rebuke that thought! Everything is under control. This is just a passing storm."

He was uncertain whether church politics caused his children's disengagement from the church. He thought that the bad behavior of his two older children (one passed away from an overdose and one was rumored to be sick with a mortal illness like HIV) posed the greatest threat to his younger children. He was afraid his three younger children were going to mimic the behavior of their elder siblings. He was so steadfast in that belief that he prohibited his younger children from having unsupervised visits with their big brother.

He was restless in his recliner chair. His thoughts were directed to the difficulties in his family life, his members' fault-finding ways, and his concern that his children would learn what was being said about them.

Santana felt stressed discussing his family life. He put his food away, put on his overcoat, donned his hat, and drove to his church office. It was the conversation with Minerva that prompted him to reassess this period of crisis in his life and commit himself to his current prayer and fasting campaign.

He raised his hands and prayed, "Lord, I wonder whether I am going to make it? What is going on?" he asked. "Lord, help me understand. Give me wisdom to know Thy will."

Ordinarily, Santana would pray on his knees. He was blessed with a fervent spirit of prayer life that would allow him to pray three, four, and even five hours on his knees or in a prostrate position as a sign of total submission to God's will. But the immeasurable stress he was enduring destroyed his zeal for prayer and seriously diminished his physical stamina.

"Lord, I want to be faithful to my call, but it is so hard," he said, as he quietly read through the names on a prayer request list pegged to a bulletin board outside his office. Members and visitors were encouraged to jot down personal needs along with their names. He would offer prayers interceding on their behalf. He would not skip a name, even if it was the name of a detractor. There were times, though, when instead of asking for a blessing for a detractor, he was tempted to overlook that name or was tempted to ask for divine retribution on the detractor, quoting the words of the psalmist, who said, " . . . smite my enemy."

But he would catch himself, asking for strength to forgive and uphold his vocational duty to pray for his flock.

"Purge my bitterness and purify my motives. Forgive me for doubting your plan and disdaining my call, for even though I smile in public, I have not served you with contentment and gratitude. Give me the strength to love those who harass and hurt me, to feel comfortable around complex and irritating people, to stand for justice, and to look after the flock in my fold with joy."

In addition to asking for strength, he asked for a revelation.

"Give me a sign. I just need one sign to know and confirm your will."

Between nods at his chair, he would occasionally lift his gaze heavenward at the Victorian-arched ceiling of his office. He then snuggled under the purple-colored, shell-patterned Afghan, sewn for him as a gift by Andrea. The rattling of the radiator woke him up from time-to-time. When it did, he would continue his prayers, whispering biblical verses that captured his emotions. Among them, was the following passage from a psalm, " Yea, the sparrow hath found a house, and the swallow a nest for herself, where she may lay her young, even thine altars, O LORD of hosts, my King, and my God."

The pastor wanted an escape. He wanted a sign.

Suddenly, he was overcome by emotions. A man with the build of a middleweight boxer, the pastor's slight body violently jerked on the chair, as if someone had discharged a Taser gun at him. There was an outbreak of spiritual tongues in an incomprehensible language which sounded something like "*kee-ha- ramba-ba-saluca, kee-ha-ramba-ba-saluca*." He repeated the sequence of vocal sounds three times. Each time more intensely.

Raising his hands toward the vaulted ceiling, he said, "Thank you, Lord, for touching me with Your divine presence. Now give me a sign. I need Your direction to lead Your people."

He continued to press God for a sign. It did not matter if it came in the form of a vision, a dream, or a prophetic utterance. He needed confirmation to validate his sense of direction.

A sign did appear. It came in the form of a silhouette, and then, it came in the form of a vague presence. The minister's eyes were so tired they shed tears, and he could not immediately discern who or what the blurry image was.

The obscure figure shared his opening remark in a sly voice and mocking tone.

"Are you meditating on the Lord or are you falling asleep on your flock, pastor?"

The pastor was roused from his reverie. He was offended that someone would suggest that he was not guarding his sheep. He gathered himself and delivered a reprimand in a husky voice.

"May the Lord rebuke that thought!" the startled pastor said.

The minister was after all a man of God, the spiritual patriarch of the church. He expected a modicum of respect when a non-member entered his office, and he expected his secretary to reinforce the previously discussed protocol on receiving visitors.

The pastor asked, "Do you have an appointment?"

The visitor, draped in a wet coat from a cold rain, refused to immediately answer the question. Instead, he quickly approached the pastor's desk. When he stood against the side of the desk, he removed his wire-rimmed glasses, and nonchalantly said, "Destiny never schedules an appointment."

Chapter Twenty-Two

A Friend of the Old Vanguard

MALDONADO'S WORDS WERE NOT the prophetic oracle that Santana wanted to hear. His presence was not the celestial messenger that his eyes were longing to see. It was obviously a depressing moment for the already beleaguered pastor. Malice, in the embodiment of Maldonado, appeared before him. It all happened within a split-second. Much to Santana's disillusionment, prayer and fasting did not provide him with a first-line of defense against another attack. His exposure to this new threat destroyed his assumptions of how divine providence works.

Nothing was to be gained at that moment by badgering God and questioning who or what was in charge of the universe. Nothing was gained by spiritualizing a problem and praying for it to go away. Ah, yes, nothing was to be gained by scapegoating Satan and blaming him for wreaking havoc in his life over a past decision. The circumstances demanded that the pastor quickly unmask the intentions of this intruder who was not a stranger to him. Although many years had passed since they were business associates sharing office space, they recognized one another easily because neither had changed much physically. Santana hadn't really been keeping track of Maldonado, and just assumed he would not return out of decency. The pastor was so bewildered by Maldonado's sudden and unheralded resurrection, that he could not react soon enough to prevent his former business partner's aggressive charge toward his office desk.

More than six-feet tall, Maldonado towered over the diminutive Santana. Maldonado relished using his height advantage to dominate the diminutive pastor. The pastor sulked before his visitor and shrank in his chair.

Maldonado smiled with his eyes but not with his mouth. The word he spoke were tinged with rancor and insincerity.

"I have been looking forward to our reunion for a long time," he said. "Many questions. Many outstanding issues. Many things we need to clarify, my friend. For the time being, I am interested in helping each other out."

The minister grasped his two hands together tightly to calm his fear. He turned down Maldonado's offer to help.

"I don't know what you are getting at, but I really don't need your help." The curt response angered Maldonado.

Wielding an extra copy of the church's annual report, which he'd obtained from the secretary and digested while waiting to present himself to Santana, Maldonado reminded the pastor of the church's financial woes. He pressed the pastor to offer him the job advertised in the paper right on the spot.

"By the look of your numbers, you are not in a position to turn down any kind of help."

What was hinted at next by Maldonado placed the pastor in a quandary.

"I know things about you that could disqualify you for this position," Maldonado threatened, alluding to the shady demise of the insurance business that had ruined one partner but not the other.

"I want the church's sexton job and I know the position is available. Your wonderful secretary confirmed that you have not hired anyone for that position."

The minister tried to dismiss him with a gracious response.

"*Guillo,* come back on Sunday. We can talk with my key people after worship," Santana said.

Maldonado sensed that his former partner was buying time in order to come up with an excuse to turn down his hiring. He rushed ahead, intent on outmaneuvering Santana. The bewildered pastor was being pushed hard into a corner by Maldonado.

"When can I start?

"I need to know right now when I can start my new job and move in," Maldonado said, not in the least concerned about his commitment to stay at the halfway house *Healing Hearts.* "And don't you ever call me '*Guillo.*' That person no longer exists for you. He died a long time ago."

The minister buckled under the pressure. "Sunday." The response sounded like a loose commitment.

"You have already succeeded at deferring my plans and happiness," Maldonado said, again alluding to the sorrow he had been carrying around.

His arms forming an X, Maldonado waved them in criss-cross motion and said emphatically, "No more! You will not treat me like a fool any longer."

The pastor took a pitiable sidelong glance at his black and white Army graduation photo hanging above the ledge of an enclosed fireplace. That same photo hung in a prominent place at the business office they'd previously shared. In the past, during their better days, Santana would make reference to the photo as a way of conveying his paternal affection for Maldonado. Santana knew that the photo carried emotional weight for Maldonado, the son of a deceased soldier.

Over time, though, the photo lost its influence on Maldonado. He no longer viewed Santana as a father figure. He came to believe his former business partner now pastor Santana had used the photo as a tool to manipulate and control the trusting younger man.

Maldonado turned his head away from the photo.

"Your secretary took me upstairs and gave me a tour of the former janitor's living space."

A miffed pastor asked, "How? When?"

Maldonado said, "You've got to be more vigilant. She even pointed out the window and told me of an available space to park my car in the church lot."

Santana clenched his jaw firmly to subdue his anger at Maldonado. He was, after all, a man of God. He understood that Christian duty prohibited him from speaking disrespectfully to a fellow human being, even his enemy.

"Our meeting has ended. May God bless you," Santana said tersely, as he rose from his chair. He walked past Maldonado without saying a word. As he did, Maldonado grabbed him by his forearm and insisted, "I need a starting date."

Breathing in a steady deep rhythm to suppress his rage, Santana gave in. "The job is yours. You can start on Sunday," he said, torn by his decision even as he spoke the words.

Maldonado grinned and relaxed his grip. He retrieved his monogrammed handkerchief to wipe off the water on his left hand. He extended his left hand of fellowship to consummate the deal. Santana hesitated at first, and, after gradually stretching his hand to meet Maldonado's cold, moist hand, his hand was firmly rotated counterclockwise into a submissive position. Years ago, when Maldonado started out in business, Santana taught him to shake a customer's hand by placing his hand always on top. It was a technique designed to establish psychological superiority in a transactional moment. Now, Santana's lesson had been turned 180 degrees around on him.

As Santana escorted the unexpected visitor out of his office, Maldonado stopped at Daisy's desk to tell her that he was the new church sexton. Daisy was thrilled by the news. She gave him a hug and a set of keys. She said, "Something tells me that you are going to need these." Maldonado twirled the keys and let out a deep belly laugh. The secretary joined him in his celebration, laughing hysterically along with him.

Daisy's contagious joy and physical attributes, in particular her dimples, free flowing hair, and cinnamon colored eyes, inspired Maldonado to smile coquettishly and recite the first verse of *Ojos Astrales*. He said, "If God one day decides to extinguish every source of light, the universe would be illuminated by the splendor of your eyes."

Daisy sighed.

Santana did not take Maldonado's poetic mood and the twirling of the keys as a benign and amusing act. He took it as a taunt. Maldonado had the master keys to the church and those set of keys symbolized power and unlimited access. Maldonado had the secretary sign his employment verification form, and with a sprightly bounce, he marched off to his car.

Maldonado said, "I can't wait to start. See you on Sunday."

Chapter Twenty-Three

The Pastor's Smooth, Shiny Foundation

Santana was anxious to talk with Daisy, but he wanted to do it without Maldonado in the vicinity. When the church's main doors shut, Santana peered through the staircase to make sure that Maldonado had left the building. Santana was now safe to tell Daisy how displeased he was with her for not informing him that a visitor was waiting to meet with him. He had asked her, and asked her repeatedly, not to send a visitor into his office without his approval. He considered that rude, and a violation of her function, especially pushy strangers like Maldonado who show up unscheduled. He had also scolded her in the past about volunteering confidential information. She would say "okay" and "yes, sir" to him, but ignored his instructions. Santana was vexed by her lapses in judgment. He was not certain whether her inability to follow his office protocol was naiveté or a passive aggressive form of insubordination. Either way, he knew that he was bedeviled by another church problem and might have to get rid of her at a more convenient time.

Santana turned to her and told her to follow him into his office.

He asked her, "Let's have a word?"

Daisy didn't like the timing of his invitation and the tone of his voice. She sensed that she did something wrong, but didn't know what it could be. She asked in a skittish voice, "Is everything alright?"

The minister did not answer. He positioned the chairs in his office so that they could face each other when they talked. He asked her to sit down and said, "When I hired you, I explained to you that the word secretary comes from the root word secret. I need you to keep my secrets and not pass out information so casually."

"What do you mean?" she asked.

Santana said, "Please take a seat."

He paused and added, "You showed the visitor a room and let him come into my office without my approval. You told him that we own the church parking lot where he could park his car."

Daisy didn't understand why Santana was making a big-deal about her sharing information about a parking lot and her decision to show Maldonado the former sexton's bedroom. The former sexton's room was common knowledge, and it was listed publicly in the newspaper as one of the possible perks of the sexton's job.

She asked, "What did I do wrong?"

She added very candidly, "He seemed like a nice man. We need a sexton around here. People are starting to complain to me me about how dirty the chairs are, how smelly the bathrooms are, and how moldy the rugs smell. He said that he was, 'a friend from the old vanguard' and wanted to surprise you with his visit."

Santana was silent. Daisy started to cry. She politely explained the thinking process behind her actions and then asked for forgiveness. Santana nodded. He was figuring out what to say next. He dreaded her loose tongue and divisive nature. She was notorious for slanting their conversations and riling up members, accusing the pastor of acting like a pulpit bully and of being angry with her for no justifiable reason. When Daisy's uncle, Chico, learned about a new office conflict, he would write the pastor detailing how poor his administrative supervision was. Chico's letters revealed to Santana how his conflicts with Daisy were being distorted.

The thought of getting another letter from Chico distressed Santana. It made him realize that he needed to visit with his confessor, Father Roberto. He rose from his chair and thanked Daisy for her time.

He said to her, "What you just said makes sense. I have to go now. I have to make a visit."

Daisy walked out of the office. Santana knew that it was going to be only a matter of time before she spread news of the new church sexton. He did not have to wait long. As soon as she sat at her desk, she grabbed the phone and called someone. Santana could hear her say something in a whispery voice about Maldonado.

He stamped his feet and in frustration said to himself, "My, Lord, she cannot hold her tongue."

"This situation is hopeless," he said. "She is not going to change."

He certainly was ready to leave the church to run an errand, but he did not want to go out in public looking shabby and spent. It was important for him to convey strength and renewal. He didn't want his opponents to know that he was suffering, and he didn't want those who still believed in him, a small remnant, to lose faith in him as their leader. Before leaving the church, he changed his clothes and then looked for a secretly hidden pouch containing a kit stocked with his personal, hygienic aids, all necessary for him to maintain his pastoral aura. His pastoral aura was designed to give him a glow of piety, renewal and strength. To achieve that aura, he applied a face scrub of a Dead Sea product, dried his face with a hand towel, spread an oil fragrance from the Holy Land over his forehead in the sign of a cross, dabbed pomade on his rumpled hair, and combed it until its texture was glassy. But happiness can never be fabricated and pain can never be masked with lotions and fragrances.

Santana walked by his secretary without saying a word. He was headed to the bathroom. Twenty minutes later, he rambled out of the bathroom and heard a faint scream from the secretary's office. He stood quietly next to the entrance to her office door which was ajar. The secretary was being comforted by Sophia, who was a Sunday school teacher and worked at *Victoria's*. She stopped by the church office to drop off her pledges, having missed two Sunday services in a row. Sophia had been traveling with her family on vacation. Daisy was sobbing, and Sophia asked her why she was crying.

Daisy said, "The pastor is always angry with me."

"He disappears and never tells me where he is going. When I ask, he makes faces and lashes out at me. All I want to know is how to reach him in case there is an emergency. What am I doing wrong?"

Sophia disapproved of the minister's behavior and vowed to do something about it.

"This abuse is going to end. I am going to bring this to the attention of the church board," Sophia said.

"Oh, thank you," Daisy said in a well rehearsed voice. She repeated, "Thank you. I am trying to do my job."

The pastor pretended that he was not overhearing the conversation, but it was unbearable for him to hear with his own ears how he was being undermined by a subordinate whom he hired and once trusted. He softened his facial look of consternation, stuck his chest out and walked in the direction of Daisy and Sophia. He was headed to his office to deposit his pouch. He smiled and greeted Daisy and Sophia, "May the Lord Bless You." Santana got no verbal response. No eye contact. He bristled at the indifference and walked into his office. Once he was behind his desk, he thought for a few minutes about how easily people are swayed. He shuffled the stacks of documents on top of his messy desk. Once he was done shuffling, he placed two pencils on one of the stacks in the form of a Tau Cross. He left another set of two pencils in the form of a St. Andrew's Cross on the other stack. If things appeared differently when he returned, he would know that someone went through his stuff. Afterwards, he walked over to his leafless plant, *Crown of Thorns*. He watered the plant, and wondered when it was going to bloom.

When the chatter outside his office ceased, the pastor knew that he could leave without facing another awkward moment. Sophia was gone, but he felt she had left behind a negative spirit in his office. The pastor left the church building without saying a word to Daisy and without disclosing where he was going next.

Chapter Twenty-Four

A Pastor's Confession

THE TEMPERATURE INSIDE THE car felt like a cold grave, and Santana's body felt like a stiff corpse. While the car's engine heated up, Santana imagined how Maldonado's reappearance presaged a gradual but certain death—maybe not literally, but it could signal the end of any one or combination of the following: the end of his pastoral ministry; the end of his marriage; the end of his life; the end of his eternal salvation. He thought the last because he harbored an intense hatred for Maldonado, and those feelings came to the surface when he met Maldonado face-to-face.

Santana stepped on the accelerator and revved up his car. He did that several times to settle down his clunker's rumbling motor. The frail engine settled down with that trick, but there was nothing he could do to calm his body's tremor. He was worried about what brought Maldonado back into his life, what stories Daisy was spreading about him, what Sophia was going to tell others, and what would happen if someone from his church ever found out that he met with Father Roberto Sebastiano, a Jesuit priest at the Holy Rosary Catholic Church.

Father Roberto knew of Santana's inward and outward struggles. He gladly met with him out of a ministerial obligation to serve as the shepherd of every person in the jurisdiction of his parish, including a Protestant pastor. The priest also had a profound affection for his former parishioner. Twenty-years ago, prior to Santana's conversion from Catholicism to Pentecostalism, he took the priest around and introduced him to the business community, civic leaders, and elected officials. Santana, who was an active member of a service club, made sure that Father Roberto was always giving the invocation and benediction at social gatherings.

Father Roberto never forgot Santana's steadfast loyalty. He would meet with Santana at a moment's notice. Father Roberto also remembered how Santana vouched for him. He urged the parishioners, who had petitioned the bishop for a Spanish-speaking pastor, to give the Italian-American a chance. It didn't take long for Father Roberto to connect with the plight of his parishioners. The priest, also a Georgetown-trained lawyer, wove legal rigor into sermons, organized peaceful rallies on justice-themed issues, and litigated pro bono cases, both small and large, on immigration, public education and housing. He quickly became well-regarded and well-loved. Parishioners cooked and baked him ethnic dishes, and they named their children after him. At any time in the parish, there were at least 20 kids with a variation of the name Roberto, such as Bobby, Bob, Rob, Robette, and Roberta. A popular sub at *Poli's Pizzeria* and house pets—goldfish, dogs and cats—were named after the man of God.

Intuitively, Santana knew that he was making the right decision by meeting with Father Roberto. The priest urged the community from the pulpit to keep calm in the aftermath of the insurance fraud case. Father Roberto even attended a protest rally outside Santana's home to plead with protestors to measure their words and refrain from judgment until the fraud investigation was complete.

Even though Father Roberto was empathic and wise, Santana didn't allow him to help him. He didn't share much with the Father, and he wasn't entirely open when he did. He didn't want Father Roberto to view him as spiritually deficient. Father Roberto asked him to visit more often, but Santana held back. He didn't want his vocational integrity to be impugned by another Pentecostal minister if it was discovered that he was entering a prohibited, Catholic and sacred space. Or perhaps worse, yet, Santana feared that if a member of his congregation discovered that he entered a Catholic building and met with Father Roberto, that information would be shared and used against him to foment his congregation's distrust.

Santana felt ashamed for living in a crossroad. He privately sought the help of Father Roberto, but publicly condemned the Catholic Church. He stoked spiritual anxiety among his parishioners from the pulpit by prohibiting them from entering a Catholic house of worship or building. He said Catholic institutions were "havens of idolatry." Santana railed against and prohibited members from attending Latino cultural events that are traditionally rooted in Catholicism, such as the Epiphany Feast of The Three Kings and the *Quinceañeras*. This was the case even if it meant depriving the kids of his own congregation from receiving free toys sponsored by *Victoria's* during the annual Three Kings Parade, and even if it meant preventing family members from getting together to celebrate culturally significant events like First Communion, Confirmation, and Stations of The Cross.

Santana underestimated the pulpit as a powerful socialization tool. His words were forcefully and authoritatively delivered, and those words influenced the life choices of his congregants. From the pulpit, he would cite scriptures to bolster his exhortations. He would say that his restrictions came from a concern that parishioners would backslide by attending a church rife with vices.

Santana would say, "Don't play with temptation. You will be bested by it."

Santana was not a trained seminary pastor, so the standard rules of hermeneutics and homiletics could not aid him in the preparation and delivery of his sermons. The most important requisite for Santana as a pastor was that he was Spirit-filled to preach the gospel and Spirit-driven in his leadership style.

Santana's gruff talk against the Catholic Church was all a charade. He wanted to appear like a hardliner against the Catholics because he was terrified about being associated publicly with a Catholic priest, all because of the growing tension between Pentecostals and Catholics over the Pentecostals' proselytizing tactics and the incendiary language against the Catholics in their religious tracts. The tracts were offensive to Catholics because they contained derogatory graphic images of the church and the papacy. Santana tried to talk his church leaders into circulating generic tracts that focused on the hallmarks of love and forgiveness, but his church secretary, Daisy, and Chico rejected his input as "not brazen enough for the truth."

Santana thought the tracts were dreadful, but he didn't want to squabble with his church leaders over them. He had other challenges on which to focus. For the time being, he found it expedient to live a life of pretensions. He put on an act to pacify his detractors and preserve the status quo.

Living in the shadows became part and parcel of his persona. He parked a block away from the parish, even though there was an abundance of parking spots available at the parish lot. He wrapped his scarf around his mouth and flipped up the collar of his overcoat to cover his face, hoping to throw off anyone who would otherwise recognize him. In a steady gait, he walked toward the rectory.

Chapter Twenty-Five

Deferred Maintenance

SANTANA DARTED INTO THE rectory of the Holy Rosary Catholic Church. Once inside the vestibule, he knocked forcefully on the parish secretary's office door. The secretary, a tall, gregarious woman, wearing a lavender, long-sleeve dress with a sash belt and jabot, was enjoying an unusually quiet day. She was stapling empty Christmas offering envelopes to the priest's monthly parish-letter. She responded to the visitor's urgent knocking with a welcoming voice. "Come on in," she said.

The secretary was happy when she saw who it was. She rose from her chair and said to Santana in a gentle voice, "Well, it is so nice to see you. It's been a while. How I can I help you?"

Santana entered with his gaze fixed on her. He bemoaned inwardly that he did not have someone like her working for him. He smiled rather timidly and asked if Father Roberto was available to meet with him.

"Is the *padre* in?"

"Can he see me?"

The secretary did not answer his questions and did not approve of a meeting right away. She got to know him well over the years, and knew by the higher than usual pitch of his voice and his back-and-forth pace that he was nervous. She sought to calm him down, reassuring him that she was not going to judge him for meeting with a priest.

"I will let him know you are here."

"In the meantime, make yourself comfortable."

Santana did. He hung his hat and coat.

An instant later, the secretary asked, "Can I get you tea, coffee, water?"

Santana, whose throat was parched and lips were dry, asked for room-temperature water.

The secretary poured water from a pitcher into a cup and explained, while she poured, that she kept her office door closed to trap the heat; the church's thermostat was zoned for the office and not for the rest of the building during the week to help the church save money on its energy bill.

"We don't close the door to make visitors feel unwelcome or uncomfortable, though it can serve as a hint for those who drop by to stir up trouble," she said jokingly. Her sense of humor made him smile.

She gave Santana a cup of water and sat down at her desk. She wrote the words "Pentecostal Preacher" on a scrap piece of paper. A moment later she folded the paper and turned her back to Santana. Before Santana could ask a second time if the priest could meet with him, she headed down the hall to a conference room, where Father Roberto was meeting with the parish council. The council was made up of Hans Schultz, the local undertaker; Antonio Poli, the owner of *Poli's Pizzeria*; and Brigid McCann, the brains behind *Victoria's* retail stores. They were reviewing the specs and the contractors' bids for the repair of the parish's leaky, slate roof. The parish council was leaning toward hiring a contractor and launching a capital campaign to match a regional, sacred-sites grant being offered to the parish. And they felt a sense of urgency to move quickly in light of the grant application's looming deadline. But Father Roberto was neither ready to hire a contractor nor interested in asking the parish for more money. He urged the parish council to slow things down.

Father Roberto knew that a capital campaign during the Advent and Christmas season was going to hurt the parish's annual holiday fundraising efforts, which were notably used to pay for the annual toy-drive, free Advent pork-roast dinner, a summer reading program, and an affordable nursery program for working-class families.

"I know my flock. People will simply redirect their giving. Instead of helping the poor, they are going to worry about fixing the building. There is not a lot of disposable income in our parish both to fix the building and help the poor," Father Roberto said.

The parish council already knew his feelings, but Father Roberto reminded them in case they had forgotten.

Very politely, Father Roberto added, "My beloved, ministry is about serving people and not preserving buildings. We can let the Diocese help us out with our needs-based repairs when the time is right."

Poli was floored. It sounded to him like the priest was losing touch with the church's historical importance, and that he was belittling the contributions Poli's Italian ancestors made as the masons and builders of the landmark church. He threw his hands in the air and became voluble, speaking for a while. Amongst the things he said was, " . . . Father, forgive me if I offend you, but fixing the building is an act of stewardship. The people will not have a sound, safe place to gather . . . "

No one agreed with Poli and that got him more agitated. He started to speak with his hands and in an insistent voice said, "If the roof deteriorates, it will start to cave in."

Poli, who called everyone "paisano" in Italian regardless of nationality and gender, added, "*Paisanos*, we are betraying the loyalty, trampling the legacy and wasting the gifts of our past members."

Father Roberto did not take Poli's comments personally. The priest thanked Poli for his frankness, and said in a quiet voice, "I know. I know."

Brigid related to Poli's and Father Roberto's individual concerns, but did not want to leave the meeting without a resolution. She had grown frustrated over talking about the same issue for six straight weeks. She tactfully negotiated a compromise.

"Why don't we hire Steve to throw a tarp over the leaky area?"

"We can deal with the problem when the weather gets warmer."

Poli shook his head and made all kinds of grunting noises. He became pugnacious and said in another rant, "This is insane. We are going to lose the grant money. We are always taking a bandage approach to fixing the church's problems and that mentality ends up costing us more in the long run. Deferred maintenance is never a wise approach to building repairs."

Hans, who was taking notes as the parish council's clerk, stopped writing. He put his pen on the table and encouraged the group to demonstrate some faith.

"I've been here 50 years. Every time we seem to be in a pinch we get a little help from an unexpected source. God always sends us an angel."

Poli slammed Hans's solution for resolving money problems as a *Pollyanna* approach, while Hans countered and called Poli's scheme for dealing with a problem a *Chicken Little* approach.

"We are creating a budget out of *Monopoly Money*," Poli said. "And we are always expecting a Hail Mary, a desperate plea, a special offering to save us."

Poli clarified that he was using a football analogy and not insulting the Blessed Mother.

The parish council, nonetheless, was animated by Poli's comments. They were in the middle of an energetic debate when they were interrupted by a knock on the door. The door opened half-way, after which the church secretary popped her head inside the room. She looked at Father Roberto for approval to enter. She got it in the form of a smile. She approached Father Roberto, whispered something in his ear, and gave him a folded piece of paper. The priest read the note and made an awkwardly happy face. He looked at his secretary and nodded. The secretary excused herself and returned to her office to entertain Santana. The members of the parish council figured that the secretary's message had to do with a pastoral emergency. They waited for the priest to adjourn the meeting, which he did in the form of a motion.

Father Roberto dismissed the parish council with a benediction, greeted each one of them affectionally, and asked them to meet with him next week. Poli remained seated with a dour look on his face. Not wanting Poli to leave the meeting upset, Father Roberto hugged Poli and uttered a phrase in Italian, knowing that a common language coupled with empathy can help disagreeable spirits transcend acrimony.

Father Roberto said, "*Tutto andrà per il verso giusto*" (It means in English, "Everything is going to work out.").

"Thank you, Father," said Poli, who got up, stretched his hands over the priest's shoulders and gave him a kiss on each cheek.

Half an hour later, from the time he entered the rectory, Santana heard footsteps and odd voices in the hallway. He became worried when he recognized Brigid's voice. She said something about talking to Steve on Wednesday and something about the church's roof amidst the approval of a male voice that sounded all too familiar. Santana immediately looked for an alibi. He froze and couldn't think of one. He paced and thought about leaving. The secretary, picking up on Santana's restlessness, escorted him in a dignified manner to the priest's study. She said to him, "Why don't you wait for him right here?"

She added: "He will be with you as soon as he returns a couple of phone calls."

She closed the door to the study and Santana sat down. He did not remain seated for long. He sprang from his chair and stared at the collection of masks hanging on a wall: a Milan (celebration) Mask, an African (fertility) Mask, a Chinese (warrior) Mask, and a *Vejigante* (demon) Mask, which he gave to Father Roberto as an installation gift, recalling memories of his native town's celebration of a *Fiesta Patronal* (A celebration of a patron saint in a town). He could never understand why the priest collected exotic, ornamental masks, and wondered if the priest staged roles and feared a personal demon.

Not being able to make sense of the meaning of the priest's mask collection, Santana turned his attention to the plethora of books in a shabby bookshelf. He seemed intrigued that some of the authors' names bore the names of his closest relatives. He had a favorite uncle named Agustín, and two books, *The Confessions* and *City of God*, were written by his uncle's namesake, Augustine. He ran his finger horizontally through the spine of the books and stopped when he came across a book that was written by an author with the Spanish version of his father's name, Francisco. That book, *The Little Flowers of Saint Francis*, he thought, had an interesting title. He ran into a book whose author had the English name of his deceased oldest son, Gregorio. The book was written by Saint Gregory, and it was titled *Regula Pastoralis* (In English, it means, "Pastoral Practice"). Latin, he remembered, was the mystical, lofty language used during Mass at his home church, and that memory gave him a warm feeling. He stretched out his hand, grabbed the book and opened it. He glossed over the pages for a minute or two and was thankful that it was translated into English. He noticed an asterisk placed on a paragraph and sat down to read the marked passage. Saint Gregory said, "Let sowers of discord consider well how they are multiplying their sins! By carrying out one wicked act they root out all the virtues at once from human hearts. By one evil they accomplish numberless evils, because by sowing discord they are extinguishing love, the mother of all virtues."

He let out a hopeful sigh and pondered Saint Gregory's words. He flipped through the book and stumbled on a curled page. He read a passage in a soft voice, "When, however, wrongdoers are in no position to harm the good, even if they want to, we should bring about earthly peace among them even before they are capable of recognizing heavenly peace. Then, at the very least love of neighbor may soften those whose unholy malice hardens them against the love of God, and they may pass on toward something better as if from a point nearby, rising to what is far away from them, the peace of their creator."

Santana stopped reading and held the book to his chest. The sublime words gave him a calming sensation. It occurred to him that he had been praying for a sign, a divine message. He wondered if the passages represented a partial answer to his personal prayer. Then realizing that the message derived from a Catholic source, he dismissed the legitimacy of the insight because it was not coming from his God. Although the wellspring flowed from the same God, he could not drink from the same goblet as his Roman Catholic brethren.

He returned the book to the bookcase and turned around when he felt that someone was standing behind him. Father Roberto had just walked in. The priest threw his arms around him and gave him a strong, bear hug.

Father Roberto let go and invited Santana to take a seat. They sat across from each other, only separated by a coffee table in the middle of the room.

Father Roberto asked, "How have you been? How is your family? When are you going to have me over for some of Minerva's rice and beans?"

Santana dropped his head. His carefully applied pastoral aura was not able to mask his pain. He mumbled in a feeble, timid, unpastoral voice how things were getting worse. He spoke of Minerva's deteriorating health. He reminded the priest how she struggled with diabetes, poor vision, obesity and asthma. He said her failing health limited her involvement in the congregation's activities and worship services, and her irregular attendance made her an easy mark for criticism. He said some of his church critics questioned her commitment to the Pentecostal faith and expressed disappointment in her limited role as the pastor's wife. Worst of all, he said some of the critics were succeeding in creating the perception that her physical ailments were an indication of God's punishment for a hidden sin or secret fault.

Minerva was dear to Father Roberto. His facial features expressed his disappointment with how things had run afoul at Santana's church. He assured Santana that divine judgment was not trickling down on his family. Knowing that Santana was apt to misinterpret and confuse conversations and exaggerate problems, he asked, "How do you know for sure that people are saying such awful things?"

Santana hesitated, but responded, "Do you know Carlos, the grocery guy?"

"Of course, I know Carlos," said Father Roberto

"He is a former congregant of mine."

Santana looked away. He felt embarrassed about convincing Carlos to leave the Catholic Church.

"Well, he told me," Santana said.

Santana laid out an anecdotal conversation that took place at Carlos's bodega. He said that two biological sisters, Norma and Gloria, talked freely and loudly to Carlos's wife, Carmen, at the counter about the pastor's family, not knowing that Carlos was stocking food items on the aisle behind where they were standing.

Norma reportedly said to Carmen, "It is not a good Christian example that Minerva is so heavy and doesn't come to church as often as she should."

Norma, along with Junior, was the *House of Mercy's* van driver. She added, "And when she comes, she does not stand at the greeting line anymore. There is something wrong with Minerva."

Norma's sister, Gloria, repeated like a *pappagallo*, "I know it. I know it," in between each sentence completed by Gloria.

Gloria sniffed. And then, she jerked tears.

"All of this controversy is getting me upset," Gloria said.

Norma tried to settle her sister down.

"Stop crying Gloria! It is not your fault," Norma said.

Norma wasn't done. She asked Carmen in a whispery voice, "Did you hear the latest on Nestor?'

Carmen was careful not to answer. She thought that Norma was try-ing to coax something out of her. Nestor was Santana's son, and she knew her husband, Carlos, and Santana were close and talked about Nestor's life situation.

Norma, noticing how tightlipped Carmen was, leaned over the coun-ter and said in a riveting voice, "He has an incurable illness, and he is not getting any better."

A gaped-mouth Carmen said, "Oh, dear," out of sheer distress, but Norma mistook her reaction to be out of moral rage.

Norma turned her face in both directions to make sure she wasn't be-ing heard. She wasn't done making critical, disparaging remarks.

"He's living with a so called 'roommate.' I never understood how the smartest and best looking of the boys ended up in a situation like that. He could have had any girl and made his family proud," Norma said.

Santana's account of the conversation at the bodega surprised Father Roberto. The priest could not understand why Norma disliked and discred-ited Santana so much, and why she was so judgmental of Minerva's and Nestor's personal life. The priest knew what Norma meant by her insinuat-ing comments regarding Nestor's "roommate." He overlooked that part of the conversation. He and Santana disagreed on the subject of human sexu-ality, and they ended up bickering on whether conscience or Scripture, or both, should inform sexual preference whenever the subject was broached. Father Roberto was a Thomist (Thomas Aquinas) and Santana was a Biblical literalist. Father Roberto slightly changed the subject of the conversation and asked Santana whether he received collegial support.

"How about the other Protestant pastors?"

"Don't you guys have a clergy association? Don't you guys meet and give each other support during times like this?"

Santana laughed. He was surprised Father Roberto did not know he lacked authentic collegiality and emotional support.

"No!" Santana said.

Santana struggled to explain how fellow Protestant pastors were aware of his troubles but were not reaching out to him. Instead, Santana said his fel-low Pentecostal pastors were visiting disgruntled parishioners and recruit-ing them, offering membership on the spot and expansive leadership roles at their churches. Additionally, some of his counterparts were intimating from the pulpit that the disarray at the *House of Mercy* Pentecostal Church was a reflection of Santana's poor decision not to bring his church under the umbrella of an established, more traditional Pentecostal denomination.

"They say that not belonging to a denomination is like a chicken running with its head cutoff," Santana said. "I'm on my own when problems take place. I have no bishop to protect me from an uprising."

Santana did not visit with Father Roberto to discuss the risks of an independent, entrepreneurial ministry or of not having his congregation affiliated with a denomination.

He wanted to discuss the reappearance of a past problem.

Santana said, "Maldonado is back."

With wary eyes, Father Roberto asked, "Who is back?"

"Maldonado," Santana said. "

He broke the name "William Maldonado" into syllables for clarity and emphasis.

Santana wanted the priest to tell him, in a nutshell, what may have influenced Maldonado to return.

Father Roberto did not take long to answer. He said, "Passion."

"Passion?" Santana questioned.

Father Roberto explained, "Passion in the form of revenge. Revenge has the same tenacity, perseverance, that love has."

The priest added, "The same passion that drove him to work hard for you is the same passion driving him to confront you to deal with an unresolved lust for revenge."

Father Roberto encouraged Santana not to blame Maldonado for his determination to exorcise his demons. The priest said that knowing full well that it was the pastor's oldest, deceased son who pocketed the money that was supposed to go for the payment of the monthly insurance premiums; the policies subsequently lapsed, and each policy holder was without insurance protection. Father Roberto was bound by his vocation to uphold confidentiality, but he tried to share with Santana in an oblique way that Maldonado was not the one responsible for the insurance debacle. Santana's own son, Gregorio, the eldest, who worked under Maldonado, used the clients' cash payments to settle an old drug debt, and he managed to make Maldonado the sacrificial lamb.

The priest knew the oldest, deceased son's deceptive practices firsthand because the son revealed the scheme to him on numerous occasions during counseling and Confession. Father Roberto tried to get Santana's oldest son to talk about his misdeed to his father or the authorities, but he died of an overdose before he had the chance to make things right.

Father Roberto tried to help Santana grapple with his deep-rooted anger, and encouraged him to embrace Maldonado's surprise visit as a gift from above to reconcile matters and experience wholeness. He said, "The people whom God places in our life are designed to teach us something about ourselves that we are ignoring, for self-awareness comes by being in relationship; and the people whom God places in our path are designed to give us a skill, a perspective, a resource that we need to help us transition from one phase of living to another."

Santana mulled over the priest's insight. It didn't take long, however, before he asked in a skeptical voice, "Even a disreputable person?"

Father Roberto said, "Most of the time we attract who we are."

The priest went on to quote from the Book of Amos.

"Didn't the good prophet once ask, 'Can two people walk together without agreeing on the direction?'"

Santana did not think the priest was being fair. He shrugged his shoulders and threw his arms up in the air as a sign of reproach.

Father Roberto did not mean to offend Santana, but he stood firm in his counsel. He said, "You cannot be filled by the Spirit if your cup is filled with anger and revenge. You need to empty the things of your life that are not pure, that are corrupt. It is the only way your cup will be filled to the brim with the outpouring of heavenly blessings. For your own sake, make room in your cup for good energy, love, peace."

The Father's words jarred Santana's memory. It unleashed a rush of flashbacks that harkened back to a confessional meeting he had with Father Roberto ten years earlier. It was like the curtains of grace were pulled aside, and on a mental screen appeared a series of scenes where he partook of vile things. He recalled the futile plots he carried out to destroy Maldonado, prior to converting and becoming a saved man. He remembered how his bad gun shots missed Maldonado in a drive-through shooting, and how his plan to have a junkie stab Maldonado with an HIV-infected needle was foiled when undercover agents nabbed the junkie and arrested him for possession of drug paraphernalia. There was something unsettling in Santana. But rather then dealing with his unresolved anger, he suppressed his toxic emotions. As soon as he snapped out of his moment of reflection, he put on the act of a victim.

Santana said to Father Roberto, "The price of serving God is steep, and the ransom for doing ministry is a perpetual sentence. Who can endure this?"

Father Roberto quoted in Spanish a saying that Santana taught him many years ago when he started his ministry at the parish. The priest said in Spanish, " 'Dios aprieta pero no ahorca.' ('God squeezes but does not strangle')."

Chapter Twenty-Six

A Dispirited Pastor

Santana left Father Roberto's office dispirited. The spiritual advice meted out by the priest did not provide the clarification of feelings and affirmation of faith that he had sought. He wanted to hear that he was justified in feeling doomed and aggravated. Life, Santana felt, had unfairly conspired against him, burdening him with a slew of calamities. Santana wanted Father Roberto to view him as a modern-day Job on the verge of becoming a spiritual martyr. Father Roberto did not agree with the manner in which Santana cast himself. The priest opined that it was hubris to question God's ways, and there was nothing pious in skirting one's past. And he went as far as challenging Santana to embrace Maldonado's reappearance as an opportunity for Santana to deal with unresolved anger.

Santana could not blot out the priest's counsel. The words haunted him. The words angered him. The words forced him to take a quick look at his rear-view mirror, where he noticed that his pastoral aura had silently drifted away. He looked wretched. At that moment, doubts about the nature of his calling and the promises he understood were guaranteed to him in the Bible started to surface. He wondered if he was the recipient of divine retribution, and if there were any merit to the criticism of his detractors. He even entertained the idea that his wife was right; he may have outlived his season in the ministry at the *House of Mercy* Pentecostal Church and it was time to move on. It occurred to him as unhealthy for his congregation and for his own well-being to look at a ministerial position as a birthright to a *modus vivendi.*

"Why am I putting myself and my family though all of this turmoil?" he asked aloud.

Then, after saying those words, he focused on an event that took place at his office a week prior to Maldonado's visit. He'd been in the middle of organizing stacks of papers when Jimenez stopped by the office for an unexpected visit. Jimenez, the church's finance committee chair and member of the deacon's board, entered the office with a handwritten chart of the church's quarterly income and average attendance on a clipboard. Jimenez claimed that he was on his way home from work when he decided that it was appropriate for him to personally tell the pastor that the finance committee met and voted not to provide him with an annual cost-of-living increase; it was the third year in a row that Santana was not going to get a raise.

Santana was surprised that a committee meeting was held with no announcement in the church bulletin or without him being told about it; the by-laws of the church were fuzzy on whether standard church committees could hold official meetings away from the church grounds.

Santana asked, "When did this all happen?"

Jimenez said, "We met at my house this past week. We wanted to keep it low key. Money issues get people riled up. We decided not to invite you to the meeting. You have so much on your plate."

Santana said, "Thank you for worrying about me, but I can decide on my own which meetings to attend."

In the past, the pastor brushed off the finance committee's salary recommendation not to give him a raise as a reflection of the church's struggling finances. To show that he was conscientious and to prove that he was in the ministry for the right reasons, he would stand up during the annual congregational meeting and decline a salary increase. Santana's resolution did not go well with his wife, Minerva.

Minerva smiled publicly when Santana declined a salary increase, but protested his decision in private as a "piety stunt" designed to win over the hearts of his congregants at the expense of his family's well-being and future. "You can't let them take advantage of you," Minerva said. "We have kids to raise!"

Jimenez looked at his clip chart. He cited statistics to justify the committee's decision.

He said, "Members are dropping out."

"The finance committee decided not to tap into our savings because the endowment is going to run out in two years, and we will be left without a church. You wouldn't want that to be part of your legacy, right?"

Santana swallowed the news of no raise with great difficulty. The timing of Jimenez's news was most unfavorable. With an eighteen-year-old son, Ezekiel, poised to enter a vocational school in a year to study plumbing, and a nineteen-year-old daughter, Miriam, who worked at *Victoria's* and was thinking about attending a fashion and business school in New York, he desperately needed a modest raise to help his children offset the cost of additional schooling. Additionally, Santana knew his youngest son, Timóteo, wanted to start taking guitar lessons at a local music school. Santana was worried about finding extra money to pay for the classes.

Jimenez wasn't done. He proposed an unusual idea that immediately raised Santana's suspicions.

Jimenez said, "Perhaps you should take a vacation with your family and reassess where God is leading you and our congregation?"

Santana felt that there was nothing benevolent in the recommendation. It sounded to him like the same political trap that was laid for one of his local colleagues, the Rev. Armando Baez. The Rev. Baez was also encouraged to go on a family vacation to allow a conflict at his congregation to simmer down, only to be replaced upon his return by an internal rival preacher over a dereliction of duty charge brought by the church trustees.

Jimenez's financial news did not surprise Santana. From where he sat on the pulpit, a trinity chair, he knew that the brass collection plates were no longer lush with dollar bills. Less worshippers translated into less critical mass to recruit new members and less enthusiasm to drop gifts into the collection plate. In addition, the displeasure of those who attended worship was evidenced by their substitution of dollars bills with the rattling of coins in the offering plate. Santana also knew from a weekly copy of the tellers' tally sheet that the groups of members who were fighting him were also withholding their pledges to apply economic pressure on him to resign.

The polemic inside the church was yielding the results the factious members sought. It was driving loyal members with either peaceful temperaments or apolitical personalities away from the church. Santana discovered this first-hand at *Felix's Fine Foods*. He was shopping for staples and ran into an inactive member, Cruzita Martinez, the mother of Javier and Juan.

"Sister, we miss you," Santana said.

Cruzita gave a heartbreaking response.

"I miss you guys as well, and I am grateful for everything the church has done for me. But I deal with so many problems at home and at work that if I am going to get more of the same at church, I might as well stay home or join another church," said Cruzita. She abruptly turned her back to the pastor and pushed her cart as fast as she could to the opposite end of the aisle.

Santana stood there motionless, watching her veer away. He wondered if he had wasted his time with Cruzita. He shepherded Cruzita through a crushing divorce, blessed her family with discretionary funds to pay for her utility bill, and raised a cash gift offering to help her pay for her mother's funeral expenses. He also spent countless hours driving her to visit with her oldest son, Juan, who was an inmate at a correctional facility in upstate New York. The more he thought about the assistance he gave to the Martinez family, the more bitter he became.

Cruzita's membership loss was one of many things that he thought about. But her departure from the church cut him the deepest. Her departure made him ask whether he was loved for who he was or loved for what he did for people.

He forced himself to drive around the city's empty streets. He pulled into an empty parking lot. There he pondered for a few minutes whether he should head to his home to be with his family and tell his wife, first thing in the morning, that she was right, or whether he should return to his church office to resume his prayer and fasting.

He did not give his choices much consideration. The adrenaline that he felt standing behind a pulpit was so seductive that he could not abandon his calling. He drove back to his office. On his way there, he purposely drove by the house of Andrea, his spiritual mentor and church confidant. If Father Roberto was his confessor, Andrea was his lay pastor. The 72-year-old Andrea was the one in whose arms, figuratively speaking, he collapsed for comfort. Andrea had been away visiting with her sister in Florida, and he wasn't sure if she had returned. There was a sign that she left at night to telegraph that she was there. She would sit by the window sill and stay up all night to knit and pray for Carmelo, her wayward son. His lifestyle choices turned her into an insomniac. As the minister drew near her brownstone home, he could see her silhouette behind a drawn shade on the second floor. Her hovering shadow reassured him that he had someone else to turn to during times when he was enmeshed in a crucible of pain. But Andrea's vigil also reminded him about the times he and his wife would stay up all night worried about his own son's struggle with addiction. He decided to return to the office to ponder his faith and religion and he would talk to Andrea about his problems on Sunday after he completed his rounds. He was determined not to leave the ministry without a fight.

Chapter Twenty-Seven

Iniquity in the Church?

SUNDAY ARRIVED. IT WAS generally a day of celebration and renewal for the pastor, but the enumerable problems he was facing, compounded by Maldonado's hiring, turned Sunday into a day of personal discomfort. He was pacing all night and his thoughts were scattered. This bothered him because he knew that some people counted on him to provide a meaningful and thoughtful homily. He knew that if he happened to have a visitor shopping for a church, he only had one chance to make a favorable impression. The Saturday evening leading up to Sunday worship, he locked himself in the study inside his home. He was so irritable that he would not be bothered, unless it was a parishioner. His family knew that it was best to distance themselves from him when inspiration was distant from him. He spent the night pacing, turning on lights, writing an outline on his hand, and hoping that a word of inspiration would come for the Sunday crowd.

It wasn't too long ago that Santana was hailed as a gifted extemporaneous speaker, consistently delivering rousing, exhortation-style sermons. In his better preaching days, he roamed the pulpit space with freedom, soared his deep-rich voice, removed and flung his suit jacket in a show of bravado, and spun like a vortex to dramatize a point; he only acted melodramatically whenever he was enveloped in a spiritual trance. But lately, the task of preaching became tedious. He fumbled through his sermons and cowered behind the lectern. He feared that the Spirit had stopped working in and through him. He was plagued by diminishing self-confidence in the pulpit, and his parishioners, those who liked him, and those who didn't, could tell.

Before Santana could give more thought to his past abilities in the pulpit, the streak of light announcing the arrival of Sunday's dawn arrived. He had to carry on with worship. He knew that he did not have the option of calling in sick, in case his absence was used as a cause for his termination. But even if there were a lay person at his church with preaching gifts who could step in at a moment's notice, the climate was rife with so much mistrust that he feared deferring the pulpit for one Sunday. He was afraid that a member with aspirations for pastoral ministry could use the preaching opportunity as an audition of his preaching abilities and make the case with a stellar sermon, demonstrating Santana was expendable. So, with great effort, Santana slogged from his house to his car to the church.

To camouflage his groggy appearance and defeatist feelings, he made his way to the men's bathroom to administer a fresh layer of his pastoral aura. He did not have a lot of time to apply his aura, according to the clock hanging on the back wall of the sanctuary. Worshippers generally arrived 15 minutes prior to the start of the standard 10 a.m. worship service. After quickly sprucing himself up, he normally stationed himself at the main entrance of the church to greet and bless his parishioners. From his second-floor office window he spotted the two church vans pull up to the main entrance. One by one, the pastor's faithful remnant, and his opponents alike, got off the bus and walked into the church. They came up the stairs and headed to the closet to hang up their coats.

Santana greeted most of his parishioners with a handshake, others with a hug. The elderly ladies always received a kiss. Regardless of how some of his parishioners felt toward him, and some did show their repugnance with perfunctory unaffectionate handshakes and cold glances, he obliged himself to greet them all in a friendly-manner. This included Maldonado, whose firm squeeze earlier in the week had crushed his hope for the future.

The worshippers, in a short procession, entered into the sanctuary area, some clutching a Bible, others holding fast to hand instruments, such as tambourines, maracas, *guiros*, and cowbells. Within minutes of promenading into the sanctuary, the sacred space was filled by the worshippers' spontaneous chatter. This was a time known as personal prayer, and it took place before the start of the official part of the worship service. During personal prayer, worshippers sat and prayed at their seats or knelt and prayed at the altar area. Some prayers were uttered publicly and collectively. Though the concurrent chatter may have sounded indiscernible or funny to an untrained, eavesdropping ear, a church insider would have said that the prayers were coherent; the prayers ranged from personal confessions to personal petitions to expressions of gratitude.

Usually, the pastor would join his congregants during the time of personal prayer, walking amidst them, and animating them to carry on with his zealous cries and citations of biblical verses. Infrequently, though, he would model a different prayer style. He would kneel and pray in silence at the right trinity chair; it was the chair on the altar that was pressed against the silk curtain that veiled a panel wall. But not on that Sunday. Santana stood in the narthex and tracked Maldonado's moves.

Carlos, who always prayed with his eyes open and in admiration of the pastor, was miffed by the subtle change in the minister's behavior. He imagined that something must be bothering him. He swiveled his head in search of Santana across the open floor sanctuary. He found it odd that Santana stood by himself and acted seemingly detached from his flock. Carlos walked toward Santana. He never hesitated in his thinking and never removed his gaze from him. Carlos had made a personal, religious promise to never abandon his pastor because his pastor never let go of his hand at the hospital when he struggled with cancer and faced his mortality; the pastor was Carlos' faithful visitor when he was ill.

When Santana detected that Carlos was heading towards him, he closed his eyes and lifted his hands in exultation, pretending to be praying on his own. Santana's feigning did not work. Carlos approached him.

Carlos then said, "Great sermon last week. I didn't get a chance to tell you."

Santana, or one of the appointed elders who patrolled the floor during prayer time, would generally rebuke a person who initiated conversation during this time. Chatting during personal prayer time was considered irreverent and distracting. Santana was a little surprised by Carlos's impropriety, but he chose to overlook the transgression.

Santana didn't think that he preached a solid sermon, but he took the compliment in stride.

He said to Carlos in a sullen voice, "Amen and amen. To God be the glory."

Santana turned around and walked away. Santana's sorrowful response gave Carlos the impression that Santana was dealing with another inveterate problem. Carlos knew that the low attendance numbers at worship that day further demoralized the pastor. Carlos sought to fix it. He followed the pastor and tapped him on the shoulder from behind. When the pastor turned around to face him, Carlos expressed his opinion on the cause of the low attendance.

Carlos said, "I do not want to trouble you, but it looks like we are going to have a small crowd today."

The pastor felt uncomfortable with those words.

He asked Carlos, "Why so negative, brother?"

Carlos responded with conviction.

"When it rains, my business has less customers, without fail."

"The church is like a business. When it rains, less people come out."

The pastor gave Carlos a dubious look. Carlos realized that the pastor was confused. He gave a clearer explanation.

"The pulpit is your counter and point of sale, and the retail counter at my store is my point of sale."

The pastor grimaced. He felt uneasy by those remarks, but he consented the point with a slight nod. He knew that Carlos respected him. He felt grateful to know that there was someone among his flock who did not blame him for the weather and fluctuating worship attendance.

Twenty minutes into the time of personal prayer, the loud chatter that marked the start of the prayer session gradually became a subdued whisper. The hushed voices cued the lead guitarist and choir director, Alfonso "Al" Arias to strum his chords in fast scales. The flamenco-styled rhythm churned out by Al and his percussionist band stirred worshippers into a frenzy of clapping, singing, dancing and playing along with hand instruments.

Maldonado was taken aback by the commotion. There was so much to absorb. Not only was this his first time seeing his insurance man partner in action in his new persona as man of God, but the energy in the Pentecostal faith tradition was new and overwhelming to the sometime Catholic, Maldonado.

He had never been this close to such a boisterous and interactive worship experience. Rather than showing dismay or acting indifferent, he acclimated himself to the style of worship, mimicking some of the worship behaviors and mumbling along with some of the songs, particularly those songs that were made up of a few verses and that were repeated endlessly. The one thing, however, that Maldonado had a hard time concealing was his discomfort with how the service dragged on and on. He twitched in his pew on several occasions, and did the best he could to endure the monotony of the service. It consisted of a blend of traditional hymns, contemporary songs, a special time for words of testimony, a collection, a sermon, an altar call, a laying on of hands for the converts and the sick, a closing song and a quasi-benediction.

Without fail, there was another formality to the church experience. Immediately after the benediction the members greeted each other in a flurry of handshakes and affectionate hugs, with the men hugging only the men and the women hugging and kissing only the women. Little by little, worshippers broke off into cliques and headed to the church's social hall. The worshippers were treated there to the scent of fried fritters sold by the fundraising committee. There was a bargain table littered with devotional books, recorded sermons from popular crusade evangelists, vinyl records or soundtracks of Christian artists or bands, Bibles, and relics from the Holy Land. The items were sold by an outside vendor who gave the church a ten percent commission for each sale.

Maldonado walked around the room and took it all in with keen interest. He was perplexed by the overflow of commercial activities inside a sacred space. He did not know that fundraising and sales were allowed inside a church. He walked around the long room and observed enough to chalk the fundraising to the self-sustenance trait. It struck him that some of the fundraising volunteers were leaders in the church, and that they were selling items in an assertive manner, pressuring members to help the church make its budget. Maldonado viewed the behavior as a latent form of aggression, because whoever monopolizes an economic niche manipulates policy and human behavior.

After decoding the fundraising behavior, he sat in a corner. His eyes zeroed in on the cliques populating the large social hall. When he finally made up his mind to join a clique, he walked up to a group and introduced himself as the new sexton. He immediately made an impression with his charm. After getting a feel for a clique, he darted to another group to listen to what they were saying. Some conversations, he thought, were strange and trivial, focusing on who sported an untamed mustache and who wore skirts that hovered above the knee and fell short of the standards of holy living. Other conversations were divisive and degrading, and it was these conversations that interested him the most. They engendered feelings of self-righteous indignation against Santana's struggling ministry, even touching upon his family.

There was one clique in particular, where the members were so close that they vacationed and ate Sunday brunch together. One person in that group said, "I am here because of the music and not the pastor."

Another person from that same group said, "We can't get young families to come and join."

And it seemed that as each person in that group spoke, the comments got worse and worse.

"The pastor's wife was not in worship today. I think this is the fourth Sunday in a row she hasn't come."

Then a man, with flattened wavy-hair, fox-like eyes, a neatly shaved mustache, and trimmed sideburns above his temples, waded into the conversation. He removed his brown hands from his long-sleeve, white *guayabera* pockets, and started to talk with overbrimming zeal.

The man, known as *Chico,* felt that he needed to prosecute Santana on behalf of God.

Chico said, "The Spirit has left this church. Without the Spirit we are not going to have souls saved or join the church, for the Spirit brings about conviction. Without the Spirit there is nothing but decay and death."

The members of the clique looked at each other in fear. They did not want their beloved church to close down.

Chico continued, "Things are going bad, and they are going to get worse. There is a grave sin being covered up in the church. We must expose and uproot that sin. And it all starts with Santana. He is the head, and as the head goes, so goes the body."

A member of Chico's clique, Jimenez, groaned. He affirmed Chico's comments by saying, "Amen to that! God is holy! Judgment must come!"

The conversation took a sharper turn when Chico bared his hand and made a chopping gesture, as if to suggest that a sword of judgment was going to cut through the air.

The clique's hostility and Chico's theatrics made Maldonado smile. He delighted in the spite shown toward Santana. Maldonado said his goodbyes and withdrew to his room. His main interest was in exploring how to further inflame Chico's clique to battle against the pastor. He knew that he could use Chico's clique as a proxy to exact his revenge.

Chapter Twenty-Eight

Church Personalities

MALDONADO WAS BARELY BACK in his tiny bedroom when he heard screeching brakes, followed by the sound of a rickety, sliding door. He wondered what those noises were all about. He looked outside his frosty window and saw a crowd of silver-haired worshippers lining-up to board one of the congregation's two church vans. From his vantage point, most of the members appeared to be very happy, particularly those who bought something at the fundraising table. But there were a few with slumped shoulders and strained faces, bound to return to their homes bearing nothing except the promise of better things to come.

The vans took off, one at a time. Maldonado set his eyes toward the vans until they were out of his sight. The departure created a mixture of relief and fear. He felt good about being alone to do his reflective journaling, but he was worried about being alone in an unfamiliar, three-story, armory-style building. Worries aside, he retrieved his rosary from his pants, and wrapped the rosary around the newly purchased figurine of Saint Lazarus, which he bought at the Botánica. The figurine sat on an antique bureau. It was surrounded by framed photos of his deceased parents, which he carried in his briefcase. He planted a kiss on the figurine, and then grabbed an incense stick and a bottle of shaman water, "*Agua de Florida*," from the shopping bag from the Botánica. He lit the incense stick and sprinkled the shaman water on the floor and walls; Petra taught him that this would purge a room of bad omens and bring him good fortune.

He turned on a table lamp and muttered a few words beneath his breath. He put on a layer of clothes before making himself comfortable on his cot. Moments later, he started to reflect on his first-ever, non-Catholic worship experience. The constant standing up and sitting down, and the frenetic raising of hands and rapid-fire clapping, seemed to him like spiritual aerobics; the esoteric language jabbered by some of the congregants sounded to him like pig Latin. The spontaneous responses, "Hallelujah!,"

"Praise the Lord!" and "He Lives!" felt to him like he was at a noisy pep rally. The worship service was poorly attended. He couldn't understand why in spite of the low attendance the few worshippers there continued to show affection and enthusiasm for their faith.

Maldonado was perplexed by other things, including the sanctuary layout. He wondered why the church was not filled with aesthetic and sacred images, while the sanctuary was stripped of all religious iconography.

He opened his journal and started to write his impressions.

Journal entry: "Concrete signs of the divine are absent, and without these signs, how can the mind transcend the temporal and dwell in the heavenly realm? How can the worshippers insist that simplicity is the way to bliss, making it possible to feel one step away from heaven?"

He did not spend enough time with those questions. There were other observations he wanted to jot down before they escaped him.

Journal entry: "I expected to see a communion table with the elements on display to make the ineffable presence of God tangible and accessible. I searched for a cross of any shape or form. None was on display to convey the Christian universal symbol of redemption. I don't understand why there aren't lit candles to create a sense of mystery and peacefulness."

Most shocking to him was the absence of statues and religious paintings. And finally, he noted, the sanctuary floor was covered with a stained rug that smelled like sulfur.

He was repulsed by the smell and unimpressed by the layout. He therefore asked himself a two-part question:

"What kind of God would call this home, and what kind of worshipper would consider this home fit for a God?"

He noticed other curiosities. He could not understand why the congregants referred to each other as brother or sister; why the men and women sat in opposite aisles as part of a piety code designed to curtail carnal passions; why the men and women adhered to a decorum that prohibited the women from cutting their hair and wearing make-up and the men and women from wearing jewelry, except their wedding band; and why the congregants attended church so often. The congregation held evening services on Tuesdays, Thursdays, Fridays and Saturdays. Additionally, they held a Sunday morning service and an evening service. On special occasions, the congregation held a revival meeting known as a *campaña*, where a motivational speaker or evangelist with healing and exorcism gifts of the Spirit was the keynote speaker. A *campaña* was sometimes a celebration of a milestone event, such as an anniversary, or a themed-rally held by one of the church's groups, such as the women's guild, the youth fellowship group or the men's society. It took place at either a home church, a host church, *or* a rented public space, such as a theater or park.

Alone in his room, Maldonado spent hours recalling and writing down his impressions in a section that followed his experience at the halfway house, *Healing Hearts*. His writing was informed by the information Daisy shared with him whenever Santana was not in the building. She helped him develop a quicker and deeper understanding of the ethos of the church. It was Daisy who helped him realize that a church community is a world unto itself.

In less than 30-days, Maldonado's entries shifted from the worship style to the eclectic and colorful personalities at the church. Some of the personalities amused him, while others intrigued him. The more he got to know the people at the church, some peripherally from his observations and others more intimately from his interactions, the more he realized they were all craving recognition and searching for higher-ground.

Entry one: The church has a frustrated preacher, Marcos Ayala, the meat cutter at *Felix's Fine Foods*. Marcos spent his work hours dreaming of becoming a full-time preacher. He hated his mundane job, and felt that it was getting in the way of his true vocation. He was a student at a three-year, adult Bible institute. His favorite class was homiletics, which taught him the basics of preaching. During his 15-minute work breaks, he would lean on a meat display refrigerator and write sermon talking-points on meat wrapping paper. He would retrieve his notes from his shirt pocket the day he was scheduled to give a sermon at his preaching course or the day he was scheduled to give a sermon at his church as the guest preacher. There were times he was not pegged to be the guest preacher at his church, but he managed to sneak in a sermonette, an abbreviated sermon, during a built-in slot geared to encourage lay participation known as special announcements or testimony time.

Few would complain about Marcos's 15-minute sermonette. They were filled with juicy, gossipy information and they were short in comparison to the pastor's one-hour, wrathful sermons. Marcos's sermonettes focused on either piety issues or ethical dos and don'ts. On one occasion, he preached about church customers he observed at his job. He criticized those who sampled grapes or berries at the fruit-stand without paying for them. He equated that behavior to stealing. On another occasion, he described church members who purchased staples on lay-away at his job or at Carlos's bodega, but somehow figured out how to string money together to buy trendy clothes at *Victoria's* and drive around in fancy cars.

But there were times when a sermonette, and these were the most effective, focused on a tragic event that was reported in *The Liberty Beacon*.

Marcos, who was a proficient English reader and speaker, would hold a copy of the paper and translate snippets of a story on the spot. The worshippers, many of whom did not speak or read English, listened in awe to Marcos's translation skills. Marcos always found a way to connect a sermonette and a news account to apocalyptic literature in the Bible. His goal was to underscore how horrific news events were signs that the rapture, Christ's return for the church, and the end of the world, were drawing near. At the conclusion of his sermonette, Marcos invariably drew a strong applause, some expressing relief that he finished, others feeding his ego; the latter were customers of his and, apparently, would ingratiate themselves for a better cut of meat or for an extra, free half-pound of cheese or cold cuts.

Entry two: The church has a bookkeeper, Charlie Mesa, and a bean counter, Jimenez. Charlie assigned pledge numbers to each donor, distributed the offering envelopes, prepared the weekly teller's sheets, made the bank deposits, and updated the church's budget on a sheet he gave to Jimenez, the church's treasurer. Mesa listed the donors in alphabetical order on a chart that he hung on the bulletin board of the narthex. Mesa's handwritten chart displayed a color-star next to each donor's name, indicating where each donor stood on a giving percentile. At the bottom of the chart, there was an index explaining what each colored-star represented. Only the top cash donors received a gold-star; there were few of those on the chart. Those who gave food-stamps as a tithe or an offering were not included on the chart to avoid embarrassing the donor.

Jimenez, the bean counter, opposed new projects that were not fundable over the long-haul. He looked for ways to trim or shutdown programs that were not well-attended, claiming that turning on the heat or lights for programs that did not support themselves placed the church at risk of depleting its savings in a few years. This could lead to the church's closing its doors permanently, and being sold to a developer, who in turn would convertthe church space into condominium apartments.

Entry three: The church historian and parliamentarian was Harry. He was the architect of the congregation's bylaws. He was elected the lead Elder of the church's governing board for the longest time; he was succeeded by Chico. Harry is no longer active on the church board, but he remains active in the politics of the church. He views himself as the sole authoritative interpreter of the church's rules. During fellowship time, he corners congregants and bends their ear with his expansive knowledge of the church's history and its inner-workings. He offers unsolicited analysis of the current board's decisions through the prism of his by-laws or his version of historical events. Sometimes Harry's analysis is complimentary, sometimes it isn't. When he criticizes the current board, it is because they collectively failed to follow one of his established rules, which he believes are set in stone. Harry's imagined proprietorship of the rules was so fixed that he opposed revision, even if an amendment was out of date.

At the annual congregational meeting, Harry put on his historian's hat and examined the church's current problems in the context of its history. In characteristic fashion, he would deliver a long-winded, anecdotal story about a pivotal event in the church prior to giving an opinion. Each story, which members suspected was a mixture of fact and fiction since the story changed every time he repeated it, would always place him as the eyewitness and first-source authority of a past event.

Entry four: The church has two volunteer bus drivers. They provide transportation to 40 percent of the members who are scattered across the city; the other 60 percent live in walking distance of the church. One of the bus drivers, Junior, was not happy with the bus route assigned to him by the church elders. He reminded the elders his route takes him through seedy neighborhoods. Even though he knew some of the players in the underworld from his former life, he feared for his safety because random shootings and gang rumbles were common. The van assigned to him was likely to leave him stranded. He is mechanically sound to tinker with the engine. He can get the van up and running, but in the process, he sometimes stained his clothes with oil and grease. He is still upset over the time he ruined his favorite tie trying to repair the engine. He pleaded with the pastor and elders to upgrade his van, but he knew this was not feasible. The church is hurting financially. His combined, two-hour route, was made more unpleasant by the passengers who acted like prigs and gossips, judging other people's spiritual flaws and moral shortcomings.

"My head wants to explode with all the non-edifying nonsense. I come to church with a heavy-spirit, upset at how they act one way in the van and another way in the church," Junior allegedly told Daisy once. *Ay, bendito.* Poor Junior. He arrives at the church service in a bad mood and leaves in a bad mood, annoyed over missing the early part of the service because people were not ready at pick-up and held back at departure time by the same people. These passengers lingered casually at the church after worship chatting it up with others or buying stuff at the fundraising table.

He seems to endure the volunteer job, according to Daisy, because it apparently makes him feel respected. There are times when his nerves are frayed, and he threatens to quit abruptly in the middle of his route, even if it means leaving the passengers stranded. Besides the van's unpredictable engine and the unrelenting gossip, what gets him most annoyed is when a scheduled pick-up declines to attend worship without having had the courtesy to alert him beforehand. Junior mimics the behavior of a no-show who stands behind his home's glass windows and gestures in a sweeping motion with his index finger that he is not going to worship. This gesture would make Junior say that a non worship attendee was, "turning on the no wipers to the Lord!" They are not saying no to me. They are saying no to the Lord."

He said, "The church's gas and my time have been wasted. When the final trumpet sounds, can you imagine a person saying, 'Lord, come back later, or come back tomorrow. I am not ready?' No wonder some of these people can't get ahead. They can't keep a commitment, and when they come to church, they are late to get back on the bus. They are not considerate of others."

Entry five: The church has a bachelor. It is Sammy, a middle-aged, pudgy man with below-average looks. He has the hard habit of latching on and trembling when giving a male counterpart a good church hug. Behind Sammy's back, the church prankster, Sergio, calls him "fruit gel" for the wobbly effects of his hugs. Sammy constantly asks for dating advice and prays incessantly for a bride. At the moment, he has no leads, though his fantasies make him think he has a chance. He has so much going on to make him suited for marriage. He is a mid-level manager at the local hardware store with a furnished apartment in the lower-level of his parent's brownstone. He drives a tricked-out pickup truck to work and a vintage Cadillac to church, and owns a vacation home on top of his parents' concrete retirement home in Puerto Rico. Whenever a single female convert joins the church, he is quick to offer information about the church's programs and is not shy about asking for a coffee date. He never gets far with his advances.

Entry six: Most of the single ladies channel their affection to the Miramar brothers. They are the two *mamitos (hotties)* of aisle five. One of the brothers, Alejandro, has an athletic physique from his intense exercise regimen. He has a pencil-thin mustache, long sideburns, and a scent of manly-man cologne. His stylish ducktail haircut he swoops backward obsessively with a comb. He is the heir apparent to the family's used appliance business. The other brother, Rafael, is an academically gifted college-student who wants to work as an accountant on Wall Street. Rafael wears three-piece suits, cuffed shirts, and buffed, blacks shoes with a wing-tip.

Entry seven: The church has fault-finders who are broken into archers and crusaders. Archers are members who deploy arrows from a moral high-ground. Crusaders are members who rail against everything that stands in their way and hinders their personal agendas. The archers and the crusaders share the common trait of focusing on the negative, of not doing anything and not allowing others to do anything either. They lambast the church secretary for missing punctuation marks in the church's newsletter; they oppose a novel idea for the simple reason that they didn't think of it or

because it threatens their status quo; they criticize a lay reader for botching
the pronunciation of a tough Biblical name or geographic place, and they
criticize the singer who sings off-key or the musician who hits the wrong
note as an accompanist.

Entry eight: The church has members who are energetic about their
religion. That energy is manifested in unabashed acts of proselytization;
these members are the evangelizers. The evangelizers coordinate revival
tent meetings, and give out the religious tracts ordered by Daisy, the church
secretary. The evangelizers preach their faith indiscriminately at work, the
barbershop, the assembly line, and the supermarket. The evangelizers feel
an uncontrollable urge to share how wonderful their church is, even though
it is currently mired in dissension and division. Some of the church evangelizers say to a prospective convert, "Jesus loves you," prior to handing off
a tract, or ask a willing ear, "Where are you planning to spend eternity?"
The evangelizers are apparently driven by an apocalyptic zeal, admonishing
a prospective convert that the rapture and the second return of Christ are
imminent. They proclaim the message, "Jesus is coming."

Entry nine: The church has traditionalists. Traditionalists are members who insist that there is a protocol for activities at the church and must
be carried out a certain way. The traditionalists are tethered to the church's
nostalgic past. It was a time when the church pews were teeming with worshippers, the endowment was growing strong, and the annual operating
budget finished in the black. Church programs were fresh and relevant. The
Achilles heel of this group, however, seems to be a blurred definition of what
is historical and what is old at the church. This shortcoming manifests in the
clutter problem in the church's crawl space. When I point it out, or remove
stuff to be thrown away, I get push back. The claim is that I am disrespecting
the memory of a deceased parishioner who donated an item to the church.

Entry ten: The church has a small, struggling fundraising committee.
The fundraisers are dedicated to finding creative ways to raise money for
the church, augmenting the plate collection. The fundraisers organize the
Sunday, post-worship, fried-fritter snacks, the dinners, the concerts, and
the bake sales. Daisy had told Maldonado that the quarterly church dinners
were popular, but were too labor intensive. The amount of work carried out
by the same people left the volunteers of the committee feeling drained and
demoralized because others didn't join and help out.

Entry eleven: There are dreamers at the church, or the Josephs, after
the biblical character, or the Josephines, a feminine version of the biblical
character. These are members who claim to have divine messages revealed
to them through the medium of a dream. Some of the dreamers dream while
they are awake, and their dreams are idealized wishes and wants of what

they individually conceive of as a better future. Other dreamers dream while they are asleep, and they individually dream dreams about future events in sensationalist and mysterious imagery. For example, one dreamer said during testimony time he dreamt about a human-sized, talking frog with six spikes, which was sitting in a church pew, changing colors. The dreamer went on to say the dream was about a person who blended into the church and misrepresented who he was. After he made that statement, people looked around and attempted to divine who was the frog in the church. To no avail. It could have been anyone.

All of the aforementioned personalities and many more permeate the fabric of the *House of Mercy* Pentecostal Church. Maldonado wanted to include other vignettes, but something curious took place. One Sunday evening, the church mouse dashed across the floor of his room and crawled under his bureau. Maldonado had heard the mouse in the recent past scratching behind the walls of his bedroom, but he had not seen it. He equated the appearance of the mouse with his grandfather who was giving him a message.

Maldonado spoke to the rodent.

"*Papá*, I promise to finish my doctoral degree. But I can't focus on that until I remove an obstacle from my mind. I have to avenge my loss. Otherwise, I will make a farce out of what you taught me," Maldonado said, who was thinking about the self-sustenance trait. Maldonado closed his journal, blew out the incense sticks and thought about the characteristics of church members and their behaviors. He concluded that everyone who attended, from the quiet one who sat in the back to the loud one who sat in the front of the church, represented togetherness and tolerance at the highest level.

"They are in this together. This is what makes a church a church. Otherwise, this place would be nothing more than a glorified version of an asylum," he said.

Chapter Twenty-Nine

Maldonado Joins Team Chico

ABOUT 30-DAYS INTO HIS sexton job, Maldonado became more comfortable with the people of the church, and, correspondingly, the people of the church became less anxious around him. He had been sitting quietly in the church pews, using his trained eyes to observe and pursue the right opportunity to exact his influence in the church without joining a committee. One Sunday, after the morning worship ended, Maldonado got up from where he was sitting in the fellowship hall and drifted over to Chico's clique. It was a pool of dissenters huddled in their usual spot, drinking coffee and bantering about what went wrong in worship. Maldonado wove his way into the circle of tightly compressed bodies and motioned with his hands that he needed to talk. The members stopped talking and gave way to Maldonado. In a calm demeanor, Maldonado spoke the church lingo.

With a smiling face, Maldonado said, "Brothers and sisters, may God bless you."

In unison, Chico's clique responded, "Amen!"

Maldonado placed his hand around Chico's shoulder, and used his free hand to motion calmly, as he floated a provocative idea. "I don't mean to trouble you all, but it would be interesting to know what would happen if the leading choir singers sat out and did not sing on Christmas Eve. Just imagine what would happen," Maldonado said.

Chico read between the lines and grinned. He savored the opportunity to unleash havoc on Santana by depleting the choir, ruining the Christmas Eve program, and placing the minister in an untenable situation. From Chico's perspective, there was nothing to deliberate and discuss; it was a straightforward, creative idea. In a fury, he volunteered the members of his clique to renege on their participation in the musical part of the Christmas Eve service.

Chico said, "Alright. Let us give in to this idea."

Maldonado slowly removed his hand from Chico's shoulder.

The members of Chico's clique, however, kept quiet. It is one thing to diss the pastor, some of them thought inwardly. It is another thing to sabotage a religious service. The Christmas Eve service meant so much to the people they cared for; it was one of the two times a year when their non-convert family members and friends attended church. The members of Chico's clique hoped the Christmas Eve service would somehow sway one of their non-convert guests to be moved and come forward during an altar call to join the Pentecostal faith on Christmas Eve, making the conversion experience the greatest gift ever.

Understandably, Maldonado's idea seemed utterly incomprehensible and irreverent, and the clique had no interest in assenting to it.

In fact, Gloria, who generally went along with everything Chico recommended, let out a gasp and made a dissenting remark.

"Eh? That is not of God."

"No way do I want any part of that."

Gloria's comments echoed those of one of the key members of Chico's clique.

Johnny Cruz, a middle-aged man, and Chico's closest friend, drew back his hands. He said he could not discredit the pastor by diminishing the Christmas Eve service. Too many others—innocent worshipers—would also suffer by being deprived of the joy.

"I agree with Gloria. This is foolish and borderline blasphemous. I don't know if I could forgive myself for doing this to our church. I don't think we should ruin an important service for the sake of making a point."

Johnny held a grudge against Santana since the day the minister mixed up his daughter's name with the name of the groom's former wife on the day of the wedding. The officiant's gaffe turned the wedding's joyous atmosphere into an uncomfortable mood. The discomfort level registered in the faces of the bride and groom as evidenced by the photos of the ceremony.

Jimenez jumped into the debate. He went over the numerous failed attempts to make Santana resign.

"We tried to get Santana to accept one of our guys as the associate pastor, but he declined. Our guy's uncertainty about taking the associate position didn't help. We tried a petition, but that backfired. People left the church in droves, and some who signed the petition remain among us but won't talk to us. We tried economic pressure by holding back our pledges and denying him a raise, but Santana stays on. This is the best idea we have heard, bar none. I know it is rude, but it is not sinful."

Johnny, Gloria and Rafael Miramar, another member of Chico's clique, said the proposal was too risky and against Biblical mandates. "The congregation is going to look around and find it convenient that the best singers who sat out are members of our clique. People will know what is going on. Who do we think we are kidding? We are going to ruin the Christmas Eve program, embarrass Santana and lose the congregation forever. Our friends in this place will turn their backs on us, more people are going to leave and bad public relations are going to put us in a deeper financial bind. We might as well resign ourselves to having to go to a new church, because this place will no longer be our home. We will have forfeited our right to be part of a trusting community. We have to be careful in the process of separating 'the chaff from the wheat' for then we compromise the wheat," Rafael said.

Chico did not like the way the discussion was turning. He thought Rafael was being weak-minded by appeasing the clique with his college-educated ideas and vocabulary. Chico dragged his foot sharply across the floor to demarcate a dividing line. He then said in a smug, pointed voice, "You must choose what side you are going to be on. Are you with me or with Santana? Are we or aren't we?"

Tension built up. Johnny sniped, quietly. Gloria followed Johnny. Rafael insisted on not hurting the weak at the church. Maldonado sensed that a conflict could unfold and, unintentionally, expose the scheme to other congregants mingling at the church fellowship hall. Maldonado placed his index finger over his lips and said in a soft whisper "peace."

Again, he repeated the word "peace," and added, "breathe in and out."

The momentary frenzy subsided. Calm was restored. The plan had been hastily conceived then rationally rejected.

"Good, my brothers and sister. We need to take it easy," Maldonado cautioned.

Maldonado, touting the fake professional credential of a lawyer, its social status and income making potential, was certain it would afford him immediate rank and influence. He didn't think people would appreciate and respect him as much had he said he was merely a research scholar. He told the clique he was a non-practicing attorney, working as a church sexton to reassess his next career move after years of handling combative, complex cases.

"The key to gaining an edge in a conflict is to stake a position and pursue that position with conviction. Going back and forth in an argument makes one look wishy-washy; it undercuts one's credibility. We are never going to bring a conflict to a resolution by placing a veneer of conviviality on a relationship that is aggrieved and estranged."

The group clung to Maldonado's words. Maldonado, sensing he was winning them over, offered his final arguments.

"If we pretend that nothing is wrong, we are always going to live with an inward split, condemning ourselves to living with a fractured community.

Acting namby-pamby is not the right way to live. Santana is responsible for the condition of this church and must be held accountable. Didn't Sophia make that point in her lesson last Sunday? She quoted the word of God when she said, 'No one can serve two masters. Either you will hate the one and love the other, or you will be devoted to the one and despise the other.'"

No one had ever heard a church janitor speak so eloquently and authoritatively about the ongoing controversy at the church.

Maldonado's power with words inspired a change of heart. Chico winked at Maldonado, thanking him for advising the group. Chico felt emboldened, knowing he had a new ally in Maldonado, an ally who possessed the power of the keys and the power of words to open and close doors at the church

"Thank you, counselor, for your fine words," Chico said.

Chico urged his group to hold the pastor liable.

He said, "Our commitment is to God and not man. We must stop enabling Santana. He needs to be held accountable for his failed ministry."

"Amen to that," said Gloria. One-by-one, the members of the clique made a commitment to support Chico's charge. Johnny, who like his son Eduardo "Eddie" Cruz, was impressed by people with titles, acquiesced. Johnny thought having a professional of Maldonado's rank in the clique was amazing. Johnny said in a fervent voice, "You are big-time! I cannot wait to tell my son, Eddie, about you. He wants to become a lawyer. He works as a guard at the library and goes to college. I would introduce you to him but he doesn't come to church. He doesn't think the church has anything to offer him. Well, that will change, thanks to you."

The mention of Eddie's name made Maldonado realize Johnny bore a striking resemblance to the security guard he met at the library.

To discourage a future meeting, Maldonado walked away from Johnny.

Rafael looked confused. He wasn't sure if the group could count on Maldonado's solidarity.

He asked Maldonado in a tone of defiance, "How do we know if you are sincere? How do we know you don't have an agenda? How do we know you are not playing both sides, a spy for Santana?"

"My goodness!" Maldonado said, at a loss for words but realizing that as a new member to an old group, he had a long way to go to prove himself totally trustworthy.

He, nonetheless, smiled. The self-sustenance theory made him realize that certainly the budding college student felt threatened. He very calmly said to Rafael, "I am giving you guys help, strategic advice pro bono. I have no financial incentive. I actually sign over three of my four monthly checks back to the church. It is with pleasure that I give you all a hand in saving your beloved church. Everything I do, I do for the love of bringing peace to the world through justice."

The members of the clique looked at Jimenez, who defended Maldonado's claim of giving generously to the church. Rafael apologized.

Maldonado accepted the apology with his signature power hand-shake, his hand on top of Rafael's. The handshake, however, didn't settle the percolating dislike that Rafael and Maldonado felt for each other. For Rafael, it was the first time he met someone at the church who was smarter than he. He resented that. For Maldonado, it meant displacing Rafael as the intellectual engine of Chico's clique. He relished that role. Maldonado knew from Daisy that Rafael impressed some at the church with his dandy attire, fancy verbiage, accounting skills and good looks. Maldonado was not impressed that Rafael was a student at a college that was known as a reme-dial school. Maldonado knew that he was going to eventually eclipse Rafael as the brains of the group by emphasizing his Ivy-league pedigree, ties to NYU and the military, and by dismantling Rafael's opinions with deductive reasoning.

Chico sensed that Rafael and Maldonado would not get along, but dismissed his assessment by reasoning that it was just a normal rivalry be-tween two talented and smart people who want to be right all the time. Without further hesitation, Chico removed a pen and a notebook from his mint-green *guayabera*. He started to tally the number of the members in the choir, counting off how many he knew he could easily influence to drop out of the Christmas Eve service. Chico knew he could count on the support of Sanchez, Gomez, Rivera, Rosario, his wife, and Martinez. Afterwards, Chico instructed his clique members in the choir to offer Al, the church's lead guitarist and choir director, lame excuses for backing out. He stressed how important it was for them to remain secretive about their plan of revolt.

"No one outside this group can know that we are acting in concert," Chico said of the clandestine plan.

Slowly, but surely, and one-by-one, the leading singers called the choral director and reneged on their commitment to sing. The defection panicked the choir director. He pleaded with his choir members to reconsider their decision. To no avail, he was brushed off and given weak excuses, ranging from having to clean the house and shop for a big meal to wanting to sit in the pews with visiting out-of-state family and friends to struggling with a lingering cold and not wanting to transfer germs to fellow choir members, thus sickening them.

Chapter Thirty

Santana IDs a Heartless Problem

RARE WAS THE OCCASION when Santana attended a weekly choir rehearsal. He only attended when he was invited by the choir director to listen to a new composition he had picked out, or whenever he wanted to sit quietly in a back pew and reminisce over a classical hymn. On a Thursday evening, the day the choir met to rehearse, Santana was using his secretary's phone and having a conversation with Andrea. He was trying to apologize for not meeting with her Sunday after he completed his rounds. He blamed an "extenuating pastoral situation," an oblique phrase he used to wiggle out of commitments, and one Andrea was tired of hearing.

She was upset with him, and he knew it. When he called and said, "God bless you," she did not respond with the standard, "Amen."

She did not reciprocate the blessing. She bluntly said to her pastor, "I was expecting you."

"I know, I know," Santana said.

Andrea didn't allow Santana's passivity to soften her sharp rebuke.

"For a moment, I thought the rapture came and that I was left behind," she said facetiously. "But when I ran into our church's paragon of holiness, Chico Rosario, at the newsstand the next day, I knew you simply didn't show up," Andrea said.

Santana chuckled at her biting sense of humor. She wasn't done.

"I am not playing. The least you could have done was to call and let me know you were not coming," Andrea said.

Santana, truly repentant, said, "My mother would have been ashamed of my poor manners. I am sorry for having you make all that food."

Andrea started to talk about something more significant than food. Food was the portal to Santana's soul; it was what she used to draw him in; to get him to relax around her table, so that she could show him motherly love, which she felt Carmelo and Hector, her deceased son, had taken for granted.

"It's not the food that I am worried about. It never goes to waste. Carmelo eats more than an earthworm, and you know I cook extra to share care-packages with my neighbors. What I am worried about lately is your inability to keep your word. You have done this three times in the last month. You can't go back on your word, because this bad habit will foster other undesirable behaviors. If I can't trust you, or depend on you, as my minister, what good is it? You can puff your mouth all you want from the pulpit with this promise or that promise, but there is going to be an unreadable question mark on your forehead. As you talk, people are going to be sitting in their pews and thinking quietly to themselves, 'you lie, you lie like the devil.' That is why the Bible says (James 5:12)," ' . . . but let your yea be yea; and your nay, nay; lest ye fall into condemnation.'"

Santana allowed her to sermonize, without any interruption, even though her message was rough to listen to and bitter to digest. He knew the old woman possessed an unshakable faith and offered a trustworthy friendship; her conversations with him never reached others' ears, and he knew, because nothing remotely close to what they discussed was ever repeated to him.

"You just gave me a well-deserved Pentecostal noogie," said Santana.

They both laughed, and talked another 30 minutes.

When they ended their phone conversation, Santana wanted to leave his office and listen to the choir working on the Christmas Eve service. He was struck by the small number of choir members in attendance, and by Al's underwhelming conducting style.

With the Christmas Eve service a few days away, Santana recognized that a weak performance by the choir would condemn him, metaphorically speaking, to the hands of the "Spanish Inquisition," an inside term he used with his wife and Andrea to describe the probing ways of his church board, led by Chico. Santana knew how vital the musical program was to stimulating an upbeat tempo, making the congregants more receptive to his sermon, and attracting new converts. He was not sure what caused the drop-off in numbers, and what led to the dispirited rehearsal. It was like a negative cloud over the sanctuary. Santana decided to sit quietly through the rehearsal, not wanting to become a distraction or reveal his concern with their performance. He knew that if he couldn't figure out the cause of the sober mood, Al would speak freely with him about it, even if it meant distressing Santana at the height of the stressful holiday season.

The rehearsal lasted into the late hours of the evening. When it concluded, Al thanked his choir and sent them off with a prayer and a hug. The choir members said their affectionate goodbyes, hugs and kisses, and exited the sanctuary crestfallen. Santana greeted each one of them, thanking them for their participation. He told them how much he looked forward to celebrating Christmas Eve with them. The choir members smiled, nodded and exited the building, but the negative mood remained in the sanctuary. Santana walked slowly toward Al, who placed a quilted cover over his digital piano and then placed his acoustic guitar in its case.

Santana sought Al out with a greeting.

"Great to see you, my brother."

Al spoke to Santana of the ongoing frustration of being unable to find his equipment where he left it. The microphone stands were scattered and lowered from their adult eye level. The amplifier cables were tangled up, and the amplifier wheeled away from his favorite spot. Al suspected the mess was created by the children who played in the sanctuary during fellowship time or the new janitor when he performed his vacuuming chores.

Santana said he would address the problem from the pulpit during announcement time, hoping this would put an end to it.

"Forget we had this conversation, pastor. I was just venting. We don't have enough kids as it is. To mention the kids tinkering with my stuff will upset the parents who will no longer bring their kids to church. Don't bother with the new janitor, either. I don't want to create a problem between you and him. The position doesn't pay well enough for the guy to quit over my complaint about my equipment. We have enough problems. We don't need to provoke a new one. This is annoying, but it could be God's way of having fun with me, wanting me to work a little more on my patience. I don't like it when things are out of my comfort level. I get angry. I feel disrespected. I expect to find the equipment exactly where I put it. But as my wife tells me, that will only happen if I live alone on a deserted island. As long I share a common space with a group of people, I have to accept that people will test boundaries. It's not like this irritant is going to affect my salvation," Al said.

Talk of feeling dishonored made Santana remember that Al's father died during the holiday season, and that their relationship was not a healthy one. Al always went through a blue phase on the anniversary of his father's passing. Santana was tender with him, telling him how blessed the congregation was to have a gifted musician lead them and how the kids really enjoyed his musical coaching.

"The kids are too important to me, and so are you. I don't want to add to your trials and tribulations. I don't want you to leave us," Al said.

Santana wanted to discuss another affair. He wanted Al to tell him why the choir was not at its full capacity.

"Exactly, what is going on?"

"Something didn't feel right, tonight."

Al opened up to Santana. He described his choir as disappointed and confused. They couldn't understand why some of their peers dropped out this week. Al said he may have made a mistake in telling them at the beginning of the rehearsal.

"There is never a perfect time to break news of this kind. I suspect some of them knew but wanted to hear it from me. The bottom line is that we lost some serious talent. I didn't have to explain that to the choir. They knew it. Some of the pieces we were practicing hinged on the abilities of my more gifted singers. Well, those plans have been scratched, and we have to revert to songs from past years. We are going to do less challenging, loftier pieces," Al said.

Santana asked, "But, why? Why did they resign so abruptly?"

"The excuses vary, pastor. But they are excuses. They don't want to do it. Some of them have a bad spirit. They sing well, but I have to constantly stroke their egos, picking songs that allow them to show off the range of their voices. It's not all of them, but a few make this job very tough. I would be remiss if I didn't point out that the ones who dropped out are connected to Chico one way or another, either through blood or a like-minded spirit."

Santana slumped his head, helplessly.

"Pastor, you are not the only one around here who knows how to pretend things are going well. I had to put on an act for my loyal choir members this evening, telling them, "Good job!" But you and I both know they sang off-key. I have my theories about an evil hand in all of this, but I have no solid evidence," Al said, making a subtle reference to Chico's sabotaging the service.

Al absorbed part of the blame, but insinuated that Chico should share in the blame.

"We are facing the possibility of an embarrassment and a fallout on Christmas Eve. I have myself to blame for not including the kids in the musical program. Kids always win over a crowd. It's too late to get them ready for Christmas Eve. I am going to learn a humiliating, painful lesson for trusting people associated with Chico. He is most likely the frog in the church that the dreamer dreamt about," Al said.

Santana had someone else in mind, but he was not going to reveal the identity of that person. He whispered, "Perhaps."

Al was one of the few loyal members Santana could count on for support. There was no doubt about it. Al, a certified public school teacher, had opportunities to lead a choir or musical group for pay on his spare time, but he chose to lead the choir for free. He felt indebted to the minister whom he publicly and lavishly praised for saving him from a drinking and gambling addiction, thus saving his marriage, family and career.

Al didn't want Santana to leave the church.

In a broken voice Al said, "It is my fault. I let you down. It's Chico's fault. He has let his faith down."

Santana was sad to see Al possessed by guilt. He gave Al three encouraging pats on the shoulder. He told Al that a *mea culpa* was not going to replace the missing choir members. Moreover, worrying about Chico's sphere of influence, whether justified or not, was not going to serve them and would displease God.

"No, Al, don't blame yourself. Guilt is destructive to one's self-esteem and self-worth. Don't blame others. That is divisive behavior, and it provides a copout for how we have contributed to the problem," Santana said.

To persuade Al, Santana knew he needed to anchor his argument in the sacred cannon. He quoted selective parts from two verses in the Bible, Romans 8:31 and Hebrews 11:6.

"' . . . If God is for us, who can be against us?' ' . . . Without faith, it is impossible to please God . . . '"

"We are going to fix this problem, together," Santana said.

"What do you mean?" Al asked, astounded by Santana's optimistic tone.

Santana started off by acknowledging he had been wrong for promulgating a policy that restricted Al's ability to buildup the choir's talent pool. Santana prohibited choir membership to inactive members, who didn't attend worship regularly and were dubbed "Cold Christians," and non-church members. Santana feared the Christmas Eve service would breed resentment among his loyal choir members, who would complain about members who only sang on special occasions in order to call attention to themselves when the church was filled to capacity. Secretly, though, Santana feared being embarrassed by a singer whom he didn't know too well and later discover the person was delinquent in church doctrine or lived a double life.

"Al, I am reversing my thinking and policy on this issue," Santana said.

Santana's change of direction stunned Al. He was both speechless and grateful, but feared the pastor was going to get flak for overturning a policy without the Chico-controlled board's approval. Al thought the pastor should reconsider his decision.

He asked Santana, "Why not wait until the holidays are over? You will have thought things through and have had a chance to share with the church board. I know God knows all, and you know best, but why the rush to change?"

Santana pondered the question carefully. The question recalled for him the words he read in Father Roberto's office. He said, "We don't have the luxury of not changing. Either we resolve the problem through action or we become the problem through inaction. The scandal of the Gospel is that God uses repentant sinners as vessels to create sacred, transformative experiences." These words helped Santana immensely.

Al said, "Pastor, I know it's you, but it doesn't sound like you. The words are coming from your mouth, but the message is coming from . . ."

"Gregory," Santana said.

"Who is Gregory?" Al inquired.

"A teacher, a servant of God," Santana said.

Santana, however, wasn't through pursuing other ideas. He returned to the subject of the Christmas Eve service. He instructed Al to come by his office the next day.

"The people on the list are going to be a blend of retired choir members, of inactive members and friends of the church. Some of them can sing a tune, some of them can't, but they have a good attitude and effort. The common denominator is that they are loyal to my ministry," Santana said.

Santana gave one more direction.

"Change the rehearsal venue to Andrea's house. She has a grand piano."

Al asked, "How about the guitar?"

"I suppose you can use one without it being hooked up to an amplifier. The neighbors wouldn't like that very much."

"Carry this out in a low-key manner. If you can, have the kids sing at the post-fellowship dinner, even if they sing the same songs we sang at the evening service. There are songs that are timeless and should be sung again and again."

Al was in disbelief. He said, "I have been praying for two years, waiting patiently for the day you would act decisively."

Santana smiled.

He said, "God does not need passive people in the pulpit."

Al and Santana offered a prayer for each other, and then headed their separate ways. Al went home. Santana went to his office. He called Andrea to share his plan, which she embraced, and he then called his predecessor, the Ol' Rev. Miguel Montes. Santana was going to plead with him to visit on Christmas Eve. Santana had tried in vain for the past two years to get the Rev. Montes to return to the congregation. But every time Montes was on the verge of agreeing to return, the Rev. Montes reminded himself of the personal vow he made not to return to the congregation until Santana was established as the succeeding senior pastor. Montes figured it would take the congregation minimally three years, without any direct or indirect contact with him, for Santana to be embraced as the sole, guiding voice of the church.

Santana knew the Rev. Montes' wife was an early sleeper, but the expediency of the moment made him take the chance of calling. He called twice. The first time he allowed the phone to ring seven times. After no one picked up, he persisted and called again. The Rev. Montes, who was emerging from the shower, picked up and was glad to hear Santana's voice.

"Look who it is," he said.

Santana did not waste any time with small talk.

"I need a favor. Don't worry. I am not going to ask for a loan or a sacrifice," he said.

"I need you to be our guest visitor on Christmas Eve. It is safe to return now."

Montes, a person who prided himself in keeping vows, responded, "I don't know. I made it clear from the pulpit that I did not want to be bothered with wedding requests, funeral services, counseling, and church events for three years."

Santana attempted to make the offer harder to resist.

"We will pay your roundtrip air flight."

"It's not about the money. I made a promise to the church, and I made it from the pulpit," the Rev. Montes said.

"Not every promise can be kept in the face of changing circumstances. You once told me that if I really needed you, you will be there."

"That is a promise, too. I need you. I need you more than ever. Our church family needs you more than ever," Santana said.

Montes grew silent. He wasn't sure if Santana was acting out of desperation or generosity.

"Give me a minute, or two," the Rev. Montes said. As he was still talking, his wife, awakened by the conversation, asked who was calling the house so late. He covered up the speaking end of the phone with his hand. Santana heard bits and pieces. The Rev. Montes finished his chat with his wife, and gave Santana a final decision.

"O.K. We will be there. But there is one condition," Montes said.

"What is it?" Santana asked.

"We are not going to preach that evening. We are on vacation," he said.

"That's fine. Thanks for being a blessing! I have one thing to ask of you both as well," Santana said.

"Keep your visit a secret from everyone in the United States, including your son," Santana said.

Montes assured Santana, "Pablo will not know. I promise."

Pablo was only attending church on special events and religious holidays. He had grown frustrated with the pressure applied by Chico's clique for him to succeed his father. The Rev. and Mrs. Montes knew Pablo had become disillusioned with religion. They did not pressure him to attend church. They knew he had endured enormous pressure as the son of a minister to behave a certain way and follow in his parents' vocation.

Santana was delighted by Montes' promise to keep the details of the visit quiet. The two reverends narrowed down the travel schedule, itinerary, and their roles at the Christmas Eve program. The evening would be well spent, but Santana did something else before he drove off to his home to tell his wife that they were going to be hosting a pastoral couple. Santana pulled out the fragrant holy oil from his pastoral pouch. He then went into the sanctuary to apply a smidgen of oil on the outside armrest of every pew. After he was done, he prayed this ritual would dissipate the oppressive, negative cloud over the church.

Chapter Thirty-One

Christmas Eve Miracle

ON A BRISK WEDNESDAY evening, worshippers poured quickly into the sanctuary, swelled the church pews and buzzed in anticipation of the annual Christmas Eve service. Santana, who was perched on the pulpit, prayed with his eyes wide open and was elated by the overall good mood of the congregation.

At about 7:05 p.m., Al started to play a gentle tune on his guitar to help the people settle in. The soft tune gradually shifted to an upbeat, uptempo tune. Santana rose from his chair, waved and smiled to the gathered crowd. He was suddenly overtaken by the spirit of the moment and his body spun freely and gracefully. The choreography impelled the congregation to rise, clap and stretch their hands above their heads. The whirlwind of energy swirling throughout the congregation prompted Al to summon his blended, ad hoc choir to come forward. They did. They processed to the sanctuary and stood in equal rows of two. As soon as the frenzy wound down, the choir led the congregation in interactive, folksy Christmas songs. The give-and-take singing went on for about 30 minutes.

If the service ended there, Santana would have accomplished his mission in creating a meaningful, inspirational service. But he wasn't done. After the singing concluded, he gave a meditation on the importance of making room in the human heart for the Christmas spirit to be born. He could have ended it there. But he wasn't done. He announced he had a special, thank-you gift for the church in the form of two mystery guests. The worshippers became quiet and looked around, hoping to identify who the mystery visitors were. But no one out of the ordinary stood out.

Santana looked at Carlos with a broad smile, and then nodded for Carlos to bring out the mystery guests. Carlos headed to the pastor's office to get the mystery guests; they had been listening to the service through a speaker in the office. Three minutes later, Santana stretched his hands toward the back of the church and said, "Praise be to God!" The congregation directed their gaze to the back. They were astonished. Norma let out a scream that sound like the cry of an alley cat. Her sister, Gloria, was equally surprised and exclaimed, "*Ay, Santo (*Oh, Holy One*).*" The mystery guests stood in the back. The congregation was in utter disbelief. They didn't expect to see the Rev. Miguel Montes and his wife, Olga.

The Monteses placed their arms around each other, walked down the center aisle, and stood next to Santana on the pulpit. Spontaneously, the congregation rose to their feet and welcomed the Monteses with a vibrant applause. Chico clapped weakly and looked over at Maldonado, who shrugged his shoulders. Maldonado didn't know who the Montes were, but he knew, by the reception of the congregation and the expression of joy in Santana's face, that Fortune had turned in Santana's favor. Chico's plan to disrupt the Christmas Eve service collapsed with a holy thud.

When the clapping faded, the Monteses motioned the congregants to take a seat. The couple thanked the congregation for an overwhelming reception. They looked at Santana and praised him for his goodwill and hospitality.

The magical, mystical evening held more surprises in store. The Reverend and Mrs. Montes took turns speaking, with Olga going first. She gave a sermonette on how the Christmas narrative is filled with the theme of surprises. She said the Virgin Mary had plans to marry Joseph but conceived through the work of the Spirit. The host of angels surprised the world order by first appearing and announcing the birth of Jesus to ordinary shepherds. Then, she personalized the narrative of Advent and Christmas by revealing she and her husband have had their lives rearranged by serendipity.

"God didn't give us permission to retire We are back in the ministry. When a blessing is in store for you, it will find you in the unlikeliest of places," she said in her gravelly voice, which earned her the nickname, "the voice of the trumpet."

Olga said she and her husband were co-pastoring for free at a small, mission-oriented church in their hometown of Cabo Rojo, Maldonado's hometown.

"One day, Miguel was fishing at a pier, and a man fishing behind him turned around and started to tell him his troubles. There was something in Miguel's persona that he found inviting, and there was something in Miguel's casual advice that helped him clear his thinking. The man figured out his problem, and, as a way of thanking Miguel, he invited us over for dinner to meet his family. During dessert time, he was surprised to learn that Miguel was a retired pastor. The surprised host told us he was leading a search for a pastor for about five years, and that his church couldn't attract serious candidates. It has 20 members, an unconventional meeting space, and a small amount of cash in its savings account. The church, however, has 40 kids who come regularly to a thriving Sunday school. The kids come from broken homes and from newly arrived Dominican families, some of whom arrive in makeshift boats and are destitute. Some of the unchurched local fisherman bring the Dominican families to us. Our goal is to run a weekday tutoring program, and give the kids free meals and free clothes on special holidays. At first, we didn't want to do this. We were content with our happy, retired lives. We were happy to lead the prayers one Sunday, then do pulpit supply another Sunday. One week became a second week, and a second week became a third week, and here we are, doing it full-time. The fascinating thing is we have more energy now than ever and couldn't be happier," Olga said.

When Olga finished, there was an instant outburst of praises. A few congregants spoke in tongues. The euphoria lasted a few minutes. Olga then gave the microphone to her husband. He very calmly said he was blessed to spend the happiest of all holidays with his extended church family. He cleared his throat and sang in his sublime tenor's voice, "O Holy Night." The congregation was mesmerized by his pious demeanor, sweet voice, and vocal evocation of the Nativity scene. The Rev. Montes had sung that same song as a soloist during the Christmas Eve service for 30 straight years. No one had ever measured up to singing "O Holy Night" after he retired. When he finished, he realized many were in tears.

Santana noticed too. He took the opportunity, while the emotions were tender and the congregants receptive, to make an altar call. It didn't take much persuasion on his part. When he asked, "is there someone among us who wants to give his life to Jesus Christ?" ten people came forward to the altar to join the church. Santana welcomed the ten and asked them to make a confession of faith by repeating after him the words found in Romans 10:9. That passage says, "If you declare with your mouth, 'Jesus is Lord,'" and believe in your heart that God raised him from the dead, you will be saved." After the public, collective confession was complete, Santana proclaimed to the new converts, "You are now saved!," and "You have been born again." The congregation applauded. It occurred to Santana to ask Montes to make a special collective prayer for the new converts. He then directed Carlos to take the new converts to a back room for a brief orientation. Carlos gathered the new converts' personal information. He then shared a possible date for their baptism at another church with a baptismal pool and gave them a free copy of the Bible. Finally, he registered them for a "speaking in tongues" conference.

Had Santana ended the service there, he would have had a victorious night. But he didn't. He had one more bold decision to make. He announced he was committing 50% of the Christmas Eve offering, which had not yet been collected, to the Montes' mission in Cabo Rojo. The Montes gave each other a hug. The congregation was delighted. Chico and Jimenez were ruffled. Maldonado was content with that. After all, he was from Cabo Rojo.

When the service ended, at least for one night hard feelings among the factions were softened. Santana's successful evening service made him popular with his congregation again, like the day he was installed as their new pastor. The worshippers filed into the fellowship hall to break bread and share stories during the annual Christmas Eve pork roast and pot luck dinner. Chico, unrepentant, did not attend. He gathered his clique and told them he did not want to hear anything about Santana's triumphant evening.

He said, "Santana survived the night with the Montes stunt. Someone must have tipped him off. Tonight is not the night to talk about what didn't go our way. Merry Christmas."

Chico walked away from his clique and out of the church. He headed into the cold, dark night to the spend Christmas Eve with his wife, Sonia, and younger son, René. Some members of Chico's clique did the same, while others joined the rest of the congregation in the post-worship roast pork, pot luck meal. It was a festive scene in the church hall. Santana could have ended his night there. But he didn't. He did one last thing. He encouraged Al to put together a group of musicians and singers (a *matutino*) and have them serenade a handful of parishioners who needed a bit of the Christmas spirit.

"Make your first stop at Chico's," Santana said to Al with a goofy smile. It was a recommendation Santana would come to regret.

Chapter Thirty-Two

Ratcheting Attacks

THERE WAS A MEASURABLE, tangible new attitude in the church. Inactive members were attending regularly, weekly donations were increasing, and people were readily volunteering to work around the church. The new attitude signaled a changing tide, not lost on Maldonado. He worried that his revenge was not going to materialize.

Three weeks into the new year, January of 1981, Maldonado could not contain his restlessness. He sat in a corner of the fellowship hall, tapped his foot rapidly, and looked attentively at Chico, apparently listening to his clique's post-worship analysis. Maldonado stopped meeting with the clique. The failed Christmas Eve's plan put him at odds with members of Chico's clique. Rafael, for example, mocked Maldonado, and derisively said to Daisy, "the sexton-lawyer couldn't even win a meter violation traffic case with his legal strategy." Rafael's remarks gained traction with members of the clique, who shunned Maldonado. Not Chico. He still kept Maldonado in high regard. Maldonado still had access to every door in the church. Chico and Maldonado had not discussed the Christmas Eve plans. Chico wanted to let Maldonado know he had prohibited Rafael from making blatantly disrespectful remarks about him. He suspected someone in his clique leaked details of the plans, and that Andrea, a well-known and influential Santana supporter, found out and preempted the clique's plan.

In the midst of the happy chatter in the fellowship hall, Carlos let out a piercing whistle. When he got everyone to hush, Carlos introduced one of the Christmas Eve converts as the new coordinator of the post-worship fellowship. The new coordinator was beaming with joy, and the congregation, with the exception of Chico's clique, showered the new volunteer with applause.

Maldonado was rankled. He looked at Chico, who seemed uncomfortable with the announcement. Maldonado gestured with his hands if they could talk. Chico nodded. They left the fellowship hall and returned to the sanctuary, thinking they were alone.

Maldonado shook Chico's hand and offered a blessing. He leaned against Chico and spoke bitter words, not wanting anyone to hear their conversation.

"It's a disgrace, but Santana has his hands on the oars, and we are splashing and thrashing. We must regain control before all is lost," Maldonado said.

The words did not stoke Chico's fears. He stood still, smiled nonchalantly, and shrugged off the concerns. "We go through this routine every year," Chico said.

Maldonado sneered and posed a question that struck a chord of anger. "Are you sure?"

Chico did not like being second-guessed. He became irritated.

"Trust me. I have been here 30 plus years and I know how it goes."

Chico claimed to have the ability to tag a person the moment he places his eyes on him.

"You know the guy wearing the floral shirt? He makes his profession of faith amidst sobs and tears, and makes huge promises to do this or that for the church. Within a month he leaves things he started in the air and goes back to the corner saloon to get drunk. You know the new fellowship coordinator Carlos introduced? She is running hot, but give her a few weeks, and she will get cold and drop out of sight till Easter. Let the conversion fever run its natural course, and then we go back to pressuring him to leave."

Maldonado liked most of what he heard. However, he didn't like the idea of stalling the attacks against Santana. He knew how to stir Chico's rage and encouraged him to change his mind.

"I think you should know Santana humiliated you on Christmas Eve," Maldonado said.

"Well, I don't look at it that way. We are a clique, a team. We were all humiliated," Chico said.

"No, I am not talking about the service. It's what he did after the service. He got a good laugh out of the crowd at your expense. I was in earshot when he sent Al to your house, to serenade you and give you a little of the "Christmas spirit," making you out to be anti-social for not spending time with the rest of us at the fellowship hall, and creating the perception you are the Ebenezer Scrooge of our church," Maldonado said.

Chico became enraged.

"I was pacing in the living room when Al showed up with his circus. I was fuming that Rev. Montes decided to accept Santana's invitation without letting me know they were returning. Our families were close, and I did a lot for him when he was our pastor. For him not to let me know he was coming to our area and not staying with us was wrong. Also, I was wondering if Pablo knew, and kept the information away from us. That was not a good situation if that was the case. Al's visit has created a strain with my neighbors. They are an elderly, white American couple, who have dinner and go to sleep early on Christmas Eve. Their kids come the next day from the suburbs to spend time with them. They weren't happy with the rowdiness. One of their kids spoke to me the next day and told me they will file a complaint with the cops if this happens again. I don't blame them for their threat. Those fools started singing on top of the stairs at the top of their lungs, banging a cowbell, shaking maracas. It was terrible! If Santana is behind this, I cannot let this go," Chico said.

Maldonado pretended to sympathize with Chico and asked him to sit down. They sat side-by-side on an empty pew. Maldonado turned to Chico and said, "Santana humiliated you. He was gloating about the whole Christmas Eve service. I can teach you how to push him out, without touching him."

"Oh?" Chico said.

Maldonado said, "You have to create a cell group made up of select members. Starting out with a select group will help you control the leaks and keep the clique motivated to battle Santana. Right now, I sense some of them are softening up. You have to meet once a week at a home, and only the cell members will know the location of each scheduled meeting. I will have Daisy help you create a schedule, and I will have her type out an outline with talking points for the one-hour, weekly discussion on a book of the Bible or one by a Christian author. You will lead the discussions. Within time, you will invite one guest at a time to join the meetings, and if we manage to influence one guest at a time through the power of ideas, we will expand our support and get rid of Santana. Cell groups are a safe and natural place to socialize new members into our way of thinking. People always get behind the regime in power."

Chico's eyes were opened to another novel way of getting rid of Santana. He thanked Maldonado, at least a thousand times, and took the opportunity to clear up some misunderstandings that lingered from the Christmas Eve service.

"I am not upset with you over Christmas Eve. I know it was not your fault. I suspect we have a rat or someone with loose lips in our group. I am trying to figure out who our Judas is. I talked to Raffy (Rafael's nickname) and ordered him to knock off his disrespectful remarks about you. I've got a son who is the same way. They get a little college education under their belt, and think they are wiser than King Solomon. These silver, gray streaks are

here for a reason. It means we have suffered a lot in life, and there is no better teacher than suffering. There is no book in the world that can substitute
for the wisdom of life's experiences," Chico said.

Maldonado was flattered. He extended his right hand and thanked
Chico.

"I don't always claim to be right, but I rarely make a mistake. Pundits
get things wrong too. There is nothing more to talk about," Maldonado said.

"That's right," Chico said.

Maldonado reached into his sport coat pocket and presented Chico
with a Senior Elder badge ribbon. Chico was elated by the gift. He immediately appended the ribbon on his *guayabera*. In turn, Chico told Maldonado
he was going to appoint him to oversee the kettle where some members of
his clique deposited their withheld church donations.

They rose from the pews and departed, but they were not alone, all
that time. Al had been praying quietly, and uncharacteristically kneeling
on a bench not too far from where Chico and Maldonado had their conversation. When Chico and Maldonado exited the sanctuary, Al searched
for Santana in the fellowship hall, but was told the pastor had just left to
do his rounds. He asked for Carlos, but was told he also left. Carlos headed
to the bodega to relieve his nephew, Javier, and his advisor, Carmelo, from
their morning shift. Al knew Sunday afternoons were slow at the bodega. He
drove to the bodega to tell Carlos everything he overheard at the clandestine
meeting between Chico and Maldonado.

Chapter Thirty-Three

Carlos and Chico Clash

CHICO PICKED MONDAY AS the day his group would meet to study a book penned by a Christian author, or one of the books of the Bible. Invariably, the one-hour discussion started with a time of group sharing, but ended with the group trashing the church and the pastor. In essence, the cell group became a launching pad for future planned attacks.

One day, mid-week, Chico was walking leisurely toward his car when he heard his name called from behind. When he turned around, he was happy to see it was Carlos, who was doing food deliveries. After a handshake and exchange of blessings, Carlos questioned Chico on the decision to create an exclusive, secretive cell group. That sort of behavior annoyed Carlos, because the group's motives was divisive.

Carlos asked, "What's this I hear that you started a new church fellowship group?"

Chico pushed back. He asked, "What's your angle?"

Carlos said, "Well, for starters, you did not discuss this with the pastor."

Chico grunted. "Wait a moment. The pastor does not pay my mortgage!"

"Yeah, but you are using church personnel and property to coordinate your program. You cannot have it both ways." The sharp comment was a reference to Chico using Daisy, the church secretary, during her regular business hours to order study guides and type up a meeting schedules.

Chico balked at the suggestion.

"Oh yes, I can. I drop a good chunk of change around here. I am one of the leading tithe givers. Just look at the chart. Plus, Daisy is a member of the cell and she does the coordinating during her off-time," Chico said, touting his silver-star status at the church.

"Chico, you know better. It's getting tense around here. The only way we can get along is if we are fair to each other and follow the rules. The only way to feel safe in any community is by building goodwill toward each other. You know the church activities must be approved by the pastor."

In a deliberate tone, Carlos quoted the Bible to tell Chico there could be adverse consequences for plotting to hurt and undermine Santana.

Carlos viewed Santana as the divinely appointed pastor from the moment Santana was anointed with oil at his installation service.

Carlos said, " . . . Who can lay a hand on the Lord's anointed and be guiltless? (1st Samuel 26:9)"

Chico flailed his hands in the air and walked away shaking his head.

He jauntily walked to his car, and once inside, took out his pocket notebook.

"This malcontent and his wife will not be invited to my cell group meetings," Chico grumbled.

"You wanna be difficult, Carlos? I am going to teach you a lesson. I am going to make you submit to my will the hard way."

And after he scratched Carlos' and his wife's names from the cell group list, Chico drove off to his home to tell his clique members by phone what Carlos said and to discourage them from shopping at Carlos's bodega.

Carlos checked-in with his gut. Something told him to call Santana. He walked over to the nearest pay-phone and dialed the church number.

Chapter Thirty-Four

Father Roberto's Good Sermon Material

THE CHURCH'S OFFICE PHONE buzzed with a persistent ring.

Ordinarily, Santana would ignore any phone call that trickled into the church's office, allowing the answering machine to record incoming messages. Santana had a phone of his own in his office drawer, but it was disconnected. The phone had been disconnected for months, and he was fine with that. He loathed being slowed down or distracted by unnecessary, long-winded telephone conversations. He knew from past personal experiences that if he fielded a phone call and held a rushed phone conversation he would be criticized for having bad phone manners. He surmised that the problems that could stem from that were not worth the risk of picking up the phone. But there was something about that phone call that was annoyingly different. It rang over and over again without going into the answering machine as it normally would after five rings. The answering machine's recording system had reached capacity because Daisy had forgotten to delete old messages. Santana did not know that. Bewildered by the caller's persistence, Santana gathered his personal phone from his drawer and connected it to discover who could possibly be calling him. He was glad he did so. The voice on the other end was from one of his favorite people. The messenger had a God-saving message to relay.

"Hello, may the Lord bless you," Santana said.

"Brother-pastor, it is me."

"I know it's you, Carlos. Who else calls me brother-pastor?"

Noticing that Carlos sounded like he was agitated, Santana asked, "Is everything alright?"

Carlos caught his breath and told the minister that he had an altercation with Chico, and that Chico had created a cell group of like-minded followers with the sole intent of creating more dissension in the church.

"It's all a ruse, brother-pastor. It's an abomination that they call what they are doing a prayer group or a Bible-study class, when I know for a fact that it isn't."

Carlos's message alarmed the pastor, but he did not want to let on.

"My Lord and savior, this is so tiresome," Santana said. "Have mercy!"

Carlos became perplexed. "Have mercy?!"

Carlos added: "Do something about it and then ask for mercy, brother-pastor."

"Preach against this behavior, or have them face disciplinary charges."

"You yourself said from the pulpit that 'in the last days many will be led astray.'"

That's not what Santana meant in his sermon when he shared that passage from the pulpit, but he gave Carlos credit for listening to his lesson and for revealing his foes' most recent scheme to undermine him. Carlos's revelation of the disturbing news made him feel like he was facing his own personal Armageddon.

"Well done, Carlos," Santana said.

"I know that I can always count on you," the minister added.

"Pastor, in fairness, Al was the one who uncovered this."

Santana gradually changed the topic. Carlos knew what the pastor was doing, and he went along with it. They discussed the weather, the bodega, their kids, their wives and their health. They ended their conversation exchanging spiritual blessings and vowing to staying more closely in touch.

Once Santana hung up, he unplugged the phone line, deposited the phone in its drawer, and drove to Father Roberto's rectory. He chanced the visit because it was dark enough outside for him to travel incognito. His biggest concern was getting to the church before the priest's secretary left the office for the day. He knew that if he got there she would be inclined to give him access to the priest's study and the books he was craving to peruse. There was something revelatory in the books that made him realize his perspective was changing. Whenever he needed an epiphany, he sought it in prayer. Whenever he needed to deflect a problem, he would perform house calls to escape. He discovered at Father Roberto's study that guidance, wisdom and comfort could be found in unconventional sources.

Santana entered the rectory and found the secretary preparing to leave for the day. She was wearing her winter coat, gloves and hat. She looked at him and told him the priest was not in. It did not matter. He was there for something other than just meeting with the priest. He started to talk, and before the words rolled off his tongue, she divined what he was going to ask.

"He is running a little late. I suspect he is delayed by rush-hour, New York City traffic. You can wait for the Father in his study."

Santana questioned, "New York City? He's got members there?"

She answered the question without telling Santana what exactly the priest was doing. She said, "Fr. Roberto has a far, wide reach. He is with a member doing ministry."

Ordinarily, the priest did not allow visitors in his office unless he was there since he had confidential files in his office. She ultimately commiserated with him and gave him permission to sit in the priest's study. Santana rewarded her kindness and trust with a kind word.

When she turned off her office lights and closed the door, Santana knew he was left all to himself to look through the books. He looked for *Regula Pastoralis*, but couldn't find it.

Santana passed his finger through the spine of the books and was captivated by the name of one of the authors, Teresa of Ávila. The name Teresa had emotional import for him. It was his mother's middle name. He pulled from the shelf Teresa's, *Interior Castle*, and randomly opened it. There was an asterisk next to a passage.

"It is absurd to think that we can enter Heaven without first entering our own souls-without getting to know ourselves . . . "

Then he flipped through the book, and found, "Let us look at our own shortcomings and leave other people's alone; for those who live carefully ordered lives are apt to be shocked at everything and we might well learn very important lessons from the person who shock us. Our outward comportment and behavior may be better than theirs, but this, though good, is not the most important thing: there is no reason why we should expect everyone else to travel by our own road, and we should not attempt to point them to a spiritual path when perhaps we do not know what it is."

Teresa's words echoed in Santana's mind and rattled his soul. He pondered their meaning.

Under his breath, Santana asked the Spirit for discernment.

"What are you trying to tell me, Lord?"

Santana's moment of introspection was interrupted by Father Roberto, who walked into his office drenched in sweat and holding eye glasses and two paddles. Father Roberto had played squash with Don Frankie at the alumni club where Brigid was a member.

"I would give you a hug right now, but I don't want to stink up your life," Father Roberto said.

"It already is," said Santana to himself, thinking about the short-lived success of the Christmas Eve service and Chico's new cell group.

Father Roberto placed his racquet ball bag against the bookstand.

"I will be with you in a second or so. I need to recharge," Father Roberto said.

He pulled a prescription pill-box organizer from the middle drawer of his desk. He popped one pill into his mouth and washed it down with a sip of water. Then he popped the other and washed it down as well.

Father Roberto smiled and said, "I need these to compartmentalize my life."

A perplexed Santana asked, "What are those for?"

Father Roberto nonchalantly responded, "One is a depression pill, and the other is a vitamin pill."

Santana made a face, expressing shock and disappointment that his spiritual hero depended on medical science and natural elements for his strength and well-being.

Father Roberto noticed Santana's reaction. To make sure he wasn't overreacting, he offered Santana the opportunity to try the pills, with no intention of giving them to him.

Father Roberto asked, "Do you want to have one?"

Santana said, "Nope. I don't need vitamins because the Lord is my strength, and I don't believe in taking hocus-pocus medication to make me happy, because I have the 'joy of salvation.'"

Santana implied that synthetic drugs fabricate happiness.

In the past, Roberto would ignore Santana's insolent comments, but he decided to give Santana a bit of his own medicine, knowing how much of a biblical literalist he was.

Father Roberto, visibly offended, asked, "Do you remember the biblical story of the blind man at the Pool of Siloam (John 9)?"

Santana nodded and said, "Yes, I know the story very well. I gave a sermon on that story not too long ago."

Father Roberto said, "It is interesting to note in the story how Jesus healed the man. Jesus healed other infirm people through the power of touch, the power of the spoken word. In this story, Jesus chose to heal the blind man by mixing saliva with dirt, making mud and placing the matter on the man's eyes. The healing properties of the matter created or recreated a new set of eyes. It was like getting a new pair of eyeglasses. As an aside, the ancient creation narrative says we were created from clay, dust."

Santana, who was excited to discuss the Word with the priest, interrupted and said, "It also says in the Bible we are going to return to dust."

Father Roberto smiled and said, "Amen to that, as they say in your tradition."

He added, "One of the enduring message of the Pool of Siloam story is that God uses the human element and the resources of the natural order to aid a person's health. The chemical properties used in medicine come from the natural world, and God is the catalyst of the natural world; and the temporal minds who facilitate our healing through innovation receive their insights from above, even though they may not know it or recognize it. To not use what God and nature place at our disposal for our well-being is to offend God and act unreasonably."

Father Roberto's words made Santana think about the insensitive things he said to his wife about the amount of medication she takes, insisting she show a little more faith in supernatural healing. He also dismissed her advice to take medication to help him regulate his fluctuating moods.

"There is a lot of good sermon material in what you just shared," Santana said.

Santana looked down and said, "God just opened my eyes. I need to apologize to Minerva. She has asked me to get medical help. I don't sleep well. I go from being too excited to being edgy around her and the kids. The other day, my daughter told me 'You are nice to everyone else because you get paid to be nice.' Those comments hurt, but they were truthful."

Father Roberto said, "I am glad I could be helpful."

He then asked Santana, "Can you help me out with what I asked you?"

Father Roberto had called Santana at his office and asked if Santana could join him at a press conference to condemn fellow Pentecostal pastors who were placing posters on utility poles near parochial schools and his parish hall. The posters promoted sensationalist preachers who were notorious for delivering scathing attacks against the Catholic Church, and encouraged church plants near a Catholic Church.

Santana said, "You must excuse me, but I can't go. I spoke to them about it and the universal feeling is, 'If there is a bar in every corner, why can't there be houses of worship near each other? Why does Father Roberto allow his people to post flyers advertising his parish's annual carnival on phone polls that are near our churches?' They strongly feel the carnival seduces people to have a drink, dance and backslide."

Father Roberto waved off Santana's remarks. He thought the arguments raised by Santana's counterparts were "ludicrous," and was sad Santana could not stand at his side. He didn't think Santana had a good enough reason not to join him. He only wanted Santana to join him in a public venue if Santana was able to bring himself to do it of his own volition.

"I guess Brigid will have to continue to pay Steve to remove the flyers," Father Roberto said.

Santana asked, "Our Steve?"

Father Roberto said, "Yes. Steve Rosario."

Santana guessed Father Roberto was disappointed with him. He realized that to help Father Roberto could bring him more problems. He excused himself and was headed out of the office.

"I am leaving," Santana said.

"Not, yet," Father Roberto said.

He gave Santana a book wrapped in green, candy-cane-themed, gift paper. He asked Santana to open the gift in private and read the dedication he wrote for him. The dedication included a verse that is attributed to Thomas Aquinas, "There is nothing on this earth more to be prized than true friendship."

Chapter Thirty-Five

Chasing Steve Away

ON A COLD WINTER morning in the city's retail district, a handful of *Victoria's* workers had just finished putting clothes hangers into Junior's truck. Luckily for Steve, two middle-aged men and two young women graciously gave up their personal break time to help Steve load the truck. Notably, the help coincided with that time in the semester when deadlines for exams and re-search papers were barreling down on him. Though the workers were not privy to the demands of college schedule, they understood that extra time for a student increased his study time and chances of earning higher grades. The workers wanted nothing more than for down-to-earth Steve to succeed and experience the kind of upward mobility that had been denied them by virtue of birth, race and socioeconomic class. The workers were impressed with Steve's respectable grade-point average, which they learned by reading his name on the dean's list notice in *The Liberty Beacon*.

Soon after Junior's departure, the workers' silence was replaced by ri-otous laughter at one of Steve's nutty comedy skits. Don Frankie, who was in the vicinity on a smoke break, sighed heavily in between puffs. He thought that the sound of cackling laughter was unprofessional. To break things up, he ordered his workers to return to the store. The way he gave the order offended everyone.

"Okay, back to work. I am not paying you guys to do charity," said Don Frankie.

The workers, with hanging heads and sagging spirits, silently returned into the store. Steve stood stiff, but he went with the flow. There was some-thing about Don Frankie's condescension that reminded him of his former college roommate. Don Frankie disliked Steve intensely and latched on to any trivial reason to justify his antipathy toward him.

Not too long ago, one of the store's workers secretly told Steve that Don Frankie had said that gathering recyclable materials for vagrants cheapens the image of the work environment. Steve ignored his alleged remarks. However, he did not dismiss out of hand the fact that they were Don Frankie's words, and that they were directed at him.

Neither the mood nor the timing of Don Frankie's smoke break was ideal, but life, as Steve saw it, presented him with an opportunity to address the facts. They were alone, and they could settle their tension for the sake of their mutual love for Brigid. Steve mustered the courage and turned to Don Frankie. "The truth is—" As soon as Steve started to talk, a voice interrupted the conversation. One of the store's workers returned to the dock holding two bloated bags of recyclable cans and bottles. Don Frankie outstretched his hands and, without muttering a word, the worker handed the bags off to Don Frankie. The worker regretted going back outside after being told to go inside.

Don Frankie asked the employee, "Do you work for Steve or for me?"

Five seconds went by before the worker answered. "You sign the checks, sir."

Don Frankie grunted at the response and said something vulgar under his breath. He placed the bags in Steve's pushcart.

"There you are. You are all set," said Don Frankie.

Steve sort of thanked him.

"Well, thank you very much. You are always so kind."

"Thank the boss for thinking of me, too," Steve said. "I am so touched by the boss's generosity and don't know how to thank her enough." Those remarks made the situation worse. Steve knew that any reference to Brigid as the boss irritated Don Frankie. He did it anyway, since he favored Brigid and loathed Don Frankie's self-promotion in the media.

Despite Don Frankie's disapproval of Steve's visits, he went by the store anyway because he knew he had the backing and favor of Brigid. That's all that mattered. Shortly after annoying Don Frankie, Steve turned his back and pushed his recyclables away. He walked in his usual gait. He was going to sell his scraps and then stop by *Dominican Joe's* for a breakfast burrito.

Don Frankie's pale cheeks burned with discomfort, and his green eyes bulged when Steve called Brigid "the boss." The next thing he did was to mutter something unpleasant and go inside the store.

"Why am I giving a nobody so much importance?" he asked himself. "This is absurd," he added.

After a few minutes, Don Frankie stopped trying to figure out why Steve bothered him so much. There was something more relevant. He wondered how to present a problem to his wife, and when it would be the easiest way and right time to do it. His only chance to address it was at work, since he and his wife had a mutual understanding never to discuss politics and business at their home. In the meantime, he went to great lengths to rehearse what he would say to her. He'd have to be like a skilled diplomat to even get the problems out on the table so they could be negotiated without destroying the marriage.

Everything stemmed from the fact that Brigid was passionate about her community and keeping it just as good for the new generations as it had been for her during her years growing up there. She was focusing on educational issues, believing that the path to betterment was through schooling and degrees. The schools were her passion. But she felt that Jersey City kids were being done a disservice educationally.

Nothing superseded Frankie's desire to know why she clung to the idea that standardized tests were a bad thing, and why she made public comments that bordered, in his judgment, on the outlandish and posed the potential to create a backlash on their business.

For years Brigid hypothesized that bullying experienced by misdiagnosed students was a major cause of high truancy rates. That belief caused her to advocate strongly against standardized exams given annually to the students in her district. One of her biggest beefs was that the exams did not reflect the day-to-day realities of the prototypical student, a flaw in the testing process that invariably led to student disengagement and poor performance. There was no way that Brigid was going to allow public appearances and political expediency to suppress her views. She publicly shared her strong opposition to standardized tests effectively at a recent board meeting, even reading a sample question that called for a prospective test-taker to gauge the distance between a marina and a destination site on a sailing trip.

"This is one of the many questions that aren't relatable and realistic. There aren't marinas or sailing tutorials in this city," Brigid said.

After getting no feedback from the audience, she added that, "the exams were unrelated to the students' experiences, completely arbitrary and a waste of everybody's time and money."

Brigid was not quoted in the paper, but someone in that meeting shared her remarks with her husband at a business function. He was not happy when he learned of his wife's opposition to standardized exams. He made his way into her office, gave her a kiss on the forehead, and addressed her as he always did, "*mamacita*."

Terms of endearment always raised Brigid's suspicion, even when they came from her sweet-talking husband. She was prescient about what he was doing. She asked her husband. "Are you still smoking?"

Don Frankie turned her question into an euphemism, playfully conflating his smoking-habit, which she worried about, with being "smoking hot," an immodest self-assessment of his good looks and sex appeal.

With a smirk, he said: "If you put it that way, I am still 'smoking'. I still look good for my age."

Brigid gasped at his wisecrack.

"Silly you," she said. "You know what I mean. You have to cut down on the cigarettes. They are not good for you."

Don Frankie stammered that it must be reasonable to think that there are other things in life that are equally damaging like mixing business with politics.

"You have to slow down on your activism," he told her.

Don Frankie wanted to sound diplomatic, but he came across as imperious. He pulled his chair closer to where Brigid was sitting, and he attempted to explain that her involvement in the standardized testing controversy was not in their best interest.

Brigid soured at his ignorance.

"Cut it out! You know that I am my own person," she said. "Besides, I am an advocate, and not an activist. I am a thinking person with a serious plan, and not just a reactionary loon mouthing off for publicity or looking for a meaningless fight."

Frankie's comments made her feel disrespected. She was irritated with him for his lack of support.

"Are you ashamed of what I stand for? Are your friends intimidated by an independent woman? Are your people resentful that a white person is trying to speak out on their behalf?"

Don Frankie was struck by how disappointed she was. He flashed a nervous smile, glanced sideways, and fumbled through pieces of fabric resting on her table. He was grasping for something material to soothe him, and to help him make a transition in his thinking. He needed a soft approach to convey a counter-argument.

"I know, dear. But you coddle the teachers and students too much. Look, when I arrived in this country there weren't all of these special programs that are expensive for the taxpayer."

"Expensive? There should not be a price tag on educating the future labor force," Brigid said.

Don Frankie leaned back and nimbly bit his lower lip, before brushing aside her argument.

"Honey, I don't think the taxpayer base agrees with that statement."

He leaned forward and gave her a copy of an enterprise story.

"The local paper [*The Liberty Beacon*] just did a series on this and the readers' feedback supports my point of view."

He turned away for a brief moment and then looked at her.

"I had to learn English and work hard to make it. That is the American way. Why change that formula for success?"

Brigid lurched toward him and grabbed his hands. Her hands were rough on the surface of his skin, but they passed on soothing energy.

She said, "these are different times."

She clutched his shaky hands and settled him down completely.

"Okay, *mamacita*. You know best. You always do."

Shortly after Don Frankie gave credit to Brigid for her wisdom and sensibility, an employee said to Brigid that a man named Maldonado left an envelope for her. The employee said the man, Maldonado, mentioned something about meeting her when her car was stuck in the snow and ice.

Maldonado wanted to make a professional connection with Brigid. He sensed that his church position could come to an end for lack of funding if Santana was fired. He was going to pitch himself to Brigid as a strong salesman and marketing professional. To prove his fashion chops, he wrote a proposal asking her to consider launching a new clothing line geared to the growing *shi shi* enclave in the city. He thought that a new line of women's and men's wool fleeces, and business cotton shirts and ties would attract the Madison Avenue and Wall Street types to her store. He even came up with a slogan for the new clothing items. It was: "*Victoria's*: Dress like a champion, feel like a winner."

The proposal had a cover memo that said, "*You are leaving a lot of money on the table by not catering to the needs of the Yuppies moving downtown. Just look at how they are snatching up brownstones and pouring serious money into refurbishing them. I know you have a heart for the underprivileged and bourgeoise crowd. While that is noble, that crowd is gradually disappearing—they are getting economically gentrified. Your store glass showcase gives you a natural exposure to the Yuppies, since they walk past your store on their way to and from work. You just need to offer something more in keeping with their upscale fashion taste. It may help if you change the colors of your mannequins and decorate the storefront's background walls with cheery, rainbow colors. I can help you keep your business and mother-in-law's legacy strong if you bring me on board as a consultant.*"

Brigid was not clueless about the changes in her neighborhood. There were bistros, gourmet coffee shops, and boutiques opening near her flagship store. She was working with Andrea to explore how to make her store appealing to the in-crowd without losing her commitment to selling affordable clothing items to her longstanding clients. She didn't get a chance to respond to Maldonado in person. She had some followup questions, but by the time she looked for him, he was gone.

Chapter Thirty-Six

A Dialectical Tension over a Stolen Car

ALONG HIS PATH TO the scrapyard, Steve felt burdened not so much by what he carried in the cart but by the weight of what he carried in his mind. He was trying to figure out why he was treated like a wretch by Don Frankie. In the middle of his thoughts, a car drove slowly past him. The car suddenly stopped, but the engine was left running. The driver tapped the horn, opened the window, and asked, "Amigo, do you need a lift?"

Steve lowered his head and was surprised to see that it was Maldonado. He was recently thinking about the scholar, wondering what had become of him. He accepted the ride.

"Sure. I am headed to the scrapyard," Steve said.

Maldonado nodded in approval.

"That's fine. I've got time on my hands," Maldonado said.

Steve smiled at Maldonado's relaxed mood. Steve quickly asked Maldonado to open the trunk, not wanting Maldonado to regret giving him a ride in the event his bags leaked.

"I don't want any gooey stuff to spread all over your back seat. I never know if people are careful when they set stuff aside for me," Steve said.

Maldonado agreed. He struggled to find the lever to unhook the trunk. Steve found it odd that Maldonado didn't know where the lever to his own car was located. Maldonado felt uncomfortable with Steve staring at him. He turned his face in the opposite direction and ran his hands under the steering wheel.

"Damn it. Where are you?" Maldonado asked. He could not figure out how to unlock his trunk. He finally decided to turn off the car and give Steve his keys.

"Here," Maldonado said. "It's one of these three keys."

Steve went to the rear of the car and managed to pop the hood open. He was surprised to see that the suitcase that once occupied the back seat was now in the trunk of the car. Very discreetly, Steve unzipped the suitcase and scrounged through it. He was stunned to see that the suitcase held women's undergarment and that the owner's tag had a feminine name. He didn't know what to think about that. He didn't say a word. He deposited his bag and closed the trunk. He grabbed a chain from inside his cart and fastened his push cart to a utility pole.

He took a seat on the passenger side, returned Maldonado's keys, and gave prompt, clear directions.

Two long city blocks into their ride, Steve made the attempt to change the radio dial from a classical to a contemporary station.

Maldonado found that behavior pushy.

"What are you doing?" asked Maldonado.

It didn't cross Steve's mind that he was doing something inappropriate. He thought the ride would be more enjoyable if they heard something more upbeat.

"I don't like to listen to dead people's music. You know. The stuff they play at funerals. That kind of music can be depressing at times," Steve said.

Maldonado didn't like Steve's characterization of classical music.

"This music is not a fad. It has endured throughout the ages. It has enlightened civilizations. Personally speaking, it transports me to a peaceful place," Maldonado said. "Just sit back and appreciate it. This is . . . "

"Bach in Cello. He's got that distinctive sound," said Steve in a rapid-fire response.

"Yes, that is Bach in D Minor," Maldonado said. "I am impressed. You've got a good ear."

"Scholar, I pick up on everything. I just wanted something uptempo to inspire me. Inspiration comes from many sources," Steve said.

Maldonado felt his music was inspirational. But he didn't want to debate that point with Steve. He needed a personal favor. He acted congenially.

"Very good. You make an insightful point," Maldonado said.

Maldonado quickly changed the subject.

"I need a personal favor," Maldonado said.

"Shoot. Be direct," Steve said.

Maldonado spoke in a worried voice.

"This car was given to me as payment for a bad loan. I took it, but I am having second thoughts about that decision," Maldonado said.

Steve couldn't figure out Maldonado's source of internal conflict.

"Did they give you a lemon? Does the car burn through gas?"

Maldonado noted that the car was reliable and good on his wallet.

"No. The car runs smoothly. It is very economical," Maldonado said.

Steve was getting frustrated with Maldonado's cryptic language and mind games.

"So, what is the problem? Why do you talk in riddles? Get to the point."

Maldonado said, "I am having a premonition. I am just not sure that this car actually belongs to the guy who gave it to me."

Steve read between the lines.

"What? Am I in a stolen car?! Are you bugging?"

"Don't panic. Don't exaggerate! Nothing has happened, friend," Maldonado said.

"Don't panic!? I can lose my scholarship money if I am involved in a felony. Let me out, man!" Steve protested.

Steve insisted that Maldonado pull over and drop him off.

Maldonado grabbed Steve by the forearm and said, "You said when I met you that your generosity is limitless for the right price."

"Yeah, something like that," Steve said.

"I will give a sizable commission if you help me get rid of this car. How can you help me?"

Steve sat in an erect posture and started to run options, demonstrating his knowledge of the underworld.

"Hmmm. If this were summertime, you could leave the car running with the windows down and a curious kid or two would take it for a joy ride. After they were done cruising, they would remove the plates and dump the car off the piers and into the river. But it is not summer."

Maldonado didn't like that idea.

"Even if it were, that is too risky," Maldonado said.

Steve shared another idea.

"I hear you," Steve said. "There is a second option, but it is more expensive," Steve said.

Maldonado's body twitched when he heard the word expensive.

"There is this guy named Carmelo. For the right price, he can get this car to a chop shop at an unknown location," Steve said.

"What is a chop shop?" Maldonado asked.

Steve explained that it is a garage where mechanics illegally dismantle stolen cars.

"The car is dismantled and its parts car are then sold to a local junk-yard. The best part of this operation is the engine's serial number is grounded off. The connection to its registered owner and to you will be gone permanently," Steve said.

"That sounds great!" Maldonado said, as he rubbed his goatee.

"How can I get a hold of Carmelo?"

Steve said, "You don't! That's my job."

"When I see cash in hand, I will call him," Steve said.

"Wait. We're here," Steve said, making reference to the entrance to the scrap yard.

Steve retrieved his bag from the trunk and thanked Maldonado. He departed with his bags and parting words.

"When you're ready, let me know," Steve said. "You know where to find me."

Maldonado grappled with the question of what to do with the car. He wondered why people carried things with them in life that were just not that easy to get rid of. After giving his dilemma some thought, he decided to keep the car. He said he would repent the theft at a more convenient time and restore the moral balance that had been eluding him.

About 45 minutes after Steve left the scrapyard with the money from his profit, he headed to *Dominican Joe's* for a burrito. He was, however, stumped to see *Dominican Joe's* food truck surrounded by police cars. Steve approached a police officer he knew and asked what was going on. The officer spoke with Steve off the record. He said that an employee at *Felix's Fine Foods* snuck out frozen meats from the freezer and sold them to Joe. The stolen frozen food was placed in garbage bags and passed off as trash. The bags were then allegedly picked up by Dominican Joe. Steve was saddened by the officer's account. He could not imagine Joe guilty of the alleged crime. After his conversation with the police, Steve knew it was time for him to touch base with Walker, his counselor. He was eager to see her anyway. He wanted to confirm a rumor.

Chapter Thirty-Seven

Confirming a Rumor

It was a dreary February morning when Steve arrived at Walker's office. He was surprised to find the forest green walls nearly stripped bare. The only artwork on display was a prized painting of Charleston, South Carolina's Angel Oak Tree; Walker won a first-place ribbon when she was 12 at a local county fair. The ribbon, though faded, was attached to the lower corner of the painting's frame. Walker's artwork, paintings and photos captured fond memories of her Southern upbringing, and were tucked away in a bunch of unsealed, labeled boxes scattered throughout her office. Walker's artwork covered the Rainbow Row, Folly Beach, Fort Sumter, and South Carolina State College from which her late father graduated. Her artwork was the only hobby she had outside her study of the Bible.

Steve felt an ineluctable void when he saw the nearly naked walls. He had heard conflicting rumors that Walker was leaving her office. One person told him she was getting a nicer office at the new building off-campus. Another told him she was leaving her full-time job to become a doctoral student in Old Testament studies. The removal of the artwork suggested there was validity to the rumor. He wanted clarity and confirmation.

Steve walked into Walker's office, collapsed on a chair, and circled the entire room with his eyes. He looked straight at the naturalistic painting of the Angel Oak Tree.

Steve asked Walker, "Are you leaving us for real, real?"

Walker dreaded the question. She stared at Steve with helpless eyes. Her silence answered the question.

Steve pressed his hands over his face. It became clear Walker was not changing office space, as he had hoped, but was leaving her job. He spoke, as best as he could, through his wedged hands, which masked his face. But a mask, whether made of flesh or anything else, can never hide true feelings.

Steve was sad. He asked, "So, are you leaving right away?"

Walker paused and then said, "Today is my last day."

Steve was disappointed. He protested, "But you never told me! I can't believe it! I thought you and I had a special bond, something special going. How can I trust?"

Walker, very calmly, grabbed a chair. She responded, "It happened so quickly. I was accepted at a program recently, and I decided to leave my position here at the college to settle some personal things. I registered the other day to start language intensive courses in the spring and summer as a bridge to my work in the fall. The department sent you a letter, informing you of my resignation and sharing the name of your new counselor, but the letters kept getting returned. It had something to do with an undeliverable address."

Steve acknowledged he had ignored the dean's advice to find a permanent legal residence.

"I am still working on it."

Walker was not happy with Steve's *laissez-faire* attitude toward important matters.

"You have been working on it a bit too long. You shouldn't have a phantom address."

She stepped back for a moment and reflected on the arc of their counseling journey. She recounted how Steve's playfulness and wild stories made her laugh during tough moments; how biblical discussions strengthened the fabric of their relationship and helped her understand her true passion and calling; how his intellectual potential was unleashed and how his new found academic confidence emboldened him to take more challenging classes; how kind and thoughtful he was to her and others; how much he wanted for things to be right with a father who had deeply wounded him; how much he loved her home-made pralines; how his fascination with her Southern artwork always took her to a good place, and how much he had grown in depth during their time together.

Walker was struck by something else. She said, "It's hard to gauge in this kind of work whether you are being effective as a counselor. Sometimes people don't experience a breakthrough right away, so it's hard to tell if I am getting through and helping a client. I worry about that because I care. Counseling is really hard work. It requires the patience and dedication of a farmer. You prepare the land, plant a seed, nourish the seed, and if the conditions are right, it takes root and blooms. Sometimes years go by before I see the fruit of my labor, a thank-you phone call or a letter from a former student, sharing how he is thriving. You, young man, have been the exception. I have been blessed to witness your growth in our brief time together. Your friendship has been invaluable to me."

Tears leaked from Steve's eyes, streamed down his face and moistened his beard. It was the first time she called him a friend.

Walker held his hand. She asked him not to cry.

Steve said the tears represent a mixture of sadness and gratitude.

He said, "You have saved my life. I thought about dropping out of college so many times and other terrible things. All I want to say is thank you."

Knowing how precious, but limited their time together was, he asked for one last counseling session.

"There are a few things that have carried over from our last meeting. Can I get one more counseling session in? You can me send the invoice to my address—wink, wink."

She laughed at his silliness.

"Of course we can talk. I will send the bill to your fake address. On a serious note, what is on your mind? Where would you like to begin?"

"I can imagine my father's saga has you dizzy, but I think I figured something out," Steve said.

"What? Tell me," Walker said.

Steve resumed his conversation. He said he realized why his father, Chico, attempted to efface his identity and favored his fair-skinned brother over him, and why his mother was incapable of standing up for him.

"Chico would try to straighten my spiraled hair by applying oils and brushing it forcefully with a wired brush; there were times he scraped my scalp. He didn't want my hair to appear like a 'bramble bush.' My younger brother has northern European hair. Chico proudly took my brother everywhere and boasted how he truly 'looked like an American,'" Steve said.

"My mother, she just sat quietly in a living-room chair and did not say a word. Not a peep, to protest my father's abuse. I figured out she was simply burnt out by my father's abuse. She lacked the self-esteem to stand up for herself because of the bad things that happened to her as a child. She certainly could not stand up for me. My father, he is a lost case. He has always been ashamed of who he is and what he looks like. I look like him. Consequently, he projects, that's the word you used, his dislike for himself onto me. I am dealing with an irreversible, enduring problem. We all have a cross to bear. I have resigned myself to tolerating my family, but I can't figure out how to undo a bad relationship, without getting personal. I haven't been able to resolve the friendship dilemma; how to pick a good one, how to get rid of a bad one. I am talking about the Eddie situation."

Walker asked if she could opine. "Can I offer my two cents on the Eddie issue?"

Steve nodded and encouraged her to talk.

Walker was very frank. She said, "It is helpful if you learn to take a forensic approach to discerning people's motives. This will protect you from placing a person on a pedestal and making a person feel superior to you.

That gives the impression you are allowing yourself to become subservient to another person's needs. Your needs matter too in a relationship. Your needs are as important as the other person's. As my grandma used to say, you can only buy a pair of shoes if they both match and fit. You can only enter a partnering relationship with someone if there is a match and fit."

Steve was intrigued and interested.

"Tell me more. How do I use the 'forensic approach'?"

Walker said, "One way of doing that is by looking at a person's global history, since it is odd for a person to deviate from his behavioral norm. A person may swear he is a new person, but don't let yourself get caught up in theatrical stunts and magical words. A person can never omit history and reverse genetics. He who claims to change is being transformed within the context of his own nature. We are who we are. If you take a forensic approach you will become more alert in dealing with people who operate below the surface. Many more Eddies will appear in your life, all with different names, ages, and incarnations. It doesn't mean that you will reject future Eddies. It means you will be better equipped to uncover their agenda, and protect yourself from getting lured into a dysfunctional trap or hurtful pattern."

Steve paused and stroked his beard.

"How do you know when it is the right time to move on? To pick a new friend?" he asked.

Walker said, "You have to pick the right person."

Steve asked, "How do you know who is the right person?"

"The right person overcomes anybody else. He overcomes generalizations, and we all have them. He overcomes class consciousness, nobody is better than nobody; overcomes materialism, buying stuff doesn't produce lasting happiness and satisfaction. You will know the right person because the chemistry will be right, and this is a subjective experience. But you will know. When you find the right person, don't be afraid to move in a new direction."

Steve let out a soft sigh. He knew how wise she was. He didn't want her to leave. He started to toss around some flattering comments.

"So, if I can ask, why are you leaving this gig to do a Ph.D? You really don't need to do a Ph.D. You are the doctor of doctors, the master of words, the motivator of motivators, even better than Oprah, and you know Oprah is my girl."

Walker thanked him, and reminded him he didn't have to praise her to know how much she was esteemed by him. She told him her decision to leave was a matter of practicality, timing and calling.

"Some of us need pieces of paper to prove how smart we are. If not, all kinds of excuses will be raised to hold us back. On a personal level, the youngest of my two children just graduated from college. Now it's my time to follow my dreams. I am going to become an Anglican priest and pursue a doctoral degree in biblical studies, specializing in the Old Testament, at Union Theological Seminary in New York," she said with a profound sense of pride.

Steve looked confused. He asked, "Why an Episcopalian, and not a Southern Baptist? Why are you studying Hebrew and not African-American History? I don't get it."

Walker smiled and said, "In America you can become whatever you want to become without having to be apologetic about it. That means a black woman like me can study a Semitic culture at a high-level, or a Hispanic person can study German Reformation studies if he wants to. Remember the thing I told you about a global track record. I looked at the Episcopal Church, and I see women priests and women in high-ranking leadership roles. You can talk all you want about affirmation, but you have to be committed to it in policy, economic structure, and organizational roles."

Steve smiled, and said, "What you said about America and its infinite possibilities is beautiful."

Walker asked, "You want to know what else is beautiful?"

"Yeah," Steve said.

Walker grabbed a copy of a Jewish Bible, a Tanakh, and read selected verses of Genesis 1.

After she completed her reading, she shared her favorite Hebrew words in that passage, and the translation of those words. She said, "I love *tohu vavohu*, which means royal mess created by a catalytic event, and I love the word *ruach* which means Spirit. Remember, whenever your life becomes upended by a chaotic mess, and whenever you feel an inner void and darkness created by a cataclysmic problem, whether that problem was thrust upon you unfairly or you brought it upon yourself, there is always an abiding, hovering presence of a loving Spirit soaring, watching over that mess; a Spirit willing to create something out of nothing, willing to give order to chaos. That Spirit is a manifestation of the Divine's love, never abandoning creation in those times of darkness and upheaval. How can people actually believe the Divine is detached from the darkness and hopelessness created by the problem of suffering and evil?"

Walker pointed to places in the world where there was a sense of *tohu vavohu*, messy places, but noted how the presence of the Spirit was acting through human agency in the form of first responders, watchdog organizations, volunteers, and donors to help restore order and give hope.

Steve was thoroughly impressed.

He said, "I like how you couched the Genesis passage in everyday language, and how your interpretation had an every-day, practical application. You are going to be a scholar par excellence. When can I sign up for your course, doctor? I am going to be a student of yours for life."

Walker smiled.

Steve then shared two words employed by Puerto Ricans that were germane to their conversation.

"I don't know much Spanish. But, I know that we [Puerto Ricans] use the word *revolú t*o underscore a chaos or mess. We tend to laugh at everything, and we tend to be resilient. We take on a messy problem with a spirit of determination that is embodied in the word *wepa*. *Wepa* can mean something like, "oh, yeah."

Walker nodded and praised Steve's intellect.

Suddenly, the chimes of a church near the college campus rang. Walker knew it was time to close her office and the college counselor chapter of her life.

"I've got to get going. There is a student-faculty celebration for me. You are welcome to join me. You were invited, but we all know where those invitations ended up."

Steve didn't refute her second subtle reference to his homelessness. He asked for a hug and she gave him one. They embraced momentarily.

After they let go, Steve said, "Thank you for everything you did for me," he said.

"Blessings to you," she said.

"Here, finish the pralines."

Steve wolfed down two, broken pieces of Walker's homemade pralines.

"Okay, since you insist, I will make the sacrifice," he said.

"You are too much!" she said.

Walker grabbed her keys and turned off the lights.

Steve let out his playful nature and started to do a silly jiggle with his head.

"Unquestionably, the best!"

"I love it," he said, as he chomped away at the last crumb. Within moments, they faded into the hallway to attend Walker's send-off party, which was arranged by a student organization. Halfway down the hall, Walker started to stride calmly and hum the hymn, *God be With You Until We Meet Again*. Steve slowed his gait and listened to the delightful tune. The lyrics reminded him of a similar hymn sung at his church during memorial services. For the first time, in a longtime, Steve gave serious consideration to returning to his home church.

Chapter Thirty-Eight

Steve's Homecoming

OVERCAST SKIES ON A Sunday morning in March, and Steve agonized over returning to his home church. He was steeped in guilt and, as a result, dubious scenarios tossed in his mind over what some high-minded church people were going to say, and how they were going to behave, once the critics spotted him inside the church. He searched for a pretext to avoid the front door. He found one in the painful comments he remembered parishioners saying about absentee members. So he walked past the church and encircled the block at least three times. After completing his third nervous walk around the church, he decided to try the front entrance to the church. He held onto the latch of the front door. He suddenly felt a paralysis in his arm that left him unable to open the door. Something strange, almost surreal, happened. An imposing force, from which he could not pry himself free, calmed his emotions and pulled him inside. Before he knew it, he found himself plodding up the stairs and on his way to the sanctuary.

Once inside the sanctuary, Steve sailed past the back pews and moved quietly into the middle section of the church, where he took a seat. He did not want to interrupt anybody out of reverence for the sacred space and the pious church crowd, deeply entranced in special prayer time. Right after the time of prayerful consecration wound down, the church became flush with joy at the sight of Steve sitting in his old pew. He had sat there out of comfort. The church had rarely experienced visitors, either new or former worshippers, ever since the revival held in the aftermath of the Montes' visit in December. This, however, was not just any ordinary worshipper. He was a young person, and the church made a special effort to shower young worshippers with lavish attention. However, this young person was not just any young person. He was the son of the opposition leader to the pastor. Amidst the flurry of joy, worshippers were curious why he was there. Some speculated as to why he was back.

Norma leaned against her sister and envisioned God as a tow-truck driver, who yanks a person against his will into the the church.

"I *betcha* the Spirit towed Steve the sinner into the church!"

"When the Spirit grabs hold of a person, it drags him back into the path of righteousness."

Her sister said, "I know it. I know it."

Jimenez thought Steve stopped by because he was in need of a material gift known as a "love offering."

He asked Johnny, sitting next him, "Is he in need of a cash blessing?"

Still others wondered to what clique Steve would pledge his allegiance.

"Is he on the pastor's side, or on his father's side (people at the church had a cursory knowledge of the strained relationship that existed between Steve and his father)?"

The cynicism of a few in the pews did not affect the overall warm mood of the congregation nor did it deflect attention away from Steve. In dramatic fashion, the congregants took turns making Steve feel wanted. Al and his musicians saluted Steve with an upbeat tune. The elderly smiled and waved at him from their pews. The rest of the congregants flooded him with affection, offering a handshake and the standard greeting, "God bless you!" Steve smiled under his disheveled beard. He was excited at the effusive goodwill bestowed upon him. Especially noteworthy was when Carlos ran through the greeters, and wrapped his hands around Steve, exclaiming, "I never stopped loving you and praying for you, my brother!" For a split second something inside Steve felt recreated. He felt joined to something outside of his body.

It did not take long for him to discover what the delirious experience all meant.

Without equivocation, he said, "I am saved, again."

Everyone in the church was happy to see Steve, with the exception of Maldonado and Chico. Maldonado realized who it was and instantly used a church pew for cover. Chico stood in the back corner of the church, and was dumbstruck by the glad-handing scene.

Chico was consumed with envy. He thought others were trying to make him look like a fool by being so welcoming to his son.

"Why are they making a big deal of this sinner's visit? This is so undeserving, so unnecessary," Chico said.

The congregation looked at Chico to see how he was going to respond. Chico knew people were glancing at him guardedly from the corner of their eyes. The attention conferred on Steve stressed him out. Chico, nonetheless, dragged himself to greet Steve. Steve saw his estranged father head his way. He had a Senior Elder ribbon attached to his shirt.

Steve's body twitched, and his eyes widened. He asked himself, "How can some people be light in public, but darkness in their homes?"

Chico puffed his chest out and brandished a fake smile. When he was close enough to Steve, he lurched over toward him and whispered, "You know it is your duty to call on your parents. You know it is a sin to dishonor your parents, neglecting them and not submitting to their authority. Your sin has gotten a hold of you."

Chico's attitude and words unnerved Steve. They almost provoked him to respond harshly to his father. Somehow, Steve managed to quickly offer a humble, but brilliant response.

"I am here, a full-fledged sinner, willing to submit myself to the authority of the heavenly Father. That's all that counts."

Chico gave Steve a scornful look, and Steve gave Chico a sweet smirk. It was an agonizing moment for Steve, who began to wrestle with the feeling that he might have made a mistake coming here. Just when he took his first step toward walking out of the church, he felt reeled back in by an unseen hand that rested on his shoulder. Turning around, Steve realized that it was the intervening hand of Pastor Santana. The mere sight of the minister overwhelmed him. He buried his sobbing face in the minister's shoulders. They wrapped their arms around each other in an embrace. It was a clear message to Steve that whatever good will was denied to him by his earth father, Chico, was of no consequence. The poignancy of the moment recalled the biblical theme of the Prodigal Son who was lost and found, and it filled the sanctuary with emotion and shouts of praise. "Hallelujah!" and "Praise the Lord!" reverberated in the sanctuary.

A moment later as the worship frenzy died down, Santana whispered, "Welcome back, son."

Steve responded. "It's great to be back home, pastor."

Steve's eyes smiled again. It was a bright spot. It was a moment where his soul experienced the joy of salvation.

Chico, feeling anger and shame, scurried to the corner where he had originally stood. After stewing for a few minutes, he motioned in a condescending manner for Jimenez to approach him. Jimenez did in his docile way.

Chico indignantly asked Jimenez, "Where is the lawyer?"

Jimenez said, "He left the service. I don't know where he went."

Chico shook his head. He wanted Jimenez to find him.

Maldonado returned to his room. He was trembling and clamored for Petra's ghost. No manifestation. No response. He had to reckon with Steve's visit to the church. Within a few minutes, he heard a faint scratching behind the wall. He banged on the wall and the noise stopped.

"I must do my part," he said, before opening up his journal and writing what he thought Steve's visit represented. The scratch behind the wall picked up again, and Maldonado rolled his eyes at the persistence of the church's mouse.

"Papá, I plan to give this up. I am going to do my doctoral work. I promise."

Maldonado, citing health reasons, had no choice but to stop attending worship on Sundays. He did anything to avoid running into Steve, whom he had heard through Daisy was attending worship more faithfully on Sunday evenings.

In the meantime, Steve eased his way back into the church. He worshipped on Sundays. He did not have the comfort level to attend on Tuesdays, Thursdays, Fridays, and Saturdays. He refused to get intoxicated by religion, even if it meant that his commitment was publicly questioned by congregants who called him a lukewarm Christian for not attending worship regularly. He enjoyed worship, nonetheless. He got to see his mother and left church happy. His happiness came in part from the pastor's sermons. The sermons were harsh, outrageous and peppered with the kind of levity that made him wheeze in laughter. Chico reproached Steve's behavior, but did not address it. His wife, Sonia, told him that if it didn't bother the pastor, he shouldn't make a fuss of it.

Steve had fun when Santana gave a sermon on Christians who often change churches and referred to them as goats, jumping from church to church. "They are not sheep but goats. Those who like to jump from church to church have to be wary that their last leap doesn't land them in hell. There isn't a perfect church. There isn't a perfect pastor. Stop changing churches, and work on changing your attitude."

Steve also had fun with the sermon Santana gave on dating. The pastor warned his members on the dangers of courting someone outside their faith community. Santana quoted 2nd Corinthians 6:14, "Be ye not unequally yoked together with unbelievers: for what fellowship hath righteousness with unrighteousness? and what communion hath light with darkness?" The minister went on to say a person who dates outside his community will find himself pulling an uneven spiritual load, and this will become debilitating. "Marriage is a partnership pulling an equal burden and striving in the same direction. Marriage is hard. Don't make it harder by marrying someone who has competing spiritual beliefs and values. Especially, if you marry a non-believer, you will have the Devil as your father-in-law, breaking bread with you at the table," Santana said.

Steve's favorite sermon involved the pastor's harsh criticism of a boyish musical group sweeping the Spanish-speaking world. Santana did not like their characteristic mane of hair. He was not happy with the young singers' insignia showing up in his congregation. Santana said the band's looks, long hair and flashy clothes, were symbols of pride.

Santana said, "We don't want *peludos*," a play of words on the name of a popular boy band, *Menudo*. He did not want the band members' long, full hair, having a negative influence on the church. "If you imitate their style or keep singing *"A Volar"* (Let's Go Flying in English), one of their hit songs, you may miss out on flying on angel's wings during the rapture," Santana roared from the pulpit.

Steve clapped. He noticed the more demonstrative he was with his praises the more the minister belabored a point and prolonged his sermon.

But there was one Sunday that wasn't funny. Santana did not make it to worship, and the speculation about the pastor's whereabouts ran rampant. Marcos was named to lead the worship and preach. He kept everyone in suspense. He deferred the closing prayer to Carlos, who announced that the pastor's family had suffered the loss of their son, Nestor Santana. Carlos explained the church secretary and the local paper would have information on the funeral arrangements in the coming days.

Chapter Thirty-Nine

Steve's Breakthrough

THE SHELL OF NESTOR's earthly being reposed peacefully inside an open casket. There was, however, something unsettling in the parlor that Hans, the undertaker, felt could turn deadly, if the matter came to light.

"There is a strong, foul smell," Hans said. He was not expressing dissatisfaction with the scent emanating from the memorial flowers in the viewing area.

Hans, fairly frustrated, rubbed his tense face. He continued to observe the interaction among the mourners. A glimmer of the problem registered with him when he noticed how the acquaintances of the deceased and the supporters of the pastor's family gathered into clusters of like-minded people. Those that didn't sat opposite each other and didn't even attempt to express a greeting or pass on a word of condolence, not even out of social obligation or blatant hypocrisy. He knew from his vast years of working as a mortician that mourners generally did not go through the trouble of treating each other that way unless there was an undercurrent of anger or a raw emotion, which if irritated, could unleash a deluge of untamed aggression.

"I will have to blame myself if something takes place," Hans said. "It can be bad for business if I don't take care of it."

Hans followed his hunch, and he headed to the front of the viewing room to make sure he was grasping the mood accurately. He pretended to be rearranging the flowers surrounding the casket. He forced himself to listen to what people were saying. He could scarcely pick things up, but he managed to hear the digs and mean-spirited comments of the hostile crowd.

"This is a dangerous situation," Hans murmured half out loud.

There was no doubt in Hans's mind that he had to discourage Santana from taking on the role of officiant at his own son's memorial service. Hans rushed to his planning office, where the pastor was rehearsing a sermon. The pastor's Reina Valeria Bible was resting on a coffee table. On top of the Bible, there was a black leather pouch that housed his essentials for the service.

With intense sympathy, Hans took the pastor's hand and said, "Excuse me, Reverend Santana, perhaps you should let someone else handle this one."

"I feel that it is my duty to help lift this burden from you."

Hans offered to read a scripted liturgy from a lay minister's manual tucked in his shelf, and to ask Evan, the newly-appointed fire chaplain, to lead the prayers and read biblical passages selected by Santana. Santana understood those suggestions as a form of moral support. It did not account for his feelings or his family's wishes with respect to who should assume the role of officiant at his son's memorial service and burial rite.

With a crushed spirit and a broken heart, Santana the minister understood that Hans was trying to get through to Santana the father, who was living first-hand the hellish torment that comes from losing a child. Hans's big concern was whether the pastor would be overcome with grief and break down in the midst the funeral service. It would be too much.

Still the pastor continued to be in denial about the level of grief and sorrow he was experiencing as a father about to bury another one of his sons, the second child, after already burying the eldest.

The physically unimposing Santana felt further diminished by Hans's lack of confidence in him. After a pause, Santana buried his hands under his thighs, closed his dark eyes, and continued: "I know that its hard for you to understand, but I have faith that God is not going to let me fall apart. I have been down this horrible path before."

Santana's remarks were an explicit reference to the time when he officiated at his older son's wake. That son, Gregorio, passed away two years earlier from an overdose, and Hans had made the arrangements.

Deep inside, though, Santana did worry. He was struggling with what words to add and what words to omit in his son's eulogy, which he had outlined on a single sheet of paper. Santana knew that the focus of the sermon was not about him. His late son did not share the normative, sexual ethic of his church's teachings. Consequently, he found himself in a conundrum. If he acted like a hardliner, he would appease most of his parishioners by not sparing even his dead son from one of the hallmark teachings of his church. If he glossed over his son's sexuality, his professional integrity could be impugned by his detractors. The tug-and-pull effect created strong tensions, which clearly anguished him.

Santana did everything he could to conceal his inner conflict and vulnerability. He withdrew into a private bathroom to take on his pastor's aura. He dabbed his forehead with anointing oil and smeared a fresh layer of pomade on his hair. The cosmetic transformation gave him the confidence to repel the devil and confront the crowd. He emerged out of the bathroom glistening in a dew of renewal and a radiant glow of holiness.

Santana, clutching his fists, said: "God is my strength."

Hans shook his head. He did not see anything noble and heroic in the minister's positive, religious affirmation. He believed that the pastor should restrict himself in the role of a mourning parent comforting his son's mother, siblings, friends and church congregants who shared his grief. He should delegate the officiant's role to someone else.

"Reverend, enough of the pretensions. I know you are hurting. You have nothing to prove. I know that you are a strong man, but this is not a contest."

"Why don't you sit with your family and let me handle the readings and prayers?"

Santana gave Hans a disapproving look. He would not change his mind.

Ah, but sooner or later, stress uncovers true motives. Hans nervously tapped the pastor on the shoulder, and made reference to a physical arrangement made on the deceased.

Hans said: "So anyway, I placed the hand with the full set of fingers over the one with the chopped finger."

Hans continued: "I thought about having him wear white gloves, but you didn't like that idea."

The words stung Santana. It caused him to bristle at Hans for being out of line.

"There are things in life that should not be covered up," Santana said.

"I loved my son. I believe that the people in attendance know what was going on."

Hans assured the minister that he had no intention of offending him.

"Oh Reverend, I accept people the way they are, too," Hans said.

Countless street rumors buzzed about Nestor purposely having a portion of his pinky removed to symbolize a covenantal commitment to his male partner.

Hans gave up on his attempt to convince the pastor to forgo the officiant's role. He flicked a switch and turned off the soft background music. Viewers, wherever they were, knew their place and took a seat in the funeral parlor viewing room. Silence cut through the packed viewing room in anticipation of what was going to happen next. Hans ventured to the front of the viewing room, with the pastor flanking behind him. The funeral director called the service to order and introduced the good reverend as an "eminent" pastor.

Santana approached the lectern and stood squarely in the middle of the room. He looked for faces that could give him reassurance and strength. He spotted Father Roberto, Carlos and Al. But not Andrea. She was not in attendance. Her absence was noticeable and disappointing. There were faces that he did not care to see, Chico, who channeled malice, and Maldonado, who, for some unknown reason, could not bear the sight of the memorial shrine. There were faces in pain and in need of acknowledgement. He looked at the front row seating where his wife and children sat, along with his deceased son's partner, Walter Wilson. He stared at them with faint eyes. He abstained from saying anything verbally, but his eyes communicated to them how much he hurt.

Santana laid his Bible on the lectern, closed his eyes and asked the crowd to join him in a moment of prayer. He instructed them to bow their heads. The gesture was designed to ease him into a worship mode. However, he wished for nothing more than for the rapture to take place and snatch him from the dread he faced. He mumbled a prayer, but no angelic trumpet sounded, touching off the Second Coming. No prophetic, cosmic intervention crystallized. No heavenly portal opened to sequester the pastor from his fear of death and the snare of his enemies. The pastor had to face life in its full embodied form and the mystery of death as well.

He did. For the sake of cordiality, he welcomed the assembled crowd. He slowly opened his Bible and somberly read Psalm 23 and selected verses from the Gospel of John, chapter 14. After he concluded his reading, he paused and asked a member of the church choir to come forward to lead in the singing of two traditional hymns affirming the promise of the afterlife. Oddly, he stood in the foreground, stared at the ceiling and endeavored to sing. He was anemically lip singing, which he was apt to do lately in regular worship services. Pastor Santana's parishioners sang in a sweet tone. Most of the deceased's acquaintances were not familiar with the words being sung, but they participated by clapping along softly.

When the hymns concluded, the pastor addressed his family's pain. He opined how death affects people and creates enduring pain, even in the face of God's promise to comfort the afflicted. He turned to the crowd and worried about sharing his eulogy. Consciously or unconsciously, it was not known, he tempered his emotions and his church's traditional view of the afterlife. He thanked God for Nestor, at least twice. He said sometimes good people go astray from their faith because the seed planted in them failed to take root, or because the plant started to plant roots but was uprooted by someone in a moral vacuum. The seed was a metaphor for a person who was a bad example and perhaps morally challenged. He was obviously using the Parable of the Sower as a reference.

With tenderness Santana said, "at the end of our temporal journey, we will have to give an account for our works; seized and wasted opportunities; for how we put our talents to use in this world." That was it. His briefest sermon ever. He managed to preach the Word without stirring up the crowd. When Santana asked the crowd to bow their heads for a closing prayer, Hans, cloistered in his office listening to the service through an overhead speaker, came forth to thank the minister and announce the proper order for the procession from the funeral home to the cemetery for the burial service.

Hans looked upbeat and spoke fluidly.

"Thank you, Pastor Santana, for your words of consolation. This concludes our prayers and service. We are going to ask that you come forward to pay your final respects before we give the family members some privacy for their final viewing."

Someone who was sitting alone against the back wall refused to allow the memorial service to end that way.

"Hold on!" said Steve, who forged to the front of the viewing room. The distinct smell of sulfur found in burning diesel emanated from him.

"I've got some words of testimony to share."

Hans stood erect and became more rigid than the corpse that lay behind him. He was about to cut off Steve's participation by asking him to share his words at the reception scheduled at the church following the interment. But Minerva, the pastor's wife, motioned to Hans with the palms of her hands to allow Steve to speak.

Minerva softly said: "You can't put a muzzle on the Spirit."

Her even-keeled temperament reigned in Hans's rushed attempt to end the memorial service. Hans acquiesced. The pastor did the same, but remained standing next to Hans.

Steve thanked Minerva, breathed heavily and raced through his opening words.

"For those of you who don't know me, I am Steve. In our church we generally have a time of sharing or testimony," he said.

Then something activated Steve's equanimity. He was able to calm himself down and share words that had a calming effect across the parlor.

"I am standing before you because I couldn't live with myself if the casket closed and we allowed this wonderful man's life to close without upholding his values and legacy. There is a story to Nestor's life that is not well known."

Steve turned and looked at the deceased. He turned again and looked straight at the crowd. Pastor Santana, sensing that something miraculous was in the air, sat next to his wife. It was the first time in years since they sat next to each other in a worship function. That included the memorial service for their first son because they were angry at each other. The pastor looked at his wife with teary eyes and held her hand. She leaned her head against his shoulder and was grateful for a moment of unity and grace, even if it was fleeting and on a wrenchingly sad occasion. The children looked at each other with delight at their parents' visible affection and support of each other. Walter was happy for his surrogate family.

Steve sprang toward the memorial shrine, which consisted of the deceased's military medals, dress uniform hat, helmet with a shield on the front that identified the company to which he belonged and his rank, and white gloves. He picked up a couple of medals and held them out in his trembling hand. Maldonado covered his face in sorrow and wiped away tears with his initialized handkerchief. Steve noticed the emotional effect he had on Maldonado. He related a series of stories celebrating Nestor's heroic role in the community. He could have enumerated many, but focused on a few.

"We all know from reading the obituary and from our personal knowledge of Nestor that he was a hardworking and dedicated firefighter, but he was more than guts and effort. He was a community hero. He did not save me from a burning building, but he saved my soul and the souls of many other young people from the dangers created by boredom and the lack of social outlets. He saved many of us from getting into trouble in the summer of 1960."

Steve asked a question as a bridge to a well-known community scandal.

Steve asked: "Ya'll remember the time when the funds for special summer programs disappeared?"

Many in the crowd nodded, and those that didn't were curious to know.

Steve's question unintentionally spotlighted Cabrera, or Dr. C, who was investigated for stealing the funds before landing a job as the senior counselor of a substance abuse facility. Cabrera, who was in the parlor and seated next to his close friend Chico, unleashed a puff of anger at the resurrection of a past scandal. Chico, full of shame, shook his head knowing his son's habit of employing satire and irreverence at places where decorum calls for a serious demeanor.

Steve was not attempting to embarrass and lampoon Cabrera. The crowd seemed to sense that as well. Steve's sincerity was palpable. The crowd appeared to understand how nerve-wracking it was to speak publicly and unscripted in a highly charged emotional situation.

Steve returned to his story-telling.

"Nestor went around the community and gave away free chalk and helped the kids sketch a tops chart on the street pavement. He then sealed off streets and diverted traffic so the kids could play safely for a few hours.

He had me go to Don Carlos' bodega to buy a bag of one-penny gums. He would pop a couple into his mouth. After chewing and making a blob, he took that slimy piece of gum and molded it into his cap. It was disgusting, and I thought that he kinda cheated with that gum trick."

Hans rushed to his office to grab a box of tissues to pass among the mourners.

Steve touched people's hearts. Now he was going to invigorate their brains.

"Besides the fun, one of the good things that came out of that experience was learning that life is like a tops chart, and one needs the force gravity on your side to move ahead. Nestor's gum trick allowed him to slide his top across the grid from box to box, and it allowed him to bump ours out of the way."

After his philosophical musing Steve crossed over to another memory. He reminded the crowd about the summer of 1961, when the pool in the ward where he lived was closed. It had been discovered that chemicals leached into the pool from a condemned factory in the vicinity.

Steve said: "I remember Nestor parking his firetruck in an intersection in order to block off traffic and create a safe playing space. He used a wrench on a hydrogen pump to open a valve and unleash a cascade of brown colored water, caused by the rust in the pipes. Then he would remove the cap off the discharge and append a cap with holes. It looked like a giant shower head, and we were sprinkled for two hours in a row, if we had a good water supply that year. Oh, how we screamed for joy, ran barefoot, and shirtless, and danced ecstatically under water that drenched us. Nestor made that happen."

The crowd was in tears. Steve, though misty-eyed, remained strong and held back his tears.

Steve reached into the left side of his cargo pants and fetched his pocket knife.

He said, "This belonged to Nestor. He gave it to me. It was from his scouting days. He once forgot to bring a sprinkler adjuster with him, and he asked me to dig out a recyclable bean can. He instructed me how to use the knife to remove the lid on each side. Then he had me append that man-made funnel to the uncovered hydrogen valve. Wow, the force of water shooting from that can was amazing!"

"That experience taught me that everything has a purpose. Even a recyclable object, with a little ingenuity and good attitude, can be a funnel of joy for those times when things don't go as planned."

He deposited the knife back in his pocket and made a self-deprecating wisecrack.

"Who knew that I was going to turn into a can collector?"

The crowd loved it, except for Chico who was ashamed and angry, and Maldonado who saw that Steve's greatness was breaking through.

Steve, feeding off the crowd, moved away from the lectern. He started to pace from one side of the front row to the other. He talked about how after he and the other kids dried off, Nestor organized their informal intergenerational stickball games.

"Nestor carried a bag of tennis balls donated by Mrs. McCann in his truck, and asked that the players come up with their batting sticks. I have to confess that I was one of the guys who removed the sticks from soaking mop heads left to dry in the halls or on fire escapes."

The crowd laughed and clapped at Steve's wiles.

Steve was not done unpacking his thoughts. He reached into the right side of his cargo pants and recovered his Gideon Bible. He wanted to share with the crowd a story about the Prophet Elijah who was taken up to heaven in a chariot of fire. Steve knew the story so well that he could have paraphrased it, but he knew that in that faith community it was taboo not to read a story from the cannon itself, 2nd Kings 2:6-14. Reading the story from the Bible was going to give Steve his authoritative standing on what he wanted to say.

Thus, Steve read from the Word:

> 6 Then Elijah said to him (Elisha), "Stay here; the Lord has sent me to the Jordan."
>
> And he (Elisha) replied, "As surely as the Lord lives and as you live, I will not leave you." So the two of them walked on.
>
> 7 Fifty men from the company of the prophets went and stood at a distance, facing the place where Elijah and Elisha had stopped at the Jordan. 8 Elijah took his cloak, rolled it up and struck the water with it. The water divided to the right and to the left, and the two of them crossed over on dry ground.
>
> 9 When they had crossed, Elijah said to Elisha, "Tell me, what can I do for you before I am taken from you?"
>
> "Let me inherit a double portion of your spirit," Elisha replied.
>
> 10 "You have asked a difficult thing," Elijah said, "yet if you see me when I am taken from you, it will be yours—otherwise, it will not."

11 As they were walking along and talking together, suddenly a chariot of fire and horses of fire appeared and separated the two of them, and Elijah went up to heaven in a whirlwind.

12 Elisha saw this and cried out, "My father! My father! The chariots and horsemen of Israel!" And Elisha saw him no more. Then he took hold of his garment and tore it in two.

13 Elisha then picked up Elijah's cloak that had fallen from him and went back and stood on the bank of the Jordan. 14 He took the cloak that had fallen from Elijah and struck the water with it. "Where now is the Lord, the God of Elijah?" he asked. When he struck the water, it divided to the right and to the left, and he crossed over.

After he concluded his reading from the Scriptures he looked at Sophia, one of his former Sunday school teachers, and credited her for teaching him the story. He then gave thanks for the reading in a form of a prayer and started to share his personal interpretation and its application.

"I have thought a lot about this story over the years since I sat as a precocious child in a Sunday school classroom. I think that every time we are taken away from this world we leave behind a mantle, and, in my mind, the mantle in the story represents our legacy. There is power in our legacy to bless others we leave behind with a double portion of our power, which can mean a resource, a skill-set, or a life-lesson."

"The story in the Bible goes on to say that Elisha, the junior prophet in the story, used the mantle that formerly belonged to Elijah to replicate a miracle carried out by the senior prophet, Elijah. Elisha was able to divide a river and cross over to the other side. In our journey, we all are faced by a river, by an obstacle, that does not allow us to cross from one side to another. What is holding us from connecting to the other side? Ignorance? Fear? Resources? Complacency?"

"Nestor has left us a mantle. He left us a legacy. If we seize it, we will have the power to move from ignorance to knowledge, from hate to love, from resentfulness to forgiveness. And I believe that the day Nestor's soul was ready to leave this world, God did not send a chariot of fire to pick him up. He sent a fire engine!"

The crowd stood up and gave Steve a standing ovation. Out of humility he gestured for them to sit down, but the applause grew louder and louder.

Amidst the adulation, Brigid was moved by the spirit of the moment. She pressed forward, embraced him, and asked for a personal prayer, which appeared to many as a conversion. If Brigid actually converted, her membership was going to give the pastor the credibility and leverage he needed to draw movers and shakers in the community.

Chico couldn't believe it. He whispered to himself, "Perhaps taking on a pastor is like warring with God. It is impossible to prevail."

Father Roberto was annoyed with Brigid, but he suppressed his feelings. He made eye contact with Brigid and winked at her. He hugged the Santanas, Walter, and Hans, before leaving the funeral home. As he exited, he asked himself, thinking Brigid converted, "How can the soundest of minds make a rash and fickle decision? Who can contend with God's ways?"

Nestor's death and Steve's preaching made Maldonado wonder what was the point in expending his energy trying to hurt Santana. He closed his eyes and heard the voice of his ancestors, Petra and Loubriel, in the message rendered by Steve. He realized something had awakened in him. He said to himself, "Even an ignoble young man can be used for a higher purpose, and even a minister is not buffered from calamity. The pain Santana has endured is more than any ordinary person should suffer in a thousand lifetimes. I don't get it. But should I even try to make sense of suffering? Human reason does not satisfy the justice of God."

Maldonado walked out of the parlor. He backed away from trying to hurt Santana. He thought about Steve's analogy of the mantle, and realized his grandfather had passed him along an intellectual concept with the self-sustenance theory. It could allow him to build a future as an academic. He was no longer interested in developing his own pioneering concept and writing an *opus magnum* for publication. He would focus instead on completing his doctoral degree, and exploring the interconnection between the self sustenance theory and the dominant one-party political systems in some Latin American countries. He proposed to demonstrate that dominance poses a threat to democratic rule.

"I am going to make my life count for something. I am going to honor papá's work. Vindictiveness will not be my path," Maldonado thought. Maldonado also reviewed his status as a felon and worried that his attachment to the stolen car and not living up to his responsibilities at the halfway house would eventually come around to not only haunt him, but throw him back in prison for violating the terms of his release. If he didn't keep his record clean, pursuing his academic goals would be a fool's exercise.

At the front of the funeral parlor something unexpected happened. Minerva hugged Steve and then prayed for him. As she prayed, Steve first felt a numbness followed by a burning sensation in his jaw line. He went to the bathroom and looked in the mirror. To his amazement, his lower teeth sparkled with gold fillings, and the fillings were in the shape of a dove or cross. Supernatural healing, such as lame people casting away their crutches in dramatic fashion and walking on their own, was part of Steve's religious experience growing up in the Pentecostal church. Steve took his experience to mean that he was marked for a special, divine purpose. He couldn't wait to testify at the church about his experience, and share that Minerva possessed healing powers.

Evan played his bagpipe as the pall bearers carried Nestor's casket into the hearse. Hans directed traffic. He asked the drivers to assemble in a straight line and keep their headlights on. Evan jumped into the hearse with Hans. Hans led the procession of cars to the family plot. The committal service prayers were led by Evan. After he concluded, Hans laid the wreaths and thanked the crowd for attending. He encouraged them to attend the post-committal luncheon. On his way to his car, Santana expressed to Minerva that something was bothering him.

He said, "Everything was beautiful today. But I would be remiss if I didn't tell you I feel hurt by Andrea. She failed me. She failed us. Where was she when I needed her the most?"

Chapter Forty

Andrea's Pastelón

ONE MID-DAY, THE SCENT of exotic spices, and the crackling sound of burning wood awoke a slumbering Carmelo. When he woke up, he twisted and turned, and ended up facing a grainy television screen. He realized he had fallen asleep with the television on after spending most of the night watching rerun western movies on a video cassette player. He staggered into the living room in a bad mood. He griped about the sound of clashing pans, but his complaints ceased when the toasty ambience created by the fireplace's warm glow made him feel homey. Then his eyes twinkled at the sight of his mother's concoction of signature Latin American dishes served in huge portions and set on a long dinner table covered in a velvet cloth. The table was sparkling with silverware and porcelain china. The china had not been used for a couple of years. It had been stored away as a luxury item reserved for a special occasion like a future buffet.

Carmelo walked toward the kitchen. He found his mother working at the sink with her back turned toward him. His voice changed from his normal, rough intonation to a soft voice.

He said, "Good morning, ma."

Andrea turned around slowly and asked, "Good morning? Do you know what time it is?"

Carmelo looked at the kit-cat clock wagging its tail furiously. The hands on the face of the clock showed that it was already late in the afternoon. He burst out laughing.

She playfully crossed her arms in mock annoyance and stared at him.

"I wasn't sure if you still existed."

They had not seen each other in a few days because of Carmelo's nocturnal habits. She was asleep when he was up, and he was asleep when she was up.

She turned around and resumed her chores. Carmelo took advantage of her about face to sample bits of *lechón* (roast pork shoulder) and *pastelón*, a lasagna-like dish layering fried plantain and ground beef. With each sampled bite he savored Andrea's homemade seasoning, known as *adobo,* in the food.

Carmelo spoke with pieces of food spinning slowly in his mouth.

"You did a good job, ma."

She paused her kitchen activity and displayed her all-knowing and fun-loving nature.

She said: "Just a good job? Food always tastes good when it is a free meal."

"Don't touch the food without washing your hands and saying a blessing over it."

The formal dining room had not been used since his father passed away. Carmelo asked if there was a special occasion. He could not understand why she had spent so much energy into preparing so much food for just the two of them.

"Are your church-lady friends coming over?"

"No. It's just the four of us."

She had a fixed custom of putting out extra set place settings in memory of her deceased husband and son when they ate together at the small kitchen table. The special, early dinner, though now at the long dining-room table, was not going to make the place settings any different.

One hour after Carmelo woke up from his sleep, he freshened up and sat across from his mother at the table. They leaned forward and held one hand. It was Carmelo who said grace in the style of a sing-song prayer she had taught him as a boy. Dinner was on a self-serve basis. Mother and son ate leisurely and quietly. The silence was indicative of how comforting and delicious the food was. Carmelo had a good appetite. He ate voraciously and helped himself to seconds.

At one point a proud Andrea teased, "You must have parasites!"

Carmelo deadpanned saying, "No, I am just possessed by a spirit of gluttony. I will eat in excess first, and ask for forgiveness later."

Andrea grinned. Carmelo chuckled. Not long after eating to the point of being stuffed, they got up from the table one at a time to clear their plates. Andrea slipped away to the stove to make a latte and serve two slices of her freshly baked creme caramel. Carmelo instantly grabbed his serving and was on his way into his room to eat dessert and lie in bed watching one of his bootlegged movies. Andrea was still in the process of serving herself dessert when she asked him to join her in the living room for a chat. Carmelo was dismayed by how serious she sounded.

He knew that his mother did not mince words. He suspected by the tone of her voice that she was going to address one of his recurring annoying habits or pounce on him for one of his peccadilloes which was recently brought to her attention. He was unaware what he had done to incur her wrath. He wanted to know who the gossip was who constantly fed her upsetting information and stirred her up. He speculated that his mother's friend, a lady from another church who volunteered at her congregation's pantry, was the gossip. Javier complained incessantly about the friend's harping on the downcast. He was certain she was the guilty party because she was coming to the house more often than usual and when she did, she seldom made eye contact with him.

He seated himself at an angle where he could face his mother without appearing defensive about any wrongdoing on his part.

He said: "Okay mom, let's get to the bottom of things. I have not been drinking and doing crap. I swear! Why are people always talking smack about me to you?"

Andrea had no clue what Carmelo was talking about. She leaned back on her easy chair and took a couple of soft slurping sips from her hot coffee. She put her coffee down and did not respond. She heard the frightened voice of the eternal child that dwells within each person spring up in protest. She glanced at the glowing black and orange embers from the fading fire in the fireplace. The next thing Andrea did was finally to reveal to Carmelo that the back-bending twinges she felt were not spasms, which she had led him to believe for a while. She said her pain was caused by an inoperable tumor in her liver. Carmelo, who was entrenched in his late father's favorite leather chair, was startled by the prognosis and started to sob. He attempted to ask forgiveness for the times he worried her, but "I am sorry" was difficult to pronounce.

Carmelo curled up in despair and exclaimed, "You can't leave me!"

To calm him down, Andrea got up from her chair and stood by his side. Carmelo's sobs became louder. Her hands gently stroked on his back.

She said: "There is nothing to apologize about. What is done is done, and what is is. All we have is this moment and each other. Peace."

Andrea went into her room and returned to present him with a gift. She wanted to reassure him that she was always going to be there to comfort him. She draped him in a hand-made shawl. It had a blue and white pattern with a pigeon embroidered on it. The pigeon was meant to symbolize tenacity. Andrea's hope was that Carmelo would remain resolute and bounce back from life's setbacks and disappointments.

Carmelo took refuge under his shawl and sat quietly for a few minutes. By then the fire was reduced to crumbling ashes. He rose from his seat and held back tears. He wasn't prepared to lose two parents in three years. He wanted to do whatever was possible to make the final stages of her life as comfortable and filled with compassion as possible. One way he figured he could do that was by encouraging her to take pain medication, which she had stubbornly refused in the past for lesser ailments.

Andrea grew up skeptical of putting anything unnatural into her body. She was determined to endure pain stoically and with Pentecostal grit. She was not one for even taking novocaine when her teeth were drilled. She recalled even as a child having a tooth pulled without novocaine. Whenever a tooth became loose, she would lasso a string around the tooth and attach the string to a door knob. Once the wiggly tooth and door knob were securely fastened, she would swing the door wide open in order to yank out the loose tooth. She loved telling her tooth removal story. She would conclude the story by sharing one of her favorite phrases, "I am going natural."

Carmelo thought about all the future challenges in light of Andrea's devastating news. He felt overwhelmed. He felt he could make life easier for his mother by asking the pastor to influence his mother to take pain medication. But he had to do this secretly. Otherwise, he would betray his family's philosophy that the doors of their home were for them only. Whatever took place behind those doors had to remain there. "There is a difference between keeping secrets and keeping your mouth shut," she would always say.

Carmelo volunteered to drop off the trays of untouched food at the substance abuse facility. He promised he would go directly to the facility and return without a hitch. "I promise that I will not stop for a drink anywhere." Andrea liked Carmelo's idea and did not have any reason to imagine Carmelo was up to one of his tricks. She handed him the keys that were hidden in a coffee can in the kitchen pantry. Carmelo took the keys, loaded the car, and drove off to the facility. Andrea called the facility and asked for the temperamental Cabrera. She did not want Carmelo to be left stranded in front of the gate as he had claimed to have been in past in order to justify a delayed return to their home. "I have to expose any false claims if a story for being late surfaces," she said.

A handful of carefully picked residents stood waiting behind the gate for Carmelo. They were to unload the car and work under Cabrera's supervision. Carmelo did not linger. He headed off to the church to meet with the pastor. Once he parked and entered the church, he found Daisy sitting at her desk organizing pledge envelopes and letters. She stopped what she was doing and gave the visitor a terrified look. Carmelo was notorious for criticizing the church and hurling criticism at the pastor over his solicitation envelopes and the tight personal relationship he had with his mother.

Daisy said, "God bless you."

Carmelo, who was raised in the church, said, "Amen. God bless you."

Daisy asked, "Is everything alright?"

Carmelo asked, "Is the pastor in?"

She said, "I never know when he is going to show up."

Carmelo knew his mother would think he succumbed to one of his vices, and she would worry if he did not return within a reasonable time. He made the decision to report the deadly diagnosis regarding her health and ultimate fate to the secretary. She sat and listened intently. After he finished conveying his disheartening news, she recommended he leave a hand-written note to highlight how important it was for the pastor to visit immediately. She didn't want the pastor to think Carmelo was exaggerating his mother's condition.

Carmelo marveled at the secretary's comments. He thought it was unusual for the pastor to disregard messages passed along by her. He found it odd, even if it were true, that she would reveal in an offhanded way one of the pastor's shortcomings. Carmelo shook his head and went along with the secretary's suggestion. He wrote a simple note that read, "Dear Pastor, mom is really sick. Please come by the house and convince her to take pain medication. Add her name to the prayer list."

He pitched one more request to the church secretary, knowing he was going to get a negative reaction.

"Keep my visit low-key. I don't want the entire church to call me and ask me to regurgitate the same information. And in case someone asks, I am fine. I don't need special prayers and counseling."

She nodded and smiled enigmatically like the Mona Lisa. But before Carmelo ever placed one foot outside the door of her office, she called Chico and shared how important it was for the pastor to make a call. As she was delivering the news on Andrea's health to Chico, the pastor whisked by the secretary to his office without saying a word. She hung up the phone, and when she saw the right opportunity, she entered the pastor's office to add context to Carmelo's note.

She explained in a forlorn tone the severity of Andrea's condition. Once the words tumbled out of her mouth, she left the pastor alone. Santana read the note and, halfway through his reading, he pitched forward his head on his desk. He fell down on his knees to offer a prayer for personal forgiveness for harboring any ill feeling toward Andrea because she didn't attend Nestor's funeral. He pleaded with God for a miracle so that Andrea's condition would go into remission. His prayer ended. He gathered up frankincense oil and a Bible. He cleared his schedule and headed off to Andrea's house. His intent was to anoint her forehead, lay hands on her for comfort and, hopefully, a miraculous healing. On his way to Andrea's house, he vented, "Lord, life is not holding much for me right now."

Chapter Forty-One

Santana's Conundrum

It took Santana a little longer than usual to arrive at Andrea's. He used up more time than it generally took him to get there because he was traveling through side streets in order to avoid getting stuck in traffic. The next challenge he faced was to find a convenient parking spot on the narrow street where Andrea lived. He was surprised to find an open spot a short walk away from Andrea's front door. Once he parked his car, he scanned through his Bible, looking for an appropriately inspiring passage to read. He knew an infinite number of biblical passages by heart, but he was afraid that he was going to get choked up and be unable to recite the passage once he was in front of Andrea. He found a passage in Isaiah and another one in Colossians. He marked the selected readings by bending the corner of each page. He grabbed his Bible and bottle of oil, and he walked quickly up the front steps. The door was ajar. He quietly walked in and looked around. He saw that there was a hat and black overcoat resting on the three-legged coat hanger, where he usually placed his own coat and hat. The style of the coat and hat were not Carmelo's taste. He exclaimed, "May the Lord bless this household!" A self-effacing woman, wearing hospital scrubs for a top, stood beside the unlit fireplace. She gave him a stern look and asked him to quiet down. The pastor felt she had censored him in an offensive way. Did she not see he was a man of the cloth, a holy man to be treated with respect and deference? He considered scolding the woman for disrespecting his status. Somehow, he tempered his impulse to lash out. He used a soft, unassuming voice in asking for Andrea.

"Where is she? What is going on?"

The woman offered a vague and inconsistent response.

"She is resting but busy hosting a visitor."

The pastor, as her surrogate son and spiritual caretaker, was perplexed by the conflicting message. Resting and hosting? At that moment, Santana made up his mind to see Andrea. He excused himself and headed toward her room. The woman did not try to stop him.

Santana stopped in front of Andrea's bedroom door and knocked before entering. He wanted to make sure she was not indisposed, unclothed or inadequately dressed. But as he lifted his fist to knock on the door again, he overheard a liturgical ritual chant he had not heard since his mother was on her deathbed over two decades ago. He peered through a crack of the door and was stunned to see Father Roberto acting in Rev. Santana's place as her pastor. Santana was confused by Andrea's acquiescence to the rite. She was receiving Extreme Unction, the final rite of the Roman Catholic Church, the sacrament administered to a believer who is dying.

Santana crossed his arms and asked himself, "What is this?" But the question sprang from vanity more than from his concern for denominational or religious protocol. And he allowed his ire about the conflict to drown out the most important thing about this moment in time: his friend and supporter was not just sick, she was very close to death.

It did not matter. It was obvious what was going on. Santana peered through the crack in the door again. His protracted stare allowed him to notice a lit novena candle with an image of the Holy Mother.

The pastor was exceedingly curious. He had no idea that Andrea was conflicted about her faith, and that her death was imminent.

Noticing the confusion and pain on the pastor's face, the woman he first encountered when he entered the home approached him and offered him words of comfort. Her words revealed that she knew who he was all along, and how well she got to know Andrea in their brief time together.

"She loves you like a son, but she asked me to tell you that she wanted a priest at her side to make peace with the Lord and with the Church, just in case."

A confused Santana asked, "Just in case, what?"

She did not want to elaborate, hoping the pastor, a former Catholic himself, would make the connection on his own. She knew the pastor's conversion story. She knew who he was and had heard his testimony explaining why he left Catholicism for Pentecostalism.

She remarked in earnest: "You know?"

Santana did not want to know. He left without saying a word. Now back in his car, he struggled to reconcile feelings of empathy with those of loyalty. He was depressed by Andrea's apparent shaky commitment to the Pentecostal faith. He was furious at Father Roberto's gaul in overstepping a religion boundary—visiting a distressed member of another flock without consent and approval from the parishioner's official pastor.

Vanity and Pride overtook Santana's sense of his pastoral mission. He was unconcerned that he had not anointed his longtime friend, he had not offered her words of comfort, nor had he been a vessel for her to unburden herself about her past failings and her son's future. In her final hours, her pastor and friend had done nothing to help her get ready for the journey ahead. Nor did he want to.

Santana said to himself: "The human heart is not large enough to be divided by two loves. Either she loves us or she loves the Catholics. She was so convincing. The energy and passion behind her fundraising initiatives. Her founding of the prayer-shawl ministry. The insightful advice she gave others. Speaking in Tongues. Her moral standing in the church and community as a deaconess and then as ruling elder on the church board. Her unmatched loyalty to my ministry."

In the pastor's eyes, everything she accomplished and stood for was obliterated with this one decision.

The next day, Andrea died. Hans, who knew the circumstances of Father Roberto's visit, called Santana to explain the last rite incident and to share the deceased's wishes. She wanted Santana to conduct her memorial and committal services with minimal participation by Father Roberto. The pastor unequivocally declined to participate in her arrangements. He stated his closeness to Andrea and the recent loss of Nestor could cause him to breakdown. To Hans's disappointment, Santana offered the names of fellow Pentecostal pastors who might be the lead officiants at Andrea's final services. Santana asked Hans to pass along his condolences to Carmelo. Hans found the pastor's decision not to attend incredibly offensive. He was going to reproach Santana for his decision, but before he could, the pastor ended their phone call saying that his decision was the principled and spiritual thing to do.

After he hung up, Santana shrugged his shoulders and asked, "What was Hans thinking? What would my members think if they saw me officiating at a service with a Catholic priest? Let me call Carlos. I need to take some time away from the office."

Chapter Forty-Two

Dual Baptism

Two weeks after Andrea's committal service, Santana grudgingly returned to work. He had been away from his office, but not away from the pulpit. He took time away to grieve the loss of both Nestor and Andrea. He had planned to take an extra week away from the office and take his family on a surprise day-trip, but he had to return to work. Daisy called to tell him his signature was needed on an insurance form which had a fast approaching deadline. The pastor thought about asking Carlos to sign on his behalf; Carlos was board approved to sign official documents. But Carlos could not be located by phone. When Santana stopped by his bodega, he was stunned to learn that the store had changed hands to an Asian. Santana knew nothing about the sale.

It was about 11 a.m. when Santana arrived at the church. As soon as he flung the main door open, he heard a faint grumble echoing through the hallway. He guessed there was bickering afloat. He shook his head in disappointment. He was not in the mood to deal with a good old-fashioned church fight on his first day back to the office.

With each step he took to the fellowship hall, the source of the ruckus became apparent. The men's auxiliary was bickering over the direction of an annual pork roast dinner. Andrea had organized it for over 20 years. The event was a staple in the community. The men were gathered around the kitchen's island table debating the following issues: deciding the color of the napkins; criticizing the outside group that had rented the kitchen for a fundraiser and neglected to clean the oven; wondering why the sink was clogged and the gas pilots not working; and considering whether naming the event in Andrea's honor was idolatrous and exploitive of a deceased member.

Carlos contended that there is a huge difference between showing reverence and giving a human being the honor and glory. Jimenez agreed with Carlos. He argued Andrea was never about cultic worship, personality praise, or showing off.

"She did a lot of things around here quietly. She was one of the gold-star givers and never allowed me to put gold stars next to her name on the chart. She made many adopt-a-cost donations and never wanted me to give her a thank-you note or a receipt for her taxes. I don't think she would be happy to know we are naming a dinner after her," Jimenez said.

Rafael groaned. He said, "Do you guys know how many people loved and respected that lady? Look at the number of people who showed up at the wake. We can potentially get all of those people through the doors if we say the dinner is in her honor."

All the while the pastor had parked himself in the staircase to eaves-drop. He overheard the gist of the conversation and decided to go directly to the kitchen to straighten things out. Daisy heard brisk steps and jingling keys outside her office and had an idea it was Santana. She tried to get his attention and give him an important message.

Daisy, not knowing Santana's mood, skittishly asked, "Can we talk?"

Santana growled. "Not now!"

Daisy, though fearful of his cantankerous moods, continued to pursue him. She wanted him to know there was an important visitor sitting in his office with a significant gift for the church. He had also missed Father Roberto, another important and unexpected visitor earlier in the morning. The priest had dropped in to tell Santana that he was being transferred to another parish. He also wanted to talk with him about the last rite incident and disclose in coded language that Maldonado did not embezzle money and defraud the clients in the insurance scandal. The priest wanted to take one more stab at revealing the truth about the fraud without naming the culprit, Santana's son, who, in conversations with Roberto had confided that he was the one who took the money. He wanted to tell Santana that the one responsible for the insurance scandal was someone close to him with a chronic addiction problem who stole the money to finance his addiction. The person, no longer alive, was the catalyst of the grievance. But Father Roberto left Santana's office feeling disillusioned. He gathered from the stack of income tax forms on the desk and Santana's notary seal on recently dated letters that he was back to doing what he did for a living before entering the ministry, and that he was currently using the church space for his side business.

Daisy tried to explain to Santana the urgency of the matter in a low voice. "But there is . . . "

Santana became rankled. He ignored her, glancing at the stairs and taking exception to her persistence.

"Again, tell me later."

The pastor turned his back on her and continued up the stairs. The contentious yakking dissipated when the men spotted the pastor heading their way. The pastor greeted them. They were annoyed by his visit and stopped their conversation. The pastor sensed their annoyance and casually made a reference to Steve's sermon at his son's wake. He expressed how gratified he was that they were keeping Andrea's legacy alive by picking up where she had left off.

"You guys get it. You are holding steadfast to the mantle she passed on to us. Thank you."

The pastor acted like he did not know they were politicking and debating in the kitchen.

He changed the subject subtly to inquire about the church sexton, because he found it odd that he was not in the thick of a church debate.

Santana asked, "Where is Maldonado?"

Daisy had been following Santana and injected herself into the conversation, knowing her uncle, Chico, was a buffer against the pastor's ordinary coarseness.

Daisy said: "He said something about moving permanently to a tropical environment."

Chico was shocked. He asked, "Did he quit? Where did he go?"

The secretary held out the set of keys that belonged to Maldonado and gave them to the pastor. It made no difference to Santana where Maldonado decided to live. He quickly walked to a window with a direct view of the church parking lot. Maldonado's car was gone. The pastor's chief critic and instigator was gone. Maldonado was traveling southbound on Interstate 95.

The only one who knew Maldonado's plans was Daisy. Maldonado had been courting her all along. He promised her he would have a place for them to build a new life once he established himself in Miami, Florida. Maldonado had his hand-written letters typed and mailed by the church secretary to a prison brother who was a cook, and who had offered Maldonado a job at the restaurant where he worked. Maldonado's plan was to relocate to Miami and go to work in the kitchen under an alias, and eventually complete his doctorate degree at a university that was starting a doctoral program in Latin American studies. He learned about the program through a magazine in the library.

Maldonado was leading the life of a fugitive, never having fulfilled his obligation to the halfway house and never having given up the stolen Chevy Coupe that had become a beloved albatross. One failure to signal, or cracked tail light or expired meter could be the beginning of the end of his freedom. Also Dr. Cabrera had been obliged to report to Maldonado's probation officer that he had abandoned the program.

Santana was thrilled by Maldonado's abrupt departure. It was the best news the secretary had ever given him. Chico was beside himself and wanted confirmation. He asked Johnny to join him for a quick visit to the sexton's bedroom, which was down the hall from the kitchen. Once they were there, Johnny let out a sharp cry. The pastor, the group of men and Daisy scrambled to see what precipitated the hysterical shout. With the exception of Daisy, they were amazed to see fragments of iconography, a pair of socks resting on a radiator, a makeshift altar, a half-burnt novena candle, the church membership card, and an empty kettle.

Daisy asked, "Why am I always second-guessed around here? When I told you guys 'he left,' did you think that I made that up?"

Twenty years before, Daisy was an Ivy-league-bound student. Julio, her father, Chico's older brother, shut down her academic prospects and professional ambitions. He contended it was a waste of time and money for her to attend college when Christ's return was imminent. Instead, Julio, driven by eschatological zeal, said she should practice piety and work as a secretary for the Lord, a position she had held since her high school graduation.

The men were embarrassed to answer the secretary's query. They could not justify their constant second-guessing of her word and work. In unison, they apologized. They were ashamed, and one by one walked to the sexton's closet to get garbage bags, a vacuum cleaner, and detergent. They returned to the room once she was gone to clean it. The pastor then held a prayer circle to rebuke and chastise the unclean spirits living in the room as a result of Maldonado's idolatrous behavior. He thereby subtly vilified Maldonado and created a bond with the men over their Pentecostal superstition regarding religious iconography.

After the prayer ended a couple of men called Maldonado an anathema. They criticized Chico for his decision to appoint Maldonado the intellectual catalyst of their secession group. Santana believed their public reproof of Chico was well-deserved. He allowed the church men to reprimand and demote Chico, relieving him of his leadership status. This incident brought so many things into the open for the pastor, things he already knew through say-so and other things about which he speculated.

Santana witnessed the dismantling of Chico's leadership at the hands of his own cohorts. He left the men's group without saying a word. He headed to his office in a jubilant mood because Chico had been demoted in his leadership status and reputation. Before he set foot in his office, he was able to tell there was a silver-haired man with his back to him. The pastor shook his head and said something under his breath about how Daisy continued to send visitors into his office without his approval.

Daisy, sensing he was upset, told him in this instance she had to make an exception.

"I tried to tell you that you had an important visitor but you brushed me off. I had to do whatever it took to keep him here. I never know when you are going to be in."

The pastor ignored her defense and walked into his office. The man stood up, gave the minister a dignified look, and gripped his hand with vigor. He introduced himself as Attorney Pat Donahue. He was Andrea's attorney.

Santana said to Donahue, "Yes, I know of you. Please, sit down."

"What brings you by?"

Donahue explained, "My client was full of God's love and her generous spirit proves it beyond a reasonable doubt. She left two iconic organizations in our community with a lump sum cash gift that will be distributed through her estate in periodic amounts. She left money to support the children's after-school program at Holy Rosary Catholic Church and to have the church's roof repaired."

Santana was not happy to learn of that bequest, and it showed on his face.

Santana's displeasure dissipated due to what Donahue said next.

"But you received the largest amount from her estate by far," Donahue said.

Santana grinned.

Donahue dipped into his briefcase and handed Santana a note addressed to him. The vastness of the bequest strengthened his faith and stirred his imagination. The church was going to receive the largest gift in her history. Santana knew the windfall would extend his shelf-life at the church. The money would chase away the demonic voices that stoked fears of the church's demise and claims that the endowment would be bone dry within three years. The attorney went through his files and gave the pastor a letter of commitment. Donahue rose from his chair and shook the pastor's hand.

As Donahue exited the office, Carlos barged in and spoke in haste.

"Brother-pastor, I need to talk with you."

The pastor gave Carlos a suffocating embrace, saying "Carlos, salvation has come our way, by way of Andrea."

Carlos said, "Oh?"

Santana showed Carlos the letter.

Carlos was pleasantly shocked. He insisted Santana call a meeting and take the lead in allocating how the money was going to be spent before others developed their own ideas.

Carlos, who worked with Jennifer Roman on the church's property committee said, "I am going to instruct Daisy to call the board members and have them meet with me after worship in order to address repairs. They are going to think that it has to do with another thing that broke and needs fixing."

But Santana was not the only one who experienced a saving miracle.

Carlos told Santana that the combination of genetics and stress over his failing business contributed to his blocked arteries. He had to have two stents inserted. Carlos left the meeting at the kitchen to tell Santana he wanted a slot in Sunday's service to give his testimony: how he miraculously sold his business in less than a week and the doctor, one of Patel's sons, who saved his life, stepped in for his heart doctor who was away on vacation.

"My heart was cured twice," he said. "I had a physical health problem and an emotional attitude problem. I was cured of racism. You know that I didn't like Indian people for no other reason than fear and resentment. Yet, one of their people ended up saving my life," Carlos said. "The Indian fellow I sold the store to is honoring me. He is going to keep the name of my store. He asked me to work for him. I could not have asked to be in the hands of a better doctor than Dr. Patel. That fella was the hands of God in the operating room. What a wakeup call!"

Santana had his own regrets and conversion story to tell. He said that he was ashamed of his resentment of Father Roberto for doing what any good pastor would do for someone in a time of distress. He was also ashamed for doubting Andrea's commitment to the Pentecostal faith and for abandoning her on her death bed.

Carlos was surprised Santana had reservations about Andrea's spiritual character.

"She is saved! She was for real!" Carlos said. "You guys can work your issues out in the future in heaven. She is going to be waiting for you over a cup of coffee, and she is going to put you in your place. Before you get your crown of glory, she is going to give you a noogie. You deserve one for doubting her."

Santana agreed he deserved of Andrea's rebuke.

Sunday after worship, Carlos did not waste any time revealing the news of Andrea's bequest to the church. The board members were pleased and moved. They rose and gave Santana a standing ovation, particularly since Carlos emphasized the gift was given in honor of the pastor's ministry. Chico, whether it was out of feigned remorse or sheer embarrassment, praised Santana for attracting a major gift. Before the board members adjourned, Carlos swore them to confidentiality until the first check was deposited. He also shared a hand-written priority list he had created of long

overdue renovation projects. Chico quickly reviewed the list and raised his
hand. He spoke of creating a committee to carry out preparatory work and
save the church some money.

Chico said, "The members will get into it more if they are hands-on
with what is going on."

Santana and Carlos liked the idea of congregational involvement, and
asked for a motion to support it. It passed unanimously. For the first time in
Santana's ministerial tenure, bad feelings within the church were resolved as
a result of a sizable donation. For the first time ever, the church experienced
a jolt of new life from living off the dead.

In consultation with the pastor and Carlos, Chico scheduled a work
day. Chico recruited volunteers to pull out the musty rug and expose the
oak wood floors beneath the carpet. The removal of the carpet left behind
a sea of sand and exposed stains on the floor. As the rug was discarded
into a dumpster, the pastor showed up with brown, paper-bag lunches from
Carlos's deli.

He indicated the lunch was for the work crew. He then asked Chico,
"How deep are the stains?"

"Do we need to simply sand it, or do we need to replace the whole
floor?"

Chico said, "Reverend, time and effort will answer those questions. My
humble impression is that there are various degrees of decay."

Chico's formality and respect made the pastor wonder if his coopera-
tion was a form of penance. The pastor allowed the crew to return to their
work and watched as they swept and scrubbed the floor. After the floors had
dried, it had the shiny surface of a buffed basketball gym. The decision was
made to leave the floor uncovered with the exception of the center aisle,
which was covered in crimson carpet.

Carlos hired an outside construction company to cut a hole behind the
pulpit's curtain and install a baptismal pool. The pool's glass was covered by
a sliding panel partition. Javier was commissioned to create a painting on
it. Javier knew how much apocalyptic literature meant to the worshippers
of the church. He painted a scene depicting believers donning white robes,
wearing splendid crowns, and crossing over a fiery chasm on a cross-shaped
bridge to a radiant, eternal city in the foreground. The homes in that city
resembled mediterranean villas. Al and his musicians bought new micro-
phones and electric instruments, including a synthesizer and electric guitar.

On the day the church held its inaugural baptismal service, Steve was
among the believers who were standing in line and poised to process down
the center aisle. Steve looked like he was a new man. He shaved his beard

and sported a fade hairdo. He was wearing a white robe and serenaded by the band and the congregation singing, "When the Saints Go Marching In."

It was a sight to behold. The partition in front of the mural opened. Behind the mural, a glass contained the clear-crystal, azure blue waters of a baptismal pool. Pastor Santana and Carlos were inside the pool, poised to immerse 20 new converts, one-at-a-time, under the baptismal waters. Each new convert, dressed in white clothes, processed in a single line. They clapped and sang the hymn, "When the Saints Go Marching In." Once the baptismal candidates were inside the pool, they were asked privately to confess a vice, a symbol of their old nature. The vice was to be symbolically buried in the water in order that the converts might take on a new nature in the form of a symbolic resurrection once they resurfaced from the water. Eddie confessed to being a huckster. Javier confessed to acts of vandalism. Carmelo confessed to illegal gambling. Felix of *Felix's Fine Foods* and Brigid renounced their infant baptism as unscriptural and were baptized a second time. Brigid, in fact, entered the baptismal waters wearing jewelry: her graduation ring. Steve was the last one in the procession. He closed his eyes, said a prayer, and was quickly dunked backward in the water. When he emerged, standing upright, he felt renewed and reborn. Steve lifted his hands upward, and spoke a heavenly language. He spoke in Tongues. For the very first time, Steve was baptized by water and fire.

Chapter Forty-Three

Steve's New Church

IN THE DAYS FOLLOWING the baptismal liturgy around the new baptismal pool, the congregation was filled with enthusiasm. On one particular Sunday, the uplifting spiritual atmosphere was augmented by a medley of songs belted out by Al and a new band he created with Javier. One of the song's verses centered on the passing of blame among church members, for those whose attitude was responsible for stifling spiritual blessings (*Tu tienes la culpa, yo tengo la culpa, de que no bajé la bendición* . . .). The other song celebrated the mystical presence of a blonde-haired Jesus blessing a predominantly brown-skinned congregation through the power of his touch (*El rubio de Galilea esta pasando por aquí, y dejalo que te toque* . . .). Steve felt the lyrics were not intelligible, but before he became too critical, he reminded himself that liturgy is not one-dimensional. It is a mixture of many things that churn the soul of a community. The simplicity and upbeat tempo resonated with the congregants. The congregation loved it when Javier led the singing. His youthful energy and inspiring voice stirred them to praise without inhibition. The congregants shook tambourines, worked their maracas, danced ecstatically, and spoke in tongues. From Steve's periphery, the church's landscape was transformed from the desolation described by the Prophet Ezekiel's vision of the "Valley of Dry Bones" to the spirit-charged community described in the Acts' Pentecost narrative. The church's membership mushroomed. Finances picked up. The church was in the midst of a revival for the second time since the Montes's Christmas Eve visit.

But periods of revival and prosperity don't last in perpetuity. Abundance and scarcity, and the ups and downs of life are cyclical. So the fanfare at the church was suddenly tamped down when the pastor announced from the pulpit that his son was going to be the new associate youth pastor. This new role for his son would put him on track to be the senior pastor's successor one day. Santana said the idea of choosing a right-hand helper came from a vision he had in one of his prayer and fast retreats. The details of the vision were fuzzy, and its timing perplexing. It was clear from the announcement that the pastor saw himself as the owner of the church.

To some extent, even if his son's hiring had come from an act of divine fiat, the laity could not resist the temptation to consider whether giving his son the position was the right decision. Would the late Andrea have wanted her money spent in this way? To make matters worse, the church's elders and deacons were not consulted on the new position. They also wondered why Steve was not considered as a candidate for the job. They also questioned why funds for the roast pork dinner, honoring his son's commissioning and laying-of-hands service, were to be taken from the parish life committee coffers without speaking to the committee beforehand.

The announcement undermined Steve's belief in the mission of the church. There was nothing that mattered to Steve other than his affiliation with the church and his growing relationship with the pastor. Steve had begun to reclaim Santana as a surrogate father. Now ecclesial nepotism threatened that relationship.

"I repent of doing so much for this place," Steve said to himself. "Damn it! Another male role model lets me down."

Right after Santana made the announcement the members clapped lukewarmly and fastened their eyes on Steve. Steve forced a smile, clapped and kept his gaze firmly on the pastor and his son. On the outside Steve was gracious, but in the inside he was angry. Steve tapped his foot nervously and gnashed his teeth. He wanted to get up and walk out of the service as a sign of protest, but he felt trapped by church and unwritten ethnic and cultural rules of docility, *ay bendito*. If he left, he could be seen as spiritually immature. If he remained in the pew, he could be seen as a wimp, lacking the backbone to stand up against an act of clerical abuse of power. He was grappling with complex emotions and was ambivalent about taking a public stand against the pastor. After all, the pastor is a symbol of divine authority.

"If I challenge the pastor, am I challenging God?"

"Am I being disobedient and sinful by not submitting to his authority and his decision?"

"Or is the Spirit communicating through my emotions that an injustice had taken place in the church?"

Never mind that Steve saw himself as an honorary pastor at the church. He felt he built up the church through his preaching, the recruiting of new members, and fundraising techniques. If the church had the extra money to fund a new position, he should have received it and and the honorarium that went with it.

Steve wrestled with his questions. For him, the questions were a form of prayer.

Steve said, "To give yourself body and soul to an institution only to be rewarded with a public slight is not only a humiliation, but it is also an open wound leading to the slow and inevitable death of hope."

He added: "I cannot get caught up in hatred for this institution."

He felt he had outlived his usefulness at his home church. Now, he reasoned, it was time for him to move beyond the church walls. He felt utterly betrayed by Santana's church.

At the end of the service, the pastor's wife, Minerva, and the church members approached Steve and gave him words of encouragement. Little did they know this was the last time they were going to share holy space together. The pastor walked past the crowd, with his son alongside, and both looked sideways at Steve. They did not stop for a moment to turn toward Steve. As much as it hurt, their failure to acknowledge him was all Steve needed to carve out his own ministerial niche. He decided to start a new church. He resolved to start a church with a social service orientation. He was going to call his new church *Door of Salvation*. His church would have a small pantry and give away food to the poor on Sundays after worship.

Steve did not want the pastor to learn of his creation of a new church by word of mouth. He wrote a laudatory letter extolling all he learned from Santana and shared his calling to start a new church in another section of the city. He concluded the letter by asking for prayers, offering his willingness to have an annual pulpit exchange and work collaboratively with Santana on future community initiatives.

He said that he did not want to say farewell from the altar. He did not want to turn a worship service into a sideshow. Steve felt that there are some things that should be left unsaid and acted upon instead. What Steve underestimated was that staking out a public position can become a two-edged sword. The congregants at his former church asked themselves, "Where is he?" "Did he backslide?" "Did he leave for another church?" "Is he sick?"

When parishioners asked Santana about Steve's extended absence, he appeared both clueless and concerned. He linked Steve's absenteeism to spiritual indifference. Santana said, "He got cold on us." He also said, "We just need to pray for him and let him be."

There was something muddled and detached in the pastor's response. Carlos, for one, asked other members, "Let him be?" and "Since when can a sheep find its way back to the fold? Sheep are stubborn by nature. They need a shepherd to protect and guide them back to the rest of the flock."

Carlos intended to find out why the pastor was not reaching out to Steve or trying to rescue him. Santana had recently preached about the necessity of searching out the wayward sheep. He had said in his sermon on the Parable of the Lost Sheep that the primary duty of a clergyman is to look out after all his sheep, with added attention to the incorrigible and wayward ones. Carlos took the lesson to heart and started to ask about Steve at the places where he usually hung out, *Victoria's,* the library, and the newsstand.

An advertisement flyer created by Javier, and information from Eddie, informed Carlos that Steve was about to start a new church at a vacant store-front location. The news made Carlos happy. He shared the news with his closest friends at the church and, unintentionally, created a groundswell of support for Steve's new church. Help was on the way and he didn't know it.

Steve could not have imagined how much work went into building a bootstrap church. Once he walked inside the storefront property, he discovered that the rental space was not conducive to an assembly. He regretted not looking at the place in person. It was a mistake to rely on Eddie's real-estate-agent friend, who showed him photos of the place. Steve now had a contractual obligation and a public commitment to open a church. He created a chronological list of priority issues. He concluded that his over-arching priority was cleaning the space. The plywood floor and plaster walls were covered in layers of exhaust dirt. The overhead lighting fixtures were defective. Worst of all, the air inside the store was heavy and moldy, and the floor was a concrete slab that made the place frigid. The place had to be repurposed before it was consecrated into a sacred place.

Steve had friends in high and low places. He contacted Carmelo and asked for help. Carmelo was eager to help. He had joined his mother's church out of love for his mother's memory and a desire to try the new baptismal pool built with her legacy money. His heart was not with Santana. He was still upset with him for not attending his mother's memorial service, and was eventually going to leave for another congregation.

One Wednesday, Carmelo tracked Steve down at the library. He offered Steve a solution for the seating problem. He offered to have Javier pickup an adequate number of folding chairs in a storage closet at the rehab center which wanted to get rid of the chairs.

Carmelo said, "They *ain't* the cushy stuff at the playhouse or movie theater, but it's a start. Plus, you don't want people too comfortable that they fall asleep when you preach."

He insisted on one thing though. He asked Steve to let him ask for the unused chairs. The obvious reason for acting as an intermediary was that the senior counselor, Dr. Cabrera, would have no incentive to assist Steve after the public humiliation he put him through at Nestor's memorial service.

"Let me ask about the chairs. After the whammy you gave him at the funeral there is no way he is going to help you out. I know that guy too well," Carmelo said.

Steve assured Carmelo he didn't intend to offend Cabrera.

"I didn't do it on purpose."

Carmelo smiled and said, "He don't know that, and he doesn't need to know that the chairs are being donated to you. So keep the whole thing quiet until the chairs are out of there and in your possession. Don't claim victory until you secure the win."

Carmelo came through on his promise. He got the chairs and had Javier pickup and deliver them to the storefront space in Carlos' station wagon. Carlos, when he found out why Javier was going to use his wagon, rode with his nephew and helped him load and deliver the chairs to Steve.

Some of the chairs were dusty and rusty. Steve spent one afternoon wiping down the unclean chairs, and scraping and painting the ones that had oxidized. But Steve did not do this alone. As word spread of Steve's storefront church, volunteers randomly stopped by to help clean and paint the inside of the storefront. With the inauguration deadline looming two weeks away, Steve decided to have a sidewalk party to speed up the renovation efforts. He had religious music playing from an amplifier plugged through a long orange extension chord to the apartment above the storefront. He provided boxes of free pizza from *Poli's Pizzeria*, and coconut and cherry ices for dessert.

On inauguration day, the church was teeming with friends, relatives and visitors, some of whom skipped their own church services to witness firsthand the beginning of Steve's journey as a pastor.

Steve was wearing a suit and tie. He was sitting on the pulpit, nerves racing and chest pounding. Noticing Steve's anxiety, Javier started to play and sing soft meditative songs. The music calmed Steve and encouraged the congregation to hum along. After settling the crowd, Steve addressed his congregation for the first time. He spoke about how his life was reminiscent of Saul of Tarsus before he became known as the Apostle Paul. He said he was on a path of hate until he had an epiphany that turned his life around. Unlike Paul who converted immediately, Steve said his conversion took place in gradual phases, and that Christ appeared to him in many places and in unconventional forms. He said Christ appeared to him on Santini Street through Brigid's kindness. Christ appeared to him on the college campus through Walker's mentoring and life-saving guidance, and Christ appeared to him at a funeral parlor through the witness of Nestor.

Steve said, "I guess a conversion is about being knocked off your horse, which represents misplaced pride."

He acknowledged his mother's and brother's presence at the service. He thanked Carmelo and Javier and a few others. He did not acknowledge Eddie, who never showed up to do any of the volunteer preparation work for his start-up storefront church. He asked those gathered to bow their heads in reverence for his first ever closing prayer as a pastor. He was interrupted by Eddie. Steve did not like it and it showed in his face.

"What are you doing?" Steve whispered to Eddie.

"I've got this," Eddie said, who appeared to snatch the microphone from Steve's hands.

Eddie added, "Ya'll are not going anywhere. Sit down."

Something moving was about to take place. Members of the community paraded forward bearing gifts. The surprise part of the service was coordinated by Brigid, but Eddie jumped in and made it seem he was behind the whole thing.

Hans was called to speak. He shared a few words and presented Steve with a signed copy of his authored memorial and committal service manual. Hans gave him a bottle of sand, which he instructed Steve to sprinkle on a casket and utter the words "dust to dust" before it is lowered into the ground.

"Every pastor will eventually bury members of his flock," Hans said.

"There are tidbits in my book not taught in seminary."

Patel came up after Hans. He publicly apologized to Steve for a one-sided misunderstanding and gave the new pastor a symbolic gift.

"Every pastor needs a staff. Here is yours," Patel said.

It was an impressive carved staff from a birch tree branch. The side of the staff had the biblical reference to Psalm 23 etched on it. The top of the staff had an ornate eagle's head at the tip. The staff stirred Steve's biblical imagination, enabling him to make a connection between himself and Moses, one of his favorite Sunday school heroes.

"Wow! I feel like Moses leading the people through the wilderness."

The people in attendance laughed and applauded vigorously. When the applause and laughter died down, Brigid shared eloquent congratulatory remarks and presented Steve with two gifts. She gave him a Pentecostal handshake and a Spanish-English dictionary. She gave him a hug and whispered in his ear that he had botched the word tabernacle in Spanish. He did not read the word's syllable correctly, uttering the word for a body part, instead.

"I guess that I have to brush up on my Spanglish. Now I know why *ya'* were laughing," he said, amidst chuckles and joyous applause.

Felix of *Felix Fine Foods* also participated. He motioned with his hands to the back of the church, and two of Felix's employees came forward with Steve's old push cart, which was brimming over with donated canned foods for the new pantry closet. Felix then publicly committed to donating a commercial refrigerator for dairy products.

Dominican Joe was out on bail and awaiting trial. He presented Steve with a customized chef coat with Steve's name stitched on it. He placed the coat on Steve and turned around to face the congregation. He asked, "Does anyone know the two most important words in a kitchen?"

No one knew the answer except his brother, Evan, who blurted out the words, "Yes, chef."

Dominican Joe said, "That's right. There can't be more than one head chef in the Lord's kitchen. The two most important words in the church should be, 'Yes, pastor.'"

Evan came forward and presented Steve with a Bible. The front cover of the Bible had the title "Reverend" and Steve's full name engraved in gold letters.

Finally, Walker came forward and presented Steve with a tallit, a Jewish prayer shawl, and a set of wind chimes, which Steve committed to hanging at the entrance to the storefront church. Regarding the chimes, she said, "When you face a messy situation, this is to remind you that the energetic and creative wind of God will make something out of nothing. You are never alone, though there are days when you will feel lonely in your ministry."

Steve said, "Whatever happens, I will survive it."

The congregation rose to its feet. They gave the shepherd a booming applause. Steve asked them to sit down, but the applause grew stronger and stronger. The adulation was a great tribute to Steve, a beloved personality in the community. An entire community witnessed the transformation of a talented young man from a struggling student and push-cart beggar to a pastor who is now pushing Jesus. Steve now has standing in the community as a religious leader. He became known as the rich mendicant for he had a treasure trove of pastoral talents from preaching to counseling to administrating to networking to bringing people together.

Steve brushed away his tears. He bowed his head to offer a closing prayer when he was interrupted one more time. Javier came forward and asked his new pastor if he could sing a song he had authored and just completed for a freshman humanities course.

Javier said, "My new pastor, Pastor Steve, and Carmelo inspired me to go to college, and I want to share a song in honor of our pastor's special day."

"The song is called, 'Trying New Things.'"

The church band started to play background music, and Javier crooned the song.

Don't be so uptight

It's gonna be alright

If you don't try new things

you will always live in blight

Let's experiment

let's go nice and slow

let's experiment,

just let yourself go

let's experiment

go with the flow,

let's experiment

it's the way to go

Don't delay the choice to try

'cause you are afraid to get hurt and cry

oh my, before you know it life will pass you by,

it will travel like lightning across the sky

an opportunity will flash and disappear

before your eyes in a whisk

listen now every choice involves a risk

Make the decision to try

you won't be haunted by the what ifs

Let's experiment

let's go nice and slow

let's experiment,

just let yourself go

let's experiment

go with the flow,

let's experiment

it's the way to go

The stanza was repeated a third time. Carmelo recognized the song from a past encounter at the bodega. He liked the completed version of the song but liked more that Javier was attending college. At some point during the song, Carmelo had an impromptu compulsion to dance in the

Spirit. He bopped up and down the center aisle. His exuberance unleashed an euphoric spirit of praise. After Javier concluded his song, the pastor gave a joint benediction and blessing for a meal. He invited his congregation to join him for a catered pasta celebration, underwritten by Carmelo, at *Poli's Pizzeria*. Steve's mother and brother were not able to attend the meal. At the receiving line, they wished him well and told him that they could not keep Chico, the patriarch of the family, waiting. Chico had told his wife, Sonia, and younger son, René, that he would pick them up across the street from Steve's church.

At the exit line, Steve's younger brother, René, looked at him with his soft blue eyes and said, "Pops wanted to come but he didn't want to betray Santana."

Steve's anger swelled. He heard his father's voice leach through his brother's remark. He wanted to take a retaliatory swipe at his father through his brother. But he didn't. It was his special day and he was not going to allow anyone or anything to bring him down.

Steve noticed his father parked across the street and said to his brother, "We all need to be where we are called to be."

Steve started to hear negative thoughts, but they were drowned out by Evan's sweet bagpipe tunes.

Chapter Forty-Four

Steve Comes Back Full Circle

Six months after the milestone planting of his own church, and the launching of his public ministry, Steve discovered that being a member of the clergy garnered him goodwill and remarkable perks. Everywhere and everyplace he set foot, he did not go unnoticed. He was lauded in public as the "The Righteous Reverend." He was given an automatic and unsolicited 10% discount by merchants on everything he purchased. Everywhere and every place he was encountered, Steve was viewed as a sage and asked for advice on all sorts of life-issues. Requests for his guidance touched upon every aspect of life. On one occasion, he was corralled by an elderly woman at an aisle in *Felix's Fine Foods*. She asked Steve for advice on a probate issue in the aftermath of her husband's passing. On another occasion his barber poured out his soul to him about his marital problems while Steve was sitting in a chair getting a trim to his fade-style hairdo. Everywhere and every place there was a high-profiled social function, Steve became the minister of choice to offer invocations and benedictions. His participation at these social functions gave him media exposure, free meals and new donors.

Steve's public persona and pastoral ministry went rogue. His rise in stature made him think he needed a more fitting clerical garb and title to match his growing professional standing and grassroots popularity. Without batting an eyelid, he started to wear a cassock and alb at the church. He proclaimed one Sunday from the pulpit, prior to the closing prayer, that he should be addressed as "Apostle Steve." Steve's congregants were puzzled by his decision to wear religious garb. Many shared with him that his change in title, though it had biblical underpinnings, simply sounded a tad Catholic. Others had a problem with the Apostle Steve title because it demonstrated a lack of humility.

Steve listened to his congregants' observations and criticisms. He nonetheless kept the changes, convincing himself that people were eventually going to get used to them. He had church stationery and business cards printed with his new title. He had the sign hanging above the main entrance to the church repainted with his new title. Apostle was painted in black and gold-trimmed, gothic-styled letters over the white background. Virtually every member of Steve's church took umbrage with the pastor's decision to alter the church sign without a congregational vote.

There was a good deal of gossip regarding the pastor's church vestments and new title. The ongoing negativity drove away 20% of the 100+ members who attended worship faithfully. The defection was hard on the neophyte pastor, though one never gleaned that from his public persona. Whenever he was asked by one of his church members about the reason a fellow member left the church, Steve would shrug his shoulders and state, "Church membership is very fluid. Members come, members go." But whenever he reviewed the church rolls on his own, he took decreasing church numbers very hard. It felt like a piece of his soul was systematically plucked away.

One Wednesday evening Steve descended the library stairs and headed toward the foyer area. He had just completed research for a sermon series he was going to offer on the book of Joshua. Eddie, who was sitting with his head titled backward, asked Steve for a bit of his time. Eddie said he wanted to talk about an instance of divine inspiration which affected him.

Steve believed Eddie was going to try to entice him to accept a new marketing idea for their inactive business. Steve made it clear he was not interested in secular work. He told Eddie he was dedicated to his vocation and that Eddie could keep all the accounts of their painting business. Eddie waved his hands to convey his disappointment at Steve's groundless assumption. Eddie said he wanted to create a new ministry partnership in the name of Jesus. Steve wondered why some people find it fashionable to reference the sacred or trot out a deity like a mascot for personal gain.

Steve said to himself, "This is all nonsense. He wants to hustle me in the name of God."

Steve frowned. He racked his brain at what good-for-nothing proposal Eddie had in mind.

He thought about three possibilities in the form of questions.

Question one: "Did Eddie want a copy of the membership rolls so that he could cold call people and sell them something?"

Question two: "Did Eddie want him to introduce him to one of the handful of well-heeled church members in hopes of getting funding for one of his pipe-dream business schemes?"

And question number three: "Did Eddie want him, as the pastor, to stand behind a pyramid-scheme product?"

Whatever it was, Steve impressed on Eddie that in no uncertain terms was he going to mix ministry with business.

Steve said, "The only new business that I am interested in is the Lord's business, church work. I now work in the Lord's vineyard."

Eddie let out an hysterical, annoying laugh.

"I want to work for the same boss too," Eddie said. "I know how much money you are raking in, and how many connections you are making. I want a piece of that kingdom too. And I know I deserve a piece of the action, because I have helped you build your congregation."

Eddie said his recruitment abilities spurred the growth of the church and his personality added "*sazon*," a Spanish word for seasoning and flavor, to the church. By *sazon,* he meant layers of richness. To make sure Steve didn't think that he was hyping his value to the church, Eddie blurted out a list of people who validated his quasi-pastoral gifts.

"Man, people walk up to me and tell me how my testimony touched them, inspired them. They tell me, no offense, every time you speak, we feel God is talking directly to us."

Then, in Eddie-like fashion, he underscored how his exclusive connections allowed him to schedule former secular musical stars, bands and soloists, now turned Christian. He also mentioned popular eccentric preachers, including the former street gang leader now turned lay prison chaplain and the preacher without a voice (a preacher who lost his natural voice to an illness and now spoke through a voice box). Eddie made connections with the frontmen of Christian bands and the populist preachers at an expanding, Spanish-speaking religious station. There he read live and did prerecorded versions of church events calendar. The on-the-air radio exposure, as minimal as it was, turned Eddie into a celebrity among the churchgoers. He used that status to build a network of admirers and followers.

Steve didn't fully trust Eddie. He suspected that Eddie scored a scheduling commission, or a payola, every time he brought an outside person to the church. He had no way of proving his hunch. He didn't bring it up though because he feared it would create a problem.

Eddie, oblivious to Steve's discomfort, used another tact.

Eddie said, "You are the serious and reverent one, the church's intellectual, and I am the fun and cool one, the church's inspiration."

Eddie, filled with confidence, employed a food analogy to show how their friendship and partnership were inseparable.

"We are like a cake. I am the icing and you are the cake," he said.

"I am the first thing people see. I am good-looking and charming. I draw them in with my sweet colors and sartorial flare. Once people have a bite of your sermons on their palate, they go crazy about you and can't put you down. They come back for more. God put us together for a special reason. Don't you see that?"

Steve just stared at Eddie. He felt insulted. However he was not going to allow Eddie to strong-arm him into a rash commitment for the sake of massaging Eddie's ego.

After a few seconds, Steve said, "I am interested in feeding my flock protein, not fluff."

"Protein is what helps develop muscles, not fluff."

Eddie dismissed Steve's assessment of what constitutes a meaningful worship experience.

His theory is that an interactive and multi-sensual form of worship is the most dynamic and appealing approach to keeping parishioners engaged and attracting newcomers. When it came to keeping worship fresh and invigorating, Eddie felt that he had a special talent. He shared a multitude of reasons why he should be given an official paid position.

"I won't charge you for what I did for you retroactively, but in the future, you have to take care of me because I have taken care of you."

Steve's face expressed disbelief. It became painfully clear to him that Eddie's volunteerism was self-interested and that he should have ended the relationship with him when he had the chance.

Eddie resorted to pushing his proposal on Steve. Steve refused to assent to it.

Eddie said, "I think you're not getting my point. Just pray about it. The Spirit is going to enlighten you."

From Steve's vantage point, he did not have to pray for clarity of conviction. He articulated in a clear way that he left his home church because he felt aggravated by an act of ecclesial nepotism. An act of ecclesial cronyism was not any better.

Eddie was angry and hinted that things were not going to end that way.

He selectively paraphrased a verse from the Bible to bolster his argument.

"God did not call me to be a tail but a head," Eddie said, referring to Deuteronomy 28:13.

"*Ain't* nobody going to stop me from my calling. Not hell with all its demons. Not even the devil himself is going to stop me from getting what is mine."

Steve somehow knew that the reference to the devil was not directed at one of the two Evelyns—the first name of Eddie's former and current wife—both of whom Eddie regularly demonized when he did not get his own way. The reference to the devil was nothing but an insult to Steve. Steve was naturally offended by Eddie's behavior. He made the hand gesture for peace and exited the library, wishing his friend a prosperous life.

"I feel sorry that you feel that way," Steve said, after which he turned around and walked away.

When Steve left the library he was greeted by fresh air that stung his face. He wrapped a scarf around his face and walked the dark and deserted streets feeling miserable and filled with misgivings. On his walk, he confessed a litany of grievances. Steve confessed aloud that it was a weakness on his part to allow his friend to refer to him on a first-name basis, and not by his pastoral title, whenever he was addressed in front of the congregants. He confessed he did not provide structured oversight of Eddie, allowing him to run programs at the church without approval. He even allowed him to serve on the board, while fellow board members expressed outrage at Eddie for cohabiting with his girlfriend, Makayla, the assistant librarian. Eddie did not have a divorce from Evelyn number two.

Steve realized it was a mistake not to end his relationship with Eddie. And finally, he realized he should have stood up against Eddie's entitled and defiant attitude at the library. After all, he was not only Pastor Steve at the church, but Pastor Steve everywhere.

Steve thought perhaps the outstanding problems with Eddie would take care of themselves, since Eddie stopped attending worship and church-related functions. There was not a whisper of gossip brought to the pastor's attention on their estrangement. But the *laissez-faire* spiritual approach of avoiding a problem requiring disciplinary intervention proved to have a cumulative, steep price. Bright and early one Sunday morning, Steve discovered in the most painful way how Eddie's veiled threats crystallized. As he was about to raise the front gate to his storefront church, he noticed an attention-grabbing poster attached to the gate. Steve removed the poster and read its contents. He dropped his keys and was shocked when he learned that a new church led by "Pastor Eddie" and music minister Javier, was going to open for worship on Sunday just two blocks west of his own congregation. To make the rivalry more problematic, the official start of worship at Eddie's church coincided with the start time at Steve's.

That Sunday morning, 50% of the congregants did not show up. Many of them were attending Eddie's installation and ordination service. Most of them, subsequently, transferred their membership to Eddie's church. The general perception was that Pastor Eddie's radio program made him hipper for younger families. In addition, his hot brunch after worship, subsidized by a grant awarded by Jones's office and the PBA, demonstrated how committed he really was to taking care of his parishioners.

No matter how much praying Steve did, no matter how passionate he was during his sermons, no matter how many house calls he did, little by little, his members rescinded their membership in writing or through absenteeism.

Pleading with his members to return to the church was beneath the dignity of his vocation.

In a moment of frustration, he said, "I am back to being a beggar, a glorified one."

The biggest blow came when Steve received a certified letter at the church from Brigid. The contents of the letter pained him in the heart.

> *Dear Steve, I am taking re-orientation classes to transition back to my home church, the Mother Church. This decision is going to help me heal my wounded soul and fractured marriage, since Frankie now goes to Mass with me every Sunday. After Mass, we go to brunch as a couple. We haven't had a date in years. I only ask that you respect my decision and pray for Frankie and me. We will pray for you. There is no need for us to talk about this further. Keep me on the church mailing list. I want to continue receiving the church newsletter, since I want to keep up with my friends, and your pastoral letter is always comforting. If an opportunity for me to support your ministry as a volunteer or a donor presents itself, I will keep you in mind.*

Love, Brigid

Steve sighed, crumbled the letter, and heaved it into a wastebasket. He tilted his head against the gate and sobbed. He lamented the trappings of the ministry and the foolishness of relying on others for his sustenance. Out of nowhere a gust of wind tinkled the chimes and made a sweet sound around him, but he was too indifferent to notice.

Steve continued to sob and said in tears, "I never knew that being a pastor was so hard."

The exodus of half of his members, particularly the loss of Brigid and some other heavy-hitting financial backers, adversely affected the operational budget and morale. Eight straight months of financial losses made the church treasurer sit down with the pastor to strategize options for keeping the church open. No matter how many hypothetical options the treasurer raised, Steve realized it was fruitless to keep the church open. He decided to close the church for good. He sent each of his active and inactive members a thank-you note for their support of his ministry and a 30-day closing notice so that stored belongings could be gathered up and goodbyes said before turning in the keys to the building's property manager.

The letter was an awakening. It made Steve realize he needed to go into Hans's funeral parlor and ask for a job. There was not much Steve had to do to convince Hans to hire him. Steve was personable, articulate and smart, and possessed a Teutonic work ethic. He also had a working knowledge of Spanish. These were the qualities Hans looked for in an employee. Over a bowl of *spätzle* mixed with sausage and sauerkraut, Hans proposed that Steve do lay, liturgical work for Spanish-speaking customers and sell on commission funeral plots and vaults at a local mausoleum.

Steve looked more to the commission-based sales. He excelled at it. Seven months into his job, he decided to touch base with his former minister, Santana. He made his way into Santana's office.

It was 11 a.m. Santana walked past the empty secretary's office. She had resigned to move to Florida. Santana walked into his office, and his dark eyes protruded when he noticed someone he did not expect to see watering his blooming cactus plant. It was Steve. Santana did a double-take and hung up his hat and raincoat. Before he could utter a word, Steve put down the water pitcher, and gave Santana an affectionate hug.

Steve said to Santana, "Blessed are the eyes that look upon your face!"

The minister, with a smile, said, "Amen and amen!"

Santana asked: "How are things going?"

Steve replied: "I did not know that pastoring was so hard."

Santana moved his head to the right. He focused his eyes on the pictures of his two deceased sons.

There was silence.

Santana asked, "What do you find so hard about the ministry? Perhaps I can help you?"

Steve said, "I didn't know that church people could be so fickle and so stingy."

"They just don't appreciate what you do for them, and get all bent outta shape over anything—a long sermon, a short sermon, a failed program, a poorly attended fundraiser."

"And when they get mad, they stop coming or giving."

Steve struck a nerve.

Santana, who already knew from Carlos that Steve's church was shuttered said, "Sometimes members do both. They abruptly stop attending and hold back in sending in their gifts!"

Steve said, "You are right senior pastor."

Santana smiled. It was not that he delighted in Steve's failure, but he knew from Steve's troubled spirit that ministry had harshly grounded him in the reality that a preacher, no matter the quality of his past work, is always a controversial sermon or a hot-button issue away from becoming dispensable.

Steve winced at Santana's words and changed the subject. He said, "I am doing other things with my ministry. I am trying to help the community."

For a few seconds neither said a word. Santana broke the awkward silence and asked Steve to elaborate.

Steve spoke, "I want to help my ministry expand."

Santana knew exactly what Steve meant by the coded words "help the community." It was a prelude to a person quite often helping himself financially.

Steve was straightforward.

"I am wondering if I could make a presentation to my friends at your church. I want to give them a hand."

Santana asked, "A presentation about what?"

Steve went into a lay sociological explanation about how Hispanics don't plan for their funerals and how he can educate them on the importance of not leaving their relatives behind with the trouble of planning their funerals.

"I am going to leave you a brochure. Please look at it. I will come back in a week or so to get your opinion," Steve said.

"Alright. I don't know how much I can help, but I will look into it," Santana said.

"Trust me. You can both help me and help yourself. Your parishioners will be grateful that you are helping them in a practical way, and I will give you an honorarium for your leads."

"The pastor's got to live to," Steve said.

Santana said, "If you have a little change, Steve's talents have endless range."

Steve smiled. He said, "Something like that."

Steve rose from his chair and went over to Santana. He gave the minister a hug and planted a kiss on him. The pastor was moved emotionally.

Steve posed one more request.

"I found this book buried under a pile of letters and started to read it while I waited. Can I check it out for a week or two?"

Santana said, "Sure. Why not?"

Knowing how odd it was for a Protestant minister, let alone a minister who disavowed academic learning to have a classic book from another century buried amidst the papers in his office, Steve asked, "Where did you get this?"

Santana replied: "A friend gave it to me. He said the author was going to be a mentor to me. He was right. You can keep it, if you like."

Steve nodded. He said, "Thanks. I need all the mentoring I can get these days. I am going to a new college. I am a little worried about the change."

Moments later, Santana looked out the window and stared at Steve as he walked along. He raised his hands, and with tears streaming down his face, offered a blessing for Steve that was based on his enduring admiration for Andrea.

Santana said, "The universe gives us the resources that we need.

She speaks, and her voice illuminates our darkened path,

her voice is distilled in the stillness and ordinary.

She presses her firm hand over ours, and in her clutch, we are safe to face the storms of our current age.

She reminds us through serendipity that miracles await those whose soul cooperates with her purposes for goodness, mercy and justice.

May she shield you from harm and cloak you with her favor to your moments end."

After giving Steve a blessing Santana returned to his chair. He leaned forward and placed his forehead on top of his desk. He was feeling worried, once again, about his future with the church. He had learned from a newspaper story that morning that Maldonado was being sought by law enforcement agents. The story had a mug shot of Maldonado and made reference to his past insurance case scandal in the city, including his past business partnership with Santana. Santana didn't know if he should hold a congregational meeting and address his past, or if he should ignore the story. He wondered whether the story could hurt his developing side business and agitate his past antagonists to rise against him at the church.

Santana connected a cord to his disconnected phone and called Hans's funeral parlor. Santana spoke with Hans and asked about Steve's work schedule. Hans told Santana that Steve was scheduled to meet that afternoon with a Spanish-speaking family to go over funeral arrangements. Hans, however, didn't want to tell Santana that Steve was living on site. Santana asked Hans to have Steve wait for him there after that planning session. Santana said he needed to discuss an urgent and discreet matter with Steve. Santana was intending to ask Steve to return to the church as his co-pastor. He figured Steve saved him from Maldonado's wrath with a sermon. He could do it again, buffering him from Maldonado's far-reaching complex legal problems, which could impinge on his reputation. Santana rose from his chair, put on his coat and grabbed his hat. He didn't think it was necessary to apply a cosmetic layer of his pastoral aura. He went after an aura of solidarity, instead. On his way to see Hans, Santana wondered if Steve was the divine sign and symbol of hope he had been praying for all along.

Chapter Forty-Five

Maldonado's Forbidden Paradise

MEANWHILE, ABOUT 1,200 MILES south of Jersey City and seven months into his new life, Maldonado cruised on the MacArthur Causeway with his passenger window all the way down. He breathed in the scent of the light, salty breeze fanning his face. He felt relaxed as he drove by trees with palm fonds waving lazily in the breeze and the water sparkling like crystal. The tropical vibe inspired an ethereal moment. But the carefree experience would not be complete unless he smoked a Montecristo and listened to classical music. He turned on the radio and stumbled upon a familiar song, *Guantamera*. He loved that song, especially when it was sung by La Lupe. He kept the dial there and listened to it. He then lit a cigar he had just bought at a coffee and cigar shop. He thanked the Lazarus figurine he had appended to the dashboard using velcro. He smoked and with each puff he released a feeling of self-satisfaction about his bighearted release of anger toward Santana. He had cause to feel liberated. He had started over in a new city, with new people and a new woman. He looked forward to the prospect of admission to a doctoral program to work on the self-sustenance theory. He was enjoying his new life in Miami even with his current low-paying kitchen job. He used one hand to steer and the other one to slide his briefcase on top of his doctoral application and the outline of his proposed thesis. He didn't want those papers to flutter away. He drove into the downtown section of Miami via the causeway and turned onto Biscayne Boulevard. Another of his favorite songs, one by Celia Cruz and "Tito" Puente, came on the air. He rattled off Celia's trademark phrase, "*¡Azúcar!*" (Sugar!). But his mambo groove ended when the song became staticky. He pulled the car over and got out to adjust the antenna. Just as he did, he noticed that there was a traffic control vehicle pulling behind him. A police officer came out of the car and approached him. The officer, built sturdy like a Corinthian column and sporting a buzz cut and dark glasses, placed his hand on his holster.

Maldonado slipped his right hand into his pocket to feel his rosary for comfort and reassurance.

The officer had no idea why Maldonado put his hand into his pocket. He instinctively snapped off the clip of his holster and drew his gun. A single shot was discharged. Maldonado collapsed and grabbed his bleeding leg. The officer walked closer to Maldonado and realized that Maldonado clutched a blood-drenched rosary. The officer asked him to remain calm and called for medical support. With the sun beaming on Maldonado, and blood oozing around him, he squinted his eyes. He couldn't bear the sight of the mess. But something paradoxical happened. That messy and painful experience morphed into a breakthrough moment. Maldonado decided to forgive the person who had caused him the most grief. He closed his eyes and saw that person in his mind. It was the image of his own face.

Addendum: Maldonado's Other Journal Vignettes

ENTRY TWELVE: THE CHURCH has prophets and prophetesses. A prophet and prophetess generally operated in one of two ways at the church, some deliver ethical criticisms of morally unacceptable behaviors after speaking in tongues and self-interpreting the divinely imparted message. Most of the prophetic utterances started with the refrain, "There is sin in the church…" Other prophets claim to have been given a message through the medium of dreams, visions, or apparitions. The visions and apparitions forecast future events. Some of the prophetic predictions were good news, such as the confirmation of someone's lay ministerial ambitions, while other predictions were full of doom. The most admired and feared prophet and prophetess was a husband and wife team, Julio and Jessenia Yomo. When the Yomos spoke their prophetic utterances, the worshippers listened in sheer reverence and admiration. One of their messages revealed an episode where first-respondents were involved prior to it becoming public knowledge in *The Liberty Beacon*. The Yomo forecasts may have come from their access to a scanner belonging to their son who was a volunteer paramedic.

Entry Thirteen. The church has a stylish person, "Mary, the fashionista." She struts around in sassy floral or butterfly designer dresses, which she buys at *Victoria's*. She is a member of the church's small gentry class, consistently earning gold-stars on the giving chart. She and her husband, a non-member, own a couple of hardware stores and rental buildings. Strikingly, the church's gentry class consists predominantly of women.

Entry Fourteen: The church has a small contingent of prayer warriors. Prayer warriors pray at least three times a day. They pray out of a commitment to personal piety and a sincere belief that an active prayer life can usher in miraculous results in logic-defying situations. The prayer warriors visit and pray for people at hospitals, nursing homes, and penitentiaries. Sometimes a prayer warrior coordinates a prayer cell at a fellow prayer warrior's home, or he will hold a prayer vigil at the church after a Friday worship service. Generally, a prayer vigil runs from 10 p.m. to the wee hours of the morning. Vigils are concluded with a light breakfast snack of hot chocolate, coffee, cheese and crackers.

Entry Fifteen: There are the knowers of the Bible, its content, its meaning, its ways. The church has a select group of teachers who pass along the teachings of the church based on their understanding of scripture. The teachers quote scripture verbatim to justify the church's opposition to worldly things: alcohol, smoking, attending a movie theater, listening to secular music, and celebrating mainstream holidays, especially Halloween, which they slam as Satanic. Some of the teachers employ stories with a moral message in order to inject fear of terrible things to come for those who do not comply with their piety codes. Among the teachers, there is a women, Sophia, who is not heavy-handed at all. She is the Athena of the congregation, reciting the books of the cannon chronologically, and quoting verbatim an innumerable amount of biblical scripture, citing chapter and verse. She leads the adult Bible class discussions, and her classes are very popular because she drops a pearl of wisdom here and there, and weaves interesting tidbits about the culture of the Bible at the time a passage was written.

Entry Sixteen: There is a custodian of the church building and its legacy. The congregation has Jennifer Roman as its property steward. She has a basic elementary education, but is a quick learner and catalyst for completing renovation projects. What is striking about her is that she volunteers to help me clean. She always insists on cleaning the pulpit, and she does it wearing a veil out of reverence. She has a common-sense approach to resolving problems. She can sway her committee, primarily made up of men, to tackle priority-based renovation projects. She has a good, patient temperament, and can listen to people bicker over the colors on a paint chart and the fabric patterns for the new curtains at the church's recreation hall.

41145482R00144

Made in the USA
Middletown, DE
04 March 2017